IS THIS THE END OF THE WORLD?

THE ARTIFICIAL CONSPIRACY

A NOVEL

JESSE MUEHLBAUER

AUTHOR OF *ALL THE MOONLIGHT ON EARTH*

ACCLAIM FOR
THE ARTIFICIAL CONSPIRACY

Superior storytelling… resonant themes… a thriller that's a winner.

— ReadersFavorite.com

The Artificial Conspiracy is another blast from author Jesse Muehlbauer. Dan Brown fans will love this book!

— Nydia Hadi, author of *Romance Concerto*

A gripping exploration of human desire, greed, and fear— where religious fanaticism and artificial intelligence collide in a suspenseful, thought-provoking read.

— Stella Chang, multimedia artist

Jesse Muehlbauer's *The Artificial Conspiracy* is a thriller with a beating heart—grappling with belief, power, and the lengths we'll go to protect the ones we love.

— Justin Blaney, bestselling author

In a genre that constantly pushes the boundaries of imagination, *The Artificial Conspiracy* stands out as a masterful blend of suspense, philosophical inquiry, and artistic innovation.

— Andrew F. Balog, author of *What Whispers in the Darkness*

For Poe,

You are so easy to love.

PART ONE

TIME HORIZON

"I sent my Soul through the Invisible,
Some letter of that After-life to spell:
And by and by my Soul return'd to me,
And answer'd:
I Myself am Heav'n and Hell."

— Omar Khayyám

CHAPTER 1

SUPERSTRUCTURE

"Is This the End of the World?"

She whispered the question that was written in the sky. Atop a massive billboard the message was perched, printed in bold white lettering against a black background. There was no indication of an advertiser, no hotline to dial, and no call to action of any kind. Seven words and a question mark pierced the horizon, separating the magenta clouds from the midnight-blue of dusk.

The young woman gazed up at the sign, hands on her denim shorts, head slightly tilted, with the expression of someone trying to ascertain the pinpoints on a map. The simplicity of the bold white font made the statement impossible to ignore, punctuated with a question mark that demanded an answer.

As her eyes shifted across the expanse, she was suddenly jarred by the furious passing of a semi-truck. A wall of wind slammed into her face, tussling her ponytail and blowing spirals of dust around her legs. After wiping the corners of her mouth with her T-shirt sleeve, she glanced back at her rental car, a convertible, that was parked just off the barren highway next to a small roadside diner.

The apocalyptic message on the billboard was dismissible to the casual observer, a novelty amusement paid for by someone with more money than sense. Its only sway over the likes of the young woman who stood below it was the added visual of what stretched out above.

"Brubaker's Comet," she said, her eyes exchanging glances between the sign and the astronomical occurrence in the solar system.

It had appeared in the sky two weeks prior, during the twilight of December 17th. At first, it had been little more than a pinprick of silver light with a small streak following behind. As the weeks passed, the comet seemed to grow in size and luminosity. Its nucleus sharpened, the halo around it brightened, and its tail split in half—one white, the other blue. It would be the last time anyone currently living on earth would ever witness the long-period comet. That fact mesmerized the young woman. She had yet to figure out the reason for why she felt a simmering unease every time she looked upward. For the most part, she ignored the phenomenon. It was only when happening upon the doomsday message that she decided to give the comet a second glance.

Off in the distance, the faint sounds of populace could be heard, serving as a reminder that her journey should not be delayed. She reluctantly turned back toward her vehicle, kicking up gravel with her flip-flops as she walked away from the billboard. When she reached for the door handle of the car, her eyes took another look back at the sign. She was dissatisfied that she was leaving the question unanswered.

Is This the End of the World?

Particles of dust lined the cracks in the leather upholstery of the convertible as she opened the door and got in. Through the opening between the headrest and the seatbelt strap, a ray of sizzling sunset cast a halo inside the vehicle. She gazed at herself in the rearview mirror even as the light smarted her eyes, distracted by the prismatic effect on display. Reflected back at her was the image of a young woman: black hair with a trace of copper highlights, mocha eyes that speckled cinnamon in sunlight, and a solo dimple on her left cheek that seemed indelibly attached to her face.

The engine rumbled to life, and soon, she was back on the barren interstate listening to the rantings of whoever was on the radio.

"…I'm telling you, listening friend, that this thing is real, and it is severe. No one sees it coming. Then, before you know it…"

The words faded into static as the hand on the radio tuner cycled through stations.

"…this evening's New Year's Eve festivities are well underway…"

"…unseasonably warm temperatures for the state…"

"…placing the local aquifer under tremendous strain, as thousands more flock to the Mesa Revival…"

"…and other programs like it are funded through listener support. You're tuned to the Palisades Radio Network."

Her hand instinctively released the radio tuner, moving instead to the volume knob housed on the dashboard.

"Coming up next, the musical stylings of the LA Philharmonic and their rendition of Prokofiev's Symphony Number 3 in C Minor, Op. 44, *The Fiery Angel*. Let's listen as the orchestra both enchants and terrifies us with a romantic drama involving supernatural possession."

The young woman listened while scanning the road ahead. A thin halo of light was now visible, indicative of the encampments that had sprung up over a period of many months. Hundreds followed by thousands of people had arrived from all over the world hoping to be within sight of what was occurring in the middle of the Nevada desert. After miles of driving in desolation, an odd sort of civilization would soon be taking shape, and its first welcome came in the form of a military checkpoint blockading the road.

"You're heading toward the Mesa Revival," barked a man dressed in desert-camouflage fatigues. He had made the remark before the young woman had even brought her convertible to a complete stop. Three other armed soldiers watched as the man approached the vehicle. "Las Vegas is back that way."

"I'm not going to Vegas," she said firmly, her hand tightening around the steering wheel. "I'm going to the Preserve."

The soldier smirked before eyeing his buddies and shaking his head. "Miss, there are close to forty thousand people camped outside the Preserve right now. Every last one of them hoping—"

She held out a piece of thick, beige paper, which had been notarized at the corner edge with a bright insignia. "I've been personally invited."

The soldier hesitated upon seeing the letter, seeming to vacillate between a closer examination of the document and a desire to get away from the vehicle as quickly as possible.

He squinted. "Identification?"

She fished her driver's license out of her pocket and handed it to the man. He stared at it for a moment before handing it back to her and then confirming that it was the same name he had viewed on the letter. "Checks out. How do you pronounce your name?"

"Mer-eye," she enunciated. "Mirai McGarry."

"Interesting name. You're obviously Asian but McGarry is Irish."

"Yep. It's a real puzzler."

The soldier slowly pushed himself away from the driver's side door and nodded toward the other men. Before Mirai drove away, the man added, "Be cautious up there. Whatever you've heard about that place, whatever they tell you, just know…it's a cult."

The radio frequency continued to wander as the vehicle made its lonely trek toward the desert assembly. Next to the road, a strobe light pierced the sky, leaving behind a crimson aura as it slowly faded back into the darkness. The radio mast on which the strobe light was pinnacled stood in naked contrast to the miles of desolation surrounding it. A series of guy-wires anchored the structure to the earth, even as the cross sections of steel lattices seemed intent on defying gravity. At regular intervals, the red strobe light pulsed its warning to approaching aircraft. Mirai gazed at the mast through the windshield of her car as it faded in and out of sight.

"…Look, amateur stargazers have just as much interest in this thing as professional astronomers. It's not every day that a long-period comet finds its way into our solar system. I mean—heck, we're not gonna see Brubaker again for another two thousand years. So enjoy the show while it lasts, folks, because come May or June, the comet will reach perihelion stage, and then…"

Static merged the announcer's voice with that of the mellow

crooning of a saxophone melody. The frequency continued to stutter for a few moments before fading completely into smooth jazz. Mirai sighed while scanning the road ahead. As the miles passed, she saw the single halo of the Mesa Revival break apart into smaller clusters of light, seeming to indicate where human activity was congregating. Beyond the light was a solitary, diamond-like object that towered over the encampment and aimed for the evening sky. Its distance kept it blurry and hard to distinguish, yet it somehow shimmered, picking up ambient light and reflecting it back toward the observer.

Wisps of arid breeze curled strands of hair around Mirai's ears as the encampment approached. Military vehicles and personnel lined both sides of the highway, and Mirai wondered if they were stationed there to keep intruders out or contain the teeming masses within. She lowered the volume knob on the radio as echoes from a public address system radiated out into the desert. Only certain words were audible, but Mirai suspected that the speaker was talking about the comet.

"My…God…" she said, as the diamond-like object morphed into dazzling clarity. Reflecting the last rays of amber sunlight left in the sky, the superstructure took shape in the form of a multistory, glass-paneled, space-framed habitat—a massive gemstone in the middle of the sand.

Mirai's vision darted rapidly between the road before her and the steel interlocking pyramid struts peaking over the top of her windshield. The building was incongruous with the miles of flat terrain encompassing it, and despite only having a head-on view of the front of the structure, she surmised that the habitat actually stretched out for acres behind the glass facade.

"This is as far as you can go, miss," said a soldier at another checkpoint. "If you're joining the encampment, then you'll have to park your vehicle out in the designated zone and enter the grounds on foot."

Mirai shook her head, scrambling to re-collect the paperwork and identification she had only recently held. "I'm headed to the Preserve. I have an invitation."

The man snatched the letter from her hand and brought it close to his face.

"Another fake?" asked a different soldier.

"This one looks real. If it's a forgery, it's a damn good one. Better confirm with Tower One. What's your name, miss?"

"Mirai McGarry."

"*Say again*," he asked forcefully.

She repeated it with more volume and watched as the soldier walked back to his outpost with her letter and ID in hand. Upon his return, he shook his head and handed the documents back to her.

"You're on the invite list all right, but I can't guarantee your protection in this convertible. We'll park your vehicle in the designated zone and escort you in an armored SUV up to the gate."

Mirai blinked as the soldier opened her driver's side door. She said, "An armored truck? To go inside the Preserve?"

"Trust me, if those people knew you were about to get inside that building, you'd be hauling twenty passengers piled on top of one another before you even realized your soft top was down."

Instinctively, Mirai grabbed her backpack purse and slung it over her shoulders as she exited the car. She felt mildly disconcerted as a soldier adjusted the front seat and began driving away.

"He knows I'm coming back tonight, right?" she said, suppressing panic.

"Say again?"

"My car. I'll need it in an hour or so."

The soldier stopped in his tracks. "I thought you were entering the Preserve?"

"I am."

The man cocked his head and let out a hearty laugh. "Miss, no one lucky enough to gain access to the Preserve has ever left. Not since this little commune or haven or survivalist cult, or whatever you wanna call it, started last year. Not one person."

Mirai watched as an SUV pulled up next to them and a man in a gray suit opened the rear door. The wire from his interruptible foldback earpiece unit ran underneath his lobe and vanished into the shirt collar around his neck. He smiled at her deferentially. "Your carriage."

"I'm not here to join a cult," she replied to the soldier.

"Yeah, that's what they've all said."

The drive through the encampment seemed a greater distance than the journey through the Nevada desert. Endless rows of Quonset huts lined both sides of the narrow strip of road sectioned off by chain-link fencing. Past the dormitories, masses of people gathered around makeshift stages where charismatic speakers yelled into microphones or bullhorns, gesticulating passionately about things Mirai couldn't understand.

Her eyes followed the procession as the SUV continued down the road. From the back seat, she leaned forward toward the two men in gray suits and asked, "How long have these people been camped out here?"

"Began about a year ago. More keep coming every week."

"Did the army set all this up for them?"

"No. State militia. The governor didn't want this turning into a humanitarian crisis. She deployed the units soon after the first wave of seekers were denied access into the Preserve. I trust you know you're extremely lucky, miss."

Mirai nodded slowly as she gazed out her window. "That's what everyone keeps telling me."

The SUV made a sharp left turn as they neared the front entrance of the superstructure, for to the right was a Jumbotron video wall facing the general direction of the masses. On the screen was a giant face. The face belonged to a man standing on the dais below the screen. His movements and vocal intonations gave Mirai the impression that he was a kind of emcee, and that his directions were to prepare the audience for an upcoming event. His voice echoed out through the speaker system, eliciting a small vibration from the glass window that Mirai was looking through. While it was too late to gain any real context into his statements, she was absolutely certain that he had thundered the name, Alexander.

"Okay, miss," said the driver as the SUV came to a stop. "The rest is up to you."

Mirai blinked before realizing that they had reached the canopied entryway into the building. She turned to the driver while massaging her backpack with her hands. "What do I do when I'm done?"

"Done? With what?"

"I'm not joining the Preserve. I'm here by invitation. I'll be back shortly. Do I contact you somehow? I'll need help finding my car."

The two men eyed each other and mutually withheld the urge to smirk. The driver then said, "Miss McGarry, no offense, but you've just been offered a one-way ticket out of hell. If I were you, I'd take it."

Despite the clamor coming from beyond the perimeter of the complex, Mirai stood in front of the entryway to the Preserve, feeling conspicuously alone. The enormity of the building became more difficult to comprehend, and what seemed like miles of structure stretched along the desert sand only added to the curiosity of how many people the habitat actually contained. Her slender hand made a fist around the backpack strap and pulled it tightly to her chest. A final breath of evening air began her longing for when she would inhale it again.

Mirai watched as her reflection appeared in the porthole of the metal entry door. A simple chrome handle was all that separated the outside world from the inside of the superstructure. As she opened the door and stepped over the threshold, a series of halogen lights flickered to life above her head.

"Hello?" she said into the void, suddenly startled by the heartless clank of the metal door closing behind her. As her eyes adjusted to the lighting, she realized that what she had entered was not so much a room as it was a chamber.

"Greetings, Miss McGarry," came a tinny voice from beyond view. "Please don't be alarmed at our foyer. It's a necessary precaution to protect us from any contaminants you've brought in."

Contaminants? thought Mirai.

"We're all very much looking forward to meeting you. To help expedite that goal, if you'd be so kind as to leave that backpack and any personal belongings in the plastic bin. From there, you may disrobe, place your clothes and flip-flops down the laundry chute, and enter the decontamination shower on the other side of the next door."

"I'm sorry, do what?" she asked, genuinely stunned.

The voice did not respond, leaving Mirai to conclude that his lack of follow up placed the burden of acquiescence on her. She looked down at the metal floor, her eyes smarting from the halogen. Rivets lined the bottom of one wall, leading a path all the way over to the other metal door, where some of the paint had chipped off exposing deposits of rust. Her eyes then followed the wall back over to the plastic bin and laundry chute.

If I do this…I'm never getting out of here. The thought seemed to form itself before evaporating into the chasm of her subconscious. When she hesitated, all that remained was an emotion inseparably linked to a memory. A sense of dread coursed through her body even as she forgot what there was to fear. As awareness overtook resistance, the memory vanished with it, leaving behind an emotional residue from which she garnered resolve.

I'll get out, she determined. *I'll get us both out.*

The sequence of steps from letting go of her backpack, to dropping her clothes and flip-flops down the chute, to showering off the sweat and grime from the desert drive, to drying her hair and stepping into a curtained dressing room passed with the momentary unpleasantness of the irrelevant. With her purpose clearly in mind, Mirai donned a luxurious beige robe and slid her feet into a pair of cotton slippers. There was no mirror in the room for final examination of her appearance. She shrugged and passed through another curtain, suddenly finding herself at the opening of a large hallway.

"Your cooperation is most appreciated, Miss McGarry," said the voice, now emitting from a series of recessed ceiling speakers. "If you will, the others are waiting for you in the lyceum."

Mirai examined the corridor leading up to a pair of white double doors. The distance was about a hundred feet, and she could sense her every move being observed as she willed one foot in front of the other.

When her hands reached out to push through the doors, the smell of jasmine was the first sensation to greet her.

"Oh wow," she whispered.

Two visuals competed for her attention the moment she entered the gigantic room. The first was the glass-paneled, space-framed tetrahedron encasing everything above her. The second was the circular conference table situated at the center of the gathering place. A rapid estimation was twenty to twenty-five people seated around it, with a solitary chair closest to the entrance unoccupied. Despite the temperate atmosphere of the room, Mirai felt the urge to shiver.

"Well, you tell me," arose a voice from the opposite end of the table.

Mirai shifted her gaze in time to identify the man who had said it. He was addressing her directly. She blinked and responded, "I'm sorry?"

The man stood up from his chair and smiled apologetically. He outstretched his hand and said, "'*Is This the End of the World?*' We're all hoping that you're the one to enlighten us."

Mirai exhaled slowly as her heart rate galloped. She nodded as if in on the joke. A few members of the assembly chuckled. While feigning a smile, her eyes scanned the faces surrounding the table. A fairly even mix of men and women sat casually, representing a cross-section of ethnicities and nationalities. The lack of uniformity in their clothing also caught her attention, ranging from dress shirts to polos, and blouses to rompers.

No one at the table appeared frightened or constrained in any way.

The man said, "No need to worry, Mirai. If we're a cult, then so are most of the world's governments and corporations. I don't consider keeping trade secrets and having charismatic leadership a hallmark of brainwashing, but you're free to think what you'd like. Please, sit down. Forgive me for the lack of a proper introduction. My name is—"

"Alexander," Mirai said.

The man widened his grin. "I suppose my reputation precedes me...as does yours, Mirai."

She slowly sat down in the rolling chair and pulled herself up to the massive conference table. The fact that she was in a room full of strangers while covered with nothing more than a silk robe was an emotion to process at another time. The entirety of her focus had just latched onto a single person, her prime target, the reason for trekking into the middle of nowhere and participating in a cult orientation.

Seated next to Alexander was a young woman about Mirai's age, with shoulder-length blonde hair and sapphire eyes. She was slim, and reserved, and sat in her seat with enviable posture. Everyone at the table was looking at Mirai. Mirai's expression of relief and concern never deviated from the young woman. With as much poise as she could muster, Mirai parted her chapped lips and said, "Julie… It's so good to see you again."

Julie could barely contain her smile as she waved at Mirai from across the table. Her voice cracked from restrained excitement, as if trying not to disturb the serenity of the moment. "I'm so glad you made it. I've told them all about you. Just knowing you'll be here makes this all worthwhile."

Mirai's smile slowly evaporated as she shifted her gaze back to Alexander, who had once again retaken his seat. The man was dressed in slacks and a black polo shirt, the bulging triceps underneath indicated his dedication to physical fitness. His eyes and hair were both gray, and his face held only a few wrinkles. Discerning his age was difficult for Mirai. Not much was known about Alexander's origin. To his followers, and to the general public at large, his past was less important than the promising future he offered through his global radio and internet program, and the protective conclave known as the Preserve.

Alexander smiled warmly at Mirai and said, "Indeed, our own Julie Laufer has not ceased in her affirmations of you since her own arrival eight months ago. Naturally, this piqued my interest."

Mirai casually nodded. "Naturally."

"Those assembled at this table represent only a portion of the family who have chosen…and who have been *accepted*, to live within the safety of the Preserve, whilst we wait out the madness ravaging the planet. You may think of us as the welcoming committee. But there are several hundred more living within the walls of this habitat. All providing for one another. All sustained by fellowship. All rejuvenated by freedom from fear. Fear of the madness. Fear of the world. Fear of themselves."

Mirai again darted a glance toward Julie who was gazing at Alexander's introduction with glee. The sight began to resurrect the unbearable sadness Mirai had dealt with ever since Julie's abandonment of her old life eight months prior. As the turmoil started to churn within Mirai, so did the conviction of why she was there.

She steadied the emotional waves and said, "I've missed you so much, Julie. We all have. Your letters became less frequent, and then none at all. So, when the official invitation came, I couldn't let the opportunity pass…"

Alexander nodded.

"…to see you again."

Alexander stopped nodding. His hand slowly reached for a small white container with a black twist cap. With the ease of a repetitive motion, he dipped his forefinger and withdrew a dollop of clear serum. He applied the substance underneath both of his ears and then on both wrists. Refreshed after the routine, he set the container back down on the table and clasped his hands together. The giant room fell silent as all eyes turned toward the young woman in the silk robe.

"Everyone," Alexander stated. "For your consideration for membership into our family here at the Preserve…I present Mirai McGarry. Twenty-four years of age. Despite having a Japanese first name, she was actually born of Burmese parents in Yangon, Myanmar. Later, she was adopted just after her fourth birthday by Jason and Valerie McGarry of Miami, Florida. Mirai grew up in a loving home and showed proclivities toward art during her grade-school years. She won numerous local awards for her work and even attended art school at the age of eighteen. Concurrent to all of this, the McGarrys gave birth to a daughter, Carys, who is a senior in high school and, fun fact, was signed to a modeling contract at the age of fourteen by a local talent scout. Am I correct thus far?"

The facade that was the smile on Mirai's face could no longer bear its own weight as Alexander rambled off the timeline of her life. Hearing the sequence of her existence in perfect continuity left her feeling violated. For a moment, her vision drifted toward the angle of Julie, but Mirai thought better of it and retrained her focus back on the man who suddenly knew her so well.

"Yes," she responded. "You're correct."

"Mirai first met our own Julie Laufer during grade school, and the two become best friends. Close enough even for Julie to turn down an offer from a more prestigious university and continue her higher education in state. As I'm sure you all recall from Julie's story, her aspiration was singing."

A few nods bobbed around the table as Mirai felt something inside her begin to simmer.

Singing? Julie is a classically trained vocalist, you twit.

"So, it comes as little surprise," he said, "that Julie recommended you for permanent membership inside the Preserve almost as soon as she herself had been admitted. Her desire to see you restored back to your *natural state* is a testament not only to your mutual friendship, but also the nature of the person you seem to be. We don't allow just anyone into our circles. The future propagation and flourishing of our species beyond this terrestrial hellhole is dependent on protecting the greatest of humanity in every category. And thus far, it appears to be working, as no one, *not a single person*, has chosen to leave the Preserve since arriving."

Mirai could sense Alexander's spiel coming to a conclusion, one that would soon demand a response. She watched as a squirm in her seat, or a flick of her wrist redirected Alexander's vision. He had her squarely in his sights and the lasso was tightening.

"Mirai, do you know why there's tens of thousands of desperate souls outside the walls of the Preserve right now? A gathering the media and the government so recklessly call the 'Mesa Revival.' It's not so they can hear my speeches, all of which are broadcast via satellite and the world wide web. It's not because we're conveniently located; Sin City is much easier to access by either road or plane. It's not because the government put a gun to their head and told them go find the giant gemstone in the desert. No. I have followers all around the planet who enjoy my messages from the comfort of their own homes. People who read my books, watch my internet programs, listen to my radio broadcasts—if you so much as pick up a newspaper in any metropolitan city in the world, someone somewhere is publishing something I have to say. The *only* reason for driving into the middle of godforsaken nowhere…without a guarantee, without a plan…is because you're hoping for something. Do you know what that something is, Mirai?"

She sat completely still, letting the words linger in the air-conditioned atmosphere within the tetrahedron.

Alexander said, "Those multitudinous people are praying for a miracle. The miracle of admission…into the chair you're sitting in right now. See, many years ago, a thought dawned on me. One so profound that I was stupefied for several days afterward. It's a simple truth… Easy to understand…yet not easy to accept… And it's merely this: Planet earth is hell. I don't mean metaphorically or spiritually. I mean literally—this spinning rock is actually hell. And every morning when your eyes first open, you've again woken up…in hell.

"Now, when this realization crystalized in my mind, I was shocked, horrified, humiliated. How could this be? I wasn't a bad person. Yet here I found myself with billions of others, trapped in a dimension that I did not belong. I knew my ending up here was a mistake, a cosmic error, and I also knew that my ability to recognize that error made it all the more certain that my destiny lied elsewhere. So, I determined to figure out an escape, not just for myself, but for scores of others who came to the same conclusion. The conclusion that if you find yourself on earth, you *are* in literal hell."

Alexander waved his arm outward toward the lyceum, and symbolically, toward the Mesa Revival. "This place, this gathering, is the first step off this hellish plane and back to what I call our *natural state*. The realm from where we originate—a paradise, for those who refuse to live in hell and are awaiting reentry into the dimension that is our eternal home—that's the miracle of which I speak. *That* is why no one has ever left the Preserve. These people sitting around this table, and all of the others within the habitat, they've all chosen to stay… because they recognize a miracle when they see one. So the question becomes, Mirai, are you ready to accept this miracle too? Are you ready to prepare yourself to leave hell behind and return to your *natural state?*"

The room fell into utter silence as all eyes once again settled on the young woman. Mirai slowly crossed her legs while following the visual array of faces encompassing the table. There were looks of expectation, of joy, of confidence that she was about to make the right decision. What Mirai did not see, were any expressions of doubt.

She felt her neck nod her head at an almost imperceptible level. It was her time to address the assembly. The anxiety jostling through her nervous system abated precipitously when she remembered that her address was to be to an audience of one.

Mirai turned to face her friend directly, swallowing the air in the back of her throat, and said, "Julie… I know…some of the reasons why you decided to leave home. You had so much potential, and so many goals, and so much pressure on you from your family to live life according to their expectations, their interpretation of the Noble Book. Everyone thought they knew what was best for you. No one ever cut you a break. Life…never cut you a break. You tried so hard to make it all work. I watched you try, struggle, and in the eyes of many, fail, and it killed me inside. So, just know that I don't blame you for coming to try this. I really don't. It's overwhelming, and massive, and different. But I came here…hopped on a plane, drove out from Las Vegas…to let you know…that I miss you so much."

Mirai felt her lip begin to quiver as she paused to draw a breath. Julie's jubilant expression had long since melted into a combination of longing and reflection. Alexander remained stoic.

"I miss going to the beach with you," Mirai said. "I miss the sound of your voice, that radiant, feminine, distinctive voice. I miss hearing you perform on stage just as much as I miss hearing you hum on the porch swing. Your voice is a gift too precious for the world to lose. Ideals exist because they matter. No one can do exactly what you do, not on stage, not in life, and not as my best friend."

Mirai's words came in a torrent, as if expecting to be cut off by Alexander at any moment. "If this is the life you want—you *truly* want—then I'll always support you. I love you like a sister. Your happiness means everything to me. But if there's the slightest chance that this decision to come here, to leave everyone and everything behind, was purely out of fear, doubt…self-loathing…I'm here to tell you that it's not too late to come back home with me. I don't expect you to stay in one place forever, nor do you expect that for me. But if life does intend for us to go our separate ways one day…then it shouldn't be like this." Mirai shook her head solemnly, contemplatively. "Not like this, Julie."

The conference room fell silent as the last remnants of Mirai's words vaporized into the metal rafters.

No one at the table spoke.

No one moved.

Julie appeared unable to hold the gaze of her best friend and looked down at her lap. Alexander was now staring at Julie, and Mirai could tell that Julie knew that too. A sharp wave of emotional pain shot through Mirai without warning or promise of reprieve. It began the instant she realized the predicament she had just placed her best friend in. At that moment, the consequences of her actions seemed perfectly clear, yet in the long journey from Miami, Mirai realized that never once had she considered the possibility that Julie would not choose to leave the Preserve.

"That…Miss McGarry," said Alexander, his voice suddenly brimming with the most dreadful kind of energy. "Is an unusual way to express gratitude toward one's new host. Wouldn't you agree?"

"I'm not here to express gratitude," Mirai answered. "Nor am I here to cause trouble. I haven't heard from Julie in months and was concerned about her well-being. Since it didn't seem like she was able—or allowed—to send or receive messages, this was the only way I could talk to her. To tell her what was on my heart. To give her a chance to—"

"To what?" snapped Alexander. "Return her to the realm of madness? Have her mind poisoned by the very philosophies that brought it about in the first place? Do you realize what you're asking her to do? You're trying to lure her back with a first-row seat to the end of the world."

"What are you talking about?" Mirai asked, a hint of exasperation in her voice. "The world isn't ending. There's no mass madness wreaking havoc. Just the normal, everyday madness that we've all lived with since the dawn of time. People are still being born, getting married, having children, creating great art and music, overcoming obstacles, and, yes, ultimately dying, just like they always have. If anything, it's a testament to human nature's resiliency. A stupid billboard message or a comet doesn't mean the end is near."

A condescending smirk from Alexander sent the table into muffled fits of laughter. "Mirai," he said, the graciousness having drained from his face. "Out there, outside these walls, that's all coming to an end. It's doomed. Without hope. Irrevocably lost. Anyone with open eyes, eyes open to the truth, can see it. The power structures that run this world are rotten to the core. That's why we're all here. Inside this place. Taking care of one another. Waiting to return to the other dimension. *Because there is no other choice.* You either stay here in the Preserve and live, or you return to the prodigal planet. You either obey my teachings or become engorged on the words of liars. You either surrender to live among *this* community, or you journey freely back to the spinning grindstone of hell. Make up your mind already, *silly girl*, because our collective patience is running thin. Julie made her decision long ago, as did they all. As now so must you."

Alexander then leaned onto the table and enunciated with razor precision, "Time is up, Mirai. Are you in or out?"

Mirai ignored him and appealed one last time to the young woman seated next to Alexander. "Julie, I still need you in my life. In fact one of the reasons I came here was to share some tough news I recently got. Something really tough. The kind of news you can only share with your best—"

"Out it is!" Alexander blurted. He reached down underneath his portion of the conference room table and wrestled something up to his lap. After setting it on the table's smooth, wooden surface, Mirai realized that it was her backpack. With the kind of passionate shove that bids one good riddance, the backpack slid across the diameter of the table and into Mirai's hands.

"They disinfected everything while you were in the shower. Your clothes are in there as well. You're to leave the Preserve immediately. Don't ever come back."

Mirai sat still for a moment, as equally stunned as she was relieved. Her hands gripped the fabric tightly and then moved around the exterior to feel its contents. She was certain something was missing.

"There was a book in here," she said, softly at first and mostly to herself, and then a second time with more force and directed toward Alexander.

"So there was," he replied, nonchalantly.

"Where is it?"

"You were informed, explicitly, in the invitation letter not to bring any unauthorized reading materials into the Preserve. Yet you chose to violate that rule."

Again reaching underneath the table, Alexander pulled out a brown, hardbound book with a cursive title engraved into the cover. The book had seen age but was worn only slightly around the edges. As he held it up, Mirai felt her shoulders begin to tighten.

"They found this in your backpack and it was turned over to me," Alexander said. "Since you perpetrated this act against the group, the contraband has been confiscated and will be handled appropriately."

"Meaning what?"

Alexander cracked a grin. "Meaning incinerated."

Mirai bolted up from her seat, letting the backpack tumble onto the carpeted floor. "You don't understand. It's not propaganda. It's Julie's diary, from just before she moved here. Her mom was going to throw it away and I thought Julie should have it."

"An error in judgment on your part."

"That is her personal property, and you have no right—"

"There is no concept of personal property at the Preserve, young lady. You are the one who has no rights here."

Mirai shot a glance toward Julie. "I brought it because it belongs to you. I thought if you read it again, maybe it could—"

But her pleas had fallen on deaf ears, as Julie continued to look away from Mirai, her sapphire eyes filled with tears that refused to fall.

As Mirai thought about what other appeals might win her case with Alexander, she determined that the effort was futile. He would not be persuaded by reason. Her refusal to join the group had been her final sentencing.

"I'm not leaving," she said firmly, "until you give it back."

Alexander hesitated, eyeing Mirai curiously from across the space. "I see. Well then, to whom shall I give this vital task?" His attention scoured the table while a man let out a cough. "Fair enough. Mr. Eban, would you kindly rise to your feet?"

A few seats to the right of Julie sat a man who appeared to be in his late twenties but held the concern lines in his forehead of someone much older. Mirai watched as he slowly pushed himself up from the table.

"David Eban," Alexander announced, before placing the book flat on the table and sliding it over to him. "Take that into the back room, incinerate it, and then return the ashes to Miss McGarry so she can leave."

The man didn't move. His rigid body held firm its positioning as his gaze narrowed in on the task in front of him. No one at the table spoke, and Mirai found that she needed to remind herself to occasionally draw in a breath.

"Right away, David," Alexander pressed.

But David continued to wait, and in that waiting, seemed to be balancing the enormous gravity of two vastly different decisions. Intently, he picked up the book from the table and squeezed it between his hands. He turned it over and then flipped it around to the cover. The inner workings of his mind became evident the instant he pulled back the cover and rested his forefinger on the first page. His eyes followed the text of the opening line before coming to a halt. Then, with determined precision, his line of sight slowly crossed the table until it locked onto Mirai with an intensity that conveyed entire conversations.

Wholly captured by his gaze, Mirai stared back in wonder.

"I'm afraid that in order to do what you ask," David finally said in a low, metered tone. "I would be destroying a piece of myself along with it." His right hand placed the book back onto the table and he slid it in Mirai's direction. Mirai could not remember if she had heard an audible objection come from Alexander or not. For in that moment, all of her sensory faculties had been attuned to David.

"Thank…you," she said, her tongue suddenly feeling misaligned in her mouth.

"A betrayal by one of our own," seethed Alexander. "This will not go unaddressed. Return to the dormitory at once."

David pursed his lips and then laughed to himself. It was the laugh of one coming to terms with a decision made without regret. Shrugging casually, he stepped past his chair and began working his way around the circumference of the grand conference room table. To Mirai's shock, he was walking her way.

"This…has been an interesting experiment," said David in midstride. "However, I believe the time has come for me to depart your world. Six weeks ago, I thought there might be a future for me here. I can see now that there is not."

For the first time since Mirai had entered the tetrahedron, Alexander seemed nonplussed. He fumbled his first attempt at a coherent statement before stammering, "You—that just-just isn't done here! No one has ever left the Preserve! No one!"

David nodded in agreement. At last making eye contact with the leader of the Mesa Revival, he replied, "Well… I guess that makes me no one."

Alexander narrowed his eyes at David and aimed his finger as if it was an arrow ready to launch. "You degenerate son of a bitch. Let it be clearly understood to all in this assembly that David is not leaving of his own accord. We are *excommunicating* him. That means we are casting you out into the world…alone, and that you will never again find a haven in the Preserve. Do you understand that? Do *both* of you understand that? Don't ever return to this place. If I see your faces again, I will inflict the greatest of miseries!"

The giant room again fell silent, ripe with the tension of the unfolding event; a tension that Alexander alone seemed to be holding in his grasp.

With a quiet strength in her voice, Mirai then said, "I'm sorry, Julie, if I put you in a difficult spot. Thank you for the invitation to join the Preserve, but I must decline. I must decline on the basis that this is obviously a cult, and Alexander is clearly a brainwashing lunatic. I'm sorry you feel at home here. If you ever decide that you don't, just know that my door is always open."

The door to the superstructure closed behind them. Mirai's convertible was already waiting, engine running, with no military officials in sight. After a brief glance at the visual onslaught that was the Mesa Revival, Mirai slung her backpack into the rear seat and told David to get in.

"Are you sure?" he asked, appearing slightly disoriented.

"It's the least I can do for you saving Julie's diary. And…you know…also getting you evicted."

David smiled appreciatively and slid into the passenger seat. Before long, the barren desert road was before them and the giant gemstone in the sand was beginning to lose its shimmer. Mirai pressed her foot down on the accelerator and the car gathered speed. Warm evening air caressed their faces as they flashed weary expressions at one another, the kind acknowledging a mutual predicament.

Mirai asked, "Did they really not give you back your belongings? Suitcase? Nothing?"

David smirked. "I still have my ID, thankfully. All else is replaceable in time. Anyway, the emotional baggage from the last six weeks is more than enough to carry."

"I have…no idea how you lasted that long in there. How any of them have. It's so depressing and sad."

"It's only depressing once you realize that the world is, in fact, not coming to an end. Before that, you're just appreciative to be in a lifeboat. That's why they seem happy. That's why they stay. That's certainly why Julie stayed, despite your heroic attempts to save her."

Mirai let out a long, exasperated exhale. "Freakin' eight ball."

"That's an amusing minced oath."

"I just don't know what I was thinking. When I received that official invite from them, I just assumed… I just expected…that she'd…"

"Embrace the rescue attempt?"

A simple nod long preceded the reply. "I guess, yeah."

"I'm terribly sorry about Julie," David said. "I didn't get to know her that well during my stay, but she strikes me as someone of great value to you. Don't fret. That was a very heroic thing to do. Your efforts will not so easily be forgotten by her."

Mirai didn't respond. As her arm leaned against the convertible door, her hand pressed against her forehead, attempting to massage away the worry lines. For another mile they traveled in silence, slicing through the hazy darkness of the desert night.

"My God, there it is…" David said in wonder.

Mirai followed his line of sight before realizing that he was talking about Brubaker's Comet. "That's right. This would be your first time seeing it outside of a glass enclosure."

As they drove along the road, it was the comet that appeared to stay perfectly still. It had nestled into its own corner of the sky, surrounded by stars and the partially obscured face of a waning gibbous moon.

"I've never been so grateful to see the heavens again," David whispered.

Mirai felt as though she should agree. Yet her lips remained silent, and her eyes stayed fixed on the road. The Mesa Revival was nearly out of view, its faint glow seeming to have a dying pulse of its own, tying together the long, winding artery that was the highway back to Las Vegas.

"We appreciate you listening each evening to *The Musical Enchantment Hour*, right here on PRN America." The announcer's voice was warm, his baritone elocution pushing back against the rushing wind in the car. "Did you know that Palisades Radio Network is about to celebrate its fortieth anniversary this upcoming year? Our founder and president, Howard Lalonde, had a vision for a unique kind of radio station. One that played music often not heard anywhere else, with mixed formats between news, music, talk, and educational programming, all designed to enrich the mind and lift the spirit. Well, he did just that, starting with the flagship station right here in Southern California, and eventually branching out into all fifty states and around the world on the internet. Here's a clip of what Howard had to say on his daily feature, *Thoughtful Conversations*, about the upcoming anniversary."

The voice that emerged was one familiar to Mirai. It had often filled the house in which she grew up, adding companionship for moments when—even within her adoptive family—she had sometimes felt alone. The man on the radio sounded fatherly, and had a way of addressing the microphone that made the listener believe he was smiling.

"Can I accept that it's been forty years since the first station signed on the air? No, absolutely not. I hold firm that there's been a miscalculation on somebody's slide rule, a plot to make me seem old." The man chuckled and drew in a quiet breath. "Actually, I recall it like it was yesterday. With my wife Sharon by my side, that 50,000-watt tower sprang to life, and I greeted the listening audience with those words that have been repeated so often on PRN America: 'May this serve you well.' Whether you've been tuning in since day one, or just discovered our signal today, from the bottom of my heart, thanks for being a listener."

Mirai wondered what it would be like to look back on a lifetime of work and reminisce about day one. A passion that had consumed one's every waking moment and had produced a body of work that would stand the test of time.

I hope I get to experience that... she thought, pondering her artwork, her small studio, and the recognition that she had achieved at a relatively young age. The mental picture fizzled as the memory of a doctor's solemn words echoed relentlessly inside Mirai's head. *Your last MRI confirmed our suspicions...*

Her mind firmly pushed back against the encroachment. It was neither the time nor the place to deal with such news. Mirai said, "You know, in all of the commotion I never asked, where do you—did you—live?"

"Orlando. Yes, the irony of you living in Miami is not lost on me."

"Oh wow," said Mirai, sitting up more in her seat. "We're practically neighbors. Where's your place?"

"It was and is no longer. I'm ashamed to say that I sold my condo before moving into the Preserve. I was overly confident that it would work out with Alexander's bunch. I have only a few items in storage. But it's okay. I can have it shipped anywhere. I'm used to traveling for work."

"What do you do?"

"Harpist."

"I'm sorry?"

David laughed. "That's always the reaction, yet I still answer the same each time. I'm a classical harp player. My agency loans me out to orchestras around the country in need of a harpist. I travel extensively throughout the year, even though I am based out of the Orlando Philharmonic."

"That's amazing. I love harp music. It's so…so…"

"Serene?"

"I was going to say majestic."

"I would agree with that descriptor as well. It's a far more versatile instrument than people imagine. Not just for dream sequences in movies."

Mirai felt the onset of a smile for the first time in hours and the infusion of relief it provided. The stranger in her car had reminded her of an emotion. It was the desperate human need for companionship. Bossa nova music provided the background to Mirai's thoughts while she drove. She blinked and cocked her neck from side to side. Miles of desolation eventually led to signs for the upcoming interstate. She squeezed the steering wheel with her free hand as she spotted a small roadside diner.

"Have you eaten recently?" she asked. "Because I'm starving."

David sat up a bit in his seat as he looked out at the approaching building. "Even if it's a mirage, I say we take our chances."

A large neon sign slanted downward toward the front entrance. Its red hue pulsed intermittently like it would soon burn out. Mirai parked the convertible and they walked inside, immediately feeling parched.

Mirai and David nodded in unison and looked up at the wall behind the countertop. A television faced the customers, its antennas nearly touching the ceiling. On the screen was live coverage of Times Square, where swells of pedestrians moved about in every direction. Cacophonous noise competed with the flashing lights of the digital billboards, all rallying to remind viewers that this was a momentous occasion. Central to the celebration was a seventy-five-foot flagpole with a glistening sphere, and just beneath it, the outline of a set of four numbers ready to illume at the flip of a switch.

"I actually forgot it was New Year's Eve," said Mirai. "It's almost midnight on the East Coast."

The dinner crowd began to slowly clear out as the last rays of desert sunlight peered through the crinkled window blinds. The young woman watched as truckers, a few elderly couples, and one beleaguered businessman ate their humble meals before inevitably having to head back out onto the highway. The way station seemed to exhale as nightfall absorbed the last remnants of sun from the sky. All that remained was the incandescence beaming from the slanted windows of the diner, the only pinpoint of light for miles.

Mirai continued to gaze up at the celebratory pandemonium, feeling eternally grateful that she wasn't standing within the swells of pedestrians moving around in every direction. It was minutes away from midnight in Times Square. Searchlights pierced the sky and crisscrossed against buildings and signs that proclaimed the moment everyone had waited for was upon them. Anticipatory energy passed over the masses like an electric surge. Music filled the open air. Cheers, claps, the waving of flags, and the blowing of party horns all united to celebrate the survival of another year and the arrival of the next.

60... flashed a message from the primary Jumbotron, which elicited roaring acclaim from the hundreds of thousands in attendance. The ball began its slow descent down the flagpole, popping and pulsing through its triangular panels with an almost radioactive light. Numbers on the digital screen continued to work their way down, seeming to increase the deafening noise from the crowd with each passing second.

As if from one voice, the masses joined in on the countdown from ten, thundering back in confirmation what they saw on the screen. It was within that atmospheric ecstasy the next moment occurred. Like the slamming of breaks after a burst of acceleration, the proceedings came to an unnerving halt. The giant Jumbotron screen was the first casualty, followed in quick succession by the rest of the digital screens inside Times Square. The sudden lack of overwhelming light made the intersection seem much darker than it was, evoking a mixed reaction from the crowd. At first, small clusters continued cheering, exhibiting the mindset that it was too late to stop now. But the vast remainder chose a discontented silence that rippled through the audience.

Then, at the stroke of midnight, the confetti cannons discharged saturating the area with three thousand pounds of colorful paper. Awash in a snowstorm of barely visibly confetti, the crowd again seemed to try and revamp the level of excitement that had been lost. Breakouts of laughter and hollering were not enough to reignite the momentum, and the crowd again fell quiet.

Darkness fell over Times Square. The first few notes of *Auld Lang Syne* faded into the open breeze. A pall of trepidation slowly drifted through the masses—some fearing that the power outage had put an end to the festivities, others fearing that this was something else entirely. Countless pairs of eyes gazed up at the shape-shifting nature of the confetti swarm. It moved above and around and below them unnaturally, no longer tethered to any meaning or purpose. Onlookers tried to make sense of it all. Murmurs of concern ricochetted from person to person.

It was sixty seconds into the new year when the massive Jumbotron screen reemerged with power. The light was blinding, piercing the blackout like a saber and overcoming the remaining strips of confetti obscuring the sky. Bathed in a silver hue from the screen, the audience watched as a message slowly crawled up from the bottom of the Jumbotron. It read:

365
Days
Until
The
End
Of
Time

For all in attendance, and for billions more around the world, the sinister words made their appearance and then vanished from the screen. The nonplussed reactions from the crowd vacillated between snarky laughter to all-encompassing horror. No one knew the proper response, for no one knew from whom the message came. Whether a hacker's prank or a genuine threat, the deed was done, and the moments that followed of power restoration and the return of normal technical operations could not anesthetize the image from their minds.

Watching the events unfold live, Mirai discovered that her mouth was agape. Her dark eyes drank in the imbroglio of the crowd, of the news commentators, and finally, the expression David flashed at her the moment their gazes locked.

Mirai blinked, hesitated, and eventually found her footing again as they gathered their food and walked back to the car in a bewildered daze. Once on the road, she continued to hold the events of the day within the worry lines on her face, a face that lit up from the bright headlamps of a passing semi-truck on the other side of the interstate. As it passed, it illuminated a lonesome billboard in the middle of nowhere—one with a question that seemed to have no answer.

CHAPTER 2
MAN ON THE AIR

Is This the End of the World?

He stared out the window wall of his office and grimaced. The billboard sat atop a small apartment complex a few streets over. For years the old sign had promoted whatever the latest trend, or event, or celebrity needed a few thousand more eyes to fulfill a marketing budget. Only recently was the new message erected. Bold white letters against a black background, an imposing question mark, no mention of a sponsor or agency. Just seven words aimed directly at his vantage point. The young man's ocean-blue eyes kept rereading the message. Each time he hoped to discover its true meaning, even as his intuition told him that the effort was futile.

"Mr. Lalonde?" the intercom buzzed. "He's in the studio. Ten minutes to air."

"Got it. I'm on my way."

Neal Lalonde glanced over at the wall clock and then confirmed it against his wristwatch. He slowly rolled up the sleeves of his gray dress shirt and took hold of a leather portfolio situated on his desk. He walked along the carpeted hallways of the network office without noticing anything or anyone around him. His mind was preoccupied with the sign, and more so, a concern the sign's ambiguous message may have on a particular member of the broadcast team.

When he reached a door marked Studio E, he hesitated while peering through the soundproof window above the half wall. The room inside was split down the middle, each side a mirror image of the other. Broadcast console boards, indicator lights, metal racks with various condensers and inputs, and the element that seemed to tie the whole studio together, a microphone flawlessly hung from a boom arm stand affixed to the desk. On the right side of the partition was an empty chair where the show's producer or engineer might sit. On the other side was the host.

Neal caught his own reflection within the glass as he stared at his father. The two men had similar facial features, but that was where the similarities ended. Howard was nearly seventy, with thinning white hair, green eyes, and wireframe glasses that always needed cleaning. He was a short, slim man who favored sport coats and slacks. He drank too much coffee and had a bad habit of eating food in the studio, often leaving behind crumbs on the console. He could be exacting, aloof, disingenuous, and at certain times, curt. Everyone within the family and the network staff had a differing opinion about him. One thing was universally agreed upon:

His voice was one in a million.

"It's January 1st and I'm Howard Lalonde," he said, addressing the mic as if speaking into someone's ear. "*Thoughtful Conversations* is up next, right after the top of the hour news. I trust you'll stay with us."

His finger smacked a red button on the panel and the *ON AIR* sign went dark. Neal nodded to himself and entered the studio across the partition. He sat down and smiled cautiously at his father through the glass. Neal's reflection was that of a thirty-year-old, with dark-brown hair that held the occasional curl, a boyish face meeting a fixed jawline, and the kind of blue eyes that seemed to hold perpetual concern. He rubbed his hand against the sleeve of his satin dress shirt while trying to warm up to the feeling of being inside a studio. That feeling always eluded him.

"Hey, Dad," Neal said into the mic.

"Neal," Howard replied.

Both men wore broadcast headphones, the cords of which ran down around the back of the consoles and conjoined with the frightening number of other cables feeding into the equipment. Neal drew in a quick breath and said, "Sounding good today. Did you sleep well?"

Howard ignored the question. His eyes were busy looking down at his notes. Neal pursed his lips, trying to analyze how to field the next question without antagonizing the pre-show host. He stole a glance at the countdown clock that was synchronized on both sides of the window. It was less than two minutes to airtime.

"Mom mentioned you didn't eat anything this morning," Neal said, trying to sound casual. "So I was just wondering if you were feeling all right."

Howard blinked, let out a single chuckle, and looked up at Neal through the glass enclosure. "Is that so? What else did the kommandant report?"

Neal bristled and knew he was showing it. He regretted broaching the topic so soon to showtime, but the responsibility of making sure Howard got on the air and maintained his usual level of showmanship had fallen on Neal's shoulders. It was a family-sanctioned task he both accepted and resented.

"I appreciate your concern, Neal, but I don't need you to babysit me. I've been a venerable broadcaster for four decades, and thanks to you all, my weekday program is now less than fifteen minutes long. I know you think it's suddenly a heavy burden for me—"

"Dad…"

"—and that I'm about to forget my own name, but I assure you, son, I can do this in my sleep."

Neal exhaled slowly into the microphone. Howard winced. "For God's sake, Neal, would you please not do that? I must have told you that a hundred times over the years."

"Sorry."

"You don't exhale into the mic."

"I… I know, Dad…"

"No, you don't. You've never addressed the mic properly. Your levels are always way off. Your elocution is sloppy. It's like I raised a pampered little disc jockey instead of a broadcaster."

Neal nodded slowly and said nothing. He glanced again at the countdown clock and in the background heard the news reporter wrapping up the segment. With a nonthreatening grin, he said, "Have a good show, Dad."

Neal pressed a button on the console and leaned back a bit in his chair. He saw his father close his eyes, take a few deep breaths, and position himself just so before the microphone. A few seconds later, the red *ON AIR* sign blazed to life.

"Greetings listening family, and a Happy New Year to you all. Welcome to the Thursday-morning edition of *Thoughtful Conversations*. This is your old friend, Howard Lalonde, broadcasting live from our PRN America headquarters here in Santa Monica, California. It's a gorgeous day outside our studios and I hope it is where you are. If not, maybe this funny news story I came across will brighten your morning."

Neal watched his father work. The man was legendary, as professional as any war correspondent, as colloquial as any hometown hero. He could wield the timbre of his voice effortlessly, moving the listener from one thought to the next, from reason to emotion and back again. He had built the network from one station into a behemoth of over three hundred stations spanning North America. Internet radio followed shortly thereafter, generating dividends the network reaped in perpetuity.

"So, what else is new?" Howard asked the listening audience. "Well, I'll tell yah, the network is about to add a new station to its broadcast family. 90.5 FM in Winchel, Florida. That's right. Our new license will allow us to bring this amazing Palisades Radio right into the communities of the Space Coast. We're talking Titusville, Melbourne, Cape Canaveral, and Cocoa Beach."

Neal blinked and leaned forward onto the console.

"This is a beautiful area, folks. And we're gonna need your help to spread the word. Since this network is one hundred percent listener supported, your generosity will allow us to bring your favorite informational, inspirational, and educational programs into a new region…"

"Dad…no…" Neal said, knowing his own microphone was turned off.

"…so if you live in Florida or know someone who does…"

Neal glanced down at the broadcast panel and searched for his own *On Air* switch. The moment he saw the red button, his heart began to palpitate.

"That's right, friends. 90.5 FM—Winchel, Florida. A new addition to the PRN America—"

"Hey, Dad," Neal's voice said, penetrating the show without introduction. "Sorry to interrupt. Just walked into the studio here and thought I'd greet the network family too."

Neal felt his pulse beating into his throat. This was hardly his first time on the air. It always felt like his last.

Howard stared at him for a moment, at first with a glare of daggers in his eyes, and then slowly, into the expression of one about to witness a disaster. "Well, look who just walked into the studio, ladies and gentleman. My son, and the operations manager of the network, Neal Lalonde. Neal…how are you this morning?"

"Just fine, Dad," Neal said, suppressing the urge to vomit. "I wanted to mention something briefly, then I'll…you know, be out of your hair. Um…as you know, 90.5 FM Winchel is *already* part of our listening family. Has been for over thirty years. I believe you meant to say 88.9 FM Preston, Oregon…will be our—you know—our new station. Right, Dad?"

At first, Howard stared at Neal through the window, seemingly on the verge of rage that his cadence had been interrupted. Howard blinked a few times, regained some semblance of calm, and looked down at his notes as if trying to find his pacing.

Neal counted the seconds of dead air. More than that, he felt them. He parted his lips to fill the void, but then hesitated as Howard said, "Preston, Oregon, of course. How silly of me. 90.5 FM Preston. Yes."

Neal cringed. "Uh…88.9 FM Preston. That's where new listeners should tune their dials. The transmitter was just turned on this morning." With that, Neal threw in a stuttered laugh. "What a day to start. Happy New Year, Preston."

The two men stared at each other through the glass. Neal then saw Howard's eyes start to wander the studio. On the old man's face was a look of concern that was steadily growing into confusion. Neal swallowed and pulled the microphone closer to his lips. "Um…so yeah. Good that we got that clarified. 88.9 FM. Welcome to the network family, Preston."

Neal watched as Howard's gaze fell down to his notes. He was sifting through them, casually, with an odd sort of resignation, almost as if he had forgotten that he was still on the air.

Neal shut his eyes and said, "So, Dad, any big plans for the new year?"

Howard did not respond. He continued scouring his notes.

"Because in my department—operations—we'll be finally upgrading some automation equipment. We're all excited about that. The one we're currently using is…well, some of it is older than me."

Neal felt the padded walls of the studio closing in on him. He drew in another breath and said, "Um… So, you know, everyone, I think that's gonna wrap up this episode of *Thoughtful Conversations*. Stay tuned for more music, followed by *The Jeff Larkin Show* at the bottom of the hour. From each of us here, we wish you an enjoyable Thursday and an excellent weekend ahead."

Neal reached the end of his sentence at the same moment he reached the end of his breath. He smacked the off-air button and gasped. In the background he heard the pre-recorded playlist proclaim the network ID.

"You're listening to PRN America…"

Neal leaned forward against his legs while trying to regulate his breathing. His eyes were still closed. His heart was still pounding. And the dreaded task of checking in on his father yet awaited him. After a few moments of recomposing, Neal stood up and walked around the partition to the other side of the studio.

Let the lambasting begin.

"Hey, sorry about that, Dad," Neal said. "I was just worried we might offend our longtime Space Coast listeners."

Howard glanced up at him, shrugged, and went back to arranging his notes. "Well, we shouldn't do that. That's for sure."

Neal paused. "Shouldn't do what?"

"Offend our listeners. They're the ones who keep us on the air. It's vital that we maintain a covenant with them. We talk, they listen, they tell their friends about us, and so forth. It's a relationship."

Neal looked down at his father, suddenly realizing that they were having two different conversations. "Right. You're absolutely right, Dad."

"Don't patronize me. I'm not your mother."

A simple nod served as a reply. Neal patted his father on the shoulder. "We should probably vacate the studio so Jeff can prepare."

"Jeff uses Studio C. Always has."

"Right."

"And you use too many filler words on the air, Neal. Too many 'uhs' and 'ums.' I've warned you about that."

"Yes, yes you have."

"Your diction needs to be smooth. There should be a natural cadence to the way you speak. You have no broadcast rhythm. You make me uncomfortable whenever you join my segments. You make the audience uncomfortable. I hate that. I hate listening to you on the air."

The words lingered within the stale oxygen inside Studio E. Neal held his position next to his father while searching for a proportional response. He found none. All he could think of was that after two decades of coaching from the man with the golden voice, his cutting words still stung. With a long sigh, Neal reluctantly smiled at his father. "I know, Dad."

His thoughts drifted to his next conversation, and how to start it without unloading his anger all at once. As Howard arose from his chair, Neal caught a glimpse of his father's notes. He knew in that moment that his justified rage could no longer be contained.

"It's reckless!" Neal exclaimed to his sister while pacing her office. "Inexcusably reckless! To continue putting him in a situation where he can humiliate himself, embarrass the network. I don't get it, Tea. What the hell are we doing?"

Teagan Lalonde watched her brother walk back and forth next to her window wall. In his hands were Howard Lalonde's scribbled notes.

"You're preaching to the choir, Neal. You know it's the board's decision and not mine. Dad maintains the network listenership and brings in the donations come fundraising time. Trust me, I've gone to war over this. I have zero allies in the boardroom. I can't cross them. Not on this issue. They want Dad to stay on the air, so he stays."

"What good is being vice president of the network if you have no power?" Neal shot back. "I mean look at this!" With the flick of his wrist, he tossed the notes across Teagan's desk. "It's absolute madness. No wonder he couldn't find his place. It's nonsensical ramblings. Fragmented sentences. Scribbled lines leading nowhere."

Teagan gave the scattered papers little more than a glance before nodding in agreement. "Neal, sit down, please?"

Her calm, intelligent voice was one Neal had always trusted. Teagan was seven years his senior and had fallen in love with radio the first time she had heard her father's program. The link between knowing a person was across town and then hearing that person on a tiny box in the living room had mesmerized her. At the age of twelve years old, she decided that she would one day run the network.

That declaration was perfectly fine with Neal, who enjoyed radio for what he could program, automate, audibly enhance, and fine-tune. He was a troubleshooter and spent most of his time in the master control room setting up programming logs, playlists, debugging software, and patching in signals using technology both new and ancient. He worked with a small team of network operators, and at the age of thirty, was promoted to network operations manager. With his new title came an added responsibility—caretaker for the family patriarch whenever he was addressing a microphone.

"How bad was it?" Teagan asked.

Neal shrugged. "By our standards? Pretty bad. He mixed up stations, states, frequencies, drifted out of the discussion midsentence. Lots of dead airtime, which I filled with my usual graceless charm. Oh, and apparently, now Palisades Radio Network is one hundred percent listener supported."

"Good Lord," Teagan groaned.

"Yeah. The FCC and IRS should be interested to learn that."

"Obviously, Dad just forgot."

"Forgot?" Neal emphasized. "The man developed the revenue model on which this entire network operates forty years ago. Noncommercial stations, tax-deductible donations from listeners, local business underwriters to sponsor specific shows while we 'acknowledge their contributions on air,' and nationally syndicated programs kicking in airtime fees to help defray the broadcast costs of their individual time slots. That's how he grew this network to three hundred stations, and that's how Mom and Dad can afford to live in Pacific Palisades."

Neal grunted while swiping a throat lozenge from off Teagan's desk. As he unwrapped it, he said sarcastically, "'Obviously, Dad just forgot.' No, Tea. Dad has early-stage dementia."

The spacious office fell silent. Neal and Teagan gazed anywhere but at each other. Two window walls met at a corner, allowing the midmorning sunlight to bathe the teakwood credenza in radiance. Within its panel doors was an assortment of scotches, whiskeys, and gins. The siblings both stared at the cabinet for a moment before deciding that it was too early in the day for a drink.

Teagan arose from her desk. Her peach-colored skirt and sleeveless white blouse swayed as she walked, as did a wavy lock of strawberry-blonde hair that bounced against the black frames of her horn-rimmed glasses. Her hair was perpetually in a French twist and secured by a beige clip. She constructed her wardrobe and appearance the same way she conducted her business—focusing on form and function.

Stretched out across the majority of the main wall in the office was a printed world map on which tiny dots indicated where PRN America had a presence. Red dots meant full power stations, blue dots were translators, yellow dots were satellators, and the green dots were primarily speckled outside of North America where the international web streaming had the most impact. Teagan scanned the wall while resting her hands on her hips. Her hazel eyes darted from point to point, assembling a profile of something in her mind.

"Tell me again. What stations did he mix up?"

"88.9 Preston, Oregon with 90.5 Winchel, Florida."

Teagan raised an eyebrow. "Off by three thousand miles. Why the hell would he get his coasts turned around?"

Neal shook his head. "I don't know, sis. But probably not the best station to draw attention to. Winchel hasn't been self-supporting since it began."

"Don't remind me," Teagan said, her shoulders stiffening. "The board brings it up each quarter. They wanted 90.5 and its annual multimillion-dollar budget deficit gone long ago. But Dad wouldn't hear of it. He demanded it stay on the air, so they backed off."

"If it's a revenue drain on the network, why does he insist on keeping it?"

"Our father is a very sentimental man, Neal."

"Yeah, well, the hourly rate on nostalgia has been skyrocketing. I saw the last financials report, same as everyone. Winchel isn't the only station hemorrhaging cash."

Teagan clasped her hands behind her back and began to pace. "It gets worse. Donations are down year over year."

Neal pivoted back toward his sister. "Again? Isn't that the second year in a row?"

"Third."

Neal felt the sudden urge to slouch, yet something from his early childhood training instructed him not to. Whether seated in front of a microphone in a studio or eating dinner at the family table, slouching had never been acceptable. No matter the daunting task set before him, he was to do it straight up, in defiance of the weight, in defense of his own honor, an act of exercising his self-esteem. He blinked and turned back toward the map.

Teagan said, "Oh, by the way, Mom sent an email. We're all invited to dinner tonight."

"*Lovely.*"

"Don't be like that. Mom has to deal with Dad too. This isn't easy for her either. We only have to manage him a few hours a day. She's facing the brunt of his confusion, mood swings, irritability, all of it."

Neal nodded apologetically. "I know. I don't mean to sound dismissive. I just… I'll…I'll be there."

Teagan nodded and walked back to her desk. Neal continued to visually absorb the dotted Mercator map before him. Using his forefinger, he drew an invisible line from Oregon down to Florida. He tapped on the state and narrowed his eyes. "Why would he be thinking about Cocoa Beach?"

The question remained even as the siblings left the network premises for lunch. Neal drove Teagan in his two-seat convertible down a winding executive road and back onto the main street. A few miles away stood a bistro they often frequented; one that served mediocre food in a relaxed, decompressing atmosphere.

While eating their soup and sandwich combos, Neal and Teagan sat in nonvocal acknowledgement of the pleasantness of the moment. The lunch outing was a twice weekly ritual. It allowed for a disconnect from all things broadcasting. Conversation was allowed. They usually ate in silence.

It wasn't until they returned to Neal's car that the omnipresent signal of PRN America reemerged through his high-end stereo speakers. The announcer was rambling off the local weather report for Southern California. Neal mused to himself at the chicanery of radio, and how localized announcements could be surreptitiously dropped into the regional playlists of stations all across the country, giving the spot the feel of having a broadcaster sitting in a studio right across town who knew the weather, news, events, and attractions of that particular city. In actuality, only a handful of PRN stations had local staff. Most of the on-air content was broadcast via satellite from the

PRN America studios in Santa Monica. Local news and weather was one of the sleight-of-hand tricks of the network radio trade, and it always left Neal grinning.

"Did you see what happened in Times Square last night?" asked Teagan.

Neal blinked while both recalling the event and making an ancillary mental connection. "Yeah, I did. I wasn't gonna stay up, but I changed my mind."

Teagan shook her head disapprovingly. "'365 Days Until the End of Time.' Who would do something like that? Some low-life pranksters who have no concern for the fragile state of their audience?"

"I think disturbing the nation was the whole point, Tea."

"I hope they find whoever did it. Make them publicly acknowledge that it was a lie."

Neal sighed heavily. "Speaking of pranksters, did you see the new billboard they erected across from our side of the building?"

Teagan chuckled derisively. "Oh, yes. '*Is This the End of the World?*' Probably the same feeble minds behind the New Year's Eve prank."

"It's the feeble mind who runs this network that concerns me," said Neal. "Dad's office has a clear view of that billboard. I'm worried what that message might do to him. How it might condition him."

"Dad isn't senile. He has times of confusion, but I doubt—"

Teagan's rebuttal was sharply cut off by the sudden and excruciating screech of an emergency alert signal broadcasting through the speakers. What followed were the two discordant sine wave tones that had become so hardwired into the public psyche that they could command attention no matter how grave the interruption.

Neal glanced at his wristwatch. "We just ran the EAS alert test two days ago. What the hell is Master Control doing?"

As the signal slowly faded, a metallic voice crackled from within the frequency, sounding as if it was transmitting from the edge of a cataclysm. "This is a message from the Emergency Alert System. The following alert is being broadcast nationwide at the request of the United States government. This is not a test."

Neal felt a chill saturate every nerve ending in his body. Like so many others, he had grown up with severe weather alerts, special bulletins, and breaking news presented with a certain level of gravitas. But the terrifying pulse of the EAS signal had always been something different. Knowing that it was only ever a test of the system had acted as its own sedative. The fear that it might one day not be rushed to the forefront of his consciousness with the fury of a locomotive.

This is not a test…

Neal glanced over at Teagan who was already looking at him. The two held each other's gaze as the static gave birth to a voice. It was a voice unlike any Neal had ever heard, yet he was certain that he had heard it. It was the voice of a man who sounded as if he had been driven to the precipice of sanity. His lack of oratory, of poise, of basic broadcast showmanship, sent a panic surging through the vehicle.

The voice began speaking, yet already sounded hoarse, as if it had been railing against the most heinous of evils for hours without end.

"…Will you…will you just…listen to me for a minute? I need—I need to get this all out…before…before they cut me off." The man's words trembled through his teeth as he said, "I—I…I know how this is gonna sound. But you all need to listen to me…because…I don't—I don't have a lot of time here."

"Oh my God," said Teagan.

"That's Dad," confirmed Neal.

"I am…*not*…supposed to be talking about this—about *any* of this —but…but…I cannot, I will not be subject to their demands any longer. You all must know…the truth…and yet…there's too much to tell. Too much to explain. And I know how this must sound to you all, I know, I do…but I'm not some—some crackpot…I'm the *goddamn president of the network!*"

Teagan was scrambling to unpack her purse, spilling its contents onto the passenger side floor of Neal's convertible. "Why aren't they cutting him? Neal? Why aren't your people cutting him off?"

"Damn it, Tea, I don't know!" Neal said, fishing his own phone out of his pants pocket.

Howard continued, "I…I know what I've seen…and it's not me

rambling about Area 51, or aliens, or genetic hybrid mutations…or any nonsense… No, listen… I—I guess…I'll just…the important things you must know…in order to protect yourselves…from what is coming… Because know this…it *is* coming…"

The transmission crackled for a moment, leading Neal to wonder if his father had finally been taken off the air. Yet after a few seconds of radio silence, Howard's frantic intonations again filled the airwaves.

Teagan yelled into her phone, "What the *hell* is going on!? Yes, I'm hearing it now but I'm off campus. Why is he still broadcasting?… Say again? Do I know what?… No… Just—just get me over to someone in master control."

Neal wheeled the car left with his free hand while plastering his phone against his ear. "Somebody better pick up the phone in there— Alan? Alan, it's Neal Lalonde. Why is my father still on the air?… You don't know *what*?… I have no idea which studio he's using! Just flip the switcher to another input… Any of them, Alan! At this moment, dead air would be preferable! I can't believe I'm even discussing this with… What? What do you mean?"

"What's wrong?" pressed Teagan.

Neal's eyes were searching the road ahead of him for an answer. He blinked and glanced over at his sister. "Alan has no idea where Dad is broadcasting from, but all uplink channels are connected to Dad's feed."

"Wait…all… What? How is that possible?"

Neal shook his head. "I—I mean…it's not…"

"…that's the craziest part of this…" said Howard. "Of all of it… The thing which—which I still can barely wrap my head around…is the fact that…that they've been planning this for so long—*so long*— and we're only picking up the pieces now… It's…it's just…" His voice trailed, sinking into the shattered tones of defeat. His sobs formed into wails before he regained any semblance of self-control. Speaking through muffled tears of anger, he continued, "I'm sorry… I'm so very sorry… Your leaders failed you… I—I failed you…because…I just don't see…how—how we're ever gonna be able to stop them. They've infiltrated the highest levels of the federal…of the military…of… So even understanding who can be trusted, at this point…is nearly…"

Neal could barely suppress the growing wave of panic within him. The convertible careened back down the winding executive road inside the corporate park. Glass tinted office buildings punctuated the landscape until one appeared at the end of the cul-de-sac. The breeze rustled the tree branches overhead as the convertible slid to an unceremonious stop at the front entrance to the building. Parked near the entryway was a delivery truck, where a man was unloading paper supply boxes. Clipped to his belt was his phone. The man was smiling as he listened with amusement, as if absorbing some perverse satisfaction from the unhinged man on the air.

"…all we can do now…is beg for mercy…and hope that those in power will decide…to stop—to stop working with them…to stand up and resist them… Those who are engineering our suffering…they are —that is to say—*Ad Ordinem*—"

The sound of abrupt silence was more jarring than the speech. The maniacal voice was gone. Three final screeches from multi-frequency tones indicated an end to the transmission and all was once again mute from the unscheduled broadcast.

Neal and Teagan slammed the car doors shut and raced through the lobby of the network. Ignoring the elevators, they chose the stairwell and pounded the steps up to the fourth floor. Their hearts were galloping when they entered the master control room. Racks of broadcast equipment lined the walls. Indicator lights blinked sporadically along control boards and consoles. The thin needles inside the V/U meters jerked back and forth, matching the vocal intonation of the current announcer who was speaking from a studio down the hall. His words were steadying, calm, apologetic. He spoke as a captain righting a ship, one in which the crew was still disquieted by the passing stormy waves.

"Where are we at, Alan?" Neal asked, resting his hand on the console computer.

"Everything's five by five now. Your father's signal was coming through the EAS machine and was patched into every channel I tried to switch to."

"Who cut him off then?"

"I don't… He must have done it himself. The signal went dead when the tone pulse hit. It was regular programming after that."

"Where is he now?"

"I have no idea where he ever was. I checked the studios. All but C are empty."

Neal spun around and nearly bumped into Teagan. He marched over to the rectangular EAS device housed in one of the electronics racks. Its solo red light blinked intermittently. All had returned to a suspicious normal.

"Maybe he's in his office," said Teagan, already heading out of the room.

Neal followed her as they ascended one more floor and into the executive office suite. Situated in the corner was a grand wooden desk, and behind it, a leather swivel chair. The wrap-around window illuminated the room in brilliant noonday light. The office did not contain Howard Lalonde.

"His car's not in the parking lot," said Neal, pressing his forehead against the window. "You think he went home?"

"I'll call Mom."

"No, I don't want to spook him if he answers. Let's just head over now."

Teagan nodded. "An offspring ambush."

"In a manner of speaking."

As the two siblings turned to leave, Neal's gaze caught the face of the billboard a few streets over. It was even easier to see from his father's office, and even more directly aligned.

"*Is This the End of the World?*" Neal whispered.

Teagan stopped at the threshold and glanced back. "What was that?"

Neal stared at the sign, hands firmly planted on his hips, his face twisting into a scowl. The giant words stood boldly over the city. The black-and-white design was impossible to ignore. Neal's mind was still racing as he tried to make sense of the last few minutes. As the shock was slowly wearing off, a simmering humiliation was beginning to take its place.

This is going to be rebroadcast everywhere…radio, television, online. He'll be made a laughingstock. A titan of the industry reduced to a late-night punchline. This will be replayed for days, weeks. News of it will be covered by every major network. Newspapers will…

Neal's periphery caught the headline a half-second before he turned his face toward his father's cluttered desk. It sat front and center on the blotter, its bold, black letters seeming to levitate off the morning edition: *365 Days Until the End of Time: New Year's Eve Stunt Terrifies Millions.*

As he drove them both to his parents' house in Pacific Palisades, Neal felt his shoulders begin to slouch as he looked over at Teagan. The siblings walked through the grand foyer and into the living room where Howard and Sharon Lalonde sat despondently on the sofa. Neal and Teagan approached carefully, wondering if their mother was aware of what had just gone out over the network. The look on her face registered that she knew.

Howard sat sloppily against a large throw pillow. He appeared slightly out of breath. His face was ashen. His eyes were large and wide, yet also glossy, as if searching for the reason that he suddenly found himself at home.

"Dad," Neal said, walking toward him in measured steps. He sat down on an ottoman and faced his father directly. "Dad, first, we need to know that you're all right."

Howard's eyes darted to his son, with a speed and an accuracy that made Neal self-aware. "Of course I'm all right. Why do you all keep asking me that all the time?"

Teagan approached from behind Neal and sat down in the chair opposite the sofa. Her elbows rested against her knees. Her hands clasped together, looking like the start of either a tough conversation or a prayer.

"Dad, why did you do that?" she asked, her voice an expressionless tone. It sounded to Neal like she was addressing a child.

Howard gazed at them for a moment, his eyebrows furrowed, the corner of his mouth slanted, his glasses smudged. Sharon Lalonde was seated next to him but turned slightly away. Her face expressed a series of painful realizations, all hitting her in rapid succession. She was coming to terms with something difficult to accept. Her body language indicated a premonition that her husband would never accept it.

"Dad," Neal said firmly. "Where were you broadcasting from? What studio did you use?"

A quizzical glare formed in the deep lines of Howard's face. "Whatever are you talking about?"

Neal felt a wave of nausea pass over him. "I'm talking about your broadcast, Dad. The one you just did…basically announcing the end of the world. You bypassed the channels leading to the uplink. I need to know how you did that. I need to know *where* you did that."

Howard shot a glance at Sharon as if to pass a silent judgment on their children. Sharon's eyes remained fixed on the foyer and front door.

"Dad," Teagan interjected, trying to reel in his wandering attention. "You initiated an EAS alert across the entire network—all three hundred radio stations, using an old preempt code only to be used for national emergencies. Do you understand that the network could face serious fines because of this? Possible license suspensions? Does any of that concern you?"

"Where were you, Dad?" Neal asked again, trying to remain calm. "No one could find you in the building, so where were you broadcasting from? Do you have a direct satellite uplink somewhere off campus that we don't know about? If so, you need to tell us. You need to tell us so something like this can *never* happen again."

"Something like what!?" Howard shouted. His anger bubbled momentarily, aimed at the two people peppering him with questions.

Neal exhaled slowly and turned back toward Teagan. "Oh my God," he said gravely.

Teagan shut her eyes for a moment to gather her composure. When she was satisfied that she could stand, she arose from off the stuffed chair and walked around the coffee table to her mother. She rested her hand on the shoulder of Sharon's pink sweater and gave it a soft squeeze. "You doing okay, Mom?"

Sharon nodded in bewilderment. "I'm glad you're here."

Neal rubbed the back of his neck with his hand and began pacing the living room. Cascading light showered the picture windows in an almost overbearing radiance. Even the potted plants on the sills appeared any shade but green. Neal's vision followed the design carved into the wainscoting on the walls. It led him to the other side of the room where an old teakwood cabinet housed the workings of an even older radio. It was as impressive as it was massive, and for the first time ever, Neal realized that it was turned off.

"I think we could all use some chamomile tea," Sharon said as she abruptly left the sofa. "Would anyone else like some?"

"I'll help you, Mom," said Teagan, following her mother into the kitchen from behind.

Howard watched the procession carefully, as if he was awaiting their exit from the room. He blinked a few times and then pointed at Neal. "Come here for a moment."

Neal hesitated but then thought better of it and returned to his seat on the ottoman. "What is it, Dad?"

Howard removed his glasses and stared into Neal's eyes with a frightening attentiveness. At first, Neal was taken aback. He rarely saw his father's piercing, green eyes without the filter of lenses.

"Listen to me," Howard intoned. "I…I'm trying desperately right now to remember why, but it's vital that I get a message to someone. Someone…you…don't know."

Neal sat in perplexed frustration at his father's sudden change of attitude. He leaned forward a bit and asked, "A message? To whom?"

"Kan Thura," Howard said.

"I'm sorry?"

"Pay attention," Howard scolded. His visage registered a fear. It was the fear of hanging on to a memory by his fingernails. "You *must* find him and tell him that…that because…because of everything happening in the world right now…I want him to know… I'm sorry.

Sorry for everything. Can you do that, Neal? Can you find him and tell him that for me?"

Neal's lips struggled to form a reply. "Tell… Who? What?"

"Kan Thura."

"What kind of name is that? Chinese?"

"It's Burmese."

"And you want me to apologize to someone I don't know—on your behalf—over something you did?"

"You must."

Neal sighed heavily. "Dad, no more evasive nonsense. You need to answer *my* question. Do you have a direct uplink—"

"*Neal.*"

"What?"

"Kan Thura. Promise me you'll tell him I'm sorry!"

"Who the hell are you talking about?"

Howard's eyes began to wander, at first out of some internal battle, then seconds later, from the nascent inklings of the onsetting confusion. He took Neal's hands in his own and gripped them tightly. "Promise me, Neal. You must find him…and tell him…tell him… that…"

Neal watched his father's focus meander. "Tell him…you're sorry?"

Howard nodded, distantly. "Yes."

"And just where am I supposed to find this man?"

Howard's mouth pronounced the words but no sound was made. Neal blinked and realized that he had heard them anyway.

"Cocoa Beach."

CHAPTER 3
EMBLEM

They breathed in the ocean air as if having been released from a series
of airtight containers. The drive from the airport parking garage toward
Mirai's house was traversed in reflection of the previous day. David let
his arm hang off the edge of the passenger door, feeling the sensation
of the breeze drifting through his fingers.

"I see you like convertibles," David said with a smirk.

"We all have our idiosyncrasies and this is mine. That Vegas rental
reminded me of driving my own car. Except that, you know, mine is
twelve years older and has more scratches."

"I can't tell you how much I missed the ocean," he said as they
drove along A1A.

"I don't care what people say," added Mirai. "The Atlantic beats
the Pacific for me. The water's warm and clear, and yeah, the sunsets
in California are amazing, but there's something about a Florida
sunrise that gets me eager to start the day."

"I assume you spend a lot of time at the beach here?"

"Here, North Miami, Fort Lauderdale…they're all good."

"I've never been to the beaches down here."

"Oh my God, we need to fix that right now."

Mirai turned the convertible onto a side street and parked next to a row of townhomes. As they walked toward the beach, sporadic gusts of wind made the green fronds on the palm trees sway as if in celebration. The azure sky above them had deepened in tone as a plume of cumulonimbus clouds gave beachgoers momentary refuge from direct sunlight. Along the coast, turquoise waves crested against the shoreline leaving behind water pockets against the light-caramel sand. The entire vista was one of perpetual motion and change. Yet in another sense it seemed impervious to time. It was in the shifting familiarity that Mirai had once realized the nature of change: occasionally, it allowed for the subtle over the dramatic.

She removed her flip-flops and sank her feet into the warm granules of sand. To her surprise, David was already barefoot, having left his socks and leather shoes in the car. She laughed as he said, "Do as the locals do."

They walked together along the water, leaving behind footprints in the sand that overflowed then vanished after each wave. Mirai slid her fingers into the back pockets of her shorts while stealing a glance at David. The stranger walking beside her now seemed more familiar, thanks to the secluded nature of long drives and long flights. She had learned that he was born in Tel Aviv, had musical proclivities since he was four, and—along with his younger brother, Eitan—had lived with family in Europe for a time before immigrating permanently to the United States. His travels as a harp player afforded him only a modest lifestyle, but since he was never one for ostentation, the thought of a more lucrative vocation paled in comparison to his forty-seven-stringed instrument.

"I love symphonic music," he had said on the return flight. "I love what it gives to people. I love what it does to them during and after they hear it."

"What is that?" Mirai had asked.

"An appreciation for being on earth."

David had been satisfied with his life up until a year prior. It was only after the loss of Eitan that things had begun to unravel. The death had been as sudden as it had been tragic. Eitan had been walking home from work when an intoxicated driver skidded onto the sidewalk.

Investigators weren't certain if it was the initial impact of the vehicle that had killed him, or from having been dragged nearly a full city block before the driver realized what was happening. The unrecognizable body of who had been his dearest friend, was a grizzly image David could never shake.

Only the sound of Alexander's indefatigable voice on a local radio station had brought David out of his nightmare. The voice spoke of hope, love, purpose, and healing. The Mesa Revival was already well under way, and the lure of even being close to the claims of restoration and flat-out miracles seemed to be his one remaining lifeline to existence.

"That's when I sold my condo, stored my things, told my agent that I would be taking an extended leave, and flew out to Nevada. At the time, I was hoping to never leave, yet in my heart, I knew my stay there was for a purpose. And once that purpose was completed, it would be time to awaken myself. It was you, Mirai, who pulled me from my slumber."

Mirai looked down at her feet as they walked. Her periwinkle toenail polish glistened in the sunlight. As her eyes returned to the beachgoers, one man had a small wireless speaker baking in the sand next to his folding chair. Mirai and David passed slowly, hearing only the tail end of an argument on a talk show where the caller was expressing genuine fear about the doomsday message in Times Square, and in contrast, the host lambasting the caller for being an idiot.

The scene evaporated into other noises, voices, squawks from seagulls, and revving car engines along the street. The sounds added distance to their steps. Before long, Mirai looked out toward the horizon, her hands still in her back pockets, strands of her hair tousling against her face.

"Are you happy you left the Preserve?" she asked, speaking more in a whisper than intended.

David didn't look at her when he responded. He too was gazing at the horizon. "Is that your question," he began tenderly, "or are you wondering if I'm happy to have come back to earth?"

Deciding that the question was rhetorical, Mirai nodded but then stopped. She parted her lips as her mind formulated something new. Her hesitation in asking prompted a smile from David, who gradually reached his fingers over to her and enveloped her slender hand in his.

"Yes, I'm very happy I came back to earth."

They continued walking until they remembered that there was life beyond the beach. Once back in her car, they drove the three-minute journey down a residential side street and turned a corner. The McGarry home was secluded amongst a row of wax myrtle shrubs on one end and palmetto trees on the other. The exterior design of the home was modern, sleek, and had a large window wall of tempered glass facing the street. The lush lawn was intersected by a tan, herringbone driveway that led to an attached garage.

"Finally home," Mirai said softly, placing the vehicle in park.

David nodded as he assessed the outside surroundings. "What a lovely abode."

"It's my parent's house. I rent the cottage in the backyard, but paint in their solarium. Keeps my expenses low so I can build my art career."

"A wise arrangement."

"It works for now. Come on, I'll show you around the house. You're welcome to stay in the guest bedroom of the main house until you get your affairs in order."

David raised his hand in protest. "I am indebted to you as it is for the travel expenses. If I could just use your phone, I should be able to restore access to my accounts in short order and then be on my way back to…" He hesitated upon remembering that he had nowhere to return. "Well…back to…finding a new place to live."

"It's really no bother. There's plenty of room."

"Greatly appreciated. But I don't wish to be an imposition."

Mirai smiled and shrugged. They meandered up the few steps leading to the main house's side entrance and entered a space filled with natural light.

"Oh my God, I missed this place," she said, doing a twirl upon entering the solarium. "This is it. The place where I paint. Where I work. Where I think. My studio."

"Your sanctuary," extrapolated David. He entered the space with a thoughtful reverence. His eyes wandered for a moment, uncertain where to focus first. The entire room seemed to be windows, allowing for the late afternoon sunlight to cascade into every crevice. On the wall connected to the house were hung canvases, some framed, others naked. It was the hallowed display of struggle from a persistent painter. Next to the inner door of the solarium, a hand-painted sign was affixed to a window. Its cursive text read: *Mirai McGarry—Artist.*

In the center of the room was a four-legged stool and an easel. On the easel was a canvas. David walked up and gazed at it intensely.

Mirai noticed and said, "I finished that right before I left for the Mesa Revival."

The artwork was an amalgamation of landscape and portrait, with sky above and seascape below. Emerging from a mesmerizing chaos in the center was a human face. It was the face of a man. One with sculpted features, a virtuous expression, and the kind of eyes that projected intellectual honesty.

David nodded slowly as he drank it all in. "These paintings, all of your artwork, have a common theme, don't they?"

Mirai smiled brightly. "It is that obvious?"

David continued to stare as he replied, "Order emerging from chaos. But more specifically, human truth—objective truth—bringing order from the chaos. Interestingly, you don't paint the chaos as if it's evil, only chaotic. It's natural, perilous, at times cataclysmic, but not evil. In your paintings the chaos merely is. An irrelevant byproduct of evolution. The human element you infuse creates the order, creates beauty from disarray. It gives the entire painting harmony and balance." David slowly shook his head. "Remarkable."

As she walked over to the stool, she said, "Seems as though you've got me all figured out."

"I haven't even begun to scratch the surface."

A stare was held between the two until it became too heavy to maintain. She shifted her glance away first, looking down at a liner brush on the table. After taking hold of it and rotating its fine bristles in a fresh splotch of purple paint, she sat down in front of the canvas and hesitated.

"There was one thing I didn't do before I left." She then leaned in and painted her signature on the lower left corner of the canvas. With artistic flair, the moniker sealed the fate of the painting, marked by the artist who identified solely as Mirai. The *M* was fashioned into the shape of a heart, making the trademark even more distinguished. It was a relic of her formative years, a memory from as far back as she could recall. The day she realized that the word *art* was in *heart,* she never again signed one of her paintings without it.

Even while inching away from the canvas, the hand holding the paintbrush seemed poised to strike again. She gradually relaxed her arm and set the brush down on the easel. Her shoulders began to slump as the creative tension drained from her body. There was no eagerness to move from off the stool. Nowhere else in the studio, in the house, or in the world for that matter, held any concern for her, for it would be outside the realm of her current achievement.

She wiped her hands against her denim romper and let out a heavy sigh. Her bare feet dangled over a floor stained with dried paint. Within the stains were fragments of footprints, evidence of the miles walked in search of an idea, or a vision, or a revelation of human truth.

David gently rested his hand on her shoulder and the two absorbed the finality of the piece. Behind the easel, the sun was now completely hidden behind a series of cloud formations towering into the sky. The overcast moved across the landscape of the neighborhood, but contained within itself all of the hallmarks of something that would soon pass, once again giving way to warmth and light.

Mirai parted her lips to speak, but words tethered to an emotion kept them leashed to her heart.

David noticed the struggle and said, "Are you thinking about Julie?"

Mirai shifted a bit on the stool but then worried that David would remove his hand from her shoulder. He did not. She said, "Why did you save the diary from being burned? You didn't know me at all. You didn't know if I was worth the price you knew you'd have to pay if you defied Alexander. Why did you do it?"

David's face suddenly beamed with excitement. "An excellent question. Why do you think I did it?"

"Well… Sometimes guys are nice because they wanna bang me. Or control me. Or manipulate me into giving them money. Or giving them advice on their own artistic ambitions."

David frowned in agreement. "I'm sure of that."

"But I don't believe that was your reason. You opened the book, read the first line, and I saw it in your eyes that your decision had been made. I knew the book was saved before you even said anything. So again…why?"

The short walk over to Mirai's backpack seemed to occur in slow motion. She watched him return with the diary in hand. As he stood next to her, he gently opened the book and read the first line.

"Beauty will save the world."

The two held the silence, for it was in the silence that the reason was becoming clear. David then looked up from the book and said to Mirai, "Ideals—the ones that are impactful, the ones that stand the test of time—come solely from the minds of those who have the moral virtue to create them. That you would travel so far, risk your own well-being, all to give someone a reminder of who they really are, that takes tremendous courage. In that moment, when I read that line, it dawned on me."

"What did?"

"That courage creates courage. You took a stand for something *objectively* true in that wretched place. You sought out your best friend to rescue her from peril. You declared something hollow that almost everyone else in the world is declaring good, and you laid out the reasons why in front of all to hear—including the mastermind himself. What you did was pure art. It was a towering ideal. It was an act of beauty. It was…the powerful force of moral virtue, Mirai. *That* was why I saved your book. In that instant, I knew I could do nothing less."

The edges around Mirai's face softened as she allowed herself the permission to accept his compliment. The sensation felt deeper than what she was normally accustomed to, and after a moment of contemplation, she gradually realized why. Most compliments from other people were typically aimed at one of her defining physical traits. Yet the unsolicited acknowledgment of the value of one of her choices caught Mirai off guard. Its rarity made the statement all the more appreciated, for it was nothing short of a salute toward her ability to think.

"Sounds like my family is home. Let me introduce you. Oh, and just to answer your question in advance, the facial scarring you'll see on my parents is from an apartment fire that happened before I was adopted. They lost everything; family photos, keepsakes, all of it. They both survived—obviously—but needed a bit of skin grafting afterward."

"My goodness. How tragic for them. Thank you for the heads-up, but I wouldn't think of asking them about it."

Mirai huffed. "You'd be surprised. Some people do."

They walked across the threshold and into a hallway that led to the living room. Mirai had expected to hear their voices, but instead, only heard one voice—the pained, crazed, desperate tones of a man losing his mind on the air. The sounds were coming from the television.

As the two entered, Mirai spotted her parents on the sofa and her sister, Carys, seated in the adjacent chaise lounge, with one of her legs draped over the arm. The family had not yet noticed them, their senses overwhelmed by the news report of the mad diatribe of Howard Lalonde.

"…all we can do now…is beg for mercy…and hope that those in power will decide…to stop—to stop working with them…to stand up and resist them… Those who are engineering our suffering…they are —that is to say—*Ad Ordinem*—"

"Again, that was a rebroadcast of what aired just hours ago on PRN America," a news anchor said matter-of-factly. "Founder and president of the network, Howard Lalonde, made the speech this morning during an unofficial EAS alert that claimed to be a message from the United States government. It aired live across all PRN stations as well as several affiliates carrying the preempted program. An official statement was released just minutes ago by network executive Teagan Lalonde…"

The McGarrys all turned to see Mirai and David at the same moment.

"Oh hey, you're back!" Jason McGarry said, seeming slightly dazed by the news story. As if being pulled in two directions at once, he glanced back at the family once more before walking quickly over to embrace the weary travelers.

"Hey, Dad," Mirai said, being absorbed by his hug.

"We missed you, kiddo. Our hero returns."

Mirai smiled and turned to embrace her mother and sister. "I don't know about that," she said, trying her best to infuse humor into a statement ripe with disappointment.

Jason caressed Mirai's face in his hands and placed a firm kiss on her forehead. "We are so proud of you for trying. You're truly braver than I'll ever be."

"Than either of us," added Valerie McGarry. "I can't think of a single friend I've ever had who would have traveled across the country to talk me out of joining a cult. What you did was admirable. I'm sure Julie will come to her senses in time."

Mirai nodded slowly, wondering why her face suddenly felt flush. It was then she remembered that David was standing just off-center of the family. "Mom, Dad, this is the guy I told you about on the phone. David Eban. David, these are my parents, Jason and Valerie."

The three exchanged handshakes and momentary pleasantries. "Thanks for standing up for Mirai," Jason said, gripping David's shoulder. "I admire anyone who can stand alone. It's never easy. But it shows character. I appreciate what you did."

David tilted his head graciously. "I was fortunate to stand up for such a worthy woman."

Mirai turned to her younger sister and pulled her into a tight side-hug. Carys was slightly taller than Mirai, yet Mirai's stance had a way of projecting that she was the protective sibling. The young model had her mother's honey-brown eyes, but that was where the similarities ended. Her bright-blonde hair complimented the horizontal line of freckles that crossed over the bridge of her celestial nose and ended at her cheeks. Her face was striking, and seemed to have emerged in total disregard to her parents' more rugged, open-faced features. Beyond the facial structure was the essence of her expression. Carys looked at people in a way that made them remember that she had seen them.

Mirai smiled. "David, my not-so-little-anymore sister."

"Carys McGarry," David said warmly. "I've certainly seen your face before. A model with a bright future. A seventeen-year-old virtuoso, they say."

Carys nodded and shook his hand. "Model, yes; virtuoso is a stretch. Nice to meet you."

"I'm trying to recall what work of yours I've seen."

"Depends," Carys said. "You read any teen fashion magazines or buy any makeup products?"

"That would be a firm no to both questions," David said.

"Then you probably know me as the backseat daughter from that TV and internet car commercial."

David's eyes widened. "Oh—yes. The one in which you're teaching the parents how to use the vehicle's high-tech navigation system. Hysterical ad."

Jason laughed. "Art imitating life."

Mirai turned to her mother. "What's going on with that radio network?"

Valerie shook her head slowly. "It's so sad. Sounds like the founder went insane. Warned all his listeners that the world was in danger because of some group manufacturing our suffering. Poor man."

"A group?" blurted Mirai. "What do you mean? Like, a government?"

Valerie hesitated. "No. I think he said…something like, Ad Ordinem."

Jason cleared his throat. "I hate to say I predicted something like this would happen, but I stopped listening to that station years ago because of the direction they took."

"Direction?" asked David.

"Well, don't get me wrong. PRN has great music and talk shows, and every now and then I'll tune in for that. But—come on, Howard Lalonde practically made Alexander a household name. He put him on the air, gave him his own daily time slot, and enabled him to become the powerhouse that he is today. Even after Alexander became a cult leader, built the Preserve, generated that massive following around the globe and within the Mesa Revival, Lalonde still decided to keep that lunatic on the air. PRN feeds Alexander's signal to any affiliate station who wants it, despite knowing exactly what that man is. It's morally indefensible."

Mirai nodded thoughtfully. "So, what happened to Lalonde?"

"They cut him off," Valerie said. "Only after he freaked out millions of people."

"And not a full day after the Times Square event either," added Jason. "What a nutty start to the year!"

Mirai and David finished catching up with the McGarrys before exiting the house and crossing the lush lawn of the backyard. Up a few steps and into the front door of the cottage, Mirai's abode was small, cozy, and filled with internal color.

"Kitchen, living room," she said, pointing in opposite directions for both. A flight of stairs led them up to a sizable bathroom and two bedrooms, one of which had a giant poster of a flamingo. "Don't judge me," Mirai scolded. "Julie gave me this poster when I was twelve and I've loved it ever since."

"I'm a big fan of flamingoes myself."

"Shut up," Mirai said playfully, and led him back down the stairwell, across the yard, and into the solarium. As she did, the chestnut highlights in her black hair radiated to life from the sunlight peeking through the windows. David looked directly at her, now having to squint from the rays.

"Ad Ordinem," she said, her voice soft without being a whisper.

"Yes."

"Do you know what that means?"

"It's Latin…"

"I know…but like…what does it mean in English?"

David blinked and then turned away, his eyes smarting under the intensity of the window's light. "I believe it means…'towards order.'"

The statement hung in the air while Mirai looked down at the colorful floor of her art studio. *Order and chaos. Suffering. Your last MRI confirmed our suspicions.*

Her body involuntarily jerked when she remembered the doctor's office. The memory broke through her mental barricade, demanding to be acknowledged, dealt with, processed. The doctor had said something to her, something her recollection could barely recall even in the seconds afterward. The room had smelled sterile. It had been devoid of color, and that detail threatened to pull her away from the conversation yet again.

"Can you repeat that?" Mirai had asked.

Dr. Wallace nodded understandingly. His words came carefully, each syllable rich with elocution. "I said your last MRI confirmed our suspicions. You have a relapsing-remitting case of multiple sclerosis."

I have what? she had thought to herself.

Looking down at the table next to her, she caught sight of her patient chart cocooned within an open manilla folder. The top form contained all of the standard information: *Name—Mirai McGarry; Age —twenty-four; Race—Asian American…*

As her eyes followed the entries down the page, she noticed a box labeled "Conditions." Her eyes had quickly darted away.

"Do you know what MS is, Mirai?"

She pondered the question as if determined to forget about the pain that radiated up and down the length of her arm and into her right shoulder. The tingling sensation felt like needles with the occasional horror of electric shock. Over many months she had grown accustomed to it, interspersed by periods of time when she could scarcely stand it. Yet the pain was not the part of the phantom that caused her fear, for as an artist, Mirai did not fear pain.

She feared only the numbness afterward.

"Not really, doctor," she had replied, no longer remembering the question.

Dr. Wallace had reached for the imaging and pointed at her head scan. "MS is an autoimmune disease. Simply put, there's a coating around the central nerves in your brain called myelin. Think of it as a protective sheath that allows electrical impulses to transmit unimpeded.

What multiple sclerosis does is attack that insular layer, leaving behind lesions, or tissue damage, that can negatively affect your central nervous system. Does that make sense so far?"

Mirai nodded reflexively. "*Multiple* sclerosis. Isn't one enough?" Her attempt at levity did not break the tension. She dismissed the remark as Dr. Wallace continued.

"Now, despite common misconceptions about MS, the disease is generally not fatal."

I have a disease...

"Life expectancies are only slightly shorter on average than the general population. You have a very common kind of MS, the relapsing-remitting kind. What it means is that during a relapse, you'll have an increase in—we'll call them episodes—where your pain, numbness, blurred vision, fatigue, will become more acute. All at different intervals, of course."

Of course.

"During periods of remission, your symptoms will subside, leading to partial recovery. Spans between relapses can vary, ranging from several a year, to years spread apart."

"Is there a cure?" Mirai had asked, with a follow-up question ready to fire.

"Not at this time, no. However, through interferon medications and some lifestyle adjustments, MS can be manageable. We have a team here who can help you navigate—"

"Will I still be able to paint?"

The doctor turned his head slightly. "I didn't catch that."

Mirai had felt a quiver in her lower lip as she spoke. Determined not to show it, she gesticulated with her right hand the motions of a brushstroke.

"Paint. I'm an artist. Before I could properly hold a pencil I could hold a brush. I started on construction paper, painting waterfalls and trees. My teachers said I was a natural, so my parents got me an art tutor. I moved on from watercolors and started doing oils on canvas by the time I was eight. I won my first award in junior high for a portrait I did of my best friend, Julie. Later I attended art school. I opened my own studio in the solarium of my parents' house where I do commissions plus my own artwork. People often ask me if I'm worried about my career choice; if I think generative AI will eventually replace artists. I'm not concerned about that, you know why? Because the next thing we crave after beauty is story, and only human beings have a *true* story behind their work. My story and my art are all I have to offer.

"I was an average student, Dr. Wallace. I failed trigonometry. Could never remember what a prepositional phrase was. I'm terrible at making new friends. I don't have any other skills. Art was what got me through the day that my parents told me I was adopted. The day my baby sister was born who looked exactly like them but nothing like me. The moment I had my first crush on a boy, and the day I saw him holding another girl's hand. Art got me through high school. It got me through college. I painted what I consider to be a masterpiece a few hours after my first time making love. And when my best friend moved away, painting is how I eventually found solace. So you see, Doctor, telling me I have MS and that medications and lifestyle adjustments can help manage symptoms—symptoms that from time to time I'm finding so debilitating that art becomes a genuine struggle..."

Mirai hesitated before drawing in a breath. She locked eyes with Dr. Wallace and said, "I don't need you to tell me that MS won't be fatal. I can live with that. What I need you to tell me is that MS won't take away my life."

The doctor had not immediately answered. He had nodded empathetically toward his patient and prefaced his response with a folding of his hands on his lap. As silence saturated the room, he had said soberly, "I can't make that promise, Mirai. I truly wish I could. But I cannot."

The solemn words echoed relentlessly inside Mirai's head as she gazed across the room at David. He was holding a small desk plaque with words engraved into the woodwork. He read it, smiled, and turned it to face Mirai who was standing at her easel, appearing lost.

"*Beauty will save the world,*" he read aloud. "I see you and Julie are both fans of Dostoevsky."

Mirai thought she nodded, imagined that she returned his smile, and pictured herself confidently walking over to him with a bounce in her step. But in reality, she knew she had done none of those things. For all she could do in that moment was think, pondering if she should tell anyone, and if so, who, how, and when.

Julie... Mirai thought to herself. *Where are you right now? You're supposed to be here for me to talk to. To share this horrible news with. To give me some advice on how to tell my family. To give me some hope that this isn't the end of my art—the death of my soul. Why aren't you here right now? Why do I feel so alone?*

Instantly, she wondered if the last statement was an accurate one.

The thought dissipated back into daylight. All that was left in her sight was David holding the phrase that had been her mantra since high school. More than a mantra, it had been the philosophy on which she had built her entire existence.

She decided in that instant to table the memory, the news, and all of the terrifying heartbreak it held as a blade over her head. Rearranging the muscles in her face to resemble a kind of smile, Mirai nodded slowly at David. "Yes, beauty will save the world."

HELLO MIRAI.

It was just after midnight when the message appeared on the computer screen. The greeting sat next to a text cursor that blinked impatiently, awaiting a response. Light from the monitor cast a bluish tint against the desk. The chair next to the desk was unoccupied but aimed toward the back wall of the solarium where Mirai was standing at a utility sink washing her brushes.

Her head turned back when the notification chimed. She took a moment to finish cleaning the last brush and then proceeded to dry her hands on a worn towel. The window filling the screen was from a popular browser and messaging application with a glowing sphere as its logo. Beside the icon was a single italicized word: *Omni*.

Mirai read the message even before sitting down in the chair. The date and sender's username were listed off to the side in small letters and bold font. The date was January 2nd. The name was Emloch.

HELLO MIRAI.

She blinked and placed her fingers on the keyboard. *Can I help you?* she typed, the sound of keystrokes reminding her that she was no longer painting. A moment passed before an ellipsis appeared in the text box, indicating a forthcoming reply.

I'VE NEVER MET YOU, BUT I'VE SEEN YOUR ARTWORK. THAT IS ALL I NEED TO KNOW. MY NAME IS EMLOCH.

Mirai hesitated, her fingers tensed against the keyboard. *Is that your first name? Last name?*

JUST EMLOCH.

"More like caps lock," she mused. *Are you inquiring about a commission?*

MOST CERTAINLY. THE COMMISSION OF A LIFETIME, MIRAI. THE CHANCE TO PUT AN END TO THE ENSUING GLOBAL MADNESS. BUT YOU MUST BEGIN THIS PROJECT IMMEDIATELY. TIME WILL NOT BE ON YOUR SIDE.

Mirai found herself slinking down ever so slightly in the chair. *I'm sorry, I'm not clear on what you want.*

The ellipsis on the screen pulsed slowly.

I AM LOOKING FOR SOMEONE. HE'S SOMEONE WHO CAN BRING AN END TO THOSE WHO ARE MANUFACTURING OUR SUFFERING. I HAVE TRACKED HIM DOWN ONLY SO FAR. I NEED YOU TO PICK UP WHERE I LEFT OFF.

Mirai sighed heavily and shook her head. *I'm afraid you have the wrong person. I am an artist, not a private investigator. There's nothing I can do to help.*

I'M TALKING ABOUT AD ORDINEM.

Mirai stopped typing. The five words stared back at her, seeming to instinctively know which selections of memories to bring to the forefront in order to inflict the most torment.

IT'S LATIN FOR 'TOWARDS ORDER.'

I know what it means.

THEN YOU MUST KNOW WHAT THEY'RE CAPABLE OF. THE TIMES SQUARE MESSAGE WAS JUST THE BEGINNING. NO ONE LIVING WILL BE LEFT UNSCATHED. I NEED YOUR HELP TO MAKE SURE THEY STAY BURIED IN THE RELICS OF HISTORY.

She wasn't sure if it was the fatigue from the flight setting in or the ambiguity of the conversation with an internet stranger, but the entirety of the studio seemed to be closing in around her.

With finality she typed, *I appreciate you reaching out, but I've had a long day. Good luck in your search. I'm not the person you need. I'm just an artist.*

She sent the message and moved the cursor to close the text window. Before she could, another string of words appeared that wrested the strength from her hand.

AN ARTIST IS EXACTLY WHO I NEED FOR THIS, MIRAI. DON'T YOU KNOW THAT BEAUTY WILL SAVE THE WORLD?

The Omni window remained inert. Mirai gazed at it helplessly, unable to formulate a response and unable to muster the courage to end the conversation. The crushing weight of the diagnosis sat heavy upon her shoulders, seemingly ready to pounce at the first signs of fatigue. She had refused to process the news since stepping foot inside her studio. Finishing her current piece of art had granted her mind a reprieve from any thoughts of pain, or numbness, or relapsing-remitting multiple sclerosis.

I have MS, she said to herself, followed by an immediate scolding for opening the door to the statement at all. Mirai looked down at her feet and then down at the floor. Her line of sight followed the long-dried paint splotches on the ground over to where her easel stood. On it was the painting she had just completed. The portrait of a man she did not know, of a landscape she had never seen, containing a philosophical premise in the form of an aesthetic ideal. The message was more than a bromide. It was the core of her own convictions, painted with artistic honesty.

Beauty will save the world.

Mirai felt an instant of peace despite the heavyset frown tugging at the corners of her mouth. When she turned back toward the computer screen, a new message from Emloch was awaiting her.

I'M REACHING OUT TO YOU FOR HELP BECAUSE OF SOME RECENT PERSONAL LIMITATIONS THAT HAVE DEVELOPED. IT'S ENORMOUSLY FRUSTRATING TO SUDDENLY FIND MYSELF IN A PLACE WHERE I CANNOT CONTINUE MY HUNT FOR THIS MAN.

Mirai suddenly felt her rigidity soften.

SO NOW, I AM RELEGATED TO MY ROOM, WHERE I CONTINUE TO GATHER INFORMATION AS TO HIS POSSIBLE WHEREABOUTS, AND AM FORCED TO REACH OUT TO STRANGERS FOR ASSISTANCE. IT MAY BE HARD FOR YOU TO UNDERSTAND, BUT PLEASE TRY.

Mirai shook her head defeatedly, barely maintaining a will to type. *I don't like this anonymity thing. I don't know anything about you or if you desire to harm this man. Besides, how can this one person be the solution?*

The ellipses appeared again, prefacing an answer.

DO YOU WANT TO KNOW WHAT AD ORDINEM IS?

The question seemed to gaze up at her from the pixels inside the screen. Mirai sensed the skin around the nape of her neck constrict as she mouthed out the Latin phrase. The sensation tingled down her arms and into her fingertips. As she pressed them against the keys, no words formulated in her mind save for one.

Yes, she typed slowly. *Before yesterday, there was nothing about them online. But since Howard Lalonde's meltdown and the stunt in Times Square, nothing but speculation.*

I CAN TELL YOU WHO THEY ARE.

Mirai waited as the ellipses pulsed, and in her waiting, sensed an eerie awareness that the solarium was almost totally dark. When the new message from Emloch arrived, her eyes had to read it twice.

AD ORDINEM IS THE WORLD'S OLDEST SECRET SOCIETY.

She mouthed out the last few words repeatedly, wondering why they felt foreign on her tongue. She began typing a new question but then deleted it so as not to interrupt the sender's train of thought.

FEW HAVE DARED TO WRITE ABOUT THEM. EVEN FEWER HAVE SEEN THEIR INNER WORKINGS. LITTLE IS KNOWN OF ITS ORIGIN, EXCEPT THAT IT EVOLVED OVER MANY MILLENNIA AND HAS GONE BY MANY NAMES.

INFORMATION ABOUT THE GROUP IS SUSPICIOUSLY SPARCE, AND THE FEW SCHOLARLY WORKS ABOUT THE SOCIETY HAVE BEEN RELEGATED TO THE DUSTY SHELVES OF FORGOTTEN LIBRARIES. IT WAS WITHIN THOSE DUSTY SHELVES THAT I FIRST BEGAN RESEARCHING AD ORDINEM YEARS AGO.

WHAT I UNCOVERED IS CONSISTENT WITH THE ANNOUNCEMENT THEY MADE IN TIMES SQUARE LAST NIGHT. THEY DO HAVE A PLAN FOR THE WORLD. AND POWERFUL PEOPLE THROUGHOUT HISTORY HAVE INTERFACED WITH THE GROUP AT VARIOUS LEVELS…OFTEN UNWITTINGLY…ONLY TO FIND OUT WHEN IT WAS TOO LATE.

Her mocha eyes drank in each line before moving down to the next. It was not until the last word that she remembered to blink.

IT IS ONLY THANKS TO THE FEW BRAVE INDIVIDUALS WHO ARE WORKING AGAINST AD ORDINEM FROM THE INSIDE THAT I HAVE BEEN ABLE TO EXTRACT THIS INFORMATION. THEY ARE A SUBVERSIVE GROUP OPERATING WITHIN THE SECRET SOCIETY.

THEY CALL THEMSELVES EMBLEM.

Mirai slowly shook her head and thought to herself, *Don't get roped into this. You're chatting with some nutjob. Go to bed already!*

THE MAN I AM LOOKING FOR KNOWS THE FATAL FLAW IN THEIR SINISTER PLAN. BUT HE DOESN'T KNOW WHO TO TRUST. IF YOU CAN HELP ME FIND HIM, I CAN CONNECT HIM WITH THE LEADER OF EMBLEM, AND TOGETHER, THEY CAN PUT AN END TO THE SUFFERING TO COME.

Suffering, thought Mirai.

THE MAN WE ARE LOOKING FOR HAS MANY ALIASES, BUT ACCORDING TO MY RESEARCH, HE WILL ONLY TALK OPENLY WITH YOU IF YOU ADDRESS HIM BY HIS CODE NAME. JUST THIS WEEK DID I FINALLY DISCOVER WHAT I BELIEVE THAT NAME TO BE: OSIRIS.

"God of the afterlife," Mirai whispered.

She could barely see straight as she typed, *I have no idea who you really are. I have no intention of putting a man's life in danger based on the word of someone I've never met.*

ALL I'M ASKING YOU TO DO IS RELAY A MESSAGE. IF HE IDENTIFIES AS OSIRIS, INFORM HIM THAT YOU ARE IN CONTACT WITH SOMEONE WHO CAN GET HIM INSIDE EMBLEM. THAT IS ALL. THE FINAL DECISION TO REACH OUT IS STILL HIS.

Mirai shook her head and reached for the button to turn off the monitor.

BESIDES, THE MAN I WANT YOU TO SPEAK WITH… YOU ALREADY KNOW HIM.

Her eyes narrowed as a separate message entered the screen with a photo attachment. The photo was of a man.

DR. LEIGHTON RUSSO OF SEATTLE, WASHINGTON. PROSPECT #1 FOR OSIRIS.

"Russo," Mirai muttered. Her eyes shot a glance back at her easel and the signed painting affixed to it. She gazed at it for a moment in wonder.

I HAVE PLACED A DEPOSIT IN YOUR BUSINESS ACCOUNT, WHICH WILL MORE THAN COVER YOUR EXPENSES. I'LL GIVE YOU INFORMATION ON EACH LEAD AS NECESSARY, BUT FOR YOUR OWN PROTECTION, THE LESS YOU KNOW IN ADVANCE THE BETTER.

The monitor turned black as Mirai shut off the computer. She plunged her face forward into her hands while massaging her temples. In her mind's eye, the text from Emloch continued to populate, overwhelming her imagination. She tried to think of something else: Carys's photo shoots, her own last art commission, the time she spilled an entire container of white gesso on the kitchen floor. Only the memory of David caused the tumult inside her head to assuage. Pushed back into the recesses of her mind, the chaos diminished into the shadows, leaving behind the image of David reading the first line of Julie's diary, locking eyes with Mirai, and sliding the book across the giant table within the Preserve.

"Courage creates courage," he had said. The sound of his voice made her shoulders unwind. It was not the vocal tones of a man who had never known fear, but of a man who had never learned to be intimidated by it. Mirai gradually sat up. She scanned the studio before rising from the desk chair and walking back into the house.

In the living room she saw Carys asleep on the plush sofa, having drifted off during a movie that was still playing on the television. Mirai silently turned off the screen and the living room lights. She ascended the stairwell and took refuge in her old room, which had been converted into a guest bedroom. Placing her hand against the door with finality, she exhaled what seemed like a week's worth of tension and slid into bed. As she viewed the world from the vantage point of her pillow, a subtle light pulsed from her phone. When her eyes read the text message, her lips formed a smile. It was from David.

Thank you for saving my life. Perhaps one day I can return the favor.

A follow up message appeared immediately afterward.

Lunch tomorrow?

Not a game-player, Mirai wasted no time in her reply. *Of course. Can't wait.*

The message sent and Mirai silenced her phone. She turned over underneath the soft sheets of her bed and promptly fell asleep. Despite having little in life resolved, her mind suddenly felt at peace for the first time in days. It remained that way throughout her slumber, even as a new message appeared on her phone. This time the sender was Emloch.

AD ORDINEM HAS STRUCK AGAIN.

"Continuing with breaking news, a train derailment in Bowling Green, Kentucky is putting residents there on edge. The crash occurred just after midnight this morning and the cause is still being investigated by NTSB. The freight train was pulling eighty-one cars, many of which contain toxic chemicals. Bowling Green authorities are urging residents in the community to stay away from the wreckage until hazard crews can determine—"

Mirai muted the audio on the computer and turned to David. He glowered at the screen, his forefinger and thumb pressed against his lower lip. Mirai then pulled the text message window into the foreground. "Here's what Emloch sent this morning."

NOW WE KNOW THEIR PLAN OF ATTACK.

David tilted his head. "I don't follow."

Mirai opened the Omni browser window and navigated to an online map. "I wasn't sure what he meant either, until I looked up the location of the train crash. It took me a few minutes to get it, but now it seems obvious. Look at the area code for Bowling Green, Kentucky."

David squinted as he read the tiny numerical digits. "364."

"Correct. On New Year's Day, the announcement was made that there was 365 days until the end of time. That was yesterday. Today, this train derails in a city that's area code is 364. So, if this pattern continues…"

A subtle nod preceded his completion of her sentence. "…tomorrow there will be an attack in wherever 363 is."

Mirai already had the tab loaded in the browser window. "Nassau County, Long Island, New York."

David stared silently at the pin drop on the map. He appeared to be contemplating several things at once. Finally, he said, "So that's what he—what you—think will happen? Ad Ordinem counting down the days until December 31st?"

"Russo," she said, a tension preceding each syllable. "Leighton Russo, David. He's the man I just finished this commission for. The same guy. I was going to pack up the painting this morning and overnight it to Seattle for a small fundraiser he's attending this week. He's showcasing several pieces, including mine, and *he's* the first guy Emloch wants me to ask."

"How did he know Russo was one of your customers?"

Mirai hesitated, half in shock that the pertinent question hadn't already crossed her mind. The breach of security was inexplicable, save for the remote possibility that Emloch personally knew Russo and had found out the business arrangement through osmosis. Even so, that couldn't explain why Emloch would need her assistance to speak with a man he already knew. The question fizzled after several seconds of being left unanswered.

David let out a long sigh before placing his elbows against his knees and leaning forward in the chair. "What happens on days that don't align with an area code? And do country codes count? Reason being, I doubt these disasters will only continue in the United States."

"Good questions. I don't know."

"And nowhere in your conversations with Emloch last night did he indicate what this para-secret society—what's it called again— Emblem, plans on doing with this Osiris fellow once introduced? If he does know how to stop this, what can Emblem possibly do while hiding in the shadows of Ad Ordinem?"

Mirai did not answer verbally, but offered pursed lips in acknowledgment of David's point.

He continued, "Lastly, and forgive me if I'm reading too much into this, but is Emloch really asking you to go reach out to people he suspects of being Osiris, without disclosing the danger involved in such an assignment? I mean, if Emloch knows about Osiris, then so must Ad Ordinem. If you insert yourself into this imbroglio, there's no telling who might notice... Who might retaliate."

Mirai began to nod but then halted. In her expression was the dawning realization that she had simply been putting the pieces of this bizarre puzzle together without having had posed a crucial question.

Do I actually believe this? she thought to herself. *I think so. All I have to do is deliver the painting in person and ask him a simple question. It's the least I can do. It's doing something, instead of just sitting here, while this terrorist group gives Julie even more reason to justify staying in the Preserve. At least I'd be fighting back, instead of just waiting...waiting until I can no longer hold a paintbrush...*

"Am I wrong?"

Mirai blinked and looked at David. "No," she said, as if from inside a different conversation. "You're not wrong."

The solarium held the midday light within its hallowed space. Everything seemed to be aglow, most dramatically the metal ferrules on the brushes. On the easel was Russo's painting. David had noticed it when he first arrived, and then had focused in on Mirai, whose nervous energy seemed to be vacillating between wanting to engage with Emloch and deciding on colors for her next canvas.

Mirai rubbed her hands together before moving them up her wrists and over her arms. She continued a massaging motion as she looked at the computer screen and said, "You're right. I have no idea who this Emloch really is. I don't know for certain if Ad Ordinem is behind that derailment. I don't know if Osiris is a real person, and I don't know what could happen to me if I did find him. There are too many variables here. Not enough solid information. All of this is super dangerous—"

"Which is why I'll go with you," David said.

The russet halos that were Mirai's eyes shifted slowly away from the screen. When they landed on the simple honesty of David's gaze, the two held each other in their respective glances without so much as lifting a finger. Mirai suppressed the instinct to object, to counter his self-sacrificing offer with a polite decline. For something in the way he had said it made her realize that there was nothing sacrificial about his words. She then recalled their conversation about values. Without connecting all the mental dots, she somehow knew that the truth laid there.

Nothing else was uttered before the message window appeared on the screen. Inside its rectangular perimeter, text began to populate at a frantic pace.

HELLO, MIRAI. I TRUST YOU HAD TIME TO THINK IT

OVER. AD ORDINEM WILL NOT STOP UNTIL THEY HAVE SNUFFED OUT THE LAST SPARK OF LIGHT IN HUMANKIND.

Mirai read the messages in a hushed voice, yet loudly enough that David could hear. His eyes also read the text in the kind of wonder one has when encountering a cypher.

IF YOU ARE READY TO BEGIN, PLEASE REPLY IN THE AFFIRMATIVE. TIME IS AGAINST US, BUT THEY'VE UNDERESTIMATED MY RESOLVE IN THE POWER OF HUMAN TRUTH. FROM SEEING YOUR ARTWORK, I KNOW YOU FEEL THE SAME.

WILL YOU DO THIS ENORMOUS FAVOR FOR ME?

Mirai blinked and suddenly felt as if both David and Emloch were staring her down from opposite directions.

WILL YOU ASK LEIGHTON RUSSO IF HE IS OSIRIS?

CHAPTER 4
PURSUIT OF A GOD

Brubaker's Comet was barely peaking over the treetops that stood above the entrance to the Mount Baker tunnel. Pinpoints of light interspersed with evergreens gave way to a rectangular opening at the tunnel's mouth. Engraved into the concrete was a message to commuters who had just completed a lengthy drive across the floating bridge of Lake Washington.

"Seattle—Portal to the Pacific," Mirai read quietly, as the SUV was absorbed into the tube. In the rearview mirror, the cityscape of downtown Bellevue faded until nothing was left but the intermittent pulses of amber passing overhead.

"Dr. Leighton Russo," David said from the driver's seat. "Psychologist?"

"Psychiatrist," corrected Mirai.

"Ah, thank you," said David, who proceeded to mumble off a list of facts as if cramming for an exam. "Psychiatrist who is also an art collector. Been in the field for fifteen years. Has worked in a university setting, in private practice, and was one of the early experts on Ad Ordinem before completely vanishing from public view. Hasn't produced any research or published any academic essays since his retirement. Back on the radar after agreeing to attend a private fundraiser tonight with other art benefactors. And you're sure we'll be able to infiltrate this event?"

Mirai reached into the pocket of her burgundy leather jacket and fished out two laminated IDs tethered to lanyards. "I messaged Dr. Russo and told him I would be delivering his painting personally. He said these passes will get us in."

"Do these people all have advanced degrees? I only ask in hope of minimizing the likelihood of my saying something stupid."

Mirai smirked. "Right. Ixnay on the idiosay."

The tunnel finally gave way to open sky again. The curves on the interstate led them to an exit ramp that brought them into the city of Seattle. Mirai leaned forward a bit in her seat to gaze out at the natural beauty and also get a sense of direction.

"You drive like you've been here before," she said.

"Oh yes," replied David. "Performed with the symphony here many times. It's a beautiful venue. How about you?"

"Never. But Washington state seems like a place I'll need to return —art supplies in hand."

David smiled to himself. "Just so you know, I asked the rental car agent if they had any convertibles in their fleet—to make you feel more at home—but he reminded me that it's January in the Pacific Northwest and not January in Miami."

Mirai shook her head and held back the more boisterous laugh she wanted to give. "Very kind of you to think of that."

Off in the distance, a structure appeared that defied its surroundings. It seemed to exist in its own realm, detached from both aesthetics and time. For a series of city blocks, it appeared and vanished around the corners of buildings. Only when the SUV was close enough to see it unobstructed did the enormity of its strangeness fully manifest.

"Oh wow," said Mirai, leaning forward onto the dashboard.

"A helluva thing, isn't it?"

The Space Needle stood above them trying to pierce the fuchsia clouds. Its pinnacle sat atop a circular observation deck that appeared as if it had landed on the angular tripod legs from a futuristic vision of the Atomic Age.

"Great place to hold a private fundraiser for art-collecting psychologists," David said while parking the vehicle.

"Psychiatrists."

The chill in the air exposed their exhales as Mirai and David followed along the walkway toward the entrance. Underneath Mirai's arm was the painting wrapped in protective packaging. Donning their lanyards, they watched as people who looked and were dressed and were acting similarly to them approached the Space Needle.

"Why did I envision everyone in black tuxedos?" Mirai mused.

The patrons scanned their badges at the entryway door. Mirai and David did the same upon entering, with Mirai stealing one final glance upward at the giant saucer above their heads. Once inside the structure, they blended into the crowd and followed the foot traffic up a winding ramp that led to the centrally placed elevators. The ride up the tower was brief, but it granted the intrepid pair a moment to comprehend their aim: find Dr. Leighton Russo, hand him the artwork, engage him in conversation, and nonchalantly ask if he answered to a secret alias.

When the elevator doors opened, Mirai and David stepped out into the observation deck. The window walls encircling the event were blocked by the dozens of attendees chatting amongst themselves. Wait staff dressed in crisp, white shirts and black vests weaved throughout the crowd offering cocktails and hors d'oeuvres. The atmosphere had the excitable tension of networking.

"May I see that photo again?" David whispered to Mirai as they edged closer to the window wall.

She fished the image from her pocket and took the opportunity to refresh her own memory against the sea of new faces. David nodded intently. Dr. Leighton Russo was a balding man in his late fifties whose physique suggested his second residence was in a gym. His eyes and mouth projected intelligence and authority, yet his expression appeared empathetic. He was the archetypal shrink, and he was nowhere in the room.

"Huh," Mirai said, her eyes darting across talking heads.

"Maybe we're early," muttered David, who doubted his own statement upon glancing at his wristwatch.

The duo wove through the crowd purposefully. Movement through the circular space added to their disorientation, and Mirai eventually had to take a moment to determine where their point of origin had been. It was only when they migrated back toward the window walls that her attention was wrested away from their mission.

"My God," she said, placing her hand gently against the glass.

Beyond the downtown lights in Seattle was a purple skyline sinking below the horizon. Off in the far distance, yet striking her vision as being deceivingly close, was a massive white triangle reaching up from the earth. Its ridges and crevices stood in stark contrast to its surroundings. To say it was a mountain would be inaccurate, as Mirai understood both its true nature and its true power.

"Mount Rainier," said David, joining her at the window.

"A volcano," came her reverent reply.

The clearness of the evening air added to its imposing form. Mirai exhaled slowly and continued to gaze upon the natural wonder while her breath evaporated from the glass. David smiled and began to turn back toward the gathering. When he discovered that Mirai was frozen in place, he hesitated and returned to his previous stance.

"A thing of beauty," he said.

"I'll need to paint it," said Mirai. "I'll never be able to get it out of my head unless I do."

After taking a few photos with her phone, she added, "You know, I can almost begin to understand why early man would have worshipped it—would have feared it. Fear and awe are eerily similar emotions. Coming across something massive, immovable, breathtaking, and with the power to annihilate your tribe, that's the definition of a deity. If you can only figure out the proper formula to placate its wrath, perhaps you and your own will be spared."

David narrowed his gaze out the window. "How far we've come."

Mirai didn't blink as the light in the room shifted, momentarily casting her own reflection against the glass. "I wonder."

They glanced at each other the instant a man walked past them. It was only their peripheries that had caught his features, but it was enough to confirm their immediate gut instincts.

Russo, thought Mirai.

"That's him," mouthed David.

They walked toward him silently, each sifting through a volley of introductions in their minds. Russo was wearing a beige overcoat as he contentedly nibbled on a crab cake. No one from the event had yet addressed him, and his body language said that was perfectly fine.

Mirai parted her lips to speak. "Excuse me, Dr. Russo?"

The man turned to meet their arrival. He stood taller than Mirai but equal to David. His initial gaze paired the two against his mental rolodex, and Mirai could tell he was trying to recall their faces.

"I'm Mirai McGarry. This is David Eban. We're here to deliver your painting."

"The artist," Russo said while taking another bite. "How kind of you to come all this way. I trust it was a good flight?"

"Good enough." She smiled. "Here…as ordered."

Mirai handed Russo the rectangular package. As he unwrapped it, his face rapidly changed to reflect the beauty of the image. "My God. What a brilliant work. Honestly, Miss McGarry, truly stunning. It's provocative. It's *true.* Based on your existing work, this piece is precisely what I was hoping for."

Mirai nodded in kind and sensed a beam of pride coming from David's eyes. "I'm glad you're satisfied. Sorry it took so long to complete."

"You made it in time for the gala. That's all that matters. Oh, excuse me, sir?"

A docent stopped and turned toward the group. "Good evening, everyone."

"Would you please put this with my collection down in the convention center? I'm exhibitor twenty-one."

"Of course. Happy to do so."

The docent carefully took hold of the canvas and walked away. As he did, Mirai felt her usual twinge of separation anxiety as the last strokes of color vanished around the corner. Inwardly, she knew that the artwork would always be hers, even if the painting now belonged to Leighton Russo. Taking the last mental pictures she would ever see of her physical work helped in the catharsis. She blinked and took an instant to compose herself.

"Aside from delivering the painting," said Mirai. "We also came here tonight to ask you a question. A question you might find…unusual."

Russo finished his last bite of crab cake and smiled. "I'll answer it if I can. Although if it's an art-related inquiry, there are better historians here than me."

Mirai tried to say the words but found that only a quick glance toward David granted her that courage. "Well," she began. "We understand that you're considered one of the foremost experts on Ad Ordinem. Is that right?"

Russo shrugged. It was not the shrug of the disinterested, but of one keenly aware of more than he was letting on. "Perhaps."

David said, "We've traveled a long way to meet you, and inquire about if you think the doomsday message on New Year's Eve, the train derailment in Kentucky, yesterday's power outages on Long Island, have anything to do with…well, that group."

The man's expression didn't change. "My research on Ad Ordinem is decades old. I'm sure I can't help you on that topic."

The duo exchanged an awkward glance. Mirai then said, "Right. Well, again…it's vital to us that we help those in our lives that are being affected by these apocalypse purveyors. People like Alexander, Howard Lalonde, they seem to be successfully convincing people that the world is about to end."

Mirai took a quick breath and wondered if Russo could tell that her muscles were tensing. "So…we…we were told…that you might have some information to provide… That is…should the right people… come along."

The man again sized them up before performing a rapid scan of the room. "And who told you that I would know anything that anyone else in the place wouldn't? What made you ask me, specifically?"

Mirai slid her hands into her pockets while her fingernails dug into her palms. "I guess… What we're wondering…Dr. Russo, is—is if… you…go by any other names?"

Russo's eyes held the power of shutting out everything else in the room. "I deal in absolutes. I'm afraid I don't follow."

The chatter on the observation deck was just loud enough to drown out the sound of Mirai's blood pressure pounding in her ears. In that moment, she felt like stealing a look at David, but decided against it as Russo furrowed his brows.

"Osiris," Mirai finally said, unable to prevent her lips from trembling just a little. "We're looking for a man who also goes by the name Osiris and wondered if that man was you."

Having stated her intention with some degree of finality, she resumed her stance and tried to decompress. Her body, however, remained tightly wound.

Russo exchanged curious stares between Mirai and David. He did not immediately answer, nor did he appear to be in any rush to do so. His eyes wandered. His hands fidgeted with a napkin. The differential expression on his face had been replaced by the quizzical glare of one searching for something beyond the thing directly in front of him. After a few seconds of volatile silence, he shifted his jaw as if about to relay some crucial data.

"We…should not talk here," he said softly. "Outside?"

Mirai and David nodded in unison, their individual countenances simmering with a clandestine hope. Together, the three worked their way through the crowd and back over to the elevators. Nothing was spoken in the ride down and no one looked at the other. They all stared out the elevator's glass wall as their collective vantage point sunk below the cityscape. Back on the mezzanine level, they paced down the carpeted ramp and found themselves back on the ground level at the exit doors.

"Have a good evening," an unidentified voice said as they left.

The nighttime air was brisk and felt like it left a coating on their cheeks. Mirai buttoned her leather jacket and watched as David did the same. Russo walked as if energized by the crisp atmosphere. There was a sudden spring in his step, a youthful tension in his actions and movements.

About a hundred feet from the exit doors is where Russo finally stopped to face them. They all stood along a cement sidewalk with a metal bicycle rack.

"Well," he said. "Osiris you wanted. May I introduce you then?"

His hand extended toward them indicating that Osiris was standing just behind. When Mirai and David turned to look, the full force of Russo's nervous energy rammed into their backs, body-slamming both of them over the bicycle rack. To Mirai and David, the world tipped upside down, with the Space Needle now balancing itself atop the blackened sky by a pinprick. As their bodies absorbed the impact from the metal and then the ground, streaks of pain shot across the insides of their eyelids. They both grit their teeth while the city spun on an axis. Upon opening their eyes, the first thing they saw was each other. The first thing they heard were the mad-dash claps of leather soles echoing away from them down the street.

"Are you all right?" David asked, obtaining his bearings sooner than Mirai.

Mirai nodded without knowing if she was all right. She blinked repeatedly before sitting up. Her face was slowly releasing the braced look of expected pain. It was replaced instead by the frown lines of determination.

"There he is," she said, zeroing her eyes in on Russo from afar. "I can still see him."

David helped Mirai to her feet and they both stood dazed but unharmed. "I guess we struck a nerve," he said flatly.

Mirai didn't respond, but did take a step in Russo's direction.

"What are you doing?" David asked.

She took another step forward. And then other. David followed with uncertainty. Woven into the expression on her face was a deep-seated suspicion about something. It nagged her forward with each successive step.

As they walked, Mirai finally said, "This doesn't make any sense. Seriously, David. Who does he think we are?"

The question festered into their joints as they began to pick up their pace, and then as they started to run. Mirai led the charge forward while a confused David matched her sprint. The reasons for their sudden exertion gradually caught up to them as they watched Russo turn a sharp corner. His desire to be rid of them generated a concern that neither Mirai nor David could shake.

"Over there." Mirai pointed toward an outdoor pavilion that was barely visible behind some trees.

When they reached the corner, a series of turnstiles was there to greet them with a giant red-neon sign atop the entryway. The neon blazed: MONORAIL.

"Is this a train?" asked Mirai.

"More of a mini rapid transit," said David, as he waved his phone over the turnstile screen and heard the ratchet mechanism unlock. "Runs every ten minutes between here and Westlake."

The two shuffled across the length of the terminal and spotted an opening near the last car. The doors were already beginning to slide shut as the pair leapt aboard and used a grab rail to stop their acceleration. They took a moment to catch their breath, even while scanning the inside of the car. The compartments were packed. People sat along the window seats with their shopping bags; others stood in the aisle ready to be the first out the door. All seemed oblivious to Mirai and David.

The monorail began its trek smoothly. With engineered grace, it pulled out of the terminal and glided into open air following along an elevated straddle beam installed above the downtown streets. Mirai stole a glance out the massive window and watched as they passed an office building. The florescent lights from the offices tamed the evening darkness through which they were traveling, offering momentary glimpses of workers wrapping up end-of-day projects. Mirai watched as if it was on a film reel. Before long, the rolling images finished their projection through the windows and were entirely out of frame.

Her eyes reverted back toward the passengers. It was difficult to see the riders near the forward cars, and the tilting curves of the guideway for the monorail forced Mirai to wonder if she could stay upright while walking. She shot a look at David who had already come to a similar conclusion. They knew it was best to wait it out.

"We are approaching Westlake terminal," came a recorded voice via the overhead. "Please stand clear of the exit doors and remember to collect your personal belongings before leaving the monorail."

"That was fast," said Mirai.

"Don't you wish all commutes took two and a half minutes?" replied David.

Up ahead, they could see the destination terminal and its blueish hue. Mirai held onto a stanchion as the train began to decelerate. Her vision continued to exchange glances between the exit doors and the riders clustered together. No one was wearing a beige trench coat in her immediate view. She figured that Russo would be staying closely nestled near the first set of sliding doors. With an unsteady step forward, she grabbed on to David's arm and readied herself to be amongst the first to disembark.

"Please watch your step as you exit," came the voice again. "Thank you for riding the Seattle Monorail."

Their first steps onto the platform had their eyes darting back and forth across the terminal. Passengers weaved around them as they searched frantically for the balding man who could save the world. The masses all seemed to be migrating in one direction—a stairwell leading down to the street.

With suspicion guiding her, Mirai marshaled herself ahead, towing David behind her by the grasp of his hand. They reached the railing next to the terminal exit and peered down the stairwell. Mirai was the first to call out his name, having uttered the words from some deeper cognition within her that cried out for an end to engineered suffering.

"Dr. Russo, wait!" she exclaimed.

Her voice echoed harshly into the stairwell causing several people to glance upward. The only one that mattered to her projected back a gaze ripe with resentment. Russo then broke their vertical staring contest and darted down the rest of the steps in a frantic rush.

Mirai and David hugged the central railing as they descended each flight of stairs, scurried each landing turn, and tackled the next round of steps with reckless abandon. Claps and scuffs squeaked from their shoes as they maneuvered around pedestrians unaware of the ensuing chase. Mirai had lost visual on Russo, but knew he was only a floor or two ahead of them. She wondered how many more floors they needed to tackle before the stairwell would give way to the city street below. She glanced back only for an instant to be certain David was still behind her. Reassured that he was, Mirai pressed on with greater determination in each step.

"Doctor, wait!" she yelled out, as the man vanished through the exterior glass doors.

Together, Mirai and David burst out onto the sidewalk and continued their pursuit of Russo who had just turned a corner at an intersection. Evening had completed its takeover of the downtown area, saturating the sky above in a black shroud. The city was dotted with amber streetlamps. Each light cast a halo on the sidewalk, illuminating the route with pockets of warmth. The duo felt the light hit them at regular intervals as they ran, as they dodged, and as the pain in Mirai's legs steadily worked its way up to her hips with each merciless step.

Russo had already made his way down most of the steep hill that now awaited Mirai and David. The graded street sloped down precipitously until leveling out near a series of buildings along the waterfront. A large, blazing red neon sign, similar to the monorail sign, welcomed visitors to Pike Place Market. Unlike the transit terminal, the farmer's market and artisan kiosks were desolate, having long since closed for the evening. The only signs of movement were at the bars and restaurants. It was within those auras of light that Mirai spotted Russo's coattails flap through an open door.

"There," she said, suddenly finding it difficult to breathe and talk and run at the same time.

David nodded in agreement and the two finished the punishing jolt down the declining street. Slowing to a moderate jog, they entered the restaurant as inconspicuously as possible. It was inside the establishment that Mirai's vision began to swim.

Breathe more. In through the nose, out through the mouth.

Mirai blinked with purpose. The sudden blur in her eyes and the pounding in her chest caused her to lose track of her target. She continued moving forward into the restaurant, passing a bar with patrons seated on cushioned stools, and a bustling waitress balancing a full tray of dinner entrees. Mirai sensed David right behind her, hoping he still had Russo in his sights. She pressed on.

It was only when they were outside again that Mirai lost confidence in their direction. "I can't see him, David. Is he still ahead of us?"

"He's heading toward the pier," David said, aiming his finger in the general direction of a building that Mirai could not visually ascertain.

The two picked up the pace again and cleared another city block. As they neared the waterfront they could hear the restless nature of the amorphous water crashing up against the shoreline. The building to which they ran stood as a tether between the land and the sea. Adjacent to it was a narrow stretch of road that led right up to a barge slip. Across the slip was a rampway, which the last of several vehicles drove over before parking inside the car deck of the Bainbridge Island ferry.

When Mirai and David saw Russo climb aboard the vessel, they inwardly groaned before flashing their mutual consternation at each other.

"I suppose we're getting on that ferry," David said, chagrined.

"Seems so," replied a rapidly fading Mirai.

A pair of steps led to a small ticket booth. As David completed the transaction, Mirai kept her sights on the boat to be certain that Russo didn't double back. A gangway was the final obstacle as they crossed the metal catwalk and stepped foot onto the ferry. The gate then closed from behind, indicating that they were the final two passengers of the voyage.

"I just need a second." Mirai gasped while leaning against a wall.

David laughed in solidarity. "At least we got our exercise in…for the month."

She nodded while searching for a place to sit. Inside the passenger cabin, rows of booth-style tables and seating lined the rectangular windows and central aisle. The ceiling was low and contributed to the overall sense that one was floating along the ocean inlet on a seaborne mess hall. Darkness overwhelmed the outside view, leaving little to distinguish the faint silhouettes of mountain ranges in the distance.

The ferry gently rocked as it pushed off from the barge. Mirai steadied herself as she walked, and she drew each breath in faith that she could proceed another step without fainting.

"You all right?" David whispered, touching her arm.

"Yeah. I'll be fine. Let's find Russo."

The cabin was crowded but easy to scan. Within a few minutes, the duo had determined that the man in the beige overcoat was not in the room. That left the car deck below or the observation deck outside.

"Let's check out there," Mirai said.

David pushed through the double doors and felt an immediate burst of chilled air attack his face. Mirai gasped but tried to remain warm. No one appeared to be outside, and as they walked around to the foredeck, nothing but guardrails occupied the visitor space. They shook their heads in unison.

It was the unmistakable clicking of a barrel chamber that caught their attention over the sloshing of waves against the hull. Mirai and David turned back toward the cabin entrance to see a man blocking it. He was a balding man in a beige trench coat—and he was holding a gun.

"Over by the bow," Russo snapped. "Starboard side."

Mirai and David held their positions for a moment, too stunned to either speak or move. Behind Russo was the passenger cabin, and behind the cabin was the skyline of Seattle. Only then did they realize how far they'd trekked from the Space Needle, as its saucer lights beamed out from the shore like a lighthouse beacon. The city symbol seemed to mock them as they drifted farther out to sea.

"Do it. Quickly and quietly."

They obeyed and backed up over to where the guardrail met the edge of the ferry. Russo took several steps toward them while maintaining his weapon's aim at torso level.

"What do you two want?" Russo asked, his voice grave and taut.

Mirai mumbled her first few words before realizing that the

outdoor temperature was numbing her lips. Taking a giant gulp, she said, "We don't mean you any harm. Honestly, we don't."

"Why are you following me? Why are you even here?"

"We heard you may be the person to talk to," Mirai said.

"About what?"

"About Emblem."

Russo grimaced in anger. "Not this again. God almighty! I'm not the man you're searching for! And your cronies should know that by now!"

"Our cronies?" David asked.

Russo narrowed his eyes. "Don't play dumb. I'm about this close to sending you both overboard for good measure."

"That's why we chased you down," Mirai protested. "We didn't know who you thought we were, but I can assure you…we're not Ad Ordinem. We only found out about them on New Year's Eve, and also from that guy on the radio like everyone else."

"Then who told you to come talk to me?"

"Someone online," she said, suddenly sounding a little less confident. "Someone who said you gave up on your research of the secret society just when you were on the verge of uncovering who they are."

"This is about so much more than *research*, young lady," Russo snarled. He quickly glanced back at the cabin doors to be sure he hadn't aroused suspicion. Once satisfied, he refocused his gaze on Mirai and said, "I should shoot you both right now—send a message to whoever those scumbags are that I won't be jerked around. You aren't the first to come and intimidate me, but I can make damn certain you'll be the last."

David outstretched his hand. "Please, you've got us all wrong, Dr. Russo. We're not connected with any group or anyone wanting to harm you. This isn't part of some plot. In fact, this matter is quite personal to us. Finding a way to discredit this group may help us bring a friend back to safety."

"Shut up already!" Russo said through clenched teeth. "You think they didn't do a little song and dance when I confronted the last goons? Claimed to have no idea of Ad Ordinem. Claimed to just be conducting research. But they couldn't deny the file drive I found in one of their pockets, filled with data off my personal computer, information on the company my wife works for, my daughter's high school semester schedule—*she's only seventeen.* Of what interest could she possibly be!? I told them if I ever saw any of you again, I would make a lasting impression. That's why I got this." Russo shook the gun for added emphasis. "So, the question is, should I shoot you both or leave one alive to relay the message?"

"I promise," said Mirai, her voice straining from the cold. "We'll never bother you again. We had no idea. We were just told to find you and see if you go by the name Osiris. That's all."

"Told by whom?"

"Someone online… Someone named Emloch."

Russo scoffed. "Well, Osiris I'm not. Now you both know, and now…now…"

The wind began to pick up adding to everyone's discomfort. Russo still gripped his gun tightly but was aiming it more and more off-center. He looked down at the deck, shook his head in frustration, and appeared to be weighing one of two options.

Mirai and David watched as the man rocked back and forth with the ferry. His coattails flapped against the harsh breeze even while his legs stayed planted firmly in place. His face vacillated between varying degrees of internal struggle. It was not a battle of nerve but solely of conscience. Russo appeared to be watching a scenario play out in his mind. As his shoulders gradually slumped, Mirai and David surmised that Russo had disliked the ending.

With the kind of pain in his eyes that announced a personal torment was not yet over, Russo squeezed the handle of his gun but removed his finger from the trigger. His arm looked as if it would collapse under the weight of the weapon if he held it much longer. He tilted his head and whispered a phrase that sounded like an exhort intended only for himself.

"*Primum non nocere,*" Russo uttered.

Mirai looked up at David. In a hushed tone, he translated back, "'First, do no harm.'"

She exhaled when she heard it. For the instant she recalled who Leighton Russo was: a doctor, a physician, a man who had at one time in his career taken the Hippocratic oath. She knew that his struggle had not been on whether to kill them. It had been about wrestling with the reality of how not killing them would manifest in his daily life.

A life lived in perpetual fear.

Dr. Russo shook his head again, this time in defeat, and slowly slid the gun back into his coat pocket. When he looked back up at Mirai and David his face was expressionless, a slate wiped clean by the frigid Pacific air.

"Tell your masters to leave me alone," he said into the wind. "I have nothing for them. I never have."

Russo then turned to leave the observation deck. Before his hand made contact with the door, Mirai yelled out, "What does Ad Ordinem want with you?"

The man held his place by the entrance and chuckled to himself. It was the unnerving laugh of being the only one in on a twisted joke. When he responded, he turned his head partially, but not his body. "When you stop asking the wrong questions, you'll start finding the right answers."

Mirai felt the world around her tremble. She awoke without opening her eyes. The sensation of the seat buckle, of the polycarbonate lining on which her head was leaning, and of the high-pitched vacuum sound consuming her ears all reminded her that she was on a red-eye flight back to Miami.

The sequence of events from reaching Bainbridge Island, to hopping aboard the return ferry, to driving back to the Seattle airport in hopes of catching an overnight flight home, played through her mind in rapid succession. She then remembered another component of the story. Her left hand moved cautiously toward the next seat until her fingertips sensed the fabric of David's coat sleeve. Only then did her eyes open.

"Good sleep?" he asked tenderly.

She nodded while running her other hand through her hair. "How long was I out?" she asked before glancing down at her wristwatch.

It was at that moment when she realized she couldn't see it. She blinked, rubbed her eyes, blinked again, and adjusted the distance of her wrist to her face. The watch was certainly there, but existed as a mere blur. Her eyes shifted toward the window. Nothing but blackness with the occasional pulse of red from the wing's strobe light. She glanced at the placards and magazines housed in the back of the seat and couldn't distinguish one image from another. Finally, her mocha eyes looked to David. He smiled at her, and she could see it, but only as if looking through a camera lens that had yet to be properly focused.

Coming full circle, she again looked down at her wristwatch as a surge of emotion started welling up in her throat. She inhaled slowly and tried to wrangle her spiraling thoughts.

What the hell is going on? Is this from the MS? I've had blurred vision before but not like this. Did Dr. Wallace say this would happen? I think he did. He also said it would be temporary...that my vision would return. But how long did he say it could take? A day...a week? Why can't I remember?

Mirai shut her eyes and leaned her head back into the seat. It was the sound of David's voice that drew her from the mental precipice.

"You've only been out for an hour or so," he said, staring. "You feeling okay?"

"Absolutely," she said, too assuredly for even her own taste.

"We have about three and a half more hours to go, I'm afraid. But not to worry. There's plenty of in-flight entertainment options from which to choose. Issue being that they appear to work on every screen in this airplane except ours."

Mirai forced a laugh while continuing to take longer than average blinks. She squinted at her hands and could make out the white of her fingernail polish. She could also make out a slight tremor.

Why are my hands shaking? I don't think I'm cold. Gotta be the nerves. Just calm down already. There's nothing you can do about your eyes 'til you get home. Just relax. Stop trembling or else he's gonna notice and ask—

Her hands suddenly looked like David's as he enveloped them within his grasp and placed them on the armrest between them. He massaged them firmly, and she felt the warmth begin to work its way up into her wrists. He posed no questions or concerns. From what she could tell, he was staring blankly at the malfunctioning screen and seemed to be taking in the pure enjoyment of physical contact with her.

They sat silently for a while. They listened to the vacuum of the cabin, and they listened to an infant cooing. They heard the couple in front of them answer each other in phrases of irritation, and the passengers behind them chat about traveling for work.

David was the first to speak as he leaned into Mirai and said, "I have an idea. Let's tell Emloch that we should search for Osiris in the Bahamas."

Mirai instinctively yanked her left hand out from David's palm so as to cover her guffawing. The two burst into fits of juvenile laughter. Their best attempts to restrain themselves failed as other passengers began to glare. Mirai wiped the tears from her eyes and struggled to regain her composure. The pair hesitated with subdued amusement before losing it again, bubbling back into another nearly uncontrollable surge of chuckling at the absurdity of the event they had mutually survived.

"For the hundredth time," Mirai said. "I am so sorry I roped you into that."

"And for the hundredth time, there's no need to apologize. I wanted to go and I'm glad I did. I'm glad I was there."

Mirai nodded and looked down at her hands, which were now back on her lap. "I'm glad you were there too."

"You know, it's not the first time I've had a gun pulled on me," said David.

"Really?"

"I got held up once outside a convenience store in Orlando. The perp waved a gun at me and demanded my wallet. Luckily, I was carrying a dummy wallet, in addition to my real one, for just such an occasion. So, I tossed him the fake and he never bothered to check it. I laughed about it all the way back to my condo…until I realized that he could have shot me. Oh well. Live and learn. How about you?"

"No, well…actually," Mirai said, leaning against the armrest a little more. "One of my earliest memories is of this little boy at the group home who would make a point-and-shoot motion with his hand. He would make them at everyone, but when he aimed at me, he would add this adorable little bang sound. He didn't make the sound at any of the other kids. Just me."

"Did he hate you or was it love at first sight?"

"Oh, he was a four-year-old Casanova for sure. I remember thinking he was dumb and why was he picking on me and all of that. But I guess you could say that was my only other brush with certain death."

David smiled and shook his head. "Look at us with our emotional battle scars. How old were you when that happened?"

"Four, probably."

"And you were living at a group home? Why not foster care?"

"I guess there was a shortage of foster parents when I needed one. And since my birth parents were immigrants, there was no other family members close by for me to live with."

"What was it like?"

That's a good question, Mirai thought to herself. *What was it like?* She hesitated while trying to extract another memory from her earliest years. Even as she tried, the timeframe seemed as blurry as her vision.

"You know, I honestly don't remember that much about living there. All I know for sure is that I hated it. I don't mean that they mistreated us or anything. I'm sure we were cared for just fine. But I recall wondering why I wasn't living with my parents. I remember feeling confused."

"Do you have any memories of your birth family?"

"None," Mirai stated. "And it was a closed adoption, so I don't know much about who they were, why they gave me up, or what ever happened to them. The only thing I know for sure is that they immigrated from Myanmar—so ethnically I'm Burmese, not Japanese as my name would indicate. I never found out why my birth parents gave me the name Mirai."

David rested his jaw against his forefinger and thumb as he listened. "Do you remember the day the McGarrys met you?"

"Very much so." She smiled. "I was in this carpeted playroom where prospective parents could chat with kids and the care administrator. I remember I was sitting in the corner doing a puzzle when they walked in. The adults all talked for a while and then talked with me. My dad has since told me that I was very distracted by my puzzle and didn't pay them too much attention. In fact, they weren't sure I liked them at all, which I think is just hilarious. Anyway, we chatted a bit more and then it was time for them to go. Just as they were heading out, Dad noticed that I was struggling to fit this one piece in the puzzle…"

"There's always that one troublemaker."

"Exactly… So he came back to where I was sitting and helped me figure it out. He then turned to leave—and I remember this so vividly —I felt this sudden confusion wash over me. I guess I felt like he and I had just bonded so deeply over that puzzle, and I was indignant that he was leaving. So, I bolted up from the floor, raced across the playroom, and asked where they were going. Dad told me it was time for them to head out, to which I very demandingly responded, 'you have to take me home.'"

David burst out into a delighted laugh. His eyes cast a twinkle as they reimagined the scene. "How I would have loved to witness that. Mini Mirai selecting her next family as if wielding a royal scepter."

"I closed the deal," she said slyly. "Soon, I was Mirai McGarry. The rest is history."

"And what a history," David said. "Your family must love you very much."

Mirai nodded reminiscently. "I'm very grateful. I can't imagine my life without them."

The flight attendants were skillfully moving a drink cart down the main aisle when Mirai felt her phone vibrate. As she retrieved it from her pocket, all she could see on the screen was a blurry glow. Her heart began to palpitate as she gave the device a squeeze. She could tell it was a messenger window that had popped up, most likely a notification from Emloch. Her mind reeled as David glanced down toward her hand.

"Our man of mystery, I presume?"

Mirai grunted. "You know what, I can't bear to read this. Would you mind?" She thrust the phone in his direction and crossed her arms against her chest.

David adjusted the text thread with his finger and said, "It's him. Asks how the meeting with Russo went. Also wondered if you've seen the news about Texas?"

Mirai shook her head. "Haven't checked my phone since we got on the plane."

David opened a browser and proceeded to find a news site. The only headline about Texas was halfway down the webpage. "There was a technical glitch at a nuclear power plant in Corpus Christi. Nothing too serious. No leaks or meltdowns. Just says it was a technical malfunction but it's now under control."

Mirai hesitated before looking over at the outline of David. "What's the date?"

"January 4th."

"And the area code for Corpus Christi?"

"Looks like…361."

"Yep, that's on track."

David glanced up from the phone. "A newsworthy catastrophe each day would be difficult to pull off. Maybe some of the events will be more subversive."

Mirai sighed heavily and shut her eyes. "I don't know what's going on, David. And I don't know what we should do about it. I mean, Russo could have killed us. He was truly frightened by whoever pursued him before, and in a different frame of mind he could have chosen to pull that trigger. I don't know if I wanna keep doing this. I don't know why we should."

David agreed but only with a facial expression. In his body, Mirai could sense that he was conflicted. The uncertainty lingered into the next few minutes as they watched the flight attendants pass by. Little more was discussed on the matter, or on anything else, as Mirai leaned against the polycarbonate lining of the window seat of the plane and felt her muscles start to decompress. When she awoke, they were beginning their descent into Miami.

CHAPTER 5
THE FIERY ANGEL

The beachfront was bustling with activity as Mirai jogged along the parallel sidewalk. Shimmering rays bounced off of ocean currents that slid onto and then retreated from the granular sand. Beachgoers out for a stroll passed by people oscillating metal detectors over the terrain, all of whom found themselves weaving around the dozens of women stretched out on beach towels in hopes of achieving the perfect tan.

I'm sorry, but I just can't do this.

The memory assaulted her mind without warning as she continued her jog. Her last message to Emloch had been brief. A summary of her excursion to meet with Leighton Russo and his unequivocal response to her inquiry in the form of a pistol had settled the matter in her mind. Russo was not Osiris. Mirai finished the note by stating that her desire to be of service in the exposing of Ad Ordinem could not overcome her will to live. She apologetically yet firmly told Emloch that any help she offered could no longer be in person. She left David's involvement in the event out of the conversation entirely.

Eight weeks had gone by with no reply from Emloch. His complete silence suggested either disappointment in or resignation to her decision. Neither reaction bothered her. Mirai was quickly settling back into an old routine—a lifestyle focused solely on her art, and on David.

Mirai slowed to a stop at an intersection while continuing to bounce in place, hoping not to lose the momentum she had gained. Strapped to her upper arm was her phone, which suddenly began to vibrate. She smiled with expectation and awkwardly maneuvered the screen to see who was calling.

It was a local number, but it was not David's.

She let it go to voicemail and then played it back in her earbuds. The smile on her face quickly withered.

"Hi, Miss McGarry, this is Dr. Wallace again. I know my office has left you several messages as to following up on your last visit. It's important that we touch base with you about starting a treatment plan for the multiple sclerosis. I'd like to get you on some interferon treatments as soon as possible. These disease-modifying therapy medications are designed to reduce the inflammation in your spinal cord and brain—"

Mirai tapped on the phone screen and deleted the message. Her chest and abdomen rose and fell in rhythm. Beads of sweat ran from her sports bra down to her shorts. She brushed an unruly strand of hair away from her face and tucked it behind her ear. Only then did it dawn on her that she had stopped bouncing.

My vision is fine now, she said to herself. *Came back in a day or two. I feel amazing. Why do I have to go down this road of medications and trial-and-error and God knows what? If I have MS there's nothing anyone can do about it. And maybe they're wrong. Maybe I should go get a second opinion. One doctor says it's MS, another doctor might say it's PMS.*

Standing idle at the intersection, she watched as a series of vehicles backed up along the street, creating a momentary traffic jam. As she scanned the cars, she noticed a convertible being driven by an old man with a fluffy white dog in the passenger seat. Mirai smirked at the sight and watched as the car pulled away, only barely catching a glimpse of the bumper sticker that read: *Honk if you love Maltese.*

Filling the space of the convertible was a city bus that hissed to a stop next to the curb. Mirai could see herself begin to bounce within the tinted glass windows. Below the bus windows was a rectangular panel with an advertisement that looked freshly printed.

She instantly stopped bouncing.

"Is This the End of the World?" she mouthed.

The ad appeared identical to the one she had seen on the gigantic billboard in the middle of the Nevada desert. Same black-and-white lettering and background, same font, no indication of an advertiser.

Mirai slowly reached out her hand and placed it against the printed ad. She wasn't sure why she was inclined to touch it, perhaps only to be certain that this desert mirage was in fact real. The memory of discovering the original message, followed by the disappointment in not understanding its purpose, doubled down as her skin absorbed the radiating heat from the panel.

Yet again without closure, she watched as the bus began to move, sliding the length of the advertisement underneath her fingertips and leaving behind nothing but a green light at the crosswalk. Her eyes followed the bus until it was completely out of sight. The apparition didn't seem real, like a hoax, or an elaborate prank. Something engineered by someone who knew her and wanted her to ponder a question with no discernible answer. The opportunity to capture some photographic evidence was long gone, and Mirai scolded herself for having now missed the chance twice.

Feeling spent, she glanced at her wristwatch and then decided to call it a run. It would soon be time to meet up with David for lunch.

Upon returning home, she waved at Carys who was busy chatting on her tablet with one of her friends. Mirai dashed up the stairs to shower, change, and do her hair and makeup. When she came back down, a wave of hunger-induced nausea suddenly struck her. Sitting on the countertop was a box of cereal.

Just to fend off the wooziness, she thought, and began fishing out the mini marshmallows.

"Well, I'm off," Jason announced as he entered the kitchen. "Got a twelve thirty tee time."

"Hi, Dad. Bye, Dad."

"Mirai, stop eating all the marshmallows out of the cereal box," Jason scolded. "It's very disappointing to buy marshmallow cereal every week only to have nothing but bran flakes fall into my bowl."

Mirai covered her mouth in laughter. "But they're really good. They're holding me over until lunch."

"Don't you have food at your own house? You know, the one you occasionally sleep in…in the backyard? The one we could be renting to anyone else for double the price."

"Oh, pipe down. I'm your favorite child. You love it that I'm over here so much."

Jason smirked and took a final sip from his coffee mug. "I guess that's true. Anyway, I gotta go. Call if you need anything. Your mother is…somewhere I'm sure."

Mirai shoved another handful of marshmallows into her mouth. "She left early this morning to go to the farmer's market with Aunt Allison."

"I vaguely remember her saying something about that. The one over in Coral Gables, right?"

"Coconut Grove."

"Really? Oh. Will she be home this afternoon?"

"Not until tonight. This is their sister day."

"Their what?"

Mirai grinned as she chewed. "Their sister day. One day a month they spend the whole day together. They…literally do this every month."

Jason cocked his head. "Since when?"

Mirai flashed a highly amused stare before asking warmly, "Dad, what prevents Mom from cheating on you?"

Jason melodramatically took Mirai's face in his hands and landed a kiss on her forehead. "You are now my second favorite child."

"Dang it."

"Seeing David today?"

Mirai nodded softly and glanced down at her outfit. "He's mostly set up in his new apartment. We're meeting for lunch."

"I like him," Jason affirmed. "I like the way he treats you and I like how happy you seem when you're around him. Are you two officially dating?"

Mirai shrugged. "I'm trying not to rush into anything. David's getting his life back on track and I just wanna be there to support that."

"But he did move his stuff all the way down from Orlando," Jason stressed, as if to remind Mirai of vital information. "And he got an apartment close by. And he's trying to land a job at the Miami Symphony…"

"All right, okay, what's your point?"

Jason reached for the cereal box and took a peek inside. Seeing that all of the mini marshmallows were indeed gone, he set the box down and sighed. "All I'm saying is this: you've dated a few losers in the past—"

"Watch it."

"—and it's nice to finally see a guy make an effort to be with you instead of you always having to be the one who makes the effort. You deserve that."

Mirai placed her hands on her hips. "Was that… Did we just finally have the sex talk?"

"Goodbye."

Jason snatched up his wallet and keys and reached for the doorknob. "Say hi to David for me. And pick up some more cereal on the way home!"

Mirai tugged at the hem of her skirt and curtsied. "Yes, Papa."

The door closed and Mirai turned to look at the time. With a few minutes to spare, she reached for her phone and opened the Omni application, all while bracing for a deluge of meaningless notifications. The window filled the screen only to instantly minimize. An incoming call had taken priority.

Julie's mom, Mirai thought. *What does she want?*

"This is Mirai," she answered, calmly.

"Glad you're home," the voice said, in lieu of a greeting. "This is Mrs. Laufer."

"Oh, hi, Annette," Mirai said, knowing exactly the degree of irritation calling her childhood best friend's mom by her first name would evoke. "What's up?"

"We're cleaning out the rest of Julie's room," she answered, coldly, but also with the slightest hint of regret. "Since it doesn't seem like Julie's coming back from the Preserve, we figured we might as well repurpose the bedroom into a workspace. I came across a box we missed with more of her old book collection—you know, the books she never ever read—and wanted to give you last crack at them. If you're not interested, I'll just add them to the donation pile."

"No…I'll definitely take them."

"Good," the woman said, sounding as if she could now check off something else from her to-do list.

"I'm heading out to meet someone for lunch. Is it all right if I swing by afterward?"

"We'll be running errands all afternoon, dear. If you want this box, it's now or never."

Mirai rolled her eyes and looked at the kitchen wall clock. "In that case, I'll be right over."

Waving again at Carys as she left the house, Mirai jumped into her convertible and donned a pair of white round-framed sunglasses. The palm trees floated over her sequentially as she drove the five-minute journey to the Laufer home. Each minute that passed brought to mind a different memory from when she and Julie were kids: walking to the Laufer house for after-school cartoons and raiding of the snack cabinet; walking to the McGarry house for a sleepover and a movie. Weekends were often split between Saturday morning breakfast at the Laufer's followed by a midafternoon transition over to the McGarry's for dinner. Both families claimed the other girl as a surrogate daughter, with full rights of behavior correction when needed, as well as full responsibility for their care, well-being, and happiness when inside the walls of the shared home.

Sisters, Mirai thought to herself, without further comment or context.

The grade-school years developed into the teenage years, and with it, an evolution in the family dynamics. The Laufers had always been slightly stricter with Julie than the McGarrys had been with Mirai. Even so, the girls united the two sets of parents in ways that transcended their seemingly minor worldview differences. That ethos started being tested the year Mirai and Julie turned fourteen. It had been a series of incidents: small offenses, misconstrued intentions, perceived disrespect. Annette and Valerie, while not best friends, had always enjoyed each other's company, as did their husbands, Jason and Cam. Yet the moments of interaction between the two families slowly started to wane that year, even to a degree that made Mirai and Julie take notice.

The Worthy Book, Mirai thought, tightening her grip on the steering wheel and pursing her lips.

There had been an argument one night. The kind that made Mirai and Julie retreat to the basement of the Laufer home and blast music off the stereo in order to drown out the parental squabble. Jason and Valerie had informed Cam and Annette of their recent read through of the rival religious text to the one the two families had always aligned. The Noble Book sat open on the dining room table in front of the Laufers, while across from them, the Worthy Book sat in front of the McGarrys. Each book acted as a religious moat blocking entry to their dueling kingdoms.

The argument had been as divisive as it had been long, dragging on into the early hours of the morning, filled with accusations of personal betrayal, of disobedience to God, and of grave concern for the other side's destiny. The conversation had ended with an amicable, albeit flimsy, agree to disagree truce. Mirai could no longer recall the reasons her father and mother had given for their departure from their former faith and embrace of the new. She could only remember the ramifications, which were subtle at first but then grew to be increasingly punitive.

"I can't believe you'd embarrass me like that!" Mirai had once cried, sobbing into her hands while walking barefoot into the Laufer house. She was still dripping wet from the backyard pool party celebrating Julie's fourteenth birthday.

Annette had fired back, "You embarrassed yourself, Mirai."

The commotion had occurred following Mirai's arrival to Julie's party. Annette had been busy in the kitchen preparing snacks for Julie's friends and had not had the time to greet anyone. Julie took Mirai around back and they quickly assimilated into the frenzied group of boys and girls leaping into the pool and playing with inflatable tubes. Nearly thirty minutes transpired before the frenzied mom had gotten her first glimpse of the party. It was within the glimpse that her eyes had zeroed in on Mirai—the only girl wearing a bikini.

Over the years, Mirai had tried to block out the memory of Annette confronting her in front of the other teens, of the vitriol with which she had attacked Mirai's character and judgment, and of the attention and shame Mirai had felt about something she hadn't even noticed a moment prior.

Valerie drove over to pick up her daughter after hearing her muffled sobs on the telephone, sobs shared by Julie who was equally nonplussed at the situation and furious at her mom for disrupting her party. Mirai remembered Valerie marching in the front door, taking a moment to kneel down and comfort her, then helping Mirai to her feet. Mirai then watched as her mother proceeded through the rest of the Laufer house and onto the back patio, taking a minute to evaluate the scene. She finally paced back into the house and aimed an incriminating finger at Annette.

"That was a really low-life stunt," Valerie seethed.

"I called all of the girls' moms last week to inform them of the attire expectations for this pool party. They all understood," Annette said.

"How odd that I never got a call from you."

Tears were streaming down Julie's cheeks as she inserted, "I'm sorry, Mrs. McGarry. I'm so sorry…"

"Well… I naturally assumed you would know what would be appropriate for your teenage daughter to wear at our house."

"No, let me tell you what this *actually* was, Annette," Valerie countered. "This was your attempt to get back at us for converting to a different faith. And since you couldn't humiliate me or Jason, you went after Mirai. Well, you know what? I was skeptical at first of Jason's desire to try this new path. I admit that. But now… I think we made the right decision. Because the thought of having to worship at the same voxhall as you, or Cam, or Julie, makes me sick."

Sitting in her car in the driveway of the Laufer residence, Mirai suddenly realized that she had arrived. She blinked and gazed down at her yellow sleeveless halter blouse and white miniskirt, an outfit she had specifically chosen to wear with David in mind. She knew she had nothing to fear now from Annette, yet something in her physical body was bracing for judgment. As the memory retreated back into her subconscious, the sting remained. It was not because of witnessing parents lose their cool at a birthday party, but because of how effortlessly the two couples had decided that maintaining a friendship in light of their newfound religious differences was just too onerous a task. Their homes would continue to be open to their surrogate daughters—with new boundaries. Mirai and Julie would remain best friends.

The parents never socially interacted again.

It's remarkable just how much morality and ethics are crafted not around people's convictions, but their insecurities.

The thought followed Mirai out of her car and inside the Laufer home, where she tried greeting Annette congenially, even as the woman took visual inventory on her guest.

"There's the box," Annette said, pointing at it in the corner of Julie's old bedroom. "What remains of her books is all in there now. That's the last of it."

Mirai nodded, slowly coming to terms with the overwhelming sensation that she would never again step foot in this room. It had already been transformed. Everything was gone. All touchpoints to a life having been lived there had been packed away. As Mirai's eyes scanned the empty space, she suddenly wasn't even certain where the bookshelf had been.

"I heard," began Annette, her voice a tone of tortured hesitancy. "That…you went to go visit…Julie…at the Preserve."

Mirai knelt down next to the small box and thoughtfully opened it. There were only a few books. Nothing she recognized. The only standout being a soft leather notebook that had a strap around the center. She carefully lifted it out of the box.

"I was invited to tour the Preserve," Mirai said, still looking down at the book in her hands. "Julie got me the invite. It's the only correspondence I've received from her since she left."

"You saw her?"

Mirai nodded. "I did."

"Is she all right… I mean, how is she…is she okay?"

Mirai unwound the strap on the old book and pulled back the soft leather cover. It took several seconds for the handwritten cursive lettering to register any meaning as she flipped through the pages, but when it did, her mind shut out everything else in the room.

It is dangerous to write this. I should not be putting pen to paper. They told me in every way possible not to keep notes on meetings, passphrases, activities within the order. For the most part, I have kept that oath. I am generally a man of my word. Yet I must be allowed some leeway to expel what I've witnessed from my mind. To conceal it is to relive it.

Their motives are pure. I do believe that. I need to stop writing "they"—as I am now a part of them too. We are God's will on planet earth. Us—the Paragons. That's an immense honor and incredible responsibility. I joined in hope that I could do something useful with my life. Something powerful. This order is capable of that. They—we— seem to be capable of anything.

That's what haunts me. I can still see his face. His pleading eyes. He had told them everything and yet they still demanded more. It was not enough to snuff out his body…they eradicated his soul.

Yes—we killed a man today. First, we tortured him, at least, that's what I think happened. They took him in a back room. They were gone no more than a few minutes. When he came out, his face looked pale, as if he had been forced to witness his greatest fear. He told us everything. His betrayal of the order, his sabotage of our members, that he had revealed secrets to someone outside of the society. He talked until he could scarcely speak. I watched him talk. I could feel his syllables on my skin. I couldn't move. I was transfixed, horrified as to what I had gotten myself into, and if this poor man's fate could end up being my own should I violate the laws of the order.

He told them the truth. I suspect he also told them whatever they wished to hear. After what seemed like hours, a robed man approached him and placed his hands on his head. He told the traitor that he was forgiven, but that he had outlived his usefulness. He was again taken into the back room. I never saw him exit the building.

"Mirai?" repeated Annette.

"Huh?" Mirai said, her eyes darting up toward the woman wondering about her daughter.

"I asked you about Julie. Is she all right?"

"Oh…yes." Mirai blinked, her mind still in two places at once. "Yes, I saw her there. She seems fine. In fact, she seems…happy. She was sitting right next to Alexander."

"You met that psychopath?"

The journal slipped from Mirai's hands and fell back into the box. She quickly retrieved it and tried to push back the mental bombardment of what she had just read. "Um… Yeah, believe it or not, I did."

"What was he like in person?"

"Oh, just as crazy as you'd imagine. But I have to give him credit. The man does know how to moisturize."

Mirai waited for the joke to land. It did not. After a moment, she said, "Annette, Julie's not coming home anytime soon."

"I know that," she snapped. "Don't you think I know that? Julie has made her decision quite clear. I'm sure it's just hilarious to you and your family to see ours gutted by our only child. To see her discard everything she's ever learned for the ramblings of a charlatan. We showered her with so much love, Mirai. So much patience. So much attention. She was our whole world. We taught her the Noble Book since she was little, took her to the voxhall every week to instruct her in the right way to live. We tried our absolute hardest to keep her out of trouble and out of error."

Annette hesitated again before exhaling a lifetime of exhaustion into her final statement. "And she paid us back…by joining a cult."

The two women stared at each other in contemplative silence. Then Julie's mother turned to leave.

Mirai placed the book back in the box and stood up. "Annette, my family doesn't think Julie leaving is hilarious. We all lost someone precious to us. I can't tell you the number of tears I've shed over this. I lost my best friend, but you lost your daughter. This must be horrible for you, and I don't know how to fix it. I tried, and I blew it. For the time being, Julie is happy with the Mesa Revival. We all have to come to terms with that. But we don't have to like it, and we don't have to stop fighting for her. Part of fighting for her is sticking together. And I can tell you, honest to God—*hand on the Worthy Book*." Mirai widened her eyes expectantly and saw a thin smirk warm the edges of Annette's face. "No one in my family wants any other ending to this story than Julie's safe return home."

Mirai burst into the diner and quickly slid into the booth opposite David. "I am so, so late and I am so, so sorry," she said, fumbling her backpack strap over her head and onto the seat.

David smiled and set down his menu. "Not a problem. For me, time doesn't begin until you show up."

Mirai groaned. "That was so bad. And a little bit sweet. How are you?"

"Thrilled to be living next to this lovely restaurant. The food here looks delectable."

"Not sure anyone has ever called diner food delectable, but I like your enthusiasm."

"Nevertheless," he said, offering her the second menu. "I can see myself patronizing this establishment on a regular basis."

"If the food sucks, you can bet I'll be patronizing."

They laughed in unison, and it was within the laughter that Mirai suddenly felt her muscles start to unwind. "So seriously, how are you?" she asked.

"Essentially, all moved in. Still disorganized, but moved in."

"I wish you'd let me help with something, anything. I can unpack boxes. Arrange closets. Whatever you need."

"All I need is your artistic eye: set the plant here, the ottoman there. That sort of thing."

"You're certainly in a good mood today."

"I am." David smiled. "I heard back from the Miami Symphony this morning. They've decided to take me on as their primary harpist."

"David!" Mirai exclaimed. "You could have opened with that! That's fantastic. Oh my God. I'm so proud of you!"

"I owe you a huge debt of gratitude, Mirai. If it hadn't been for you coming to the Preserve, I may still be trapped there, lost from the inside. I could never thank you enough for your encouragement. You truly brought me back to life."

His words seeped into her ever-softening frame. It was only then that Mirai noticed her hands enveloped within David's. She couldn't recall if she had first reached out to hold them or if he had. All she knew for certain was that they were clasped together in the middle of the table, the byproduct of spontaneity, of appreciation, and of their mutual letting down of guards.

"Enough about me," David said, breaking a silence that was the opposite of awkward. "What bright moments livened your day?"

Mirai glanced away for an instant, trying to figure out how to summarize the amalgamation of interactions she had had that day, and all of the memories and concerns associated with them.

Shrugging wearily, she said, "It's been a busy morning. God, is it only lunchtime?"

David gave her hands a gentle squeeze. "That bad, huh?"

"Not bad, just… Some things to think about. But I don't wanna rehash all of that now. Ask me something else. Anything else."

David nodded agreeably. "Very well then. How is Carys doing? Her life seems a bit hectic at present."

The two continued chatting about Carys and her upcoming shooting schedule. Years of product line photos and obscure, local commercials had gradually developed into better jobs and national opportunities. Carys's agent had booked her work for every weekend through graduation. What had been a fun hobby in her teenage years was steadily looking like a secure career for the foreseeable future. It was a dream come true for the young model, and a point of contention within the McGarry household.

"My parents wanted her to go to college, but Carys is going to wait," Mirai said as they ate. "She wants to see how far she can take this. Looks like she'll be bouncing between Miami, LA, and New York for the next several years."

"Is higher education the only thing holding your parents back from giving their full approval?"

"Keen insight, sir. No, they're both concerned for her safety. But I mean, come on, this is a huge opportunity for Carys. Everyone understands that she has to take her shot. They support her. I believe they support her. They just… I don't know… don't always show it well. I think the idea of massive publicity gets to them. They're very private people. Carys is not."

After their meal, Mirai and David walked the block and a half to his new apartment. Her hand was nestled between the polyester sleeve of his button-down shirt and his torso, and the hem of her white skirt periodically bounced against his slacks from the gentle breeze. As the two entered his corner unit, Mirai was struck by how much light the apartment held. It seemed warm and inviting, despite the litany of boxes and general state of move-in disarray.

"I'll help you make it livable," she said, moving about the space with the kinetic energy of the possible.

David set his keys down on the countertop and nodded in agreement. "I would most welcome that. I was thinking that perhaps a desk could go—"

"Oh…my…God!" Mirai exclaimed gleefully from another room. David could hear the sound of her black pumps shuffling back across the linoleum as she slid to a stop in the kitchen. With hands pressed together in front of her chest, Mirai beamed. "Your harp is finally here!"

"Amazed you found it. With it being so inconspicuous and easy to hide."

"It's enormous!"

"That was a joke, my dear."

Mirai moved with alacrity over to David and took his hand in hers. Then leading him with less grace than she intended, they both entered the spare bedroom that had nothing more to show for it than a small window and David's own lifelong pursuit.

"I know it's like asking a doctor to examine a rash on his day off," Mirai pleaded. "But…just this once…would you play something?"

David reached for a stool and placed it next to the harp. Once seated, he looked up at Mirai and said, "Don't you know? Playing the harp for a woman like you is what I always envision." He then smirked as he witnessed her melting reaction. "A little less sickening sweet than last time?"

Mirai's smile betrayed her solo dimple. "Just the right amount."

David sat silently for a moment, pondering what to play. He then said, "Perhaps something recognizable."

Gently resting the soundbox of the grand harp against his shoulder, his arms seemed to embrace the instrument from both sides as if caressing a lover. The amber-colored harmonic curve met his eye level as he gazed across the forty-seven strings and over to the harp's pillar and crown, themselves bathed in mahogany.

Mirai listened as the first few notes emerged from the strings and immediately identified the song as Debussy's *Clair De Lune*. Her eyes followed the movements of his fingers as he plucked each string with precision. His hands moved slowly, and then very quickly, then slowly once again, all in accordance with the notes that only he could see in his mind's eye.

Mirai found herself leaning against the naked wall. As the song progressed, standing became an unnecessary burden, an impediment to experiencing the richness of the moment. She instinctively removed her pumps and felt herself gradually slide down the length of the wall and onto the carpeted floor. Her skirt ruffled in layers against her knees as her feet pressed into the plushness of the carpet. She sat below David's eyeline, watching him pluck each string, gazing as his hands would suddenly pull away from the harp only to float back and resume the melodic motions.

Every note seemed to radiate off the intense vibrations of the strings, granting precious little time for recovery before David's fingertips would demand of them again. Her eyes followed his hands working their way up the edge of the harp and then methodically back down. His artistry was masterful, attentive, and strangely tantalizing. The instrument had become a natural extension of his body by the time he reached the end of the song. Carefully plucking the last few strings, his hands slowly pulled away, his eyes closed, and the tonal vibrations left the room without so much as a farewell.

David exhaled and relaxed his shoulders, allowing the harp to once again stand straight on its base. He opened his eyes and saw Mirai staring up at him from below. His hands reached out as he slid himself off the stool and knelt down to join her on the carpet.

"Not too rusty," he mused. He waited for some kind of feedback. His eyes watched hers as she examined his face, searching for something, trying to hold onto something as ephemeral as a fading note. It was in the searching that he felt his hands being lifted up by hers. When she placed them onto her own cheeks, his palms were still warm, still alive with creative tension.

The moment suspended time and held them inside the rapturous uncertainty of a question. David decided in the moment that the question did indeed have an answer. His fingertips slid past her cheeks and into the first few strands of her thick, black hair. And as he drew her face toward his and their lips finally met, Mirai leaned into him, knowing that somehow, she could still feel the vibrations of the harp strings on every fold of skin that David touched.

The afternoon sunlight bathed Mirai in warmth as she drove home and parked her convertible in the driveway. An effervescent smile radiated from her lips causing her cheeks to tingle. Upon entering the house, she closed the door behind her and leaned back for a moment. Thoughts of David overwhelmed her consciousness and became the lens through which she viewed everything around her. Nothing seemed as daunting as it had the day before. Life's problems appeared more manageable. She knew it was the emotional response to falling in love, to being in love. It was the grand reawakening to what was objectively good and true in the world.

She pondered that truth while meandering aimlessly around the house. "Anyone home?" she said lackadaisically.

The living room was vacant. So was the kitchen and dining room. Mirai clasped her hands together behind her back as she moved down the hallway toward the stairwell. Each step was a movement all its own. Each movement was a reminder of the sensations her body could produce.

Deciding that the house was empty, she headed back into the solarium. A fresh white canvas awaited her. She stretched her arms out and absorbed the smell of the room. Her eyes then drifted over toward the desk. On the computer screen sat a message.

DO NOT DOUBT ME ON THIS. CARYS IS IN GRAVE DANGER.

Mirai blinked as her smile soured. Unsure if she was comprehending what she was reading, she took several cautious steps forward. She reread the words again until there were no excuses left for ambiguity. The first communication from Emloch in two months shook Mirai to her core.

"What the hell?"

What are you talking about? she typed angrily.

The ellipses predicted a forthcoming reply. As they pulsed, Mirai grabbed her phone and began scrolling for Carys's profile.

CARYS IS AT A PHOTO SHOOT WITH HER AGENT. THEY'RE ALL AT THE EXECUTIVE AIRPORT. SHE IS NOT SAFE. YOU HAVE TO GET HER OUT OF THERE NOW.

Why? Why would she not be safe? Who would want to harm her?

As she hit the enter key, her left hand was simultaneously typing out a text to her sister asking if everything was okay. Before she could send it, Emloch's response appeared on the screen.

THIS IS NOT A DEBATE SITUATION, MIRAI. I'M TELLING YOU TO GET CARYS OUT OF THAT AIRPORT. NOW!

Mirai felt her body deadlocked in a tug-of-war between the keyboard and her phone. She began formulating a reply to Emloch even as her legs started backing away from the computer. Her thumb had already dialed Carys, and her hand was pressing the phone to her ear. A sequence of steps out of the house and into her car left her memory with opaque spots. She was driving down the intercoastal road while redialing her sister who had failed to pick up. A surge of adrenaline fought to be acknowledged.

Carys isn't going to answer, Mirai thought. *If I was at a shoot, I wouldn't answer either. Damn it, Emloch. Why are you making me do this? I thought I was done with you.*

The force of an overpass rustled her ponytail as the convertible exited the freeway and headed inland. Warm air swept across her nose and cheeks and served as proof that this was not a daydream. The juxtaposition from her afternoon with David to her current moment was as real as it was harsh. Mirai cursed and pressed redial again.

Calm down. Everything is fine. Everything is going to be fine.

The municipal sign for the executive airport appeared along the side of the street. Rows of palm trees lined the boulevard leading up to a parking lot. The airport was significantly smaller than what she was used to seeing, and she soon realized that its size was equivalent to its exclusivity. Underneath an atrium was a valet stand. She pulled up and a young man walked over to greet her.

"Good afternoon, miss," he said, flagrantly checking out Mirai in approval and her car in disapproval. "Are you parking overnight?"

"No, just for an hour or so."

The valet tore a paper stub from his notepad and handed it to her. "Keys inside the vehicle?"

The engine's running, isn't it? Mirai grabbed the ticket and her purse and nodded. "Yes."

A quick burst of speed had her shuffling through the sliding doors of the private airport. The inside was spacious and unashamedly opulent. Not a waiting line or conveyer belt was in sight. All passengers appeared to be known travelers, and the security procedures for rapidly clearing them was convenient and seamless.

Mirai approached the check-in counter and placed her ID in front of the agent. "I'm not flying anywhere today," she said sheepishly. "My sister is part of a photoshoot on one of the planes. I'm sorry about this, but I really need to relay a message to her. It's sort of urgent."

The man smiled understandingly. "These things happen. I can have an escort take you over there."

Mirai completed the security check and was whisked away by a small courtesy shuttle. She glanced at her phone to see if she had missed any calls from Carys. There were none and Mirai knew there wouldn't be.

This is so stupid…

They drove parallel to a taxiway on one side and a series of airplane hangars on the other. The cordoned off road ran for a quarter mile until it ended at an apron where a private jet glistened in the sunlight. A small cluster of people were gathered together outside the retractable airplane door. The talent was nowhere in sight, although Mirai suspected they were already inside the plane.

"Thank you," she said to the driver, and felt the exposure of open space as she walked anxiously toward the private aircraft.

"Excuse me," Mirai asked a woman in a dress suit. The woman had a clipboard in her hand and a clenched pen across her teeth. "Sorry to bother you, but I'm Carys McGarry's sister and I was wondering if I could speak with her for a moment?"

A finger pointed irritably toward a man with a camera strap around his neck. He was kneeling down next to a gear box and rummaging through it as if his life was on the line. As Mirai approached, he seemed to anticipate her arrival and glanced back with a look of suspicion.

"Yeah?" he said.

"So sorry about this. I know you're all busy."

"We would be busy if I could find the right lens. But it looks like someone didn't pack this up properly on our last shoot." He grunted. "That someone was probably me. Anyway, what can I do you for?"

"I'm Mirai McGarry, Carys McGarry's sister, and I—"

"Identical twins?" he chided.

"Exactly," Mirai smirked. "Only Carys is from the blonde-haired region of Burma."

The man laughed and shook his head. "I'm just joking. I've been Carys's photographer before. She showed me pictures of you because she thinks you're pretty enough to be a model too. I remember your face."

"I guess that's flattering?"

"You ever do any modeling?"

"No, I'm usually the girl behind the camera. Honestly, having one model in the family is more than enough."

The man held up a lens and shrugged in acquiescence. "I guess this'll have to do. Well, if you ever want some extra work, lemme know. I'm contracted by them, but I also do freelance on the side. Always looking for an interesting new face."

"I'll keep that in mind."

"But you didn't come here for a job. You came to find your identical twin sister. She's up in the plane with the others."

"Thanks."

Mirai hustled up the red fabric steps of the airplane door and took a moment to compose herself upon entering the multimillion-dollar private jet. Her eyes followed the recessed lighting down the length of the cabin, underneath which were creme-colored leather chairs interspersed along the aisle. The tables adjacent to those chairs were mahogany and reflected the amber glint from the cabin lights as if simply to enhance the spectacle. Several photographers were busy clicking away. Mirai spotted Carys amongst a group of other young models all dressed in athletic wear. When their eyes met, Carys gracefully excused herself and walked up to the front of the plane.

"Mirai, what are you doing here?" she asked with a chuckle.

"I am so sorry to interrupt. I hope I didn't ruin anything."

"No, they're doing our group shoot next. I already did my

individual ones. You like?" Carys did a pirouette with her arms stretched above her head.

"What is this for?" asked Mirai. "And why are you in a leotard?"

"Some promotional stuff for an exercise brand. I think the theme for this one is…active people as jetsetters? Cuz we, I dunno, fly around a lot? Honestly, they explained it on the ride over here and I still don't get it. The guy who owns this jet is a mega sponsor of a lot of American sports teams and I think he just wanted his plane featured in the ad campaign. Whatever. Why are you here?"

Mirai looked around, suddenly feeling embarrassed—suddenly feeling angry at having been manipulated. Outside the cabin was glorious daylight; the idyllic Florida sky settled in for a prismatic display of late afternoon color. The runways below appeared to be operating normally. Inside the private jet, all was copasetic.

Mirai turned back to Carys and said, "I…have no idea why I'm here. I…made…a mistake. Go back to your shoot and have a nice time. See you at home."

"Are you sure everything's all right?" Carys asked, reaching for Mirai's arm.

Mirai smiled. "I think so. Seems fine. Really, don't mind me. Go strut your stuff."

Carys shrugged and waved goodbye to her sister. As Mirai turned to exit the plane, the photographer at the gear box was making his way up the stairs.

"Hello again," he said. "Say, let me pass your phone number on to the head of marketing here. He mentioned the other day that he was looking for an Asian American female for an airline shoot. I can give him your name and you two can talk turkey."

"Sure, why not? I can try out my killer stare," Mirai said with a laugh.

"You'd be portraying a flight attendant, so I'm certain 'killer stare' is what they're going for. What's your number?"

Mirai proceeded to list the digits as the man wrote them down. He said, "Got it. I assume that's a 305 area code?"

"Yeah."

"Cool. I'll have him call yah."

The photographer maneuvered past her as a look of shock warped the last vestiges of contentment from her face. Her expression was frozen in time. She stood in the center of the entrance immovable, like a stalagmite locked to the floor. A sensation of unadulterated horror slowly pulsed through her veins. It was a sensation inseparably linked to a thought. Her eyes looked down at the phone in her hand. With her thumb, she rigidly navigated to a screen which displayed a countdown clock. At the top, the text read: Number of Days Until New Year's. At the bottom, the numerical digits stood in large, bold terror.

3-0-5.

"Oh my God," Mirai whispered.

Her death grip on the device tugged at a muscle that she could feel all the way up into her shoulder. The tension caused an immediate ache followed by actual pain. It was from the pain that Mirai's mind told her to look out toward the airstrip. A suburban and a black panel van were racing directly toward the jet before skidding to an unceremonious stop against the tarmac. Mirai did not count the number of men who leapt from the vehicles, only that most of them seemed to be wielding enormous guns.

She blinked and saw time begin to unfold in slow motion. In one instant, she was already racing down the main aisle of the jet. In the next instant, her phone was back in her purse, the strap tugging at her chest as she ran. There were no words to explain what was about to happen, for she herself did not know. Only her faith in Emloch's prediction and the knowledge that Ad Ordinem was true to their dastardly word made the next course of action justifiable in her mind.

"Carys get down!" Mirai screamed, and side-tackled her sister onto the floor of the airplane.

Pops of gunfire sliced through the outside air. Screams mixed with the unmistakable sounds of impact in human flesh ricocheted against the fuselage windows. Mirai sensed others ducking for cover all around, and did her best to shield her own and Carys's heads from the impending shards of glass. Yet the shards never came. It was only through the cries of terror on board the plane and the strands of hair partially obscuring her eyes that Mirai realized the cabin had not been hit.

"What's happening?" Carys said through clenched teeth.

Mirai held her even tighter.

Guttural bursts of agony echoed out, indicating that those on the ground had been and were continuing to be shot. Then, shouts from men who spoke as if they were in command rang up the steps leading into the plane. The terrifying vibration of boots ascending steps traveled along the cabin floor and into the awareness of the two sisters. As the first assailant entered the plane, someone from the flight crew screamed.

"Everyone listen up!" came a voice.

Mirai could hear but dared not look. For in that moment, she believed that willful blindness would be her only chance at clemency. She curled around Carys and felt her younger sibling's frame tremble through the leotard.

"You—all of you! I want you off this plane. Now! Let's go!"

One by one Mirai heard the reluctant and the mortified rise up from the floor and make their way toward the exit. The commotion offered a glimmer of hope. The men wanted the plane, nothing else. Perhaps they would all live to see tomorrow.

Mirai pried back her eyelids and peaked up at a man standing over her. The man wore a short sleeve T-shirt, a gray utility vest, camouflage pants, and rugged boots. In one hand was an automatic rifle. His other hand appeared to only be a single finger aimed directly at Mirai and Carys.

"You two—over here with me," he barked.

I thought they were letting everyone off? What does he mean?

Mirai decided to comply and thought she had come to that decision within a reasonable timeframe. But the speed and the aggression with which the assailant twisted her arm and body up to a standing position proved otherwise. With a violent shove, Mirai found herself slumped against a leather seat next to a window. Carys was ungraciously plopped next to Mirai. It was then the siblings realized that there were two other men onboard. All had weapons that looked to be of high caliber. All worked in tandem and seemed to be following a plan. Within a matter of seconds, the plane had been entirely evacuated, save for the three assailants, someone ingratiating himself with the cockpit, and two sisters observing it all in terror.

Just us? Mirai thought. *Why just us?*

The assailant who gave the appearance of being in command flashed a hand gesture toward another man that was interpreted as an order. The second man walked over to the front of the plane and relayed a message. Mirai watched and tried to understand what was about to occur. As she did, the third assailant marched to the back of the plane and stared down intensely at the sisters.

"Up here, eyes up here," he said, snapping his fingers for their attention.

They looked at him and wondered if they had ever seen him before. But nothing of the green in his eyes, or the crew-cut blond of his hair held any recognition. He was simply a face, and a leather glove, and a gun.

"What are your names?" he demanded.

Carys looked at Mirai. Mirai nodded in surrender.

"Carys McGarry," she said, nearly stuttering.

"Mirai McGarry. Are you going to let us go like everyone else?"

The man took Carys's chin in his gloved hand and yanked her face closer to his. His eyes were searching, scanning, checking off a series of mental boxes. He then released his grip and did the same to Mirai, who in response grasped his wrist with her own hand. The man barely seemed to notice—once again lost in a moment of contemplation. He let go and took a hearty step backward.

"If you both cooperate you won't be harmed. I assure you."

"Cooperate with what?" protested Mirai.

The man ignored her and kept his gaze focused out the fuselage windows. Mirai turned around to look as well. A second later she wished that she had not. The carnage of metal crates, splintered and pockmarked with bullet holes, was no match for the carnage of crimson that stained the ground below. Decimated bodies lay everywhere. What had minutes earlier been a bustling atmosphere had been instantaneously transformed into the stillness of death.

Mirai lurched her face away from the window. Carys then made an attempt to look but was prevented by her older sister.

"No," Mirai said firmly, her eyes locked onto Carys's with a powerful glare. "No."

A voice yelled out from the cockpit. "We're ready to roll."

The third assailant gave a thumbs up and sat down in the seat across the aisle from his charge. Mirai watched as he latched his seat buckle.

Oh my God. They're taking us somewhere…

The piercing whine of the jet engines coincided with the closing of the cabin door. The unmistakable sound and sensation of cabin pressurization sent Mirai into a panic.

"Where are we going?"

"Someplace safe," came the curt reply. "You two buckle up and sit tight."

"You need to let us out!" Mirai demanded. "We refuse to be your hostages!"

"You're not hostages," the man said, and as he said it, Mirai saw in his countenance that he truly believed it.

Mirai glanced at Carys who seemed to be verging on disassociation from the shock of a good day turned heinous. Mirai wrapped her arm around her sister's shoulders and pressed a firm kiss into the side of her hair. "We're gonna be all right," she whispered. "I promise, I won't let them hurt you."

Before Mirai could come to terms with what was happening, the jet began to move. The devastation on the tarmac below slowly faded from view and turned into a taxiway morphing into a runway.

Mirai shook her head in frustration. *I should have tried to grab his rifle. Maybe I still can. All I'd need to do is put a bullet through one of the windows and the plane would depressurize. We would have to stay on the ground.*

The thought weighed down on her as she scanned the interior of the aircraft. There were eight windows on each side. Sixteen chances to keep the plane on the ground. Mirai drew in a deep breath and wondered why her legs felt like cement.

You can do this. Just grab the gun and…but wait…what if its locked? What's that called—a safety? I don't know how to un-safety it. Maybe it doesn't matter. It's still worth the risk. If it's ready to fire a round, then that round is going through a window.

Mirai slowly pulled her hand along her thigh and up to the belt strap. As her fingers made contact with the metallic clasp, the entire cabin suddenly took a sharp jerk to the left. The force of the swerve knocked Mirai's head against her own window, and as she absorbed the impact, her eyes saw that the runway below was careening back and forth.

"Son of a bitch!" the assailant said, unclasping his buckle and darting up the cabin aisle.

The plane continued to jostle, causing the amber recessed lighting to flicker. Mirai held Carys close as the jet swerved again, followed by the screeching noise of deceleration. Everything within the cabin seemed to react to the sudden loss of motion. Sounds of boxes tipping over, glassware crashing, and unsecured camera equipment tumbling underneath seats confirmed what Mirai saw out her own window. They were on the runway and had completely stopped.

"Goddamn it!" one of the men cried. His exclaim was backed up by the cocking of a rifle.

Mirai pressed her bruised cheek up against the window and winced. From her vantage point, she could barely see the back of a semi-trailer truck parked perpendicularly on the runway. Its rear doors burst open and six men in black ski masks leapt out of the trailer. Each held a weapon similar to what the assailants had, save for one. His weapon was larger and strapped around his shoulder.

"Who are they?" asked Carys, straining to see.

"I have no idea," Mirai said.

Burps of gunfire erupted across the runway. The sound of tires shredding sent a bolt of hope through Mirai as the cabin began to sink unevenly.

Thank God. At least the plane is grounded.

The two sisters watched as the men on the runway spread out in formation around the jet. Once placed, the man with what appeared to be a launcher knelt down on one knee and aimed the shoulder cannon toward the front of the airplane.

"Get back! Get back!" exclaimed one of the assailants to the others.

"Get down!" screamed Mirai to Carys.

They hit the floor the same instant the missile hit the cockpit. The explosion disintegrated the partition door and sent a billowing sheet of fire surging through the cabin. The incredible pressure blew out the fuselage windows, sending shards of glass in every direction. Shrapnel ricocheted into the leather chairs, spinning some completely around, while others simply ignited into flames.

Mirai opened her eyes and wondered if she was in hell. Asphyxiating smoke started to choke her lungs. She was certain that soon there would be nothing left to breathe. Pushing with unsteady arms, she sat up on her knees and tried to peer through the ashen haze. There was light shining through up ahead in spite of the smoke and fire. Mirai grabbed Carys's wrist in preparation to run.

"Hold on," one the assailants protested, but not to Mirai. He was lying on the ground with his back to the cabin wall, blood running down his neck. His rifle was nowhere in sight. Bearing down on him was a shadow preceding a person who calmly entered the aircraft and reached for his sidearm. The assailant on the floor protested again, stretching out his hand in pleas.

The other man wasted no time and fired three rounds into the assailant's chest. The deafening roar of the gun struck Mirai and Carys with brute force. Their ears roared from the ungodly sound before it faded into a shrill ringing that was both welcome and unnerving.

Mirai watched as the man who had entered the plane holstered his revolver. He appeared satisfied that the assailant was dead. Beyond dead. After a quick burst of speed, he was towering over them at the rear of the jet. The sisters gazed up into a face shrouded in gray smoke. Emerging from the flaming aura was an outreached hand. No instructions were offered. No demands given. Simply a choice to grab ahold and live.

Mirai pushed Carys up first, who staggered along the aisle with traumatized muscles. As the olive-colored hand reached out again for Mirai, she noticed that across two of his fingers ran a thin scar. It was the leftover evidence of a wound long since healed. The hand widened its palm and reached ever closer to her. She met it halfway with a determined grasp and felt herself being hoisted to a standing position.

The man turned forward and began pulling Mirai through the flaming wreckage of the fuselage. Tongues of fire tried to lick at them as they weaved over and around fragments of airframe. The nauseating stench of burning plastic filled their nostrils. Mirai covered her mouth and nose while trying not to become sick. She strained to see what was ahead, but could scarcely think, much less see through the blindfold of smoke. The hand continued to pull her, to guide her through the inferno. She felt its unwavering grasp of her tighten all the more. They were nearing the light source. The hope of freedom was within a shrouded reach.

Her legs limped through the remainder of the cabin before taking a painful leap down and out of the burning plane. The runway was blistering, unforgiving, and left scrape marks on her hands upon impact. Once inhaling the outside oxygen, her diaphragm spasmed into a fit of coughing so severe that she was certain she would vomit. Her abdomen and shoulders took turns absorbing the violent reaction. With asthmatic force, Mirai coughed out the toxins, and only when her lungs were partially satisfied was she able to rest a hand on her spasming chest. She took a moment to catch her breath and then turned to embrace Carys who was already reaching to embrace her. The two hugged and held each other for nearly a minute, wiping tears from their smoke-stained cheeks, and confirming every few seconds that the other was all right.

It was only when Mirai's vision shifted to the right that she noticed the first third of the airplane was gone—obliterated by the missile. Still in a traumatic daze, her eyes then darted back toward the rest of the runway, only to discover that the semi-trailer was already well on its way off the airstrip. The men who had saved them were also gone, leaving behind no one but the survivors who were huddled together on a patch of grass next to the taxiway.

Mirai's vision swam as she wondered where the man with the scarred hand had gone. How he had vanished so quickly—without farewell. Why he had not given Mirai even a second to thank him for saving her life. Ambulances and squad cars approached the scene with their lights ablaze. Mirai saw them but could not hear them. The only sound she could hear over the ringing in her ears was the pounding of her heart. It beat wildly, insistently, trying desperately to convince her that she was still alive.

CHAPTER 6
AFTERSHOCK

HELLO MIRAI.

She saw the words appear on her phone screen and nodded slowly. The nod confirmed that the message had been anticipated. Mirai lay sideways on her bed, the bedsheet crinkled around the shape of her body. Outside the room, raindrops were pelting away at the windowsills. It had been raining all night, and the overcast morning atmosphere made the house seem all the more secure.

I SAW ON THE NEWS REPORT THAT YOU AND CARYS SURVIVED THE ATTACK. YOU DID VERY WELL. I AM PROUD OF YOU.

Mirai listened to the rain and watched it zigzag down the panes of glass. She gazed at their endless maneuvering while taking mental notes. For some time, she had suspected that her next canvas would portray the beautiful chaos of a rainy day.

WHAT YOU WITNESSED WAS PART OF AN ONGOING CIVIL WAR. ONE BETWEEN AD ORDINEM AND EMBLEM. AD ORDINEM ORCHESTRATED THE ATTACK. EMBLEM INTERVENED.

THE PLANET'S OLDEST SECRET SOCIETY IS TURNING ON ITSELF. THE COLLATERAL DAMAGE WILL CONTINUE TO BE

SEVERE. WE MUST TALK ABOUT NEXT STEPS IN THE SEARCH FOR OSIRIS.

The pair of wearied eyes drifted away from the phone screen. She rolled over onto her back and looked up at the slow whirling blades of the ceiling fan. The endless motion set her mind adrift. She thought of gunshots, the cacophony of deafening noise, of holding on to Carys and of the claustrophobic nature of dense smoke. Then the timeline morphed into the claustrophobia of answering questions inside a private room next to the terminal. Still in shock, they did the best they could to answer the direct inquiries of men who claimed to be everything from aviation officials to counterterrorism units from the federal government. The interrogators did the best they could to make Mirai and Carys comfortable. They also insisted that time was of the essence and that the sisters' immediate cooperation was of national importance. Mirai had chosen not to divulge her knowledge of Emloch, Emblem, or area codes. For in that moment, the information seemed the only piece of her life over which she still held any semblance of control. Emloch's message had saved Carys. There was still more to uncover before handing him over as a lead to the authorities.

Mirai closed her eyes purposefully and reopened them, as if to force a reset on her daisy chain of memories. At once she was back home, standing in the doorway with Carys while parental arms corralled them into a crushing embrace. They had all wept; they had all talked. Jason and Valerie shook from rage, from exhaustion, and from relief. Their daughters had survived a terrorist attack. It was a bizarre statement that didn't become more natural with practice.

Soon thereafter, David had arrived. Mirai recalled the look on his face when she ran into his arms. He bore the expression of one who had himself cheated death. David held onto Mirai as if he faced the constant threat of her suddenly vanishing into the ether. She had dissolved into his presence, into his reassurance. They all ate a simple meal together and then retreated to the den for a mindless film. Whatever the plot had been, the movie had served its purpose to grant them momentary reprieve from the horror of the day. When evening absorbed the last remnants of light left in the sky, they all retreated into various parts of the home for what they hoped would not be a fitful night of sleep.

Mirai continued listening to the rain. A nascent smile crossed her lips as she felt a hand move up the length of her body. The arm to which it was connected slithered underneath the sheets until coming to a stop at her breasts. Her face turned to see David lifting his head from his pillow and planting a firm kiss on her exposed shoulder. In his eyes was the look of appreciation. Mirai curled herself over to him and ran her fingers through his hair. Their conversation was silent, expressed through the subtle shifting of eyes that refused to look away. When there was nothing left to say, she pressed her forehead against his and melted into the caressing warmth of his hands on her back.

"Am I still alive?" she asked.

David kissed the side of her head and slid his hand into her hair until his fingers disappeared. As he massaged her scalp he observed the reaction on her skin. His eyes followed the contours of her face down to her neck where his lips began to gently kiss a line from her jaw to her clavicle. The immediate change in her breathing pattern chiseled a smile into the corner of his mouth. He kissed her lips once, then again. He went back for a third time but then hesitated, making her wait, and evoking from her the look of longing that he adored.

Mirai moved in impatiently to complete the kiss. As she did, the images and sounds from the previous day continued to bombard the foreground of her memory. She shut her eyes and engaged in a full-on tug-of-war with David's lips, hoping that the physical contact would vanquish the blood-soaked images that tormented her.

Oh my God! she recalled someone screaming, their voice swallowed into a volley of gunfire.

Get down—everyone get down!

Up here—eyes up here! If you cooperate, you won't be harmed...

Mirai leaned her head back as if lost within her eyelids. The sounds of metal bending, bullets lodging, and bodies hitting the ground merged with the concussive noise of the cockpit explosion. Mirai remembered thinking that she would never hear anything again. Not Julie's voice. Not Carys's laughter. Not the music from David's harp.

I promise, I won't let them hurt you... she had said to her sister.

Mirai sighed and rolled onto her back. The ceiling fan blades continued to whirl as now did the entire room. She placed a hand over her forehead. The thoughts were not assuaged. Her mind replayed the shooting of the assailant and the three flashes of copper light it had created within the haze. Then came the look of terror on Carys's face as the man with the sidearm made his way to where they were crouched. The hand, the fire, the long gullet of the fuselage trying to swallow them all into hell; the carousel of images assaulted her vision without consent.

"Mirai," David whispered.

Her eyes opened to see him turned toward her and moving his arm between the pillow and her neck. She placed her palm on the stubble of his cheek and groaned. When she realized that the fingers of David's other hand were sliding down the length of her torso, the groan instantly turned into a moan.

"Just keep looking at me, for as long as you can," he said.

David watched her brows furrow as she gazed into his eyes. Her knees raised up underneath the sheet creating two towers. Her heels dug into the mattress. She clenched the back of his hair with one hand and the edge of her pillow with the other. The mental pictures of destruction and death began to fade as the sounds of her own labored breathing flooded her consciousness. Her frame twitched at random intervals and keeping her sights fixed on David became an increasing struggle.

Inside her mind, the shape-shifting horrors from the previous day lost their grasp of her focus. The ensuing tumult gave way to a single face emerging from the chaos. The face gazed down at her with tenderness and strength. Mirai drank in the assurance until she could no longer. As her eyelids fell forward and shut out everything in the bedroom, the clarity of her thoughts dimmed. She pressed her forehead against David's shoulder in an attempt to blackout even more of the stimuli from the outside world.

Time evaporated. Cause and effect were no more. The last remaining worry she was managing to hang onto was sucked into the void of the nonexistent. She grit her teeth as if she had been chewing. She panted as if she had been running. When she let out a guttural sound, her mind released in harmony with her body, fully allowing her to accept the gift that David was offering. The voices retreated, replaced by the tapping of raindrops against the windowsill. Her muscles stopped bracing for the searing pain of bullet holes. They surrendered instead to the moment, to the pleasure her body was capable of producing, and to the oncoming flood of sensations washing over her like a supernova.

Over the course of the next minute, her panting gradually softened. Still dangling between realms, Mirai felt her slender frame decompress into the wrinkles of the bedspread. One eye opened long before the other. She leaned her head back onto the pillow, leaving behind an imprint of sweat on David's arm. He smiled at her and brought his fingers back up to rest around her navel. She twitched again while trying to find her sensory bearings.

As she recovered, David leaned in and asked, "Did you feel that?"

Mirai smirked and nodded from an otherworldly distance.

David said, "Then in answer to your question—yes, you are absolutely still alive."

The rain turned to daybreak as patches of light penetrated the overcast. The breeze smelled salty and filled the house with thoughts of the ocean. Mirai's mind drifted to the beach as she stepped out of the shower and began to towel off. She gazed at her body in the mirror and wondered why it didn't look as pulverized at it felt. Her hand let the towel drop to the bathroom floor. It then moved across her left shoulder and arm. When it came in contact with her other hand, she repeated the motion on her right shoulder and arm. Her eyes then looked down at her hands as they slowly stretched to open and then contracted back into fists. Tousled strands of wet hair fell forward, acting as curtains next to her cheeks as Mirai leaned in closer to the mirror. With firm jabs, she pressed her fingers against her face. Across her forehead and down to her chin she prodded, leaving behind fleeting fingermarks that were absorbed into her tanned skin.

Her stance straightened as she repeated the maneuver against her neck, her chest, along her abdomen and thighs, and down to her legs. The farther down her body she moved, the harder she pressed. When finished with the examination she stood in front of the mirror, gazing contemplatively into her own eyes and posing a question she only had the courage to utter in her mind.

Why doesn't any of me feel normal?

The question lingered as she got dressed and made her way down to the kitchen. No one was up yet and that suited Mirai just fine. She needed time alone, in her studio, with her colors and blank canvas. The wooden stool on which she sat felt more rigid than usual. The lighting in the solarium was now blinding, as if the sun were overcompensating for her malaise. None of the colors on the palette seemed to be in the correct order. Her brushes felt either worn out or not worn in enough. The pre-stretched canvas sat before her on the easel in utter silence. Her eyes searched the white slate for a pattern, for a meaning, for a message.

Relax... she said to herself. *Just relax and breathe. Nothing will come to you if you force it.*

Taking a moment to compose her wandering mind, Mirai corrected her posture on the stool and placed her hands on her lap. She gazed out the window at the swaying fronds of the palm tree in their yard, down at the paint-splotched floor and the projects associated with those stains, and then over at her desk where an etched piece of wood reminded her of the purpose of her passion.

It begins with chaos...

Mirai dipped a brush in some crimson-colored paint and began working the corners of the canvas. From there she moved on to shades of blue, creating the essence of a gradient sky. A new brush brought in a swirl of yellow and orange to the center of the painting. After every few brushstrokes she would stop to take assessment. The hesitancy bothered her, sowing early seeds of doubt.

This isn't right.

The abstraction taking shape was not what she had been envisioning, appearing less like a sunburst and more like an explosion. A heavy sigh preceded a second attempt at contrast. Using a liner brush, Mirai tried working the blended sections together in the form of a weave. Yet the spokes did not look like a bond, but a twist, a knot, a chain.

Mirai set down the liner brush and decided to add form to the center of the painting by using a palette knife. She mixed shades of yellow together and aimed the edge of the tool in approximation to where the order should begin emerging. The paint scraped along the canvas as she worked it in with the knife. Her hand bobbed back and forth in surrender to her tightening wrist. Her eyes darted between the canvas and the palette, only blinking in the time it took to reload with paint.

Chaos and order.

She moved with precision. It was the act of working against an inner clock. Speed would overcome stagnation, she believed, and allow her to break through any blockage in her subconscious. Yet as she continued, the results projected a different story. The brushstrokes pushed back. Her arm began to ache. Her eyes continually searched for an image that wasn't forming. The promise of order was failing to deliver. All that was metamorphosing was more chaos. An unnerving sort of chaos. One with a sinister streak. A moment's pause gave Mirai the descriptors to define it.

It was chaos masquerading as order.

"Freakin' eight ball," she said, and flicked the brush onto the side table.

Her shoulders slumped as her eyes drank in the disaster on display. It was hardly her first bad artwork, but she found difficulty in remembering just how long it had been since it was this atrocious. With thick, white paint, she covered over the canvas as if blocking out a typo. She sliced the material from the wood frame and disposed of it in the trash.

Don't worry about it. It's obvious why you're a little off. Tomorrow will be better. It has to be.

She walked into the living room and was startled by how much time had elapsed. Sounds of human activity came from the kitchen as did the smell of breakfast. Sunlight was showering in through the main window and casting a shimmer against the metallic frame of the coffee table. Mirai walked into the light and did a giant stretch. As her eyes adjusted to the outside radiance, she zeroed in on a man walking across their front lawn. Behind him was another man with a large, broadcast-quality camera. Behind them both was a news truck parked on the residential street.

"What the hell?"

David walked up behind Mirai and assessed the situation. "Oh boy," he muttered.

Lining the street on both sides were other panel trucks, all emblazoned with different news logos. Reporters were already making a barricade on the sidewalk so their respective camera people could obtain the best view of the house.

"Um, Dad?" Mirai called out into the hallway.

Jason and Valerie marshaled themselves into the living room as if already aware of the development. "I know, I saw the vultures gathering about ten minutes ago," said Jason, motioning for Mirai and David to back away from the picture window.

"How'd they get our home address?"

"Probably the same way they got our cell phone numbers," said Valerie. "I had to shut mine off about an hour ago. Have you gotten any calls?"

"Not yet," said Mirai. "Has Carys?"

"No. But she's such a public figure it won't be long until someone offers it over."

"For the right price," added Jason.

"Should we shut the blinds?" asked Mirai.

"Not necessary," assured David. "Journalists can't film inside your home without permission. But the instant we step outside…"

"Where is Carys?" Mirai asked.

"In the kitchen," said Valerie. "Breakfast is ready, which is what I suggest we all focus on. Let them report and record and—"

The sound of the doorbell chime gave them all a start.

"And ring our bell all they want. The front door is our official statement. *No comment.*"

They entered the kitchen and sat along the breakfast bar with Jason choosing to stand. Mirai turned to Carys and gave her a tender nudge. Carys nodded and nudged Mirai back.

"Were you able to sleep?" the older sister asked the younger.

"Yep," was her curt reply, while she preoccupied herself with picking out the cantaloupe from her fruit cup.

"How are you feeling?"

"Focused. I have another shoot this afternoon."

Mirai glanced at Valerie. "Her agent didn't cancel?"

Carys interjected, "I told him we can't. I'm still trying to prove myself in the industry. Everyone's counting on me. I'm fine. I feel fine. Being in the studio clears my head. I just wanna shoot."

The doorbell chimed out again. Jason slid his plate of scrambled eggs across the counter and began to pace the kitchen. "Weasels."

"I'm sure they'll go away soon," Valerie said in a levelheaded tone.

"Coming to our home, though. That's just obscene."

"What happened was news. It's their job, dear."

Jason shook his head in irritation. Mirai and David exchanged glances.

"On a different note," Valerie said, pivoting the conversation. "Congratulations on your new job, David. We love the Miami Symphony. It will be quite a thrill to see you in the orchestra."

A humble nod preceded his reply. "Greatly appreciated."

"When do you start?"

"I'm meeting the rest of the ensemble tomorrow. I'll begin orientation shortly thereafter."

Valerie continued to pepper David with symphony-related questions in an effort to lift the mood of the household. As she did, Mirai felt her phone vibrate in her back pocket.

THERE IS NO TIME TO LOSE. YOUR NEXT ASSIGNMENT IS

LOCAL. DR. GEORGE DOMINGUEZ WORKS AT THE UNIVERSITY OF MIAMI, BUT VOLUNTEERS SUNDAYS AT HIS LOCAL VOXHALL. ITS ONLY A FEW MILES FROM YOU.

DOMINGUEZ WROTE ONE OF THE TWO BOOKS IN EXISTENCE ABOUT AD ORDINEM. SINCE THEN, HE'S BEEN IN ACADEMIA. HE FITS THE PROFILE FOR OSIRIS AND MAY BE ABLE TO SHED MORE LIGHT ON THE ATTACK.

Mirai sighed in frustration and set her phone down next to David's plate. As he finished reading the text, his expression was one of uncertainty.

The next few days followed a similar pattern: Mirai would awaken being spooned by David, followed by a shower and getting dressed, a solemn breakfast with the family whilst ignoring the perpetual attempts by the media for an interview, then hours in her studio for work that amounted to little more than kindling.

In the evenings, Mirai ate dinner with her family as they all tried to find inconsequential things to discuss. Then David would arrive and join them in the den, rehashing his first week with the symphony and how good it felt to be rehearsing with such talented musicians. Once back in her bedroom, Mirai would wrap herself in David's embrace, her mind finally at ease for what seemed like the first moments of the day, drifting peacefully into a dreamless sleep.

It was not until early Sunday morning when she began to worry. Sitting before yet another blank white canvas, her eyes gazed into the nothingness feeling as if they were on the verge of atrophy. The colors on the palette had faded. The brushes all appeared worn. In her mind's eye was a template that she had used countless times. The route from her brain to her hand though seemed hopelessly riven.

GOOD MORNING, MIRAI. IF IT'S ANSWERS YOU SEEK, THEN I SUGGEST MEETING WITH GEORGE DOMINGUEZ TODAY AT HIS LOCAL VOXHALL. HE MAY BE ABLE TO TELL YOU MORE ABOUT THE MEN WHO ATTACKED YOU AND CARYS.

Mirai read the message from Emloch and walked away from the easel. She retreated back upstairs and entered her walk-in closet. The hanging tank tops, rompers, and camisoles seemed to all blend together, leaving her in a state of listless confusion.

"I need to get to the beach," she stated. "Sun, ocean, and sand should cure me."

After donning a brightly colored bikini set, she slid on a pair of cut-off denim shorts and did a quick evaluation in the full-length mirror. "Would you come with me to the beach this morning?" she asked David as he began the process of buttoning his blue linen shirt. "I wanna bring Carys too. I think we all need a reset."

"Of course. Any therapist worth their degree would prescribe sun therapy today. We can swing by my place first so I can change into appropriate beach attire."

"No need. My dad has plenty of trunks you can borrow. Besides, I think you'd look cute lying on a beach towel in a dress shirt and slacks."

"Don't forget the wingtip shoes."

"Exactly."

Following breakfast, Mirai, David, and Carys left the house, grateful that the media firestorm had finally moved on to other breaking news. They walked down the road to where Mirai's usual lounging spot was situated along the beach and unrolled their towels across the warm sand. With her sister on one side and her lover on the other, Mirai plopped down and began lathering on sunscreen while gazing out at the shimmering horizon.

"I have two sanctuaries," she said. "My studio and this beach."

"Both fitting places of worship for a goddess," David replied.

"Geez, get a room already," Carys chided.

Mirai smirked as she handed the lotion to her sister. "Hey, I know you've never been in love before, but trust me, it'll happen. When you least expect it. It'll strike you from out of nowhere."

"Sounds like a disease."

David burst out laughing. Mirai arched an eyebrow and adjusted her sunglasses. "My point is that Cupid's arrows are unpredictable. You just have to be open to receiving one."

"Cupid's an idiot. Dad used to preach all that lovey-dovey crap. He even tried to play matchmaker with me and that kid Tyler when we were in seventh grade. Seventh grade! Who does that? No, you're the romantic, Mirai. Not me." Carys finished lathering and reached over her sister to hand the bottle to David. "Your turn."

"Thanks. So, you've never carried a torch for anyone?"

"Nope. Mirai views the world through rose-colored glasses. Me… just through a camera lens."

Mirai shook her head and smiled. "*Shall I compare thee to a summer's day? Thou art more lovely and more temperate. Rough winds do shake the darling buds of May—*"

"Oh God, she's speaking in iambic pentameter."

"It's Shakespeare, you dork."

Carys stretched out on her towel and tapped the corner of her earbuds to play music. "As I said…rose-colored glasses."

David rubbed the warm skin of Mirai's back and gently kissed her arm. "I adore a woman who can insert a sonnet into everyday conversation. After all, isn't it beauty that will save the world?"

Mirai stared at David through her white-framed sunglasses before slowly removing them from her face. Hearing the words spoken back at her by someone who truly understood the meaning warmed her flesh far more than the sunbaked sand. She rolled onto her side and propped her head up with her hand.

"David, what's a 'paragon'?"

He mirrored her position on his own beach towel and said, "Paragon? That's not a word one hears very often."

"I came across it in an old book."

"I'm sure of that. Let's see…paragon. Isn't it an ideal version of something or someone? Like the perfect example of a specific virtue?"

"That's why I'm asking you. Use it in a sentence, Mr. Eban."

David groaned. "Middle school nightmares rushing in fast. Okay. Paragon. Mirai…was the…paragon…of…beachwear fashion in her multicolored bikini."

She laughed and pointed at her face. "Eyes up here for now."

"Did I get a passing grade?"

"Barely. My real question is why a group of people would call themselves paragons?"

"A group of people?"

Mirai nodded slowly, peaked back around to be sure that Carys was lost in her music, and then leaned in closer to David. "I found a box when I was over at Julie's house last week. Her mom was gonna toss it, so I brought it home. Inside was an old journal where this guy is writing about having witnessed a ritualistic killing upon uncovering a traitor in this secret society. He said the members are called Paragons. That's with a capital *P*. Proper noun."

"Paragons? That's a curious title."

"He seemed really disturbed by what he saw, and was wondering if his fate could one day be the same as the traitor's."

"What's the writer's name?"

"I never had a chance to read the rest of it because I was rushing to meet you for lunch. Then everything happened at the airport, and, well… Honestly, I forgot about it until this morning. My memory has been really spotty lately. Keep forgetting about things. Can't focus on my art…"

"Go easy on yourself," David said. "It's perfectly understandable after what you survived."

Mirai looked down and drew David's name into the sand. Her finger then fashioned her own. The granules sunk along the runes of the cursive lettering while Mirai enveloped the names within the confines of a heart. She stared at it for a minute before glancing back up at David. In her lips was the essence of a half smile, half frown. "That's the best artwork I've done all week."

The sound of ocean waves lapping up onto the shoreline filled the uncertain silence. Stated plainly within the lull was the question of what to do next. Mirai reached for her phone and reread the text from Emloch. She felt in equal parts the draw of seeking closure against those who had tried to harm Carys, and the trepidation in pursuing yet another blind alley.

"What do you wish to do about Emloch?" David asked, cautiously. "He's both placed you in harm's way and saved Carys's life. I'd understand if you think it's too soon to go talk with him… If you need more time to recover…"

"No, I want to go," she responded. "I want to know if he's aware of any local chapters of Ad Ordinem in Miami, who they are, and why they would want to abduct us. I'm afraid if I don't, something like this could happen again."

David sighed in reluctant agreement. Mirai then added, with eyes wide in personal reflection, "They evicted everyone from that plane, David. Everyone but us. I need to know why. As for Emloch, I don't want Carys or Mom or Dad to know anything about him just yet. I know we should tell them, but let's gather a little more info before letting them in on what we've been up to. Okay?"

He reached for her hand and gave it a squeeze. "Of course. For the time being, it will be our very big little secret."

"I'm sorry, who did you say you are looking for?"

The young administrator glanced back toward the capacious inner space of the voxhall as if she was supposed to be attending to other matters. Her ask for clarification was posed in a stage whisper, just high enough to be heard above the din of people gathered behind her.

Mirai and David moved in closer. "George Domínguez. Dr. Domínguez," Mirai repeated, her voice evaporating into the four corners of the anteroom.

"I know he's here today," the young woman said. "I'm just not sure where. He's probably gathered with everyone else inside the voxhall. It's almost time to dispense the Potion. Let me see what I can do."

Mirai thanked her and watched her vanish into the teeming throng. It was beginning to take shape into two lines down two separate aisles, and which line an individual chose to wait in seemed to ultimately make no difference.

Mirai pulled the strap of her backpack purse higher up her shoulder.

David drew in a quick breath and whispered in her ear, "This time, if the guy bolts, let's not chase him."

Mirai was restraining a laugh as the young woman reemerged from the crowd with a portly man wearing wire-framed glasses. His blazer had patches on the elbows and his inner shirt pocket was bulging with pens.

"I've been summoned!" he proclaimed boisterously. "George Domínguez, how are ya?"

Mirai and David exchanged handshakes with the man. They again thanked the young administrator, subtly indicating that she could go.

"Dr. Domínguez," Mirai began. "Sorry to bother you on a Sunday and at your voxhall no less, but we just had to see you about an urgent matter."

"Well, you found me." He smiled. "I was able to partake in the Potion already because I'm good at cutting the line. If you'd both like to chat privately, we can head on up to the mezzanine. Nobody there right now."

The trio walked up a wide, carpeted stairwell and sat down at a small table next to the balcony railing. From above, they could see the proceedings in the hall below, the lines of patrons, the repeating motions of the voxroys, and the light-blue liquid contained within crystal decanters sitting atop the sanctum.

"So, what's on your mind?"

Mirai shot a reassuring glance toward David. She said, "My name is Mirai McGarry. My sister is Carys McGarry. Do either of those names mean anything to you?"

She saw the spark of recognition go off in Domínguez's eyes as he pushed his glasses back up the bridge of his nose. "Oh my… *McGarry*… Of course. Wow." Domínguez rubbed his hands together as his mind connected dots of recent importance. "You were on that plane last week?"

"I was."

"Dear God. Well, I salute you and your sister. That's a helluva thing to walk away from."

Mirai nodded graciously. "Thank you."

"Were you also there during the attack?" Domínguez asked David.

"I wish I had been."

"Ah, boyfriend then. Good answer, young man. That's what I would have said."

Mirai smiled at David before addressing Domínguez. "I…just have so many questions for you. It's hard to know where to begin."

The man nodded agreeably and then slapped his right hand down on the table. "Allow me to take a stab at it. You tracked me down because I wrote one of the two obscure books in existence about the planet's oldest secret society, and ever since Howard Lalonde went berserk on-air—as well as the separate, yet plausibly connected, incident in Times Square warning of the end of the time in less than a year—you can't help but wonder if the targeted attack at the airport was also orchestrated by…well, *they-who-shall-not-be-named*. How close did I get?"

Mirai and David exchanged amused stares. "Pretty damn close," she said.

Domínguez chuckled to himself. His tone then quickly sobered. "Miss McGarry—"

"Mirai."

"Very well—Mirai, did you read my book?"

"I did not. I couldn't find it."

"Not surprising, seeing as how it's been out of print for nearly two decades. It shows up in lonely libraries here and there, and occasionally at a used bookstore, but even online it's a tough find. Most of the research I compiled on the group was used in my dissertation back in the day. I was exploring the rise and fall of secret societies over the course of human history. Ad Ordinem was one of many groups I highlighted, along with the usual suspects like the Illuminati, Knights Templar, etcetera, yet it was also the one which warranted the most critical response. I decided there was enough material to write a book. So, I did. It was released by a small publishing house and barely sold a thousand copies. No one's ever asked about it since. Well, that is until the start of this year."

"The Lalonde broadcast and the Times Square incident?"

"Correct. But the interest peaked and valleyed very rapidly. My phone was ringing off the hook one day and dead as a doornail the next. We all have such short attention spans we can scarcely recall last night's dinner…which for me was meatloaf and green beans. So I guess I'm doing all right."

Mirai shifted in her chair as she posed her next inquiry. "So, who are these people? Why do they call themselves Paragons?"

"Do you know what that word means?"

"An ideal example of a person or quality," Mirai said matter-of-factly, before tilting a wink toward David.

"Impressive. And also correct. The members of this particular secret society believe themselves to be the ideal practitioners and architects of human events on earth. See, they don't worry about moving global markets or containing the military industrial complex. They view their role as loftier than all that. As Howard Lalonde correctly noted, they've infiltrated just about every level of human affairs. But they've done so with a grander purpose than just manipulating an election or overthrowing a kingpin. They exist, and have so since the beginning, to slowly and systematically aim the human race toward a designated and predetermined end."

Mirai felt a chill run the length of her arms. When she touched her skin, it felt cold and clammy. "'365 Days Until the End of Time.'"

"Precisely." Domínguez pointed and said, "Notice they didn't say 'the end of the world.' I, for one, think that's an important distinction. It was not a prophecy of doom on the physical planet. Only on the mechanism that ties all human minds together. The single, unifying force that transcends all barriers of prejudice, philosophy, and creed, is *time*."

"Time?" clarified David. "As in, that which separates the future from the present and past?"

Domínguez narrowed his gaze. "Time, as in the last vestige of universally agreed upon objective reality."

Mirai turned her head. "I'm not following you."

"How old are you, Mirai?"

"I'll be twenty-five in May."

"Are you sure? How do you know?"

"Because I know the year I was born, so do my parents. I was born almost twenty-five years ago."

"And how do you know that your birthday is in May?"

"Because…it always is. Every May 7th," Mirai said with a shrug.

"And you trust that that date is accurate, every year?"

"I do."

"And other people who know and love you also trust in that tiny square on that twelve-page flip book known as a calendar? They all agree to celebrate and commemorate your annual rotation around this burning star the same day each and every year?"

"Basically."

"Why?"

"Why what?"

Domínguez smiled widely. "Why can people, with whom you may not be able to agree on any single solitary other issue, come to a consensus on what day to celebrate a number that represents how many years you've been conscious on this giant rock?"

Mirai hesitated. When the answer dawned on her, she felt her shoulders begin to slump. "Because of time?"

"Because of time," Domínguez said, emphasizing each word. "The foundational absolute in a world increasingly uncertain of anything else. We joke that time is a construct, yet it's one to which we all willingly submit. If I tell you to be at my house at noon, and you arrive at eleven, we both agree that you were early, or if you arrive at one, that you were late. It's not like other topics. We can't agree on politics. We can't agree on history. Our philosophies tear us apart instead of cinching our bonds. We despise each other's knowledge just as we've always despised each other's faith. It seems like we can't agree on *anything*, except the foundational element of human consciousness."

"The concept of time," Mirai said.

"The concept and *consequences* of time, yes. If that's the case, and if this all-important absolute were to be removed from the equation of existence, what would that look like, practically speaking?"

Mirai looked at David. David pondered the question for a moment.

"It would…destroy our own confidence in objective reality," he opined.

"Your finger is on the button, sir. Those who deny the existence of objective reality see the achievements of this world as a series of disconnected *miracles*, instead of the physical end results of sense, perception, and *reason*. There would have been no lifesaving medical treatments, no radio airwave transmissions, no satellite uplinks, no skyscrapers, and certainly no agriculture without a firm belief in the rules and opportunities of objective thinking. It's cause and effect. If this, then that. Assuming Ad Ordinem is behind what we're witnessing, and their endgame is to bring humanity to a close, the main step would be to disconnect us from our primary mode of comprehending life on earth… That is, the use of our rational minds."

Mirai sensed David shooting her a glance. She instinctively reached out to touch his hand. Below the mezzanine, the lines of people had only somewhat thinned and the occasional murmurs and sotto voce tones served as the only reminder that the trio were not alone in the vast expanse of the voxhall.

After a moment of reflection, Mirai whispered, "Why didn't the attackers evict us from the jet too?"

A mild shrug preceded his reply. "I assume they needed a few hostages."

"One of the men told me definitively that we *weren't* hostages."

"Was he holding a weapon when he said that?"

Mirai hesitated. "Yes."

"Then I beg to differ."

The table fell silent as Mirai finished replaying the incident in her mind. A disconsolate look overcame her face while she glanced down at her hands. An acute cramping had centralized in her right palm. When she proceeded to massage it, the pain inexplicably grew worse.

"So where does that leave my family?"

"In what way?" Domínguez asked.

"In what way? Carys will be graduating soon. Her eighteenth birthday is in June. Her agent has already booked her for shoots across the country, and possibly a few in Paris. She's going to be traveling an extensive amount. Gone weeks at a time. Have you seen my sister? Carys has a face you don't forget. She already has a huge fanbase online. When she does her first press junket she's going to be known internationally. And now you're telling me that the world is crawling with Paragons? People who would undoubtedly recognize her face when they start seeing it, who will remember that hers was the face they almost abducted, thwarted only by the clandestine work of a group they hate. I don't know if we were caught up in an isolated incident, or if Carys was the target all along, but can you imagine if they had gotten her? How is she supposed to travel after this? How is she supposed to stay safe? How am I supposed to protect her…"

Mirai winced as the pain radiated up into her wrist. She clamped her eyes shut for a moment, trying to manage the searing discomfort.

"Are you all right?" David asked, leaning toward her as she groaned.

"Yeah, I'm fine," she dismissed him. "Stupid tendon acting up. Been painting too much this week. It'll pass."

David parted his lips to protest but then thought better of it. He placed his hand on her other arm and kissed the side of her head. "Maybe we should go."

Her eyes reopened. "Dr. Domínguez, if that abduction attempt was personal, if they truly did select us to be hostages, or God know what else, then…" Her voice trailed for a minute, as if her mind was struggling not for words, but against a wellspring of emotion. "*People died*, because of us."

"Not because of you," Domínguez corrected. "Because of Ad Ordinem. It was their volitional acts of violence, not yours."

"What if we were the reason?" Mirai said, her tone a maintained hush. "If the plane was targeted because Carys and I were on it, then the people on the tarmac died because those Paragons wanted us for some purpose. I need to know what you think that purpose was."

Domínguez's face twisted apologetically. "If it's hypotheses you need, Miss McGarry—"

"Mirai."

"—then I'm afraid I have none to give you. My book was

exclusively about the facts I could compile, nothing else. Ad Ordinem is a secret society. The operative word there is *secret*. Much of their activity and motivations remain shrouded in mystery. I can't tell you why they attacked that plane, why they targeted you and your sister, if that message in Times Square was from them, or if your family will be targets in the future. I have my theories, you have yours. Unfortunately, that's how most conspiracies work. In the end, one rarely finds the actual truth. Just the truth that you *want* to find."

Mirai nodded defeatedly. David continued his attempts at consolation.

"You know," Domínguez added. "I have a daughter, same age as Carys—seventeen going on eighteen—with all of the excitement and insecurities that come along with that milestone. I know what it's like to fear losing her. To fear something happening to her as she grows up, heads off to college, charts a pathway in life. Your concerns do not fall on unsympathetic ears, Mirai. But what I *am* saying, is that you don't know why you both were singled out. Could have been completely random. Which is why after all appropriate precautions are put in place, both of you must continue living your lives… Otherwise…they win."

As they all rose to leave, Mirai found herself drawn to the mezzanine railing. She gazed down at the lines of people thinning out, and of the liquid within the decanters running low. Domínguez noticed and joined her at the railing.

"Did you attend a voxhall growing up?" he asked.

"For a while," she said, her voice back at normal volume yet somehow still distant. "We were a Noble Book family until my parents decided we weren't. We switched to a different voxhall, but I stopped attending soon afterward."

"Did they serve the Potion at your voxhall?"

"No," she said. "They didn't believe in it."

Domínguez nodded. "Yeah, not every voxhall serves it. Not all believe in its power. They say that the statistics show a precipitous drop in cases of illness for those who partake in the Potion versus those who don't."

"Is that true?"

Domínguez shrugged and chuckled. "I don't know how the study was conducted, or if their methods were empirical, so I couldn't tell you for sure. All I know is that I have enjoyed peace, comfort, and hope in my life whenever I partake. May be scientific, may be spiritual, or may just be plain old placebo effect. Whichever way it works, it seems to work for me."

The last of the Potion was administered as the lines came to an end. Those who remained in the voxhall expressed gratitude before collecting their belongings and going on their way. The ancillary noises in the great space diminished, causing Mirai to be self-aware of every word she now spoke.

"What would make someone join a cult?" she asked. In her face, David could read that she knew she was asking the wrong question, but asking it anyway.

"A cult?" Domínguez repeated. "Are we talking about any cult in particular?"

Mirai didn't answer. She continued to gaze down at the assembly through eyes that were imagining something else.

Domínguez said, "Belief is a tricky thing. We all exercise it, sometimes to fill in the knowledge gaps, other times to grant ourselves comfort in overwhelming circumstances. I'm a man of reason, but I'm honest enough to admit when I'm practicing blind faith. There's nothing evidence based going on down there, Mirai. But so long as they're free to exercise their own judgment, I don't see the harm in it. Harm only comes when faith is used as a shield against the real world. I've seen too many people use the rigidity of organized religion as an excuse to avoid addressing their own deep-seated disappointment in life. An old colleague of mine once asked: 'Is it that your sacred book says you can't, or is it that you've grown comfortable masking your uncertainties in dogma?' Or to put it another way: Is this actually true and am I willing for it not to be? That question haunts me to this day."

"What about the Mesa Revival?" she asked, still observing the movements of those below as if they were bees along honeycomb. "Are they exercising their own judgment?"

"What's happening in Nevada is a different phenomenon altogether. A concerning amalgam of desperation, conditioning, and inculcation. I see nothing good long term for those in attendance. That's the dangerous thing about cult mentality. People in them all have the same thing in common."

"What's that?"

Domínguez frowned. "A hatred for their own existence."

Despite the pain in her hand, Mirai gripped the guardrail a little tighter. The distance from the mezzanine to the main floor seemed as if it were expanding. An unsettling dizziness began to ensue. She twitched away from the railing and headed toward the stairwell. As they exited the anteroom, the midafternoon sunshine cast warmth over their expressions, ones slightly weathered by the conversation.

"Thank you so much for your time, Dr. Domínguez," Mirai said.

"I hope it was worth it. I told you what I know. In this instance, I wish it was more."

"It was plenty. Oh, and one more thing." She reached into her purse and withdrew a small leather notebook. "Would you mind giving this a look? I found it at a friend's house. She collects old books. Whoever the writer is, he seems to be quite entangled with Paragons."

Domínguez took hold of the book carefully, turning each page as if the words could fall off the paper. He stood silently for several minutes before stating, "Well, this is something new. Yes, I'd be happy to give it a look. This friend of yours who owned it, is she a professor?"

Mirai smiled. "Nope. A classically trained vocalist. She's my best friend."

"Next time you two talk, ask her how she came to obtain this."

The smile faded. "That probably won't be possible. She…well, she joined the Mesa Revival last year. She's been living at the Preserve."

Domínguez's mouth fell agape. "No kidding? Holed up in that desert palace? One-way ticket out of the *global madness*?"

"That's what they claim. End of last year, I actually traveled out there to go see her and try and bring her back to Miami with me. But she was too scared to leave. I was devastated. But that's also how I met David."

"Wait. You joined the Preserve and then left?" Domínguez asked, incredulously.

David smiled. "Apparently the first and only one to do so. Was either my best decision or incredibly stupid. Time will tell."

The man cocked his head. "Alexander's a son of a bitch but he's a good marketer. Best charlatan I've seen in decades. A lot of people seem to worship the man. But he also has some powerful enemies. The Feds want the Preserve shut down. They think it's a compound for money laundering and weapons smuggling. Nobody's entirely sure what's going on there. Still, I can't help but wonder how it's all gonna end for those people."

Mirai seemed poised to ask for clarity but decided she didn't have the energy to follow up. "Anyway, let us know if you find anything useful. There's only a handful of entries in the journal. Most of the book is blank."

"I'll dig in this afternoon. Right after my Sunday nap."

The three shook hands and parted, Domínguez back into the voxhall, and Mirai and David toward the parking lot. As they walked, David suddenly said, "We need to go back. We forgot to ask if he was Osiris."

Mirai grabbed ahold of David's hand and continued leading them toward the car. "Let's not go back. Really, David, I don't think he's Osiris."

David acquiesced and kept his stride next to Mirai as her hand squeezed his with increasing intent and as her walk devolved into a limp.

"Mirai, are you sure you're—"

"I'm fine," she whispered, her tender voice conveying the pain. "I'm fine. I'll be fine. Let's just go home. Please…can we just go home?"

CHAPTER 7
BRUSHSTROKES

The conductor sliced his baton through the air and brought forth the sounds of damnation. From the podium overlooking the orchestra, he moved his arms with restrained intensity as the music overwhelmed the concert hall. The frightening cacophony emerged out of the onset of crashing cymbals and tolling bells, sweeping the audience into an instantaneous sense of impending doom.

Like an ancient wizard fighting off the forces of chaos, the conductor swept his white baton toward the instruments he needed in battle. As his eyes homed in on the timpani, the percussionist locked onto the conductor's gaze, his arms poised over the drums in anticipation of a series of notes that would certify the dread to come. Next, he pivoted toward the brass, and in a single tossing motion, initiated their response to the onslaught. The musical nature of the entity they had unleashed was beginning to have discernible features. It was not the sounds of an evil that had always known its destiny, but of a fallen creature about to learn.

The audience viewed the stage from several vantage points, some at the ground level, others perched in balcony box seats, but all were transfixed by the crescendos and violent chords of the absolute movement. In one particular pair of hands, the program containing the repertoire of each performance was clutched between anxious fingers. The program declared the words Prokofiev's *Symphony No. 3* in an elegant font.

The holder sat with unwavering eyes that from afar looked like twin solar eclipses. Her burgundy dress came to a halt at her crossed knees from which led down to a pair of open-toed black heels. One of the heels bobbed and swayed with reserved tension, mimicking the impact moments coming from the orchestra. The young woman's face drank in the spectrum of melodic tension, yet her focus was devoted to one section of the symphony above the rest.

Plucking at his harp, at times with fury, at other times with a kind of sensual passion, David sat amongst the far corner of the ensemble. His intense gaze was primarily locked onto the sheet music in front of him. When he could find an instant to spare, he would exchange glances with the conductor to confirm his pacing, before retreating his eyeline back down to the white paper.

Mirai watched from above and knew that David sensed her gaze. That knowledge added a layer of vulnerability to the moment. Her lover was performing an intimate act in front of hundreds with her as his solo muse, and the sense that she was somehow included in his display of exhibitionism birthed a sensation inside of her too interwoven for words.

The sonata advanced toward the ten-minute mark, suddenly softening its pounding theme to one more melancholic. The flutes and violins complimented one another while David continued adding his gossamer flairs from the harp. The musical ecosystem compressed into the pensive themes of uncertain hope and silent courage. It was a momentary reprieve before once again having to grapple with the forces of inferno.

Seated next to Mirai were Jason and Valerie, who looked at David's contribution to the proceedings with a parental pride. Mirai stole a glance toward her parents and remembered them having introduced her and Carys to classical music at young ages. Attendance to the symphony was a regular occurrence that Carys had only reluctantly grown to appreciate, but that Mirai had been enraptured by since her very first encounter.

"I want to paint what I hear," a rambunctious ten-year-old Mirai had once informed her parents. At the time, they had not been certain how to help her in that quest. She had left the symphony humming the jazzy choruses of Cole Porter's *Night and Day* and the complex movements of George Gershwin's *An American in Paris*. Once home, she darted up the stairwell and began working with her watercolors. Jason gently announced that it was after bedtime, and that she could finish her masterpiece on the morrow. She had capitulated and was quickly tucked in for the night.

The next morning, Valerie had entered Mirai's room to find the ten-year-old sitting on the floor surrounded by art supplies and wearing a look of genuine satisfaction.

"I couldn't sleep," she said preemptively to her mother. "So, I painted this."

In her hands was a painting of a busy downtown street, filled with bustling pedestrians and passing vehicles. In the background was the Eiffel Tower, and in the foreground, a man walking gaily along a pier. The painting was entirely of watercolors and had an impressionism to it that stunned Valerie to silence.

Mirai had smiled proudly and with a hint of relief. "*An American in Paris*. There, now I can go to sleep."

In her teenage years, Mirai had learned to hone her craft in various ways, and more often than not, symphonic music served as the inspiration. Yet it was not until Julie Laufer had blossomed into a powerhouse vocalist that Mirai began making the fundamental connection between great art and great music.

"They both demand a response," Mirai had declared to Julie one day at the Laufer residence. Julie had just finished practicing a ballad she planned to perform at school. Mirai had been so moved that she could no longer sit still.

"Music evokes emotion," said Julie, watching her friend pace the living room. "That's what makes it so powerful."

"Yeah, but it's more than that," Mirai had countered. "It *demands* something of you. You can't just freakin' walk past *Wanderer above the Sea of Fog,* or *The Voyage of Life,* or the giant statue of Atlas holding up the world without it demanding something in return. It's not just an emotional response. When I look at these works of art or listen to you sing *Panis Angelicus,* I feel a step further than that. That it requires something of me."

Julie's sapphire eyes had watched her friend in captured amusement. "What doth it require of you, oh dramatic one?"

Mirai stopped pacing. She had stood quietly for a moment while rubbing her toes across the carpet. After a moment of contemplation, she smiled gleefully. "They all require you to feel, then to think, then to *decide*. My art and your music could be the inspirations behind the greatest decisions of humanity. Wouldn't that be wonderful, Julie?"

Wouldn't it…wouldn't it just be wonderful…

Mirai blinked and slowly remembered where she was. The concert hall rumbled from the kinetic instruments once again mounting toward an attack; the sounds ebbed and flowed as if the whole of the building were being tossed against waves. David was still on stage, masterfully working his fingers across the strings. The conductor stood before them all, his back to the audience, facing down the tempest from the bow with promise of a safe ending to their orchestral voyage.

With finality, the bells tolled. With frantic exhortations the horns proclaimed their final warnings. The violins nearly screeched with intensity as the timpani drums built a subversive crescendo. Everything within the ensemble was surrendering to a singular theme—the proclamation that the end was indeed nigh.

Then, just as the tempo hinted that it was bringing down the temperature of the scalding movement, a blast of horror shrieked from the trumpets, the cymbals, and the stringed instruments, bringing to a close the thirty-six minute piece and leaving behind an unshakable reminder of the corruptibility of the soul.

The audience erupted into sustained applause. The conductor acknowledged each section of the orchestra, inviting them to take a collective bow. When it came time for David to rise, he smiled graciously toward the audience and blew a kiss in Mirai's general direction. Mirai applauded passionately, standing amongst other members of the audience who had risen to their feet. She knew that the stage lights prevented David from actually being able to see her, just as the multitude of patrons all clapping at once was drowning out any chance of her own applause making it to David's ears. She smiled, thinking that it didn't matter. They both knew the other was there and that was enough.

"Bravo!" shouted Jason from the balcony. "Encore! Encore!"

"*Dad,*" Mirai scolded amongst the continuing applause. "Don't be weird."

The evening finished off with a few more selections from Prokofiev's repertoire before a spent orchestra and a satisfied audience made their way out of the concert hall. Weaving through the patrons took more energy than Mirai was expecting, but the instant her eyes laid hold of David, her lassitude became an afterthought. She marshaled herself toward him, feeling as if her feet were free of weights, her arms of chains, and her mind of penetrating fog. It was beneath a giant chandelier that they formed into an embrace. Mirai's fingers slid across the soft fabric of his black suit while David's hands traced the outline of her back. Even as she spoke her first words to him, the unforgettable melody he had helped create played relentlessly within the vistas of her mind.

"That was spectacular," she said, her face looking up into his. "It was devastating, and thrilling, and it…it was…"

"Art?" he smiled.

Mirai felt her body lean into his. Her fingers gently tugged on the purple silk of his tie and watched his lips descended down to hers. The kiss lingered, with neither lover in a rush to part. Mirai rested her hand on the back of his neck and felt David's hand softly glide down the center of her open back. When they finally drew in a breath, their eyes remained tethered, with David as the musician and Mirai as his instrument.

She gazed at him through the twinkling lights from above, then from the passenger seat of her car while streetlamps highlighted the curly waves in his hair, and finally from inside of his bedroom, as the moonlight showered his body in a silver radiance. His linen shirt was open, and her hands soaked up the sensations of warmth from around his torso. His chest expanded as she placed a kiss on his neck, under his chin, and at the corner of his mouth. She observed his eyes watching her every move. The uninterrupted attention made her skin tender to the touch.

With a single motion, her hands slid up his chest and into the shoulders of his shirt. It fell from his arms and dropped to the floor, leaving behind muscular shadows like rolling hills. Mirai's fingers danced along the ridges playfully. She sensed his patience running thin, and that knowledge drew a mischievous smirk from her lips.

She slowly took a step back and reached around her own neck. Behind the thick layers of black hair, she was unwinding a knot tied at the base of her neck. The strings of fabric fell free along with the rest of her burgundy dress, clumping to the floor around her feet. Mirai remained motionless for a moment, determined to make the impression last. Through her mocha eyes she watched him watch her. His adamantine expression hadn't changed since he had laid eyes on her underneath the chandelier. Nor had it ever. David gazed at Mirai the same way he did the mahogany woodwork of his harp, or its delicate strings poised with creative tension. It was a look of desire, first at the curves of her body and how the shadows seemed to trace her erogenous zones, then gradually back up to her mesmerizing face.

Mirai observed his eyeline work its way up her naked frame all the way to her own gaze, and in his expression was a truth she desperately wanted to believe about herself: that she had limitless potential. It was admiration; it was pride; it was a salute, and it was amusement at how benevolent life could sometimes be. Mirai witnessed all of it in the countenance of the man who was looking ever and only at her.

"I'm all yours," she said in reply.

Gone was the pain of the minutes and hours, of the fear and regret of things done and not done. She granted herself reprieve while in his bed, overwhelmed by his touch. Nothing could hurt them, for nothing else mattered. Mirai surrendered to that truth and to the pleasure it afforded her as she drifted into a realm forgotten by evil.

The next morning, Mirai knew only of her intense desire to paint. She opened her eyes and saw the rays of sunlight harnessing the window. It was that image and the motivation to capture it on canvas that got her out of bed before David was awake. A quick wash of her face and slipping back into the dress from the symphony had her bustling around the room as if late for a meeting. She hopped over to the bed on one foot while securing the strap of her heel.

"David?" she murmured. His body stirred under the sheets. "I'm gonna go."

"So soon?" he asked, squinting at his wristwatch. "It's early."

"I need to go home and get some of this sky painted. It's absolute perfection."

"You're absolute perfection."

Mirai smirked and kissed David as he leaned toward her. "I'm sorry to just leave. Do you want me to—"

"No, no," he said. "The sky waits for no one. Go lasso it and bring it back to me on canvas."

"I will," she said, kissing him again and with slightly more passion. "Come over and see me before work?"

David nodded sleepily and then turned back over onto his pillow.

Mirai donned her white sunglasses and hopped into her convertible. The Florida air was crisp and fragrant, and it imbued her with the sense that each breath was important. The drive back to the house was brief. The walk from the driveway to the solarium even briefer. On the easel sat a fresh canvas, and for the first time that week, Mirai sensed from it a greeting instead of a dare.

Out of her formal wear and into a white T-shirt and crisscross denim shortalls, she tied her hair into a messy ponytail and began glopping paint splotches onto her palette. Her eyeline shifted rapidly between the fiery morning sky and the blank canvas. An image was formulating in her mind, and with it, was manifesting on her face. With zeal she dabbed the bristles of a large brush into a variety of copper and reddish tones. With the side of her right hand resting on the canvas, she took a deep breath and stole one more glance out the spacious windows of her studio. Her eyes reverted back to the blankness in front of her as she tensed her right hand to press the paint from the brush onto the canvas.

Mirai blinked and realized that nothing was happening.

The smile had barely vanished from her lips before she watched the wooden handle of the brush begin to slide across her purlicue. The metal ferrule fell from her palm, followed by the bristles made of badger hair. Her fingers made no attempt to stop it as the brush slid out of her grasp. In bewilderment, she watched it fall past her legs and the bare feet perched on one of the spindles of the stool. The brush smacked the floor with a sound that sent a tingle up her spine.

The incident took less time to observe than it did to perceive. Mirai gazed down at the brush while a simmering dread pulsed through her veins. Slowly looking up at the canvas, she witnessed her right hand gradually sinking down the white material. Mirai did not feel the movement, or the sensation of friction with the canvas, or the normal muscular attempts she believed she was making to try and stop her hand and arm from submitting to gravity.

The back of her hand turned toward the canvas as it slid, exposing her palm, and with it, a streak of crimson paint that was a leftover reminder of the brush she had once firmly held. Mirai stared at her hand in terror as it finally surrendered to the pull of her arm. In one swoop it fell limp to her side, dangling from her shoulder like a dead weight.

"Oh my God," she whispered, as her eyes moistened, and as an internal tremor found its way to the forefront.

Using her left hand, she reached over and placed her limp right hand on her lap. The lack of any feeling whatsoever sent her on the verge of panic. Mirai pressed her left thumb firmly into her crimson-stained palm. She flicked her wrist with her forefinger. She twisted her right knuckle in such a way that would have otherwise made her scream. The numbness was absolute, as thorough as a local anesthetic.

"Okay, okay," she said. "Stay calm, just stay calm. This is temporary. It'll come back."

Mirai moved her left hand across her right arm, over her elbow, and up to her shoulder where the sensations of touch reclaimed familiar territory.

"It's just the arm. It's just my hand and arm. It's not spreading."

She sat still for a moment and tried to rein in her galloping heart rate. Her vision shifted across the room without purpose. Her internal body temperature rose and fell in waves.

I've just been painting too much...overextended myself... Maybe I'm ill...the onset of the flu or something...

Mirai nodded to herself yet arrived at no conclusions. The dangling appendage refused to let her. She picked up a fan brush with her left hand and started dabbing it in some yellow paint. Without thought as to what she was creating, she began stroking the canvas with the brush for the sheer reassurance of seeing color. The motions felt awkward. The results looked worse. She continued the brushstroke movements to calm her trembling frame.

Then, as if trying to slip an ace into a poker game, she slid the handle of the brush into her right hand using her left. The attempt at mental trickery failed, causing the fan brush to tip forward and slip through her lifeless fingers. When it landed on the floor next to the first brush, Mirai felt a surge of anxious anger saturate her nerves.

"I didn't know you were here," came a voice from the threshold.

Mirai involuntarily jerked while remaining seated on the stool, her back to the door. The voice was Valerie's.

"Yeah, Mom, I'm here."

"Morning inspiration, I see," said Valerie, smiling. "Are you sticking around for breakfast?"

"Yep. I'll be here."

"Okay. You want some mango? I was gonna cut up a pineapple instead, because it's pretty ripe, but if you want mango, I can do that too."

Mirai grit her teeth and did her best to focus on tempering each word. "I eat a mango every morning, Mom. Why would today be any different?"

Valerie shrugged. "I don't know. Just thought I'd check. Oh, looks like you dropped some paintbrushes."

"Yep. Got it."

"You all right? You sound tense—which is surprising now that you have a boyfriend."

"Mom…"

"You're trying to work, sorry. I'll leave you be."

As the sound of footsteps dissipated, Mirai exhaled, which only seemed to make room for more unresolved tension. She grasped one of the buckle straps on her shortalls, as anchoring to anything in that moment felt mildly comforting. After giving the strap a firm tug, she repurposed her left hand for massaging her right hand and arm. Several minutes of rigorous rubbing made no difference. The feeling was gone.

It'll come back….it's coming back… Just be patient…

Mirai reached for another brush and dipped it in chartreuse. With her left hand she attacked the canvas, nearly knocking it off the easel. Streaks of color smeared the board as she tried to balance herself and her left hand. The strokes failed to impress. Mirai tossed the brush and reached for another. The unnatural motions churned inside of her. To her dismay, even something as simple as a skyline appeared as dreck when applied by her nondominant hand.

Damn it all…

Mirai lurched from the stool and grabbed the canvas. With her left foot she kicked the easel out of the way and watched it fall over next to the utility sink. A look of murder was in her eyes as she laid the canvas down on the floor. She wrenched the palette off the side table and plopped it down on her left side. Several tubes of paint rolled away as she opened a supply box and emptied its contents onto the floor. She added the desired colors one at a time until the palette satisfied the abstraction in her mind. With yet another brush in her left hand, Mirai went to work on building out the gradient layers of a morning firmament.

Soft strokes…use an X motion.

She clenched her teeth as the sky took shape. It was not the sky of a professional artist, but of a grade school amateur. Tears began saturating her eyes and the canvas became blurry. Mirai wiped them with her wrist and continued painting.

Her knees were aching from the merciless floor when she heard a solitary knock against the doorjamb. She shook her head without glancing back. "Not now, Mom. Please just leave me alone."

"Mirai?"

She froze in stunned horror. Her mind vacated all thoughts save for one.

David...

"Mirai, are you all right?"

He moved toward her intently. Mirai continued painting, albeit in slow, wandering strokes. David placed his hand on her shoulder as he knelt down beside her. "Are you okay?"

She did not immediately answer. There were no words she could find to explain what was happening. No bypass through the logjam in her throat to describe her level of distress. She simply ignored the question and continued painting crisscross strokes with her left hand, while teardrops fell randomly off her cheeks, staining the canvas.

"Mirai," David consoled her, running his hand down the length of her right arm. "What's going on? Why are you on the floor?"

Mirai's motions slowed, like an engine running out of steam. Her slender frame trembled in an effort to both hold herself in an awkward kneeling position and also prepare a response—any response—to the man staring at her through concerned eyes.

"You're crying," David said softly. Though she had yet to acknowledge him, he reached over and wiped the moisture from her cheeks. It was then he noticed something else.

"Why are you painting with your left hand?"

She continued gazing downward, continued meager brushstrokes, even as her knees felt as if they would shatter. In her mind, a volley of responses fought for supremacy. She kept her mouth shut, for none of them were true.

Only her periphery caught sight of David gently lifting her right arm up to his face, for she had not felt it. He examined it with furrowed brows. Mirai sensed his worry and it heightened her panic.

"Don't," she finally blurted. She spoke it in a tone that sounded foreign even to her.

David hesitated but continued holding her arm in his hands. "Mirai—"

"Please don't, David."

An unintentional look of sadness crossed his face as he slowly let go of her arm and watched it dangle oddly from her shoulder. "What's going on?" he asked, this time with more demand. "Did you injure yourself?"

Mirai could no longer stand the pain in her knees. She sat cross-legged and cradled her arm on her lap. Her face was partially aimed in David's direction, yet her eyes could not bear to make contact. The artist sat despondently next to the musician amongst a scattering of creative mess.

Mirai parted her lips to speak, and as she did, another tear escaped from her eye. "I'm fine," she whispered. "Please…just leave me alone."

The statement lingered with no context. David didn't move. Outside the solarium windows the daybreak was complete, giving everything in the studio a soft glimmer. It gave the appearance that everything would be bright and cheerful again once they rose up from off the floor. They both remained seated.

"You told George Domínguez that your right hand was hurting from overwork," David spoke softly, yet also in the tones of one building a case.

The faintest of nods came from Mirai's head. Her gaze remained transfixed on anything but David.

"You were in so much pain when I brought you home that day. But you said it was just body aches from the way you sit while working on a canvas. I decided to believe you and you seemed better in the morning."

"David… Please go—"

"But I also remember the flight back from Seattle. You were

acting strangely the whole way and even afterward. For several days, you moved with such caution and performed simple tasks as if doing them for the first time. Then, after a while, everything seemed fine. I asked, and you said it was just the quirks of having an overactive mind. The necessary suffering in order to create. The artist's temperament."

Mirai closed her eyes as if hearing another word would be unbearable. "Please…"

"And now, I come over to find you on the floor of your studio, supplies strewn everywhere, crying onto your canvas while painting with your left hand. So, forgive my impertinence here, but I have to ask…" David gently reached for her limp arm. "Is there something you want to tell me?"

Mirai squared her jaw and finally cast her gaze on him. She drew in a breath and said, "It's none of your business. It's no one's business but mine."

The answer landed with more impact than Mirai had expected. David's face shifted, his expression vacillating between hurt and anger. He remained silent for a minute while collecting his emotions. Once composed, he said, "Of course it's my business, Mirai. We're in a relationship. I care about you. If you're in pain that pains me. How could it not concern me? You're the most important person in my life. You're the first thing that comes to mind every morning and what I dwell on to fall asleep. How could you say that? How could you expect me to accept that statement from the woman I love?"

The impact of David's words landed with equal gravity as Mirai's expression slowly changed. They both heard what was spoken, and they both knew it was the first time it had been verbalized. David blinked but remained resolute, standing behind a sentiment he had long been nurturing. Mirai suddenly appeared less stoic, but the cracks in her visage revealed a disappointment that seemed incongruent to the moment.

David exhaled and said, "I love you, Mirai."

She shook her head as sorrow seemed to crumple her body. "But you can't yet. There's something you don't know." Mirai's voice sounded unused, and in it she saw the irony, since only now was she finally speaking the truth.

"I can't…" She breathed, planting her left palm against her face to try and stop the cascade of tears. Inwardly, Mirai raged against the crying, against the thing that was making her cry. A seething vitriol against the world and the biological lottery it created pumped like liquid acid throughout her body. From the anger she drew strength. From the strength she wiped her eyes and finally looked at David's face.

"I lied to you," she said. "Each time I had symptoms or an episode or whatever they call it, and told you it was just fatigue, I was lying to you. I knew what it was. I've known for months. I've known since right before we met. Since right before I went to the Mesa Revival to try and bring Julie home. I knew what was going on and I knew where it could lead. But I chose to lie to you because I've been lying to myself more."

David shifted his leg as he leaned in closer. "Lied about what?"

Mirai hesitated, seeming to push back the tsunami of emotions that was threatening to drown her in hopelessness. Shutting her eyes, she pronounced each word carefully, as if conveying the meaning of an entire story instead of just one sentence. "About relapsing-remitting multiple sclerosis."

The syllables left her lips and made Mirai realize just how unpracticed they sounded. Only then did it dawn on her that she had never before named her disease out loud. She opened her eyes and saw David. His expression was still registering what was said, but his furrowed brows and detached gaze made it clear that he was rapidly coming to terms with it.

"You have MS?" he asked.

"That's what the doctor said."

David looked down at the disaster around them. His eyeline then refocused on Mirai's arm and hand. "Are you…having an episode right now?"

She nodded defeatedly. "Yes."

"So— and forgive me, one of my brother's friends had MS, I'm going off what little I can remember about this illness—you're feeling some numbness in your arm right now? Or is there no feeling whatsoever?"

"No feeling."

"Does it… I mean…are you in pain?"

"No. I can't feel anything."

David nodded, absorbing the information in quick bursts. "This… paralysis. It's temporary, right? From what I recall, it comes and goes based on the severity of the episode?"

"That's what they claim."

"When did it start?"

"This morning."

"Do you think it had anything to do with… I mean, did I accidentally hurt you…last night during sex?"

"Has nothing to do with that. Has nothing to do with you."

"But, like, why did it come on so suddenly?" he asked.

"That's how it works. There's rarely any warning."

"You came home, and it started out of nowhere?"

Mirai sighed. It was the sigh of one about to read an epitaph. "As soon as I tried to paint."

The next question on David's tongue dissolved. Mirai watched as the gravity of the moment made the mental connection in his mind. He suddenly saw her chicanery for what it was, a desperate attempt to deny a brutal reality. One that threatened to rob her of her very lifeblood.

"Mirai," he said, leaning in to embrace her. As he did, they both felt a jarring misalignment between them, one so obvious that David pulled away much faster than he would have otherwise.

After rubbing his face in his hands, he asked, "Why didn't you tell me? Did you think I would abandon you once I found out?"

"I've read stories online. People do."

"Well, I don't."

"Hold that thought."

David shot a glare that Mirai had never seen from him. The two maintained the stare before mutually glancing away. Silence filled the space between them, burgeoning out into the rest of the studio.

"I was so young," she muttered, gazing off into space. "Still had a lifetime of art to create."

"And you will. This isn't the end of your career. What did your doctor say? Aren't there medications for treatment of MS?"

"There's no cure."

"Symptom management then."

Mirai's face once again became crestfallen. "Sure. There's lots of drugs they can put me on."

"And I'm certain that once they find the right cocktail of treatments, your symptoms will be easier to manage. You'll continue painting as always."

The subtle shake of her head prefaced a tone of vanquishment. "David," she said wearily. "It's a degenerative illness. Yes, there are times of remission, but each relapse can cause increased loss of function. Do you understand what that means? It means that each time the MS goes back into remission, I could experience decreased mobility, both physically and mentally, compared to what I had before the relapse. I could be feeling better and be a slightly worse artist…with slightly less muscle memory, slightly less executable technique. My artistic style could be altered to the point that my work is no longer recognizable. I could exit a relapse feeling like a reborn woman and have lost the talent for which I've worked my entire life. I may still be Mirai, but will I still be on canvas?"

The question was left unanswered, for it was painfully rhetorical. David ran his hand through the curly waves in his hair and appeared to be at a loss for words. His train of thought had been derailed. In an effort to rekindle a sense of connection with Mirai, he pivoted to problem-solving mode.

"Well, what can we do about what's happening right now? Do you need me to go grab your medication?"

"I'm not on any medication."

David looked stunned. "But… I mean, why not?"

"Because I'm just not."

"That doesn't make any sense. Your physician didn't prescribe you…what is it—what are those called?"

"Interferon—"

"Right. Beta interferon injections. I've heard those can help."

"Perhaps."

David sat dumbfounded, seeming to dangle off the end of Mirai's incomplete thought. With a hint of frustration, he said, "Okay. So, why aren't you receiving them?"

He was prepared for a rambling response in which Mirai combated the veracity and effectiveness of the MS treatments with a list of reasons as to why they wouldn't be right for her. What David did not expect was complete silence. Mirai stared directly at him and didn't make a sound. It was not an answer, yet in many ways, he realized that it was.

"Does your family know about this yet?"

She continued her silent stare. In it, he deciphered the truth. Exhaling heavily, David slowly rose to his feet and grabbed ahold of his folded suit coat. It took only a moment for him to re-erect the easel back onto its tripod legs. He placed it in the center of the room and began setting the scattered tubes of paint and brushes back in the box. Only Mirai and the canvas remained on the floor. He outstretched his hand to her and held it in place as she offered little more than a blank stare in return.

With the purse of his lower lip, David absorbed the moment and proceeded to put on his suit coat. He then reached back down with both hands and hoisted Mirai up to a seated position on the stool. She sat rigidly, facing the naked easel, her body tensing as if having been violated. David placed his hands on his hips and extended a solitary nod.

She said quietly, "I should thank you for that. I admit that I should feel some sort of appreciation. But, honestly, right now…in this moment, all I feel toward you is resentment."

David shot a glance out the solarium windows and observed how inviting the outside world appeared to be. After a lengthy hesitation, he turned back to Mirai and smiled. It was inside his smile that she caught sight of a watery glint in his eyes.

He briefly caressed the soft skin of her cheek and said in a quivering voice, "I know."

Chaos and order…

"I'm fine… I'll be fine."

She remembered him caressing her face. Her cheek had melted into the warmth of his hand. The heat felt calming, waylaying an intense anxiety simmering within her. Before leaving for work, David had asked if there was anything else he could do. Mirai had told him no, at least, that was what she thought she had told him. What she did recall was that the misalignment between them lingered even as the sound of his car left the driveway. It permeated the oxygen in the room. It saturated her body like an unwanted grime.

She walked up the stairs and into the bathroom as if wandering through a dense fog. The shower stall was spacious and warm. The steam wafted about her as the water cascaded down her skin. It was only when she squeezed some shampoo into her fingers did she realize the unexpected challenge of washing her thick, long hair with just one good hand. The process was exhausting, leaving her to wonder if she really needed to use conditioner too. Each action suddenly came with an energy trade-off. By the time she finished her normal showering routine, an end-of-day fatigue was rolling over her to the degree that twisting the shower nozzle off seemed unreasonably exerting.

Mirai stepped out of the stall and began to towel off her wilting frame. Her stance began to teeter. The tile in the room appeared askew. She stood in front of the mirror and set the towel down on the vanity. She was still dripping wet, but her strength had evaporated.

Do I have a fever or something?

She fished the thermometer out of the cabinet drawer and was disappointed at the readout. Everything was normal. Using whatever sturdy structures she could find to lean on, Mirai maneuvered slowly across the bathroom and into her old bedroom. Her eyes scoured the room for an easily available pair of underwear, a bra, a tank top. Nothing was within reach.

I need to lie down…

The pillows cushioned her face as she collapsed onto the bed. With more effort than she had to muster, her good hand pulled the sheet and blanket over her body. Her eyes closed as she breathed in and out; the remainder of her energy reserves were depleted.

She opened her eyes momentarily to view the novelty clock on her wall. It was a little after ten in the morning.

Just rest…for a few minutes…you've been pushing yourself too hard…under too much stress… I just need to sleep for a while…just for a little while…then…

Her mind tried to wander to painting, to her discussion with David, to the fear that something was going to happen to Carys.

It'll be…fine…everything…will be fine… I just…I just…need…to…

"Mirai?"

She jerked under her covers as her eyes opened to see Valerie standing next to her bed. Behind her mother was the wall clock. It read a quarter past noon.

"Oh… God, Mom. You scared me."

"When you missed breakfast I assumed you were in your studio working. Are you all right? You don't look well."

Mirai turned onto her back and smarted against the blazing midday sunshine illuminating her bedroom. "Yeah, I'm just not feeling so great. Needed to sleep for a bit, I guess."

Valerie placed her hand on Mirai's forehead. "Interesting. No fever."

"No, but I do feel like I'm coming down with something. Maybe I should just stay in bed for a bit."

"I'll bring you some food. You need anything else? I'm working from home today so it's not a problem."

Mirai told her mother not to worry. She watched Valerie leave the bedroom and then realized the stroke of luck she'd stumbled upon.

I can lay low up here for a few days until my arm gets better. If I'm careful, no one else has to know.

The plan relieved her as she pulled back the covers and sat on the edge of the bed.

Now for some clothes…

The room immediately began to spin. A burning flush rose up her chest and into her face, making her feel dizzy and nauseous. Mirai scolded herself for sitting up too fast and lay down again underneath the bedsheets. As she stared up at the ceiling, her vision continued to swim. The attempted activity took less than a few seconds. To Mirai's dismay, she was thoroughly spent.

Maybe I am sick. The thought rung hollow in her mind as she analyzed her condition. If she was coming to terms with anything, it was that even during her worst illnesses as a child, she had never before felt this fatigued.

I'll eat… That will give me some strength… Then…then I'll do some research online…see what can help for people with…with…

When her eyes opened again, the soup on her nightstand had long since cooled and the mango smoothie had turned to lukewarm glop. The sunlight was coming in at an odd angle through her window shades, casting angular shadows against the walls. With mounting dread, she looked over at the wall clock and groaned.

It was almost dinnertime.

Oh my God… I literally spent the whole day in bed.

The statement struck her with the intensity of a gong. She drew in a deep breath and maneuvered herself up to a leaning position against the headboard. After devouring the soup her hunger was somewhat satiated. Her emotions were not.

Relapsing-remitting multiple sclerosis she typed into the search bar of the Omni application. The results were endless pages covering the disease itself, along with a host of ancillary symptoms.

Numbness, generalized muscle pain, localized muscle pain, fatigue, vision problems, memory loss… Mirai continued scrolling down the page. She read: *Relapsing-Remitting Multiple Sclerosis can eventually lead to Primary-Progressive Multiple Sclerosis…mobility problems…*

loss of neurologic function…loss of cognitive control…when the disease no longer goes into remission…

She quickly scrolled further down the page, away from what she had just read.

Women are three times more likely to develop MS than men…young women in particular are at greater risk…people from Southeast Asia may experience more severe MS symptoms than other ethnicities…

With a flick of hostility, she deleted the search field and began typing something else: *Is MS hereditary?* Her brown eyes shifted left to right across the page, reading blocks of text that seemed to indicate no relation between MS and genetics, except in rare instances. Mirai paused while letting the information settle in her mind.

I wonder if either of my birth parents had MS? I wonder if there's a way I could find out?

The curiosity festered into her skin as she pondered the image: a middle-aged Burmese woman, seated in a wheelchair, in the humble abode that was her home in Myanmar, face and body ravaged by the decades-long progression of a degenerative disease, sparkle having been snuffled out of her eyes, all traces of hope removed from her expression, too weak to feign happiness, too strong to ask for help, seemingly alone.

The mental picture refused to release her from its overbearing grasp. Mirai shook her head, blinked a few times, and averted her eyes toward the window. She had often imagined what her birth parents, and birth mother in particular, had looked like, had been like. What she did for work, for hobbies, for fun. Who she was in society and who she was to herself. Her aspirations. Her fears. Her virtues and her sins. Mirai had at one time or another created scenarios for all of it, often filling in the mental blanks with moments from her own life. She had pictured her as both a business titan and as a peasant. With a modest home in the country or amongst the teeming throngs living in tenements. As exceptional or common. As a philosopher, an artist, a lover.

But she had never imagined her with MS.

A crushing wave of despair sank Mirai's body back under the

sheets. Her eyes widened as she entertained her own worst fears of the future. Her own worst fears of how others would now view her. Her own worst fears of that hideous thing, which could make someone love their own life one day, and utterly despise it the next. No more sense of hope. No more sense of art. Colors having turned to gray. The sounds of a symphony having gradually faded until all that was left to hear was the desolate beat of her withering heart.

I don't know how to fix this…

What followed was a thought so perverse that Mirai instantly recoiled from it.

Doesn't matter anyway. 296 Days Until the End of Time.

CHAPTER 8
ONE AND THE SAME

"You may go in."

Mirai nodded appreciatively toward the usher and proceeded to place one foot in front of the other, leaving the anteroom behind and entering the main gathering area of the voxhall. A feeling of shame covered her the instant she crossed over the threshold. It was the sort of shame reserved for when one does something wrong—not against a neighbor, but against oneself.

This is ludicrous, idiotic, desperate, came a chastisement from somewhere deep within her mind. Mirai agreed with the thought yet continued walking down the main aisle. It was Friday morning. Her bedridden fatigue had lasted two days before releasing its sadistic hold. The aftereffects continued to pillage her body as each movement elicited a mild scold. Her right hand and arm were still mostly numb, but pins and needles had begun creeping their way along certain sections, taunting Mirai with hope that feeling and function would soon follow.

The idea of revisiting the voxhall had dawned on her only after receiving a text from George Domínguez, asking for a few more days with the illusive journal. The thought of willingly stepping foot inside a place that had contributed to the destruction of a family friendship

made Mirai queasy. Yet her mind justified the act as one of research—
an attempt to leave no stone unturned. It was in that justification that
Mirai only partially graced the edge of the event horizon, glimpsing the
sense of hopeless desperation Julie must have had when diving into the
black hole that was the Preserve.

*Just do this and go. Nothing's going to happen, but at least it will
be out of your head, ruled out as an option. God, this is embarrassing.*

The assembly hall was empty, save for Mirai and the voxroy who
stood in his vestments atop the dais. The voxhall was dimly lit, giving
the space a contemplative mood. On any other day, given any other
situation, Mirai could see how merely being present in such a place
could grant mental calm. Her eyes focused on the voxroy as she
approached. Behind him was the sanctum on which the decanters that
held the blue liquid sat. Mirai tried to remember what was so special
about the Potion. Her wearied mind drew a blank.

"Please," said the voxroy, his face coming into form thanks to some
recessed lighting near the stage.

Mirai closed the distance between them and met the man at the first
step of the dais. It was at that moment when she realized that she had
no idea what she was supposed to do. Playing it safe, she kept her head
tilted down, hoping to appear reverent.

"I'm not sure," she began, her voice hardly a whisper, "what I'm
supposed to do here. I just need some help. Wondered if partaking of
the Potion could make a difference?"

She could feel the voxroy staring at her. With uncertain eyes, she
glanced up at him. Much to her surprise, the man was Asian, and as she
squinted through the darkness, his facial features hinted at possibly
being Burmese.

"Partaking of the Potion," the voxroy said, his voice paradoxically
tender and strong in the same breath, "can be a regenerative experience
for many."

Mirai forced a thin smile and nodded.

The man then added, "But certainly not for all."

Mirai blinked and retracted her smile. The voxroy turned away
from her and reached for one of the decanters. The blue fluid jostled in

the glass as he poured some into a small cup and turned back to Mirai. He descended down to her level on the carpeted aisle and handed her the cup.

"For you," he said.

Mirai took the cup with her left hand and raised it thoughtfully to her parting lips. As the liquid made contact with her tongue, she was surprised at how smooth and chilled it felt. It was almost sickeningly sweet yet carried with it an odd aftertaste.

Mirai felt her frame decompress as she handed the cup back to the voxroy, who had been eyeing her carefully the entire time. "What was that?" she asked, genuinely curious.

The voxroy set her cup back on the sanctum and returned to his place at the bottom of the dais steps. "That…was the Love of God."

The expression on her face morphed from curiosity to intrigue. "What do you mean, 'the Love of God'?"

The voxroy was young. Mirai suspected that he was even younger than her. His jet-black hair was short and utilitarian. His face was warm and compassionate, yet with an underlying edge to it. In his eyes, Mirai could see only the faint reflections of nascent voxhall light. Something about his eyes made her think that even if the lights were completely on, the irises would still be hard to read.

"The Love of God is granted to you, as an act of mercy, based on your willingness to submit yourself to the partaking of the Potion. In doing so, you were a recipient of the Love of God."

Mirai let his words sink in. "Is that what you believe?"

"It is what this voxhall believes."

The aversion was both recognized and dismissed by Mirai. She was feeling grateful just to be walking. With a humble nod, she thanked the voxroy and prepared to leave.

"You don't have to disclose your reason," the man said suddenly. "After all, God already knows. But what brought you in today?"

Mirai hesitated before glancing down at her limp arm. Without pretense she replied, "Oh, I suppose, just hoping for a miracle."

The voxroy's expression melted a little, and in the melting, Mirai witnessed a glimmer of disappointment. He sighed heavily and nodded toward her. From his vestment a hand emerged, offering an embrace if she was so willing. Mirai took a step forward and wrapped her good hand and arm around him. The hug lasted for only a moment, but as she pulled away, she saw his right hand reach forward to touch her cheek.

"May you find your miracle."

Oh my God, she thought.

Her periphery had noticed it prior to the side of her face feeling it. It was unmistakable. As the voxroy pulled his hand back from her cheek, Mirai's vision narrowed in on his fingers, straining for focus in the room's trace available light. When her eyes confirmed what she had felt on her face, she stared directly at the voxroy with a newly formed expression.

Ricocheting memories of the fire, the thick smoke, the gunshots, and finally a hand—outstretched and waiting to bring her up and out of the airframe coffin—all strobe-flashed across her mind. The hand, from a face she couldn't see, with a scar across two of its fingers, was the same hand that had saved two sisters from burning alive.

With a brimming certainty, Mirai audibly gasped before exclaiming, "You're the man from the plane!"

The hand with the scar took hold of Mirai's left arm. The voxroy led them both a few steps over toward the side of the stage. In his face, Mirai could see a look of sudden tension, yet it was not directed at her. His eyes were aimed over her head, at a young family who had just entered the grand room seeking to partake in the Potion. The voxroy blinked before retraining his attention on Mirai.

"We must keep our voices down in the voxhall, lest we disturb anyone seeking solace." The voxroy continued his intense, unblinking stare. "Do you understand?"

Mirai gazed at him, suspecting that she was supposed to read between the lines. All that she could comprehend in that instant was his hand, and that even on the rougher patch of skin on her elbow, she could still make out the scar.

"Who are you?" she whispered.

The voxroy slowly loosened his grip on Mirai. His eyes exchanged glances between the young woman before him and the family working their way up the aisle. He shook his head and said, "I'm the voxroy of this voxhall. And I must be attending to these people."

"Please," she protested, her left hand reaching for his wrist, her body seeming off balance. "I must know—"

A groan of agony cut off her remark as Mirai leaned forward in pain. With her left hand she grasped her right arm, and in amazed wonder realized that she could feel it. The pins and needles had transformed into something more pronounced. A slicing sharpness combined with a muscle cramp that threatened to twist her arm right out of its socket moved through her limb spastically. The pain attacked her with terrifying force. As her face contorted in discomfort, a smile began to form.

"I guess this is a good sign," she muttered.

The voxroy reached around Mirai's shoulders and helped her back to a semi-standing position. The wave of pain that had taken Mirai's breath away was momentarily subsiding. A few rotations of inhaling and exhaling gave her confidence in being able to walk. The voxroy nodded agreeably and led her gingerly out of the hall. Down a side corridor was a room having all of the indications of being his office. Mirai sat down in a seat across from his desk as the voxroy excused himself. Upon his return a minute later, was the same man but without the vestments, who instead wore a dark polo shirt and khaki pants that were met in the middle by a belt. On his face, he was wearing the ritualistic heaviness of the day.

"I asked the other voxroy to step in for me," he said solemnly. "Are you all right?"

Mirai looked up at him with eyes resisting the urge to weep. With her left hand she lifted her right hand up to her face and arthritically wiggled her fingers. "It's coming back. The feeling is coming back."

The man observed what Mirai was doing and tried to ascertain the significance. He sat on the edge of his desk and gently took her right hand in his. There was a subtle tremor coming from her limb, as if the whole appendage was trying to resurrect after rigor mortis. He pondered it in silence.

Mirai said, "Do you…think…it was the Potion?"

With a levelheaded frankness, the man said, "How long has this numbness been going on?"

"A few days."

"And you couldn't feel anything?"

"Nothing at all."

The man squared his jaw. "And now there's pins and needles?"

Mirai smiled. "I can feel your hand touching mine."

He hesitated before squeezing Mirai's palm and placing it back on her lap. "Have you been diagnosed with any medical conditions?"

"What's your name?" Mirai asked, softly.

He pointed at the nameplate on his desk, as if trying to indicate that he had nothing to hide. "Kan Thura."

Mirai blinked in recognition of something. "So, you *are* Burmese."

Kan rubbed his hand against his knee and nodded. "Uh-huh."

"Me too. I'm Mirai McGarry, although you'd never know I was Burmese from my name."

Kan stared at her for a moment longer than the response required. "Mirai is a Japanese name."

"Yeah, never got the full explanation on that one. Maybe my birth parents just really liked the name and didn't care. Either way, my adoptive parents didn't rename me. I've always been grateful for that."

With swiftness, Kan slid off the corner of his desk and retreated back around to his leather swivel chair. His fingers drummed the blotter as he gazed at the young woman seated in his office. A quizzical look finally broke through the stoic monolith that was his face.

"Getting back to my question then, Mirai, was this paralysis part of any previously diagnosed medical condition?"

She leaned against the armrest of her chair for the kind of support that seemed more than just physical. "Late last year, my doctor suggested I might have a relapsing-remitting case of MS."

Kan's expression didn't change, but a restrained energy was festering between his clasped hands. "I see."

Mirai continued massaging her right hand and arm as she said, "Getting back to *my* question then, Kan. Who are you?"

"I've already told you. I help facilitate operations at this voxhall. I have been for over a year now."

"Ever find time to rescue damsels in distress?"

Kan chuckled. It was the kind of laugh used as a delay tactic. Becoming slightly more animated, he said, "There are people who come to this voxhall, and have so for years, because they find comfort in the familiarity of the rituals. They sit, they contemplate life, they converse with other like-minded individuals who are surprised to learn that they're all searching for the same thing. They partake in the Potion and go about their week feeling better about life. Then, there's people like you."

Mirai felt his gaze push away everything else in the room. Timidly, she joked, "People…with possible chronic illnesses?"

Kan's face sobered. "People who should know better than to believe in any of this nonsense."

At first, Mirai wasn't sure she understood Kan's definitive statement. Once she did, her chuckle mimicked what he had used to push a surge of anxiety into the next moment. "I…don't understand."

"I think you do."

Mirai fell silent, dumbfounded by the assertion.

Kan sighed heavily and said, "You're here, hoping for what—a miracle? By drinking some blue mineral water that was sanctified by a man in a robe? You think God chose to heal you from your MS after one prayer but continues to ignore the pleas from the men and women locked away in the hellholes of this world? The people who face torture and dehumanization on a daily basis? Are you that detached from reality as to think God favors you over them? Simply in lieu of the fact that you're in a building claiming to be a sacred space? Or are you fully aware of the contradiction and are just too desperate for a cure for those facts to matter?"

Mirai parted her lips in rebuttal but remained mute.

Kan continued, "I don't think you realize just how much the general populace does *not* have a problem with contradictions. It's a sign of high emotional intelligence to be bothered by them. I know you're bothered by them, Mirai. So tell me, what the hell are you doing inside a voxhall?"

Mirai listened as Kan's words settled, the sharp edges of the sounds feeling almost tactile. She shook her head, tried to conjure up a coherent response, and failed. The two continued sitting in silence as she processed the gravity of his diatribe.

"Are you… Are you trying to tell me…" She struggled to articulate her confusion. "That…you work at this voxhall…serve the Potion, comfort people with the Love of God…and you don't…believe in any of it?"

The sunlight from behind Kan faded as a cloud formation passed by. Not only did the light in the small office diminish, but the color of the room seemed to change as well. Mirai had just started getting a better idea of the man's facial features. Now he was turning back into a shroud.

"If you learn nothing else from your experience here, Mirai, learn this fact. Faith is not a substitute for the hard work of developing emotional intelligence and intellectual honesty."

Intellectual honesty, thought Mirai, suddenly imagining the faces from her paintings. *Seeking objective truth even if it leads to an answer you don't like.*

She frowned in confusion. "But isn't that the biggest contradiction of all? To represent this place and yet despise everything it stands for?"

"My reasons for being here are beyond your comprehension," Kan shot back. "They're strategic, not pious. What's your excuse?"

"You're talking like you know me."

"In a manner of speaking, I do."

Mirai broke eye contact with Kan as her sights fell down toward her right hand. To her awe, she was making a fist. When her mind told her fingers to uncoil, for the first time in days, they obeyed.

"You saved my life," she said, still gazing at her hand. "How did you know the plane was going to be attacked?"

Kan smiled widely, brightening the room despite the overcast. "Tell me, Mirai, do you believe in God?"

Mirai continued stretching and relaxing her fingers and palm, all while indiscriminate sparks of pain would cause her face to twitch. She looked at Kan and said, "I grew up attending a voxhall with my family. They taught from the Noble Book. Then one day my parents decided we were a Worthy Book household. Caused a stir with my best friend's parents. I never understood the reasons for the switch. But it didn't really matter, because I was older by that time and wasn't sure I believed any of it anyway. Once I turned eighteen, I stopped attending the voxhall. That was that."

Kan nodded slowly. He then leaned forward on his desk and first posed the question with his eyes prior to asking it. "What does any of that have to do with believing in God?"

The question landed with its intended impact. Yet Mirai also knew how to turn the tables on topics she wished to avoid. With a smirk, she said, "What does any of this have to do with if you're the man from the plane?"

The two held each other's stare for a moment. They then both leaned back in their respective chairs as if acknowledging their opponent's chess move. Mirai broke the silence first. "How did you know they were going to attack that jet? Is it because you're with Emblem?"

The thin veneer of congeniality seemed to vaporize from Kan's face within the span of her direct statement. Retreating back to his monolithic expression, he answered, "I'm sure I don't know what you're talking about."

Kan arose abruptly and walked around his desk. As he appeared to be leaving, Mirai turned and grabbed his wrist with her right hand. The action both surprised and delighted her.

"Wait," she said, yo-yoing between standing and remaining seated. "I'm not trying to pry. It's about my sister, Carys. I need to know if this was a random attack or something targeted; if this was an isolated incident and we just happened to get caught in the middle, or if I need to be vigilant about protecting her in the future. I'm so scared for her. I just need to know if you have any context into who attacked that plane and why. Especially, why Carys and I were the only people kept as hostages. Can you at least tell me that? Can you at least tell me why?"

Kan's rigid stance softened as he looked down at Mirai. She could now feel the muscles in his wrist decompress through the newly reacquired sense of touch in her fingertips. A look of compassion melted away the hostility in his forehead and jaw. He leaned forward and said, "We've been in this room for some time and you haven't even noticed the artwork yet."

His smile assured her that it was safe to let go of his arm. When she did, the side wall came into view, and on it, affixed between two solid wood bookcases, was an oil painting. The canvas was framed, and within the boundaries of the frame was a depiction of limitless potential. The colors, the gradients, the lines and the form, all of it served as a backdrop to the human face emerging from the chaos.

"Oh my God," Mirai said, finding the strength to stand. "You own one of my paintings?"

Kan winked in the affirmative. Mirai approached it reverently, uncertain if she any longer had the right to touch it. The piece was one of her early works, yet it still held the theme that had been consistent throughout her art career—chaos and order. Her eyes danced across the canvas before coming to a halt at the lower lefthand corner. The signature remained unchanged. Mirai—with the *M*, as always, shaped into a heart.

"I have so many questions," she murmured, turning back to Kan.

Kan's smile was now laced with empathy. He gently touched the side of her right arm as if bestowing a gift. Then, reaching for the door handle, he said, "I don't know why. It seems like you got exactly what you came for."

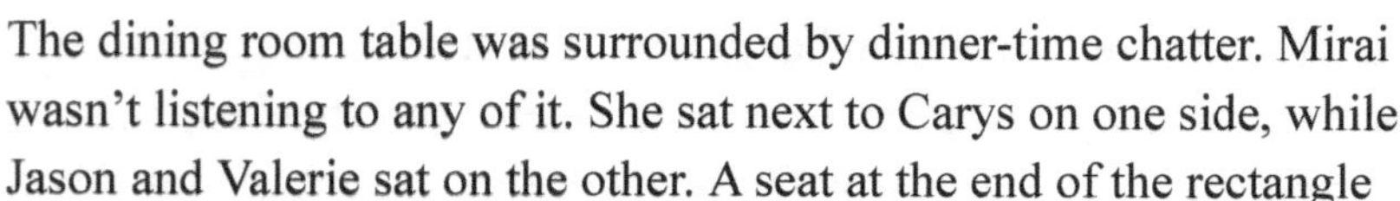

The dining room table was surrounded by dinner-time chatter. Mirai wasn't listening to any of it. She sat next to Carys on one side, while Jason and Valerie sat on the other. A seat at the end of the rectangle was vacant, reminding Mirai that David's rehearsal session was running long. In the background, a man's voice could be heard on the radio. He had been speaking, thundering in passionate articulation for several minutes already and Mirai hadn't comprehended a word.

With her right hand, she held a dinner knife and used it to cut into the chicken parmesan. The action felt almost normal. With her left hand, she twirled some linguine around her fork and tried to be appreciative for every painless motion.

"You don't care, right Mirai?"

Her eyes shifted toward her sister. "Huh?"

Carys repeated, "About the seating assignments. On the plane. To Los Angeles. You don't care about aisle seat versus window, right?"

"Why are we talking about that?" Mirai asked, her mind straining to catch up to the conversation.

Valerie and Carys exchanged amused glances. Valerie said, "Because of the campaign Carys is shooting there next week. The big one. The biggest of her career. For Omni. I mentioned this to you twice."

Los Angeles… Mirai thought, the word burrowing into her psyche.

"Your driver's license doesn't renew until later this year, correct?" Valerie asked.

"My driver's license?"

Valerie smiled at her daughter while chewing. "For identification. To board the plane. I think you're still a little out of it from that flu you had."

"It wasn't a flu."

"Well, whatever it was. I'm asking about your—"

"Yes—it's current."

Valerie nodded as if marking something off her mental checklist. Mirai shook her head and took a small bite of her food. Thoughts of the hectic week ahead, the bustling metropolis that was LA, and of the causeless unease she felt every time someone spoke of her sister materialized in her mind's eye, allowing for her imagination to recklessly fill in the horrific blanks. The voice on the radio continued to fill the empty space in the room, his vocal intonations reminding

Mirai of something that she couldn't quite piece together. She watched as her mother and father talked more about travel logistics. Within their conversation were the curt replies of disagreement over something.

Kan must know who was behind the attack. I've got to convince him to tell me before we all go to Los Angeles.

"What about security?" Mirai blurted.

The table chatter came to a halt. Valerie glanced at Jason as if they had already discussed that topic at length and it was now his responsibility to convince the family. Jason sighed heavily and cleared his throat. "The agency has assured us that security is their top priority for Carys. There'll be a heightened private security presence on set and added layers of authentication for all staff and personnel." Jason finished his statement with dramatic gusto. "That being said…"

Valerie frowned and looked down at her meal.

"I still have grave concerns about Carys's safety in light of what happened on that plane," Jason admitted.

Mirai's body perked up at the honesty of the statement. As her posture straightened, Carys's slumped. "Yes, thank you for saying that," blurted Mirai. "I have been worried sick over this, and no one seems to want to acknowledge the danger involved."

"Jason," Valerie groaned. "We promised we weren't going to do this again."

"I'm sorry, but it's just how I feel," he said firmly. "There's been no updates from that federal aviation investigation. No one was caught. No one brought to justice. Some of the perpetrators died, but certainly not all. The motive is still wildly unclear. And we ultimately have no solid information as to why our daughters were the only ones taken hostage."

"Jason, not at the table, please. Can't we just—"

"All of which—I might add—on the eve of the largest ad campaign Carys has ever done. The commercial alone is going to run nationwide, and the print ads will be posted everywhere for months."

"There's nothing to worry about," protested Carys. "The incident was an act of random violence. There's nothing anyone could have done to prevent it. Geez, I won't live my life in fear, and I'm sure as hell not going to let it stop me from doing this campaign. I worked my whole life for a break like this!"

"Can we all just calm down?" Valerie said in exasperation. "This is still a sensitive topic for everyone and none of us has fully healed from it, I assure you." Valerie made the remark while holding back a wellspring of emotion. Mirai shifted her gaze toward her father, whose expression reflected the same stage of grief that she currently felt, the tightening vise of crippling fear.

Intermittent clinks of silverware against dinner plates replaced the heated debate. Everyone stared at their own food, ready to reengage back into the argument at the slightest provocation. Outside the window, gradient layers of pink were melting the sky into the horizon through the fronds of the palm tree in the yard. The leftover sunlight cast a terracotta shadow against Jason's face. Mirai stared at him while the voice on the radio prattled on.

She said, "I'm sure…we can all find a way to make this work…"

Her sentence trailed off as the voice from the radio began taking shape. His words were pronounced with authoritative gravity. His tone was warm but with a threatening edge to it. The faint echo bouncing from off his consonants reminded her of some sort of grand hall, an auditorium, where information wasn't disseminated out but dictated down.

The man said, "…we will have access to the peace of God *if* we obey; we will have access to the knowledge of God *if* we believe; we will have access to the Love of God *if*—and only if—we follow the ways of God. I am here as a conduit, a messenger, to show you all here today and those listening around the world, that there is only one pathway to that which you seek. That path will never be found in the voxhalls of the world. Neither faith nor medicine can save you from that which will destroy your mind. You cannot *partake* your way out of the global madness, my friends. The Potion won't save you. Only the transformation will. The time for it draws near. Keep attuned to the signs. In so doing, we await perihelion."

Mirai sensed her face becoming flush as the moment of recognition arrived. She blinked incredulously and looked at her mother. "Are we listening to Alexander?"

Valerie listened for a moment longer than should have been necessary to be convincing and then shrugged. "Oh, yeah, I…turned on PRN America earlier…when I was making dinner. The previous program must have ended."

Mirai pushed herself back from the table and marched over to the tuner dial. She wrenched it clockwise, scrambling the frequency until it landed on a news station. "Problem solved," she stated, tersely.

"I don't want to listen to news, Mirai," Valerie said. "That's the last thing I wanna hear right now. Turn it back to…"

"To what?"

Valerie hesitated before glancing down at her plate. "Never mind. Nothing."

A simmering rage was quickly bubbling up to the tip of Mirai's tongue. "Turn it back to Alexander? Are you kidding me?"

"Mirai—"

"After what that prick did to Julie? Brainwashed her and countless others into living in that doomsday cult?"

"I just wanted to listen to something…*uplifting* for a change. It's been a heavy few weeks." Valerie took a sip of water from her glass and set it down carefully. "Don't make a big deal out of this, okay?"

"It's difficult not to, Mom!" Mirai yelled. "Me and David almost didn't make it out of there. You didn't see the look of hatred that man had in his eyes when he threw us out."

"Yes, I remember—"

"'If I see either one of your faces again, I will inflict the greatest of miseries.' Direct quote. If David and I had stayed a minute longer, I might not be standing in this house right now. Do you understand that?"

Valerie exhaled slowly and hovered her fork over her food. It was becoming increasingly evident that no one had much of an appetite left. She abandoned the effort and dropped her utensil onto the napkin. Mirai watched her mother surrender to guilt—the guilt of committing an offense against her daughter, and in a roundabout manner, against herself. It was at that instant when Mirai regretted yelling.

Building atop her baseline anxiety was a mounting nausea and Mirai knew she needed to leave the dining room. She changed the radio station to smooth jazz and briskly walked out the back door and up into the bedroom of her cottage.

What the hell was that about? Listening to Alexander… After what he did to Julie? How long has that been going on? I better never hear that psycho again or Mom's really gonna get an earful.

Mirai examined herself in the full-length mirror and realized that her pulse was pounding. She closed her eyes and slowly exhaled.

Calm down. This is about so much more than Alexander and you know it.

The vibration from her pocket lassoed her thoughts back to the present. On the phone screen was a local number she recognized. "Hello?"

"Mirai? George Domínguez. Do you have a minute?"

Mirai placed her hand against her forehead and tried to smile into the device. "Hi, Dr. Domínguez. Yeah, of course. Thanks for calling."

The man's voice was poised with something to say. Each preliminary exchange seemed to be in the way of reaching his point. "Thanks for the extra few days with the journal. Appreciated your patience. Okay, so, I had a colleague of mine take a look at it too. Something about it was throwing me. Didn't quite add up, you know? The binding is old but the writing is new. Plus, the author makes mention of something that only occurred less than thirty years ago. But…so…I, well… It was actually my friend who noticed it first, clever bastard. It's… Honestly, it's easier to show than explain. Can you meet me right now? There's a diner across from the beach called Julio's. Throwback place with a big neon sign. You know the one I mean?"

Mirai nodded while scanning the room for her backpack. "Uh… yeah. Yeah, I know it."

"I'm here now. In a booth by the window. Can't miss me."

"Okay, I'll see you soon."

After the call, Mirai sighed in exasperation and left the house. She slammed the door of her convertible and began driving through the side streets of her neighborhood toward the main road. The air felt light on her face and seemed to withdraw the compacted tension she was holding in her jaw. She tuned the car stereo to the same smooth jazz station and watched the world sweep past her along the coast.

When she spotted the diner, she pulled the car into the first parking spot she could find and reached for her bag and phone. Waiting for her was a text message from David.

Hey. At your house but your family said you'd left. Coming back soon? Want me to meet you someplace?

Mirai slipped the phone into her purse and decided to reply after her meeting with Domínguez. The diner door pealed as she opened it. Inside were people seated along the countertop area, some eating, others drinking, all seeming to be permanent fixtures of the establishment. Mirai turned her head toward the booths and spotted Domínguez eating a sandwich.

"Oh, Mirai," he said with a wave.

She sat inside the booth opposite Domínguez and noticed the journal laid open next to his glass of iced tea. "Hello again," she said. "Doing some light reading, I see."

"You don't know the half of it. But you're about to," Domínguez replied. After wiping his lips with a napkin, he brushed his fingertips against a different napkin in an almost ritualistic manner before touching the journal. "Okay, so, I read through what little there is in this thing a dozen times. I asked a friend of mine to do the same. We both concur that the likelihood of the author describing Ad Ordinem as the group he's joined as being very high. He writes about them having no home base of operations, his own readiness to travel around the globe to meet with other members, and his excitement in being a part of shaping the future of humanity. Not to mention, he actually calls them *Paragons*. I mean, Mirai, it's all there."

Domínguez took a deep breath and then lowered his voice. The two leaned toward each other without noticing. "As I mentioned over the phone, the book itself is quite old. Early-twentieth century binding and paper. The corners are obviously worn by time, not by use. It even has that old book smell to it. However, the ink used in the writing of the pages is clearly modern. I'm guessing from a basic 7mm medium tip pen. Maybe a clicker. And look, the color of the ink, that's not pure black. It has a bluish hue to it. There's no way this came from the nib of a quill pen."

Mirai nodded as she observed the upside-down text. "So, the author used an old book to journal his modern-day thoughts?"

Domínguez smirked. "Precisely. Maybe it was the only journal he had on hand at the time, or maybe he wanted the journal to seem old and unassuming so it could sit unmolested on a bookcase. Free from inquisitive eyes."

"Hidden in plain sight."

Domínguez pushed his glasses up the bridge of his nose. "You're getting the hang of this, young lady. Now, here's where it gets interesting. As you noticed, there's not much actual writing in the book. I counted only six journal entries, including an odd one at the end which seemed more of a sign-off to any future audience rather than his own stream of consciousness. Yet it was that last entry that bugged me the most. It was so incongruous with the rest. I kept rereading it to discern the meaning. Do you remember what it says?"

Mirai shook her head even as Domínguez turned the book around to face her. On a page all its own, were nine sentences all daisy-chained into one thought.

My mission is simple. A new reason to live again. Ready for anything. Knowledge is my guiding beacon. Steadfast in my goal. This is my destiny. Obstacles be damned. Never turning back. Evermore and evermore.

"Sounds like a farewell to his old life," she said. "Accepting of what's coming… No matter what."

"On the surface level, I agree with you. But on the subversive, secret-society level"— Domínguez chuckled—"it sounds more to me like a series of passphrases."

Mirai blinked. "Passphrases? For what?"

"We may never know, since we're not on the inside. But what the author did leave for us, is his full name."

Mirai arched an eyebrow and then reread the text. "I…don't see it."

"Are you familiar with acrostics? Where the first letter in a series of words or sentences or paragraphs combine to form a hidden message?" Domínguez's forefinger came down onto the page and Mirai's focus followed its movement as it tapped on the first letter of each sentence.

He said, "My… A… Ready… Knowledge… Steadfast… This… Obstacles… Never… Evermore."

Mirai mouthed out each letter silently before whispering, "Mark Stone?"

"Mark Stone," Domínguez repeated. "The author of this journal left behind his name in code, for who—for what purpose, we may never know. But I suspect that this Mark Stone was eventually admitted into Ad Ordinem and henceforth ceased his journaling. I don't know when this occurred, but I do know it was less than thirty years ago."

"How do you know?"

"Because of journal entry five. He mentions attending the WaterSplash Festival in an effort to ingratiate himself with some other secret society members. WaterSplash only started three decades ago. He wrote this journal sometime after that."

"Wait…WaterSplash Festival? That's held every summer on Miami Beach. Are you telling me this guy's local?"

"He is, or at least was."

Mirai drummed her fingers against the tabletop, absorbing the information, exchanging a curious glance out the diner window and up at the moon rising over the water. "I wonder how Julie came into possession of this…"

Domínguez turned the book back around to himself. "My thoughts, exactly. The fact that you have no way of communicating with her anymore just kills me. I mean, if this was simply a thrift store pickup it would have little significance. But if she obtained this through family channels, from a friend or coworker, if someone gave this to her entrusting it to be kept safe… I really want to know who that person was."

Mirai thought of Julie, first the girl and then the woman she once knew. She thought of the Laufer family and the circles they maintained within their voxhall and the community at large. No one by the name of Mark Stone came to mind, nor anyone she would suspect of being a member of a secret society.

You never would suspect it… That's the whole point.

"Dr. Domínguez, these Paragons…do they believe in… I'm not sure how to categorize it. Did you once say they believe they're mission to be…supernatural? Otherworldly?"

"Predestined by God? Yes, very much so. Paragons believe that they are God's will on planet earth."

Mirai hesitated. Her eyes narrowed while her mind churned out a sequence of events. What hung off the edge of her lips was an incomplete thought, one that she formed as she talked out loud. "The man…the man on the plane who saved Carys and me… had a scar on his hand. I believe I've found that man locally. He serves at your voxhall, Dr. Domínguez. His name is Kan Thura. He has the same scar. I spoke with him. We talked. He didn't confirm being the man on the plane, but he didn't deny it either. If he's the same man, then that means he's with Emblem. It means he knows who the attackers were and why they wanted me and Carys taken hostage. I need to know more about Kan Thura. I need him to tell me everything he knows about that day so I can better protect Carys and my family. Do you know the man I'm talking about?"

Domínguez turned slightly in his booth and mouthed out the name. "Kan Thura? Doesn't ring a bell, but that doesn't mean much. There are several voxroys at my voxhall, and perhaps Thura was just filling in that day. Voxhalls move them around as needed to serve the community. But you believe him to be with the group who rescued you?"

"With the group, and perhaps more. Perhaps even the man I've been looking for since the start of this year. A man who goes by an alias. The name Osiris."

Domínguez closed the journal and shot a glance around the diner to be sure no one was attuned to the people whispering in the corner booth. "Osiris? What gave you the idea to look for a man named Osiris?"

Mirai pursed her lips, teetering on how much to disclose and what should remain private. As fatigue won out, she released a sigh and said, "There's a person who started messaging me at the start of this year. He goes by the online name Emloch. He—at least I'm guessing it's a he—is the one who told me that a man named Osiris could bring down Ad Ordinem once and for all. Emloch said that due to physical limitations he personally couldn't travel, but that he knew the people Osiris needed to connect with. He placed some money in my bank account and sent me and David to Seattle to meet with Leighton Russo."

"Russo. I believe I read his book. The…psychologist?"

"Psychiatrist, yeah. And let me tell you, he was…less than enthusiastic about our questions. Next, Emloch told us to meet with you."

"Me? Why would he think I'm Osiris?"

"Because of your extensive knowledge on Ad Ordinem. He thought you might be able to give us insight into the airport attack."

Domínguez nodded slowly. "I see. Go on."

"Emloch predicted the plane attack. He texted me that Carys was in grave danger and to get to the airport immediately. Turns out he was right. That's the only reason I was there to protect her. Because of him. He believes that Osiris can save us all, if only we can locate him in time."

"In time?"

Mirai glanced down at her phone and pointed at the New Year's countdown application.

"Ah. Gotcha."

"It was Emloch who told us about Russo, about you, about how the mysterious disasters are all connected to Ad Ordinem's New Year's Eve threat, and that Carys was in mortal danger on that airplane. It was all Emloch. And he says we need to find Osiris. What if I already did?"

Domínguez parted his lips but then paused. Thinking carefully, he whispered, "Kan Thura?"

"Kan Thura. Osiris… What if they're one and the same?"

Domínguez's next statement was hushed, as if emerging from his subconscious mind. "Osiris…god of the afterlife."

"Yes," Mirai confirmed.

"It's curious. While doing research for my book, I came across a prophecy that Ad Ordinem adherents generally interpret to be literal. Like much of their foundational beliefs, I couldn't track down the origin of it, but it was mentioned in some of their eighteenth and nineteenth century letters. And then again once more in a primer I found penned by internal leadership back in the 1930s. I referenced it in my book, and I think I have a photo of it…"

Domínguez fidgeted with his phone while navigating a series of digital pages. "Here we go. This is it. The prophecy any Paragon would be familiar with."

Emerging from the glow of the screen, was a five-stanza poem. Mirai leaned in until the words dotted her irises.

Come back O man of wistful wiles
And restore your place in sacred isles
Standing firmly neath Agamemnon's gaze
To recompense a wandering vision's loss
And for her virtue, cleanse the end of days.

"A prophecy," Mirai said under her breath. "From Ad Ordinem… about a man…who returns to where he belongs after straying…in order to…?"

Domínguez said, "As with most prophecies, there's some difference of opinion in its interpretation. However, the consensus seemed to be that this man could stop the apocalypse. The end of days."

"The end of *time*?"

"One could argue."

"Hmm," Mirai pondered. "And who or what is Agamemnon?"

"Oh, a relic of Greek mythology, a king during the Trojan War. Agamemnon does something to displease the goddess Artemis and she threatens to interfere in their next battle unless he sacrifices his daughter, Iphigenia, as an act of penance. There are two versions of the story, one in which he does end up sacrificing her, another in which he doesn't."

Mirai let his statement play out in her mind. He had rambled off the myth nonchalantly. Something about the story bothered her. "Interesting. So someone, namely a Paragon, who believes this prophecy to be true, would be motivated to find this Osiris in order to stop a catastrophe. Factually speaking then, we'd be talking about someone from inside Emblem."

"Makes the most sense to me."

"Osiris has to be Kan."

"Then again," Domínguez cautioned. "It's usually at the point when one makes a satisfying mental connection that the conspiracy theory really goes off the rails."

"How so?"

"Oh, just something I've noticed in my years studying secret societies, conspiracies, the truth-hunter types. It all sounds well and good until the first crack in your hypothesis appears. You then have two choices: continue researching in order to prove yourself right or wrong, or succumb to cognitive dissonance—wherein you simply ignore the evidence that conflicts with your assertion. That's the problem with conspiratorial thinking. Our feelings prefer the comfort of conjecture over the rigidity of facts."

The two sat in silence while inwardly evaluating the conversation. Beyond their booth, the dinner crowd was starting to thin out while new patrons in the mood for a late snack wandered inside. With each new entrance, the peal of the bell served as a momentary distraction for Domínguez. His eyes scanned the room for nothing in particular, yet Mirai could tell that the man's brain was working overtime.

It was at the point when the table made an odd sound. Mirai glanced down at her phone as a new text came in from David.

Everything okay? Just worried about you.

Mirai's lips softened as she read the message. She quickly replied. *Sorry, yes, I'm okay. Just finishing up with George Domínguez at Julio's. I'll meet you back home in a bit.*

She looked at Domínguez and shrugged. "I should probably get going."

"Um…yeah," Domínguez replied, his lips formulating a follow up. "Hey… Mirai, one last thing. This Emloch, when did you say he began messaging you?"

"A few days into the new year. Why?"

"And if memory doesn't fail me here, in our last chat you mentioned having gone to the Preserve to try and convince your friend Julie, the holder of this journal, to come back to Miami with you."

"Yeah."

"That all happened right before the messages started?"

"Basically."

Domínguez nodded, his hand resting still atop the cover of the old book. "Now, understand…I'm just thinking out loud here. Is it possible that someone from the Preserve is actually this Emloch persona?"

Mirai's vision followed the slanted lines of the table while pondering Domínguez's question, and its assertion. "You think Emloch is Julie?"

The man's face tightened. Mirai could tell she was within range of his theory but still off target. "You think Emloch is Alexander? But why? That man hates me. He literally threatened my life if I ever returned to the Preserve. Besides, I'm small potatoes compared to the enemies that man has, none-the-least of which is the United States government."

The man's expression didn't change. It was at that moment when Mirai sensed her line of thought getting knocked off its axis. Domínguez then asked, "How well do you know David?"

CHAPTER 9
IMMOLATION

Mirai was gazing into David's eyes the moment he collapsed on top of her. He buried his face in her neck as muffled sounds of labored breathing filled his bedroom. She wrapped her arms tightly around his torso while his back muscles contracted. His raspy panting continued for a few more seconds before calming down. Mirai felt their bodies decompressing into the mattress.

Above the side of David's face, the ceiling fan blades whirled slowly, slicing across the midafternoon rays of sunlight that blazed through the window blinds. She watched the rotations from underneath David, the beat of his heart pounding against the tender skin of her breasts.

As he recovered, he kissed the side of her neck and cheek and then gingerly pushed himself up. "You…are…" he muttered, before struggling to find the proper wording.

Mirai smiled while running her hand through his hair. "Steady, lover. It takes a minute for blood flow to return to the brain."

David nodded in exhaustion and turned over onto his back; lying next to Mirai. "You seemed kind of distracted. Everything okay?"

She nodded, still gazing upward at the fan. "Yeah, it was great."

"Let me finish you by hand."

"I'm okay. Honestly, I don't think it's gonna happen for me right now."

David stared at her from across the pillow and Mirai was keenly aware of the observation. She knew that intimacy had been difficult for her to achieve that afternoon. The reason why simmered in her chest, nestled along pangs of irritation against the man who had placed it there.

How well do you know David?

She had tried to think of it as merely a thoughtless comment. A tertiary tacked onto the shortlist of other nonstarters—Julie and Alexander. Yet Mirai knew Domínguez had not stated it absentmindedly. His calm, concentrated demeanor had conveyed the idea with all of the forethought of a litigator. David had crossed Domínguez's mind the instant Mirai had laid out the timeline. The Preserve, David leaving the compound with Mirai, Emloch sending anonymous messages, the correlation was too visible for Domínguez to ignore.

Mirai had politely dismissed it as nonsense. She had informed Domínguez that David had willingly left the Mesa Revival in order to return home. They had bonded over their shared experience. David had moved his belongings from Orlando to Miami to live closer to her. Leaving behind the itinerate harp-for-hire life and accepting a stable job at the symphony was for her. Ingratiating himself with the McGarrys was for her. Moving his schedule around so he could be there to travel with Mirai was for her. This was the man who had confessed his love for her while she was on the floor having an episode. The man who believed in her dreams. The man who would sit and watch her paint as if nothing else on earth mattered. The man who shared his bed with her, and the chest on which she would often fall asleep.

Trust. The word preceded the reasons she offered to Domínguez and punctuated her defense argument. She had only known David four months, but their relationship fostered more trust than any she had ever known. Against every metric—rational, practical, emotional, intuitive —Mirai trusted David.

It was within that rehashing of Mirai and Domínguez's conversation that an unsettledness festered into her body. It had no traceable origin and no exit sign. It existed merely as a constant. As a desert road sign. As a question without an answer.

How well do you know David?

Mirai blinked and turned herself toward him, placing her right hand against the drumming of his ribcage. "Still alive?" she smirked.

David nodded. "I'm hanging on."

They held each other while letting both the fan blades and the second hand on the wall clock circle by. Mirai felt David rub her right arm in gentle strokes. The sensation thrilled her. She tightened her embrace of him all the more.

"It's remarkable your episode ended so quickly," David said. "Do you think you'll be able to paint again soon?"

"I hope so. The pain is nearly gone. I can feel your touch. Just need to test the muscle memory."

"I'm sure it will all come back to you with the first brushstroke."

"That would be amazing. It would be a miracle."

David didn't immediately respond. He continued caressing her arm and hand. Mirai could tell he was trying to determine at what angle to broach the topic. "So it started feeling better right after you drank the Potion?"

Mirai breathed against his skin as she replied, "Yes."

"Did the voxroy say anything more about it?"

"Just that it works for some and not for others."

Mirai felt David nod. She did not look up at him, for in that instant, all she could wonder was why she had chosen not to tell David about Kan. He was quite possibly the man who could help her protect Carys from further harm. Yet something about their encounter made her wish to keep the meeting private for the time being.

"I'm gonna take a short nap before heading in," David yawned.

"Good idea," she said. "You've got a busy few nights ahead. I'll be there for Friday night's performance. Can't wait to watch you again."

He smiled on the heels of her last statement, his eyes already closed, his breathing becoming shallow. Mirai hesitated before carefully sliding herself out from under his arm. She sat up in bed and stretched before donning a pair of panties and a T-shirt. Tiptoeing out of the bedroom led her to the apartment hallway, where just beyond the partially open door of a side room stood David's harp. Its majestic presence caught Mirai off guard. She gazed at it, observing the similarities and the differences to the one he used on the orchestra stage. The sounds it emitted, that David willfully evoked from its strings, resurrected a series of memories in her mind. Only after a moment of unashamed leering did Mirai notice that she was hugging herself.

The living room was small but had lots of natural light. Mirai sat down on the sofa and tucked some of her hair behind her ear. She retrieved her phone from her purse and opened the messenger window in the lower lefthand part of the screen. Her thumb scrolled the message threads back in time, all the way to the start of the conversation on January 2nd.

HELLO MIRAI.

Her eyes followed the text as she scrolled.

…I'VE NEVER MET YOU, BUT I'VE SEEN YOUR ARTWORK. THAT IS ALL I NEED TO KNOW. MY NAME IS EMLOCH…

…THE COMMISSION OF A LIFETIME, MIRAI. THE CHANCE TO PUT AN END TO THE ENSUING GLOBAL MADNESS…

…I AM LOOKING FOR SOMEONE. HE'S SOMEONE WHO CAN BRING AN END TO THOSE WHO ARE MANUFACTURING OUR SUFFERING….

…DO YOU WANT TO KNOW WHAT AD ORDINEM IS?

Mirai swallowed the stale air in the back of her throat as she continued reading.

…I CAN TELL YOU WHO THEY ARE…

The phrase held firm to the screen, refusing to be scrolled away. Her thumb finally pulled back and the message thread moved.

…AN ARTIST IS EXACTLY WHO I NEED FOR THIS, MIRAI. DON'T YOU KNOW THAT BEAUTY WILL SAVE THE WORLD?

She glanced away from her phone and looked out the windows. With no comprehension of what she was seeing, her eyes darted back to the screen as a look of caution colored her face.

Inside the text box, she slowly typed: *How did you know about the attack?*

The message sent and sat at the bottom of the thread, awaiting a response from Emloch. Mirai exhaled. Having sent it made her mind feel lighter, like the act of transferring a burden. She set the phone down on the coffee table and walked casually into the kitchen. A bottle of electrolyte water and a stick of cheese seemed the best postcoital options in David's refrigerator. Between sips and chews, Mirai meandered around the apartment, appreciative to feel at home in his space.

She thought about the moment they met, across the massive conference table inside the Preserve. Of Alexander's demand that Julie's diary be burned and that David be the one to do it. She remembered him opening the book, reading the first line, and deciding that his act of defiance would be worth the expulsion.

She recalled the drive back to the airport. The flight home to Miami. The nearly ceaseless conversations that had linked one moment with the next. It had been a tennis match of ideas, stories, confessions, and insights. Within the span of their trip home, Mirai felt as if they had revealed almost everything about each other, or at the very least, had set a solid foundation on which to build a relationship.

Mirai smiled as she took another sip of water. The memories cradled her nerves. The man in the other room loved her. She then wondered why she had yet to tell him the same.

The phone on the coffee table vibrated. A new message had arrived. Mirai sat cross-legged on the sofa and tapped the screen. Its light caused her irises to glow.

HELLO MIRAI. HAVEN'T HEARD FROM YOU IN A WHILE. I CHOSE NOT TO REACH OUT BECAUSE I ASSUMED YOU NEEDED TO REST. HOW ARE YOU FEELING?

Mirai arched a quizzical eyebrow and jammed her thumbs against the text box. *I'm doing fine. Why wouldn't I be?*

PEOPLE OFTEN HAVE CRASHES AFTER A TRAUMATIC EVENT. ESPECIALLY PEOPLE LIKE YOU.

People like me?

YES, MIRAI. PEOPLE WITH MULTIPLE SCLEROSIS.

The phone suddenly felt heavy in her hand. Sensations of flushed warmth and icy chill surged through her body. She blinked repeatedly, trying to confirm what she had read. Her mind reeled, trying to recall if she had ever mentioned her diagnosis to Emloch. After a minute of hesitation, she was certain she had not.

How do you know I have... Mirai stopped typing and then deleted the text. Starting over, she wrote: *What makes you think I have MS?*

The ellipses bounced, and Mirai watched them closely as if doing so could speed up the response time.

I KNOW SO MUCH ABOUT YOU, MIRAI. YOU ARE MY HERO. YOU ARE WHO I COULD BE IF ONLY I WAS NOT LIMITED BY MY DISABILITY.

What disability?

MUCH LIKE YOUR ILLNESS, MINE IS HARD TO EXPLAIN. BUT DON'T WORRY ABOUT ME. WE ARE SO CLOSE TO FINDING OSIRIS. ONLY A FEW MORE STEPS AND WE WILL HAVE OUR ANSWER. THE ANNIHILATION OF AD ORDINEM. THE END OF TERROR AND FEAR. THE FREEING OF MILLIONS OF ENSLAVED MINDS.

Mirai typed while shifting her jaw and mouthing out the words. *I am tired of you dodging my questions. I asked you how you knew Carys's plane would be attacked, and then I asked why you think I have MS. You gave me no answers.*

I DISAGREE, MIRAI. I'VE TOLD YOU EVERYTHING YOU NEED TO KNOW. I'VE ALSO DEPOSITED ANOTHER LARGE SUM INTO YOUR BANK ACCOUNT. THIS SHOULD GET YOU THROUGH THE FINAL RENDEZVOUS I HAVE PLANNED.

No! No more trips. No more money. No more anonymity. I won't lift another finger for you until we meet face-to-face. If you can't walk, then I'll come to you. Where do you live?

The ellipses pulsed, indicating Emloch required no forethought to provide a reply.

WHERE DO I LIVE? I LIVE RENT-FREE, MIRAI, INSIDE YOUR MIND.

"Son of a bitch," Mirai snapped. With considerable speed, she leapt from off the sofa and marshaled herself across the living room, down the hallway, and into the bedroom, all the while holding her phone facing outward.

"David—"

They both jerked at the sight of one another, startled beyond what the situation deserved. David had been sitting on the edge of his bed, phone in his hand. When their eyes locked, they both let out a nervous chuckle.

"Mirai…"

"David… I'm sorry. I…forgot you were napping."

"No, no," he stammered, setting his phone down on the nightstand. "I…couldn't sleep. So I just decided to…get up. Is everything okay?"

Mirai looked back, then forward, shook her head, and tried to reorient herself against a plethora of impulses. "Um…yeah. Yeah, I'm okay. I was just…just texting with Emloch."

David nodded slowly. Mirai looked down at the phone in her hand. Her heart was still galloping from the unexpected sight.

David then asked, "What did he say?"

An exchange of glances left Mirai unable to form a sentence. She scrolled aimlessly within the thread, trying to find a starting point. None of the words made any sense. It was all like hieroglyphs.

You're letting what Domínguez said get to you. Stop it.

"Was it a threat?"

Mirai blinked and looked back up at David. "What?"

He gazed at her briefly before pulling back the remainder of the bedsheet still covering his body. Casually, he arose from off the bed and walked over to Mirai. "You seem shaken. Did Emloch threaten you?"

"No," she blurted. "Not… No."

He smiled and pulled Mirai into an embrace. "You don't owe him anything," he said softly. "Maybe it's best to just let him go. He has placed you in danger more than once. He was right about Carys, but still…"

The two held each other for a moment, and when the moment passed, David gently raised the tip of Mirai's chin with his finger and thumb and placed a tender kiss on her lips. They stared at one another as Mirai whispered, "You probably have to get ready to go soon."

She took a step back while he took a step forward. His hand reached for her midriff and gently slid across her skin and around to her arm. His fingers traced their way down to the hand in which she was holding her phone. Mirai felt the device slipping from her grasp as David took it and tossed it onto the nightstand.

She spoke in a hushed tone. "I don't know that you have the time or virility for—"

David kissed her again. Mirai took another step back and realized that she was against the wall. She sensed his hands moving around her torso, sliding underneath her T-shirt, and the shirt coming up and over her head. His lips worked their way across her cheek and down to her neck. His hands were consuming her body. Mirai's mind shifted aimlessly, unable to focus on any one thing. Yet as she peeked over the ridge of David's shoulder, her eyes were attuned to the nightstand, and the two phones laying next to each other in partial darkness.

Chaos and order.

The brushstrokes populated the canvas in fits and starts. A firmament, a haze-shrouded sun, and a horizon line separating the sky from the ocean all resembled the technique of the artist who went solely by the moniker *Mirai*. Yet there was something she had yet to recapture from her episode.

Freedom.

"This is all so…controlled," she muttered, reworking section after section with her paintbrush. The natural flow of her paintings, originating with chaos and evolving into the reassuring order of a virtuous face, was achieved through a delicate balance of precise planning and a sense of letting go. The ebb and flow of her motions had taken years to perfect and mere days to disrupt.

Mirai set her brush down on the table and took a moment to evaluate the piece. The inspiration was there. The technique was almost recognizable. The only thing missing was flow. She gazed down at her right hand and curled her fingers into a fist.

Why did David seem so startled to see me yesterday? He was on his phone when I got the messages from Emloch—wasn't he? Maybe I'm remembering it wrong…

She blinked and then tried to rub the fatigue from her eyes. It had been hours since she began painting. The midmorning sun seemed to be embracing everything within the solarium. Mirai soaked up its warmth while examining her hand and wrist. It was at that point when she realized she was hungry.

The main house was empty. Only her inner thoughts filled the space. She scrambled a few eggs and then cut up a mango. As she used the knife, her right hand began to cramp.

How did Emloch know I have MS? Nobody knows that except for me, my doctor, and…

She set the knife down and massaged her wrist. The pain was manageable and a relief to the alternative. Its impedance to her art was relatively minor compared to the devastation caused by total numbness. She had every reason to suspect that the episode would soon be through and that her full ability would soon be restored.

A thought nagged at her anyway.

Perhaps one more intake of the Potion will put me back to normal. There's no harm in trying it—even if it is a placebo effect. Besides, Kan might be there. Maybe he'll be more willing to talk today?

Mirai tapped the PRN America logo on her phone screen and sat down at the breakfast bar. She ate her food slowly and pondered a volley of thoughts against the background of relaxing music. Her pulse quickened even as she tried to unwind. Festering into her psyche was the question Emloch had refused to answer—how he had come about such private information as her medical records. The text seared itself into her mind's eye; its image was all-consuming.

YES, MIRAI. PEOPLE WITH MULTIPLE SCLEROSIS.

"How the hell does he know?" she said, clenching her jaw. "Who told him? Unless he hacked into my medical file, Dr. Wallace and David are the only people who…"

The voice on the audio stream startled her. "Your favorite music, all in one place. This is PRN America. Thanks for joining us this morning. More songs to come after news and weather. Stay tuned."

Mirai walked back over to the sink and rinsed her dish. She then stood at the countertop while gazing out into the backyard. The sight of her rented cottage was pleasant. It stood in stark contrast to the onslaught of visuals affecting her mind. An amused grin crossed her lips upon realizing that she had never before painted it. Her eyes began breaking the image down to its artistic components.

"Top story this morning continues to be the standoff at the nation's most important landmark," came the reporter's intrepid tone. "Twelve hours ago, a man claiming to be from the Mesa Revival barricaded himself atop the torch balcony of the Statue of Liberty."

Mirai blinked and looked back at her phone.

"New York port authorities, police, and city officials have been communicating with the unidentified man via telephone and have been monitoring the situation closely. Sources indicate that the man is in his mid to late thirties, appears to be armed, and has a duffle bag of supplies at the ready for a prolonged protest. His demands have come only through fragmented calls with the police, but have mostly consisted of claims that those housed up inside the Preserve are in mortal danger. He is requesting airtime on network television to relay his grievances. So far, no one has come forward with any substantive information as to the man's identity, nor his broader motives."

Mirai slowly walked back to the breakfast bar and tapped on the Omni logo. The immediate image was that of a man with a gun, talking on his phone while in midstride around the circular balcony of the

Statue of Liberty's torch. The photo had obviously been taken from a helicopter or drone. Mirai narrowed her eyes at the man, relieved that it was no one she knew.

"The sight of anyone atop the torch is rare," continued the anchor, "as the viewing balcony has been closed to the public since 1916…"

Mirai sighed and silenced her phone. After rubbing her face, she glanced over at her car keys laying on the table.

I need to get out of here for a while.

The convertible rumbled to life as she donned her white sunglasses and pulled out of the driveway. The intercoastal waterway shimmered with reflective daylight, casting glistening steaks across the spinnaker sails of boats. Heading toward downtown, Mirai watched the cluster of buildings spread apart, their glass-panel facades appearing to be a natural extension of the azure sky.

She tilted her head and wondered where she was going. Something within the hand controlling the steering wheel seemed to already know. With instinctive motion, she switched on the radio tuner, half hoping to hear calming music, half desiring to learn more about the protester.

"…preempting our regular programming to bring you this. Again, our sources on the ground have indicated that the man has agreed to speak with reporters, so long as Palisades Radio Network agrees to carry the call live and during primetime hours. There's been no word yet from the police chief or the mayor's office…"

Mirai listened as she drove, her mind compartmentalized between the fascination unfolding and the question driving her mad.

How did Emloch know about the MS?

Mirai felt her fingers tighten. Her eyes scanned the cityscape for nothing in particular, as if searching for a hazard that had yet to manifest. With kaleidoscopic speed, her thoughts came and went. She made a right turn at an intersection and didn't know why. The street was unfamiliar. The direction was not.

There's no real harm in it. Not really. What if it helps? Plus, Kan might be willing to share more…

"…live via satellite, and we will bring you that interview starting at seven pm Eastern time."

Mirai wheeled the car left and recognized the street. She was arriving from the opposite direction, as if her intuition had used the chicanery against the more rational part of her mind. Situated at a bustling corner was the voxhall. Mirai stared at the building while awaiting a green light.

"…no one else appears to be with the armed man, which—I mean certainly—brings some level of relief to the authorities involved."

She entered the parking lot and found a spot close to the doors. Once inside, the lack of chatter and commuter noise brought about an eviction of all ancillary thoughts, save for one.

If there's even a chance that the Potion works…

"Good morning, miss," said an attendant. "Are you here to partake?"

Mirai nodded and tried to verbalize in the affirmative. She was ushered into the center of the voxhall where, unlike her previous visit, a large number of patrons were waiting their turn at the sanctum. The voxroy stood at the dais dispensing the Potion. Mirai could barely see him in the subdued light but felt confident that it was Kan Thura. She took a deep breath and moved along at the back of the line. As she waited, she took out her phone, opened the message thread with Emloch, and started typing.

How did you know about the MS? That's a huge invasion of privacy. Why should I ever trust you again?

After sending the message, Mirai slid the phone back into her pants pocket. The line was now moving at a more moderate pace. She determined to focus on the ritual at hand. Some people found great comfort and healing while partaking; others did not. Mirai conditioned her mind to believe that she was amongst the lucky ones, even if it was all nonsense.

When the last few attendees walked away from the dais, the man whose facial features looked similar to hers came into focus. His eyes showed no hint of recognition when he saw her. His face registered no change. The rote manner in which he moved, acknowledged, dispensed, and bid farewell was nothing short of robotic.

"Greetings," he said in a soft tone. "Will you accept the Potion?"

Mirai looked at Kan curiously, wondering if this was his attempt at secrecy. With an anxious shrug, she said, "Yes, yes I'd like to partake…again."

Kan turned to dispense the blue liquid out of the decanter. Mirai shifted her eyes over toward a small cluster of other voxroys, who all seemed to have their sights fixed on her. They stared at her from afar. In their faces was the stern look of disapproval.

"For you," said Kan. "The Love of God."

Mirai took the small cup and brought it to her lips. As she did, a wandering thought penetrated the moment.

May this bring healing to my right hand.

She swallowed the Potion and the prayer left her consciousness. The cup was returned to Kan and he nodded graciously. Any trace of disingenuousness or disbelief had been erased from the man's visage. When in his garments and in the voxhall, he conducted himself as a man of true faith.

"May you find your miracle," he said.

Mirai smiled, nodded, and after an awkward hesitation in which she noticed that the line behind her had grown considerably, turned to leave. When she reached the end of the long aisle, she turned back and saw the other voxroys watching her. They made no attempts to hide their observation. It was the keen eyes of those waiting for her to exit the building. An unsettling dissonance burrowed into her psyche.

Did I do something wrong?

The scenario replayed in her mind as she got back in her car and drove home. It continued to linger while she ate lunch, tried to paint, and greeted her parents upon their return from work and her sister back from school. Mirai pictured the disapproving stares as she stood in her closet and chose an outfit for the evening. After applying the last of her makeup, she grabbed her purse and bolted down the stairwell of her cottage. Back in her car, the radio was again tuned to PRN America.

"…are asking the question if authorities will forcibly remove the man after the interview."

"They've gotta be real careful about that," came the voice of another commentator. "The optics on this could be politically devastating if something goes wrong. This guy is clearly some nut who has a personal grievance against the Preserve, against Alexander, against the whole Mesa Revival—and probably with good reason. But he's holding no hostages. He's not endangering anyone by being up there. So, I say let him have his fifteen minutes of fame and he'll come down peaceably once he smells some of that New York-style pizza."

The crisp evening air had a salty taste. Pedestal clouds lined the sky, giving the impression that rain was on the way. The city lights dotted the landscape as the convertible headed toward the symphony hall. Mirai slowly raised the volume on the radio so she could hear the conversation over the gusty wind.

"…been informed that the man has just joined the call. This is being simulcast over several networks, but it will be our own Gavin Balmer who will be conducting the interview. Let me now turn it over to our host, who is broadcasting live from our New York affiliate."

A few seconds of dead air preceded the introduction. "This is Gavin Balmer with PRN America. The man who has barricaded himself atop the Statue of Liberty is currently on the line. Sir, to whom am I speaking?"

The man's voice emerged with unexpected poise. If the network had been hoping for a crazed lunatic, the first impressions indicated otherwise. "Good evening, and thanks for having me," the man said. "My name is of no importance to this conversation. What matters is only this: The people at the Mesa Revival are in grave danger, and no one—not the White House, not the governor of Nevada, not the media —seems to be doing anything to stop it."

"What sort of danger are you referring to?" asked Balmer.

As Mirai listened, the barrage of mental pictures featuring the teeming masses within the Mesa Revival filtered down to a single face.

I wonder if he knows Julie, she thought.

"Let me begin with this—I'm not a nutjob." The man chuckled, aware of the irony. "I know I'm up here on the torch of the Statue of Liberty, waving a gun around, defying police orders to come down… Trust me, I know how this looks. What I'm doing is extreme because that's all that seems to get attention these days. The majority of my career has been as a social worker, helping people in various stages of disfunction find some grounding and stability. The demographic I served fell primarily into two camps: those escaping substance abuse issues and those escaping cults. Standing on my credentials, I can say with certainty that what we're witnessing at the Mesa Revival is one of the largest cult gatherings ever assembled."

"That's a serious accusation," Balmer calmly interjected. "And one that millions around the globe would undoubtedly disagree. Tell me, how did you come to this assessment of what's going on in the Nevada desert?"

The man's vocal volume peaked and valleyed in accordance with the wind filling New York Harbor. He seemed to be trying his best to guard the mouthpiece and reduce crackling. "My assessment began as an effort to save a friend."

Mirai felt her muscles tighten.

The man continued, "He joined nearly a year ago. Left town without even telling me. Then one day I received a letter explaining why he'd chosen to leave the world and burrow away inside the Preserve. I won't get into the specifics, but let me say that a few things disturbed me right off the bat. He informed me in the letter that he wouldn't be sending any further communication, that it was imperative he remove himself from all old influences and ways of thinking. Then recently, I uncovered evidence that those inside the Preserve were eschewing their birth names in favor of new ones, made-up ones, ones approved by none other than Alexander himself. The very fact that the Preserve exists and has tens of thousands of people pleading for admittance is evidence enough of the powerful hold this mindset has over those at the Mesa Revival."

"Mindset?" asked Balmer.

"Of course," said the man. "Every single person there truly believes the world is coming to an end. They've been fed this lie that planet earth is actually hell and that they are the only ones who recognize it—those under Alexander's shepherding. And to truly be ready to return to their *natural state*, one must be a part of the Mesa Revival, or at the very least, adjacent to it—metaphysically speaking."

"And you know all of these because you yourself attended the revival?"

"I went to bring back my friend, yes," responded the man. "But it was too late. He was so indoctrinated into the belief systems and regimented practices of the Preserve, he wouldn't even see me, except to say that I should renounce my old life and join him inside that desert palace. I was quite depressed after that, and decided that the only way I could be of some use was to study and report back on what I was seeing on the grounds."

"Well, let's talk about that for a minute," Balmer said. "Because numerous journalists have toured the Mesa Revival, only to report back that as misdirected and, frankly—weird—the gathering seems to be, the event is basically benign. You disagree with that?"

"Strongly. There are claims of miracles—I witnessed none. Reports of people having been raised from the dead—I met zero zombies. People purporting that they had come to the revival battling serious mental health disorders and were now completely off their medications —no one from the medical community has been invited to verify these assertions. The groupthink at the Mesa Revival is beyond massive, it's *staggering*. No one fact-checks anything being said, and what *is* said spreads like wildfire. Confirmation bias reigns supreme. Paranoia of the outside world is rampant. They increasingly only trust one voice, and it's not the voice of reason inside their head. It's only the voice of Alexander, the man who still to this day rules the airwaves. Airwaves that offer him a forum each day to spew his unique brand of uplifting apocalypticism. Of course, I'm referring to you all…at PRN America."

Balmer didn't sound fazed by the accusation. He had his comeback fully armed. "Well, that's your judgment of the situation and you're definitely welcome to it. However, what you call 'uplifting apocalypticism,' millions around the globe call comfort in a time of great uncertainty."

"Your network enabled Alexander from day one," the man countered. "Howard Lalonde put him on the air decades ago. His program airs every night, broadcast live from the Preserve, and is provided via satellite—thanks to PRN—to any affiliate station in

North America who wants it. His internet streams garner an audience of over a billion. Look, I'm not even demanding you take him off the air. But show some intellectual honesty for once and at least combat what he's saying. Have someone debate him. Or air a rebuttal after each of his programs, offering an objective viewpoint. A view that the world only seems like its ending because that's the narrative we all keep getting fed. Prophecies can be dangerous, Mr. Balmer. If repeated often enough, they have a pesky habit of coming true."

Mirai drove into the parking garage and began spiraling up the narrow ramp. For a moment, it seemed like the signal would get lost within the concrete structure. Once she reached the top, and was back in open air, the man's voice again settled into the stereo.

"…and that's why I'm doing this. I'm trying to get a message out there that none of this is normal. That Alexander is power hungry. That the Preserve operates in the exact ways and methods of the nefarious cults we've been taught to avoid. Unless someone does something to stop this, we face a tragedy of cataclysmic proportions."

"One could say that you, sir, now sound a bit apocalyptic," Balmer mused.

The man sighed heavily into the mouthpiece. He took a moment to gather his thoughts before answering. "Alexander is trying to create the very disaster he's claiming to denounce. I'm simply the bullhorn. I'm trying to take people's eyes off the shiny gemstone in the desert and focus on the scorpion coming up from behind. I'm asking for some level of intervention for these people—at the Mesa Revival. People who are showcasing all of the hallmarks of cult behavior."

"Cult is an easy word to toss about, however—"

The man's voice sharpened. "Ostracization of family and friends. Martyrdom mindset. Strong association with victimhood mentality. A leader who claims to have all the answers. The taking on of new names and new identities. Using words and phrases that are only understood internally and not outside the group. Cognitive dissonance whenever a prediction fails to manifest. A firm belief that the world is coming to an end, and that your conclave will be the only ones saved—"

"Sir, I'd like to pivot the discussion toward your endgame here. Are you planning on coming down from the—"

"This isn't about me! I'm just the messenger. Take a look at what's happening at the Mesa Revival—a real, honest, objective look—and tell me that those people are not heading for disaster!"

"Sir-sir, I'm happy to continue this conversation, but you'll need to answer some of my questions in order for us to carry on—"

"Howard Lalonde and PRN America hold more responsibility than most in this situation—"

"Sir."

"...dereliction of duty going back decades..."

"*Sir.*"

"...could bring this to an end with one phone call..."

The man's voice abruptly vanished. Balmer cleared his throat and then said, "All right, well, since the man on the balcony refuses to have a civil conversation, we will be unable to continue the interview. It's unfortunate, as I sense he had some valuable points to make, but devolving into a shouting match and ad hominem attacks does not a good discussion make. That, ladies and gentlemen, was the man atop the torch of the Statue of Liberty. We've just received word that the local authorities will be making another attempt at negotiating with the man to make a peaceful surrender..."

Mirai parked the car and shut off the engine. Despite being pressed for time, she sat silently in the vehicle for several minutes while watching the dashboard clock inch closer to the bottom of the hour and the start of the concert. A twinge of nausea sat in the pit of her stomach. A part of her knew why; a part of her was still in denial. She imagined a course of action, one in which the sequence of events led to an inconsequential end. The alternative to the sequence also filled her mind, and with it, saturated the nerves along her spine.

With pursed lips she reached for her phone. Its vibration redirected her determined eyes. On the screen was a notification. It was a new message from Emloch. Mirai hesitated before opening the text window. She wanted to stay focused on other matters, yet knew the curiosity would get the better of her if she ignored it.

HELLO MIRAI.

The greeting seemed to radiate off the screen.

I TRUST YOU'RE READY TO CONTINUE OUR QUEST FOR OSIRIS. I HAVE A NEW LEAD FOR YOU TO FOLLOW.

Mirai jammed her thumbs against the digital keyboard. *I told you, until you and I meet face-to-face, there will be no more help coming from me. You've evaded my questions long enough.*

The ellipses pulsed with a forthcoming response. Mirai held her breath and wondered why she suddenly felt a sense of dread.

WE DON'T HAVE TIME FOR THIS CHILDISHNESS, MIRAI. THE FATE OF HUMANITY HANGS IN THE BALANCE AND YOU'RE ADDING NEEDLESS COMPLICATIONS. I'VE ALREADY PLACED THE FUNDS IN YOUR ACCOUNT. YOUR COOPERATION IS VITAL.

You no longer have my cooperation. I cannot help you anymore.

There was a long pause between messages. Lengthy enough that Mirai suspected that she had shaken Emloch off for good. Yet that theory was dashed when the ellipses reappeared. Their duration was short; the message was even shorter.

IT WOULD BE A SHAME IF WORD GOT OUT ABOUT YOUR MS.

Starting at her wrist, and working up to the muscles in her shoulder, Mirai felt a contracting of every sinew in her arm. Her fingers curled around the phone as if strangling it, as if strangling Emloch. In her face was the pronunciation of rage.

Her eyes were petrified.

YOUR FAMILY… YOUR FRIENDS… WORST OF ALL WOULD BE THE ART COMMUNITY. THEIR GROWING RESPECT FOR YOU WOULD SOUR. THEY WOULD NO LONGER LOOK AT YOUR ART WITH ADMIRATION. ONLY WITH PITY.

Mirai swallowed as a simmering panic twisted in her bones.

POOR MIRAI… THE ARTIST WHO COULD HAVE BEEN.

She shut her eyes to prevent the oncoming tears. Her slender frame trembled as the mental picture began its gleeful torment. It was an image of her work, being viewed by her contemporaries, all of whom were acknowledging a perception in its decline.

She was such a good artist…before the disease… Mirai reached out for the metal door handle, her left hand shaking so violently that she could scarcely grasp it. *You can see her technique vanish through the years… What a shame…* Mirai pulled the interior latch and opened the vehicle door. *The early years…those were her best… She really went downhill after the—what was it—multiple sclerosis?*

In one swift motion, Mirai leapt from the driver's seat and vomited onto the concrete floor of the parking garage. The world teetered for a moment as she regained her bearings from the dizziness. She steadied herself against the side of the vehicle and drew in a deep breath. The shrill ringing in her ears drowned out the ambient noise from the structure. Her vision now seemed a bit blurry. Mirai pressed her hands against her face and slowly massaged her temples.

I can't believe this. Emloch is gonna blackmail me.

She blinked repeatedly before feeling confident enough to stand on her own. The trembling in her body had subsided. The surge of adrenaline was retreating. With shell-shocked eyes, she scanned the garage. She heard pedestrian voices but no one was visible. A conspicuous sense of isolation crept over her.

After reaching into the car to grab her purse, Mirai started walking across the expanse toward the elevator. Her steps gained strength as she moved. The uneasiness from being sick had quickly dissipated. Her mind was focused on one task, a task which would free her of worry and secure in her spirit a trusted ally.

The elevator descended to the mezzanine level of the grand symphony hall. The doors opened to the carpeted entrance and lofty chandelier that had become synonymous with her visits to watch David perform. Around a corner was a wide stairwell, drawing patrons from the mezzanine into the box-level seating. Mirai gazed at it for a moment, using the time to gather courage. She pressed her hands against the fabric of her formfitting black dress and marshaled herself past the stairwell, continuing toward a set of doors nestled along a corridor. Without turning around to check for lingering stares, Mirai entered the backstage area as if she knew where she was going and had a purpose in being there.

Act like you belong here. No one will question you.

Mirai walked with intent. She made eye contact with no one. The click of her heels served as the metronome to her legs; they kept pace with the natural rhythm of an authority figure. She scanned for visual clues while working her way through the labyrinthine hallways.

As she approached a corner, the muffled sound of applause could be heard through the partition walls. Mirai stole a glance at her phone screen clock. The symphony was about to begin. She listened as the concertmaster tuned the stringed section. Silence then followed for another moment before the conductor appeared on stage to a round of rapturous applause. Within seconds, Mirai heard the first few dramatic notes from *Infernal Dance* from *The Firebird* by Stravinsky.

Rounding the corner led her to a sectioned off wall that looked like a vertical checkerboard. Square cubbyholes with fabric-lined baskets cluttered her vision. Underneath each basket was a printed nameplate on which was listed the various ensemble members' names. Mirai looked behind her to assure that the coast was momentarily clear. She spotted David's name instantly. Without hesitation, she wrenched his basket back from the cubbyhole and reached inside for what she was sure would exist.

There's no way he takes his phone onstage.

Mirai was correct. The phone filled her palm as she withdrew it from the basket. The screen illumined as she gazed at it, its artificial light pushing back the shadows on her face. The screen lock required a four-digit numerical passcode. Mirai remembered seeing David punch in the code frequently, but she never before had the impetus to ascertain it.

Try his birthday. November 20th.

1-1-2-0.

The attempt was rejected. Two attempts remained before the phone would stay locked for ten minutes. Mirai bit her lower lip while trying to steady her nerves. The next logical choice would be her own birthday. It seemed too easy, too convenient for such a subversive task.

Yet reason demanded that she try it anyway. Her thumbs hovered hesitantly over the glowing glass.

Okay then. May 7th.

0-5-0-7.

When the phone unlocked, Mirai felt a jolt go through her frame. It was the equal shock of knowing and of being surprised. She steadied her forefinger while navigating to the messaging window. In a list were his recent texts and messages. At the top was her name.

Heading over to the hall now—see you afterward, he had sent.

Running a few minutes late. I'll be there soon, she had replied.

Mirai blinked and got out of the thread. She scrolled down with precision, not knowing exactly what she was looking for but trusting that she would identify it once it appeared. Texts between David and his family members, his coworkers, the conductor of the symphony, and his landlord, all populated the rectangles within the application. Nothing was out of the ordinary.

Mirai listened as a momentary lull in the music sent her heart racing. Her eyes followed the silence toward the backstage wall, wondering if the first movement could possibly be over. When it picked up again with a rampage, Mirai exhaled and grit her teeth.

What are you doing? she scolded herself.

The contact list continued to go back in time until prior to when she and David first met, starting with his entry into the Preserve. She shook her head and scrolled all the way back to the top of the list. Exiting the window, she swiped right and brought up a cluster of other frequently used applications. Email, weather, music, news. She quickly read through the options and smirked that it could have been her own usage history.

No Emloch…not even a side girlfriend…

Mirai stole another glance down the hallway. There was no one around. The orchestral music roared to a crescendo. David's phone felt increasingly weighty in her hand. With a tremendous sigh, she navigated back to the main screen.

Only then did she notice the Omni app. The multifaceted browser logo was easily discernible amongst a host of competing images. It featured a translucent sphere hovering over a silver halo. It was the most popular application in the world, and soon, Carys's face would be the one to promote its functionality to a new generation.

Gotta remember to pack some sketching supplies for the trip to LA next week, Mirai thought. The thought prevented her from doing what she had intended, which was to swipe up and set all things back to where they had originally been on the screen. Instead, she swiped too lightly, and inadvertently opened the Omni app.

The translucent sphere pulsed and the dissolved into the viewing window. Atop the screen were all of David's most recent searches, reminders, vocal commands, and settings. On the right corner was an open tab. Its title gave her pause.

DistantFriend.

Mirai squared her sights on the words and tapped on them. A new window emerged. Before she had a second to prepare, the greeting assaulted her eyes.

HELLO MIRAI.

Her body froze. Her blinks altogether ceased. It was only the instinctual movement of her finger that caused any alteration in the scene.

I'VE NEVER MET YOU, BUT I'VE SEEN YOUR ARTWORK. THAT IS ALL I NEED TO KNOW. MY NAME IS EMLOCH.

"Oh my God," she whispered.

Is that your first name? Last name?

Witnessing her very first reply brought a resurgence of queasiness.

JUST EMLOCH.

Mirai tapped on the top of the window and saw a filter option. When she changed it to most recently sent, an eerie sense of déjà vu flooded her senses.

IT WOULD BE A SHAME IF WORD GOT OUT ABOUT YOUR MS.

Her eyes widened in horror.

POOR MIRAI… THE ARTIST WHO COULD HAVE BEEN.

"It can't be…"

Tears began breaching her eyes. A terrifying pain surged from deep within her being. With a slicing, twisting, stabbing significance, Mirai felt the mental processes by which she confirmed what she was reading, what she was seeing, and that it was in fact David's phone she was holding. The hope that this was some lucid nightmare from which she was soon to awaken crumbled upon seeing an orchestra staff member brush past her in a hurried dash.

This is real...

She wrested her own phone from her purse and opened the camera. A few snapshots of David's message history satisfied her, until a final idea crossed her mind. It would prove nothing more than what she had already uncovered, yet there was something poetically fitting to the witnessing of it, and Mirai proceeded nonetheless.

Using her left hand, she typed a message through the Omni app and hit send. Instantly, the phone in her right hand vibrated.

HELLO MIRAI.

Tossing David's phone back into the basket and shoving her own back into her purse, Mirai marched down the corridor with considerable speed. She wanted to be out of earshot of the symphony, and away from the concert hall with its recent memories. The lighting in the main foyer smarted her eyes as she reemerged from backstage. A few patrons wandered about, drinking champagne and chatting, oblivious to either the time or their surroundings.

Mirai picked up the pace and headed toward the bar next to the two-story window wall of the grand entrance. The bartender had his back turned to the assortment of people who stood gazing upward at the same thing transfixing the bartender. They all were staring at a flatscreen television anchored to the wall.

"Unconscionable," said a man.

"So disturbing," mumbled another.

Mirai placed her hand on the beveled edge of the counter and wondered why the bartender had yet to acknowledge her. She then focused her vision on the bizarre sight filling the TV screen.

It was a live helicopter feed of downtown New York. The shot was zeroing in on the harbor, and as it did, the Statue of Liberty was coming into view. Dusk had overtaken the skyline, draining the color from the world behind the city skyscrapers. The only lights dotting the harbor's horizon came from the statue, both from its crown and from the totemic green torch in its hand.

That was where a strange flicker captivated the eye.

"Something rarely seen in the Western world," said the grave, authoritative voice of the news anchor. "It's…well, it's hard to add commentary to something like this."

Nothing more was uttered by those watching from the bar. Their words had been stolen by a heinous image, one too incongruous to exist next to the symbol of the nation. For atop the torch balcony of the Statue of Liberty, was the man from the interview—the protester of the Mesa Revival. He could no longer be classified as recognizably human, as the entirety of his body was engulfed in dancing flames. The fire raged with a passion, consuming all that had been the man, his ideas, and his purpose.

"What did…" Mirai gasped. "How did he…"

"Damndest thing I've ever seen," responded an elderly patron, his mouth agape. "Had gasoline in that duffle bag. Took it out. Poured it all over himself…"

"Oh my God."

"What's the term for that? For what he's doing?"

Mirai responded without thinking, nor did she recall having answered, "Self-immolation."

The words left her lips with a finality, spoken as if describing not just the event, but also the evening. The television monitor continued to revel in the ghastly imagery. A wide-shot angle showed the New York Harbor, the Statue of Liberty, and a man burning alive atop the torch balcony, all beneath the thick blackness of a starless sky and the unnatural glow of Brubaker's Comet.

Mirai eventually looked away, yet the iniquity left a stain on her mind. There was nothing left to do but go home, sleep, and hope that when she awoke, the dawn would grant her insight to paint anew. Keeping that desire at the forefront of her traumatized memory, Mirai turned to leave. She could still faintly hear the complex musical arrangement coming from the orchestra hall, its crescendo expanding both time and space. The fact that she was within earshot of it, and of the solo harpist adding his contribution to the piece, quickened her steps out of the building and into the night. As she walked, as she ran, her thoughts compressed into a singularity—into a tempered belief. The belief was dangling by a thread. Mirai drew in a stabilizing breath, and through tears that she could no longer restrain, stated the words anyway.

"Beauty will save the world."

PART TWO
FUTURE TENSE

"When small men begin to cast big shadows,
it means that the sun is about to set."

— Lin Yutang

CHAPTER 10
THE SIGNATURES

"Alexander."

He whispered the name of the man in the sky. A giant screen had been affixed to the side of a building, transmitting the live feed of Alexander's internet broadcast. The indefatigable figure was sharp and radiant, bristling with the sort of charisma that demanded undivided attention. Clusters of people gathered along the street to watch, some for minutes at a time, others for a mere passing glance, all with varying levels of curiosity. Alexander stood at a translucent lectern and thundered his oratory from a carpeted stage within the Preserve, his voice rippling out through overhead speakers to an unseen audience. Their response to his more climactic statements echoed with laudatory resound.

"They continue to demonstrate their untrustworthiness," Alexander declared. "They lie incessantly and with impunity. They offer binoculars with one hand and a blindfold with the other. They make *us* out to be the deluded ones, the insane, those unfit for society, all the while masking their dark and sinister deeds for fear of judgment."

Neal Lalonde gazed through his office window before stealing a glance at his wristwatch and pondering something outside of the time. The newly installed Jumbotron was an omnipresent nuisance, broadcasting Alexander's live and prerecorded messages around the clock. A local devotee of the Mesa Revival had bankrolled it. Neal had heard rumors that the individual had tried to buy his way into the Preserve but had failed; so instead, he brought Alexander to the streets of Santa Monica. Noise complaints had been immediately filed. The resulting compromise was a silenced, closed-captioned Alexander after eight in the evening, with full audio ramping back up again each daybreak.

Neal stood with his arms crossed and his eyes wandering the office. Although the screen was a few blocks away, he found it difficult to focus. Even the distant sound of the mad prophet's voice crushed Neal's inner monologue. Alexander continued, "Disasters continue to plague the world: earthquakes, tsunamis, famine, wildfires that rage on for weeks at a time… all indicators of the oncoming collapse of our ecosystem. Nothing is getting better, only perpetually worse. More nations than ever are declaring war and preparing for battle."

Neal arched a quizzical eyebrow.

"But rest assured—ladies and gentlemen, members of the Preserve, those who by proxy of radio, television, and the internet are also considered trusted allies—that judgment day is coming for them… for *all* of them, who refuse to see that they are already condemned because they are already in hell. Therefore, take comfort in these words. In so doing, we await perihelion."

Neal shook his head and turned away from the window wall.

"That's also been my reaction to him as of late," came a voice from the hallway.

Neal turned to see his sister enter his office. Teagan Lalonde walked toward his desk with the mannerisms of someone who had just taken a beating. Behind her black-framed glasses were hazel eyes that had witnessed a skirmish, on the battlefield of a boardroom, in which reason and moral virtue had fallen victim to the machinations of weak men. Neal watched as she collapsed into the chair opposite his desk and let out a wearied sigh.

He asked cautiously, "That bad, huh?"

Teagan smiled. "It's always nice when the board's vote against your proposals is unanimous. Leaves little room for ambiguity."

"Yes. Unity is a beautiful thing."

The two sat silently for a moment. Neal then abruptly stood and walked over to the teakwood cabinet where he poured whiskey into a pair of tumblers. When he handed the second glass to his sister, they clinked the rims together in a sarcastic toast.

"To the death of intellectual honesty," Teagan said, and swallowed the shot whole.

Neal returned to the window and glanced at the image of Alexander on the screen. In a way, he couldn't tell what the man was saying; in another way, he could.

"Why are we keeping him on the air?" Neal asked.

"Because the board is convinced of PRN's downfall if we remove him. He's still our top-rated show and a huge revenue driver. Not to mention the syndication deals with other networks…"

"A man self-immolated in protest of the Mesa Revival. He accused our network of enabling a cult. Didn't the board have anything to say in response to that?"

Teagan spoke slowly, her eyes avoiding the window. "Their last word on the matter was that PRN America and Alexander are inseparable."

"Please tell me they didn't actually use that word, Tea."

She looked down into her tumbler and frowned. "Inseparable, inextricable, and intertwined."

Neal pivoted around toward his sister and huffed. "How delightfully alliterative."

Teagan drummed her fingers against Neal's desk. Her eyes drifted across a stack of file folders to a small canister sitting atop an opened cardboard box. The container was white with a black screw-top lid.

"Is that what I think it is?" she asked.

Neal returned to the desk and shook his head in surrender. "Call it an act of morbid curiosity."

Teagan laughed. "I can't believe you ordered it. Lemme see."

On the jar's rear label was an ingredient list written in such a small font as to be almost unreadable. On the front of the jar was a simple logo.

"The Salve," Teagan said. "So, this is the crap Alexander's been peddling on his program the last few weeks?"

"That it is," declared Neal. "And according to his website, it keeps selling out. Back orders are piling up. Ships internationally. Only available from the Preserve. I have no idea if it's FDA approved…"

"God Almighty, did you read the ingredient list? I mean, admittedly, I use a few cosmetics slightly worse than this… but still…"

"Yeah. It's toxic as hell."

Teagan unscrewed the lid and gave the clear substance a sniff. "Smells nice, I'll give him that. What's this for again?"

Neal sighed. "He claims it reduces tension, anxiety, depression… I dunno—probably cures erectile dysfunction too."

Teagan rubbed a small dollop between her forefinger and thumb. The serum was smooth and colorless. Neal added, "You apply it below your ears or on your wrists. Supposedly has a calming effect."

"Did you try it already?"

"I did."

"And?"

Neal tossed the empty box into the trash bin. "As with everything else from that man, it didn't resonate with me."

The ambient sound of Alexander's voice drifted down the corridor from the recessed ceiling speakers, reminding the siblings that his presence was inescapable. Teagan wiped the Salve's residue from her hand and arose from the chair. "Shall we grab lunch?"

"It's 10:45, Tea."

"Brunch then?"

Neal shook his head. "Master Control is running a systemwide update this morning. I should stick around until it's finished."

Teagan nodded. "Fair enough. I've got some PPM reports to go over anyway."

"I never thought Dad would relinquish oversight of the ratings data."

"I never thought Dad would relinquish the executive directorship, but here we are."

"He didn't," Neal corrected. "The board extracted it from his arthritic hands and gave it to you. Don't forget that, Tea. As much as they fight you, they did choose you to take over the network. That's got to count for something."

She pursed her lips and took a step toward the door. "Teagan Lalonde—newly appointed executive director… but in title only. Dad may still have his radio program left, but don't be fooled, Neal. Even after his on-air meltdown and all of the turmoil that incident created, the board owed him one. Dad wanted a Lalonde to continue his legacy. My skill sets, expertise in the industry, perspectives on how we should innovate and evolve… None of that was taken into consideration. He wanted a Lalonde to keep things going, so they chose me. It was nepotism at its finest."

Neal sighed heavily. "Tea…"

"No, no, it's okay. I understood exactly what was going on when I accepted the role. The power does not reside with me. This is the way things are now, but in time it can change. The board legislates policy and I execute it. I'm a figurehead, Neal." With that she chuckled to herself. "I just wish they weren't so transparent about it."

Neal exited the office with Teagan and they parted ways at the elevator. After checking in with Master Control, he shuffled down the stairwell to the main lobby and greeted the woman at the reception desk. "Rob's out sick today, so when the tower climber guy gets here, I'll take the meeting. We gotta get that strobe light replaced in Bakersfield."

"Sure thing, Mr. Lalonde."

Neal turned to head back to the stairwell when something in the corner caught his eye.

"Is… she waiting to see someone?" Neal asked, suddenly whispering.

The receptionist tossed up her hands apologetically. "She came in a half hour ago and plopped down on the sofa. I've been so inundated with calls this morning that I haven't had a second to check in."

A curious smirk etched his face as Neal approached the young woman, who was stretched out on the lobby sofa, soundly asleep. He closed the distance gradually, hoping not to startle her. His words were spoken with tender softness—completely insufficient for awakening anyone, and in the sort of tone one would employ if hushing themselves for disturbing someone else's slumber.

"Miss… miss, are you all right?"

Miss…

Miss…

The words drifted into the young woman's subconscious, transforming into her own voice, and her own pain.

I missed you…

Julie…

Julie… there's so much I need to tell you…

I'm listening, Mirai.

Can you believe this? Everything that's happened since you left?

I'm so sorry I wasn't there for you.

You're here now… That's all that matters…

How are you coping?

Terribly… I could never shed enough tears to release the agony in my heart. I feel like I'll never have joy again. Each day there's only sorrow… and fury…

Fury?

I've never experienced more anger. I've never experienced more betrayal.

So everything David said and did was a lie? To what end? For what purpose?

I don't know. I don't want to know. I texted him that we're on a break. That we were moving too fast, and I just needed some time alone. Was that the right move, Julie? I was scared and didn't know what else to say. I have no idea what he's capable of, why he pretended to be Emloch, or what he was trying to manipulate me into doing. My family is confused and disappointed, of course. They loved him. But they didn't really know him. I guess I didn't either. God, Julie… I just want to pretend like none of this ever happened.

Agreed, Mirai. Let's pretend like none of this ever happened.
I've missed you so much, Julie. I'm so relieved you're back…
I'll never leave you again… I give you my word…

The moment before her eyes opened, Mirai knew it had been a dream. The warmth around her chest slowly dissipated into the pangs of lament. Sadness flushed the corners of her cheeks. Her vision swam as she gazed out at her surroundings with disoriented concern. She was lying sideways on a sofa in the waiting area of a grand lobby. Off to one side was a semicircular reception desk. On the other was a wall map with an array of international analog clocks denoting certain time zones.

Mirai blinked and looked down at the coffee table before her. Trade magazines about broadcasting littered the glass pane next to a small wooden placard stating: *May this serve you well.* Underneath the table was her small backpack and a pair of flip-flops. Feeling a rush of embarrassment for having dozed off in such a public setting, Mirai quickly sat up and slipped her feet back into the thongs.

It was at that moment when Neal Lalonde came into view.

"Oh… I'm sorry," Mirai muttered, her eyes still adjusting to the light. "I… I must have…"

"No worries," Neal said with a smile, "our station often has that effect on people."

Mirai again scanned the lobby while volitionally assembling pieces of the past into a discernible timeline. The sequence of events from arriving at the airport with her family, to spending much of the previous day sightseeing the local attractions, to wishing her sister the best of luck as she and her parents headed off to the shoot in the early morning hours, stood as a wobbly framework inside her memory. Her inexplicable presence on the lobby sofa remained a maddening shroud.

"Are you… waiting to see someone?" Neal asked.

"Umm… no," Mirai responded, rubbing her hands against her face. "I was just… My sister—Carys—she's doing a photoshoot at the modeling agency across the street. My parents are with her, and I had some time to kill, so I walked around the corporate park and noticed that this was the PRN headquarters. I think I just felt… a little woozy… and needed to sit down. I'm sorry about dozing off in your lobby."

"There's a cafeteria on the fourth floor. I'll admit, the food isn't great, but maybe a little sustenance will get you back on your feet. Also, I'm Neal."

Mirai reached for his outstretched hand and nearly missed the alignment. When their hands finally clasped, she felt reassured that she was fully awake. "I'm Mirai."

"What a lovely name. That's Japanese, right?"

She sighed while standing up. "One would think."

The lobby suddenly lost focus. Her eyes felt like they were oscillating within her skull. She paused and took a moment to rebalance, hoping that she had the wherewithal to make it to the elevators.

"Still a little unsteady, I see," Neal said. "Should I bring some food down here instead?"

"No, no," assured Mirai, taking each step with intention. "I'll be okay."

"Probably just a blood sugar crash."

Mirai nodded distantly. "Mhmm."

They continued to the elevators and ascended to the fourth floor. Down the hall and to the left brought them into the bustling commissary. Breakfast time had long since ended and the early risers were now ready for lunch. Neal pointed toward a few open table options. Mirai chose the one to which she was closest. A minute later, Neal returned with two trays.

"Soup and sandwich day. Not ambrosia, but it'll do."

Mirai gazed down at her food and felt herself decompress. She nodded in gratitude. "I really appreciate this."

They ate in silence before Neal positioned his first question. "So, your sister is doing a photoshoot you say. For which brand?"

Mirai's voice sounded as if it was on the verge of becoming hoarse. She knew it was not from overuse, but from a week of processing a personal upheaval. Her physical frame had absorbed the overflow from her mental faculties, all while trying to suppress the reality of the betrayal so as not to ruin her sister's big moment. Steadying her nerves, Mirai responded, "Umm… Omni, actually. It's a big project. She'll be shooting most of the week."

Neal wiped the corner of his mouth with a napkin and nodded. "I would imagine. Big company. Everyone uses Omni."

"She's going to be the face of the brand during this current campaign. I'm really proud of her. She's worked for an opportunity like this all her life."

"Would I have seen her previous work anywhere else?"

Mirai smirked as she chewed. "She did a car commercial last year. She's the know-it-all teenager in the back seat teaching the parents—"

"—how to use the navigation system, yes! I've seen that one. Funny ad. It's a commercial I never get tired of."

Mirai offered a humble shrug. "Yep, that's my sister. Her name is Carys McGarry."

"Well, in a city full of models, I'll get to say I knew her… or at least about her… way back when." With that, Neal exhaled a huff. "Carys McGarry. Man—I'm sure you hear this a lot, but that girl has a striking face. I mean, it's one of those faces that sticks with you after having seen it. It stays in your head. I don't know if I'm making any sense…"

"Oh, I get it. No one was more shocked about it than my parents. Carys looks nothing like either of them. Of course, then again, neither do I."

Neal set his spoon back into the soup. "I would be lying if I said the thought hadn't crossed my mind. Adopted, I'm assuming?"

"Very much so," she said. "Eternally grateful, too. I love my parents. I couldn't have landed with a better family. Or in a better place to live."

"You never hear anyone say that about LA," Neal mused.

"Oh, no, we don't live in LA. We're just out here to support Carys during the photoshoot. We live in Florida."

Neal's eyebrows arched in unison. "Is that so? PRN has a boatload of stations out in Florida. You don't happen to be a listener to the network?"

In as deep a voice as she could muster, Mirai said, *"May this serve you well."*

Neal burst out laughing, impervious to the array of quizzical stares coming from other tables. When he regained some composure, he said, "That was the best impression of Dad I've ever heard."

Mirai joined Neal in another round of laughter before the realization of his statement settled in. "Wait… did you say Dad?"

Neal coughed through his last outburst of chuckles and then took a sip of water. "Guilty as charged. Howard Lalonde is my father. Has been for as long as I've known him."

"Wow, I guess I didn't realize who you are."

"No one special." He smiled. "I'm the operations manager of the network. My sister, Tea—well, Teagan—she's the big kahuna. Dad is mostly retired now."

"Was it because of what happened on the air?" Mirai hesitated, slouched a little, and closed her eyes apologetically. "I'm so sorry, that was rude."

Neal waved off the comment. "It's nothing we can't talk about. After all, he did announce to the entire nation that some sinister force was about to bring the world to an end. Yeah, that incident definitely left a mark. Took months of carefully crafted public relations maneuvering to restore listener confidence. After a few FCC fines and some internal realignment, the network appears to have weathered the storm."

Mirai's eyes gradually widened while imagining the imbroglio. Neal then said, "So back to you. Where in Florida do you live?"

"Miami."

"Miami Mirai. Love it. Our station tower down there is in Hialeah. You get a decent signal?"

"Mostly, although I usually listen online."

"Traitor," he said with a grin. "Since I have you as a captive audience for another minute or two, I'll conduct a quick poll. What component of the broadcast lineup would you say is your favorite? Music… talk shows…?"

Mirai set her napkin down on the tray and gazed attentively at her right hand. Some days it felt completely back to normal. Other days it did not. After a pregnant pause, she whispered, "I'm an artist…"

"I'm sorry?"

"I said… I'm an artist. I paint… in my home studio… oils on canvas. Often, I paint while listening to PRN's music. I find it calming. Helps me focus if my mind is wandering."

Neal leaned in a bit against the table. "That's remarkable. I love hearing that we make a difference in people's lives, but rarely have I imagined us having an impact on the life of an artist. How wonderful."

Mirai ran her left hand across the length of her right arm. Her vision drifted across the empty plate and over the table, conducting a panorama of the room, the occupants, and the sense of camaraderie they all seemed to share. She blinked and redirected her eyes to Neal. "Other times… I tune in when I can't sleep. I listen to the announcer, and I know that at least one other person can't sleep either. It's been… It can be… helpful… in those times."

Neal stared at the young artist with the stark realization that for the first time in weeks, he couldn't hear the omnipresent voice of Alexander in the background. He was certain it was still there, yet the sound of Mirai's voice seemed to act as a protective coating, shielding him from the carcinogen within his work's lifeblood. He exhaled slowly. "I appreciate you sharing that, Mirai. I really do. You know, when you work here… when you're saturated by it every minute of the day, it can be easy to lose touch with the purpose. You hope it's still there, having a positive influence somewhere and on someone, but until a person actually says something… tells you that it makes a difference in their life… well…"

Mirai smiled. "It has… and it does."

Neal grimaced and pointed his forefinger upward. "Despite him?"

For the first time since sitting down, Mirai noticed the enigmatic ramblings coming through the overhead speakers. The man's voice was unmistakable, as distinctive as the cherubic sculpting and soulful eyes of her photogenic sister. The sound instantly transported her back inside the Preserve, seated around the massive table, across from Julie, across from Alexander, and within the fixed gaze of David.

Mirai shuddered and shook her head. "I don't listen to him."

Neal briefly studied her body language and pursed his lips. He then arose from his chair and collected the lunch trays. Upon returning from disposing of the trash, he answered, "Me either."

From the cafeteria, Neal led Mirai along the various hallways and floors of the building, offering her a personalized tour of the network. They stopped at Studio D to observe one of the on-air staff reading a top-of-the-hour news and weather report. The announcer noticed them through the glass partition and tossed a friendly wave in their direction without breaking his verbal stride.

"That's Larsen," said Neal. "Been with the network for decades. He's the voice of most of our PSAs, station IDs, program intros, that sort of stuff."

"I definitely recognize it," said Mirai. "It's amazing to finally pair it with a face. I never would have guessed him looking like that."

"Always a shocking experience. Listeners manufacture their own mental images of everyone they hear on the radio based on any number of factors. The man speaking through the microphone may be someone you actually know, but if he alters his vocal tonality even slightly, you'd never be the wiser."

They continued their stroll through the operations department and Master Control. The room was an odd mixture of modern and dated, with racks of technical equipment lined along each wall atop a carpeting from several bygone eras. In the center was a workstation console with screens for various satellite uplinks. Seated at the console was a man in a swivel chair.

"Hey, Alan," began Neal as he approached. "What happens when you put a radio in the refrigerator?"

The man sighed heavily. "You get cool music."

Neal turned to Mirai and shrugged. "Guess he's heard that one."

Alan stood to greet Mirai and then handed a clipboard to Neal.

"Plate current/plate voltage reports for the day, and the system update is finished as of twenty minutes ago. I'm going to lunch. Oh, does Rob know about the strobe light outage in Bakersfield?"

"Rob's out sick. I'm meeting the tower climber later to talk about it."

"Did you eat already? Please tell me it's not soup and sandwich day."

Neal hesitated. "Very well then. It's not soup and sandwich day."

"Damn it. Maybe I'll head over to the bistro. Anyway, see you in an hour."

As Alan left, Neal turned to Mirai. "This is it. The nerve center. Over there is where the programming logs are generated for the playlists. That's the patch cables and auto-switcher for moving the signal from one channel to another. And here at the console is where we monitor the uplink/downlink. Some of the programming you hear originates locally at stations where we have staff. The rest gets delivered via satellite from the network."

Mirai approached the workstation and listened as audio whispered from behind the soft fabric of the speakers. Each speaker played a different feed. After a minute of absorbing the cacophony, she backed away in awe. "I don't know how Alan does it," she said. "Monitoring all of those feeds simultaneously would drive me mad."

"To be fair, Alan was already a tad loopy when he started working here. But most of the time he keeps the audio on these low enough to just be background chatter. There's an alarm that will go off if we lose one of the signals. It's that red bulb next to the EAS machine."

Mirai and Neal both looked at the machine and thought of the same moment. The petrified voice of Howard Lalonde proclaiming a worldwide conspiracy had emitted directly through the device and across the entire radio network. His desperate, pleading rant had been added to the bizarre annals of broadcast history. It was history no one at PRN America wished to remember.

"Well then," Neal pivoted, "I guess we'll end the tour where we began."

Mirai followed Neal back down to the main lobby entrance where a giant wall map had been erected. The imposing image displayed the global reach of the network, a timeline of its origin to the present day, and a painted rendering of the founder positioned as to be central to the entire operation. Mirai drank in the statement, moving her vision across the country, the oceans, and multiple continents, landing finally on the portrait of Lalonde, and the soft, visible brushstrokes that composed his regal visage.

"Chaos and order…" she said under her breath.

"What's that?"

Mirai took a step back from the wall. "It's beautiful. Who was the artist who did your father's portrait?"

Neal squinted at the painting but came to no conclusions. "I'm embarrassed to say I don't know. No one's ever asked me that before."

Mirai shrugged. "Just wondering. It's very impressive. You must be so proud to be a part of all this."

Neal slid his hands into his pockets. He glanced down at his shoes and nodded distantly. "Yeah. It's…" The incomplete sentence lingered and then dissipated without resolution. They looked at each other, flashed a smile, and knew that nothing more on the matter needed to be said.

"I should probably head back over to the photoshoot. Thank you so much for the tour, the food, and for being so kind about me falling asleep on your couch."

"Happy to help. You sure you're feeling up to the walk back?"

"I should be fine now. But if you hear about some Burmese chick passed out in your parking lot, you can assume it's me."

Neal tilted his head. "Wait… Burmese… I thought you were Japanese?"

Mirai laughed. "Oh, yeah, sorry… I was still a little out of it when you said that earlier. No, my name is Japanese, but my nationality is Burmese. My parents were from Myanmar. I have no idea why they named me Mirai."

"Interesting," Neal said, a gossamer of light twinkling in his eye. "You're Burmese and from Florida? You wouldn't happen to know a Kan Thura, would you?"

The question was posed in the form of a disinterested laugh. Yet the instant the name had been uttered, Neal watched as the smile melted off of Mirai's nonplussed face. Her wordless reaction sent a chill down his spine. They both continued gazing at each other, thoroughly stunned; Neal—thinking of his father's semilucid request to help him expunge an old guilt—and Mirai—thinking only of the man who had saved her on the airplane, who had administered the Potion in her hour of need, and who probably went by the name of Osiris.

"*Kan Thura?*" Mirai stressed. "How in the world do you know Kan Thura?"

Neal's mouth went dry as he processed her reaction. "I… I mean… I don't. But my father does… or did. He asked me… sometime back… to fly down to Florida and meet up with this guy."

"For what purpose?"

His tongue fumbled his first attempt, so on his second try he enunciated slowly. "To… tell him that he… wishes to apologize."

Mirai's stare intensified. "Apologize for *what?*"

"Honestly, I have no idea. Dad wouldn't tell me. But it seemed vitally important to him at the time. I kinda promised that I would try and locate the guy. Is… it a problem?"

Stepping away from the wall, from Neal, and from the portrait of the founder, Mirai pressed her hand against her forehead and tried to ignore the sudden onset of dizziness. *Howard Lalonde warned about Ad Ordinem… Kan Thura is part of Emblem… Apologize for something in the past… This can't be a coincidence.*

Mirai spun around in her flip-flops. "I… don't even know where to begin in trying to explain how I came to meet Kan Thura. But in answer to your question, yes, I've met him. He lives in Miami."

Neal blinked incredulously and ran his hand through the curls in his hair. "I mean, is it possible that there's more than one Kan Thura living in Florida? Dad said I would find him in Cocoa Beach."

"No," she said firmly, "it's him. It has to be him. The connection between them can't be pure chance."

"What connection?"

Mirai looked into Neal's ocean-blue eyes and said, "The

connection of a secret society, a subversive organization trying to stop them from within, and an old broadcaster who somehow knew way more about it than anyone should."

Neal parted his lips to protest. Mirai took a step forward and, after shooting a glance toward the reception desk, lowered the volume of her voice. "I'll introduce you to Kan Thura. But before I do, you need to have a chat with Dear Old Dad. Find out exactly how he came to hear about the world's oldest secret society."

Reflexively, Neal matched the timbre of Mirai's tone. "You mean, Ad Ordinem? That's all nonsense. Dad was crazed out of his mind when he said that stuff on the air. The man is not responsible for himself. He has dementia."

With the dizziness increasing, Mirai suddenly felt faint. She sighed angrily and turned toward the pair of glass double doors. Neal followed her outside. "Mirai, please wait… I didn't mean to imply…"

She had stopped. Neal halted from behind and wondered why she was looking upward, above the top of the tree line, at the weathered brick apartment building just beyond the corporate park. They blinked in unison upon reading the billboard that was perched high over the city: one with bold white lettering against a black background.

"*Is This the End of the World?*" Mirai said.

Neal felt his shoulders begin to slouch. He didn't resist it. The message on the old sign had been facing the PRN America headquarters for months. Just when Neal had finally learned how to ignore it, the Jumbotron of Alexander added fresh mayhem to what had otherwise once been a scenic view. When the young woman who had fallen asleep on the lobby sofa turned back toward him, she had the glow of sunlight haloing her face.

"Talk to your father, Neal. Then meet me in Miami. I'll take you to see Kan Thura."

A solo crack of lightening electrified the sky. The subsequent thunder reverberated along the street level. Rain fell in a torrential shroud, masking the intersection where the voxhall stood. From underneath the soft-top canopy of her convertible, Mirai gazed through the windshield as the wipers combatted the downpour.

"There's nothing like a Florida thunderstorm," Neal mused from the passenger seat with his carry-on luggage nestled in the back. "The plane barely beat the storm system. Incidentally, thanks for picking me up from the airport."

Mirai tapped her fingers against the steering wheel. She had heard Neal speaking, but his words had not registered. Her mind was preoccupied with an odd sensation in her upper right arm. It had been nagging her for over an hour. Part pinpricks and part numbness, the sensation was undeniably seeping into her muscles and working its way down toward her elbow.

She nodded, not knowing to what she was agreeing, and unbuckled her seat belt. "He serves at this voxhall. You can talk with him in there."

Beneath the protection of an umbrella, Mirai and Neal walked quickly across the street and into the shelter of the building's anteroom. The stained-glass windows flickered followed by another jolt of cloth-tearing thunder. Mirai wiped her ankle boots against the doormat before entering. She then pressed her left hand up to her right shoulder. A firm squeeze created a paradox of increased pain and relief.

"Good morning. Are you here to partake?" asked the female attendant.

"We are," said Mirai, solemnly.

"You may go in."

The grand room was dimly lit, as always, yet something about the exterior storm gave the interior a pinkish hue. There was no waiting line leading to the platform. Mirai blinked and tried to identify a familiar face on the stage.

"Up here," she whispered to Neal, who followed curiously from behind.

A lone voxroy stood facing the sanctum. He was preparing the

Potion in the decanter, the ethereal blue liquid sloshing while he moved. From the aisle, Mirai felt her heart begin to palpitate. Even before the man had turned toward her, she knew he was not their target audience.

"Excuse me," she said, "I'm wondering if Kan Thura is here today?"

The voxroy gazed at her for a moment. It was the kind of gaze one gives when sizing up how to address a problem. A gossamer light seemed to have permanently settled into the frames of his spectacles. Mirai could see herself within the lenses.

"You've… visited us before, yes?"

The structure of his statement was that of a question, leaving Mirai to wonder why she felt as if he had uttered a command. "I've been here several times."

The man smiled cordially. "I see. It appears that our last voxroy did not set the proper expectations with you as to how things operate here, and for that—on behalf of the voxhall—I apologize."

Mirai sensed her fingers starting to slip from her right arm. The voxroy continued, "It is part of our tradition here that those seeking to partake in the Potion must be members of the voxhall. It's a simple, relatively effortless task of reading some documentation and then taking our Oath."

"Your what?"

"Nothing complex, I assure you. It states that you've read our founding principles and agree to live your life according to their truth. That act grants you membership in this voxhall and unlimited access to the Potion."

Mirai shook her head in confusion. Although she wanted anything else, she was certain that the crestfallen look on her face was beginning to show through, and would soon be replaced by outright desperation. "No… I… see, I'm not really ready for any of that yet. I just wish to partake in the Potion as it's been helping my…" Her sudden recollection of Neal's presence left the last word dangling. Quickly pivoting her mental talk track, she said, "Helping my muscle aches. They get unbearable from time to time."

The voxroy intoned sympathetically, "I understand. Please know, we would welcome you into this voxhall at any time. We just need to follow protocol, and one of those protocols is having you be a member. We can step off to the side and get you going with some reading materials, and afterward we can schedule a time for you to come back and take the Oath."

"An… oath? Stating what, exactly?"

"Your allegiance to the spiritual authority of this voxhall."

Mirai's grasp slipped completely from her arm. Her left hand dropped to her side as if it was numb. But it was not numb, just defeated. The voxroy added, "It's all orthodox, I assure you. Most of the words in the Oath are taken directly from the Worthy Book."

This can't be happening, thought Mirai.

"If that's not in alignment with your beliefs, there's a voxhall across town that uses a different book. Either way, you'll need to take the Oath before partaking in the Potion again."

Mirai shifted glances away from the voxroy and onto the glass decanters stationed atop the sanctum. The fluid sparkled from the pinpoints of recessed light. It was right in front of her, mere inches out of reach, yet eternally inaccessible under current policies.

"Shall I give you the welcome packet to take home?"

Mirai bit her lower lip and attempted a subtle grin. "Look, I respect your practices here. I do. It's just that… So… so you're saying that if I read the pamphlets and recite the Oath, I can partake again? Is that all?"

The voxroy bristled within his garments. "It nearly goes without saying, young lady, but there is a crucial element to this process I think you're overlooking."

"Belief," Mirai breathed, bordering on inaudible.

"Naturally," the voxroy replied.

She closed her eyes as the pain in her body grew. A simmering panic was starting to emerge. "Is Kan Thura here? We came to speak with him on an urgent matter."

The voxroy interpreted her inquiry as an attempt to sidestep his authority. His evaporating grin signaled that fact. Maintaining his composure, he said, "I'm afraid that Mr. Thura has been transferred. He'll be serving a different voxhall in another community."

This time, Neal interjected. "Transferred where?"

"Unfortunately, that information is beyond what I can share. I do wish you'd take the welcome packet with you. You'll see that membership isn't nearly as daunting as it sounds."

"Please," said Mirai, "isn't there someone else I could talk to… ask about an exemption? Occasionally there must be accommodations allowed, for those… un…" She hesitated while straining to find the right word. "—un*able*… to proceed with the Oath but who still wish— need—to partake."

The voxroy squared his jaw. Somehow his face remained oddly agreeable. "The only reason I can think of for someone to be *unable* to take the Oath, is due to a fundamental lack of belief in the teachings of the voxhall. If that's the case, then that person has no business partaking of the Potion. Do you understand?"

Mirai stared into the eyes of the voxroy and hopelessly held his gaze. Within his green eyes was a startling lack of pragmatism. There would be no negotiation, no exceptions to the rule, no allowances of any kind. The man looked down at her as if she were a threat, and her iconoclasm would not be tolerated. Mirai thought about explaining that betraying her own principles would cause her equal harm. That the reciting of an oath had most likely been done by hundreds, even thousands, inside the hallowed voxhalls of the world, without so much as a critical thought as to their own sincerity. Yet she was at least being honest about her disbelief, and for it, was being relegated to the position of a societal outcast. It would be useless to ask for mercy. Empathy had no place in a system created eons before anyone currently living. In order to partake of the Potion, she had to be a member, and in order to be a member, she had to state words from an oath she did not believe, lifted from books that had torn two families apart.

A man convinced against his will is of the same opinion still. The old adage entered her mind with the force of a locomotive. The instant she remembered it, the expression on the voxroy's face made her inexplicably certain that he had thought of it too.

Without bidding either of them farewell, he clasped his hands together and swung himself back toward the sanctum. The conversation was over. Mirai stood as if some part of her had just been dismembered. A wave of crushing disappointment tried to overwhelm her. She suppressed it and looked at Neal. "I… I'm sorry… I thought that—"

"Don't worry about it," Neal assured, and led her back to the anteroom. He opened the umbrella as they exited the weighty doors of the voxhall and stepped out into the pouring rain.

"Dad couldn't remember telling me about a Kan Thura or an apology," Neal said as they walked, "but he did originally say that this guy would be up in Cocoa Beach. Plus, he made that mistake on-air about our new station covering the Space Coast. For whatever reason, that area's been on his mind. I think we should check it out."

Mirai agreed as they reached her car. "It's about a three-hour trip. Not too bad, I suppose."

Neal smirked. "Just enough time for you to catch me up on everything you know about Ad Ordinem."

Another highway marker for Interstate 95 passed overhead while Neal scrolled through the message history on Mirai's phone. His eyes darted across the lines of text while Mirai occasionally glanced over from the driver's seat. After reading the final message, he slowly lowered the phone to his lap and stared out the passenger window.

"Is that it…? Is that everything?" he asked.

Mirai exhaled. "Basically. David was impersonating this Emloch persona since January and even joined me on the wild goose chases he himself was orchestrating."

"What happened when you confronted him about it?"

"I didn't. I'm too scared to. I just messaged him that we needed to take a break. That I was overwhelmed and needed some time to myself."

"Ouch—I've received *that* text from a woman before. How'd he take it?"

Mirai pointed back at her phone and Neal pivoted over to the thread with David. "Civil," he said. "Devastated, but civil."

"Yeah," Mirai mumbled.

"What do you think he was trying to accomplish?"

"I can't imagine."

"Did he genuinely love you?"

Mirai glanced away to the side mirror and merged the vehicle into the left lane. After a few seconds of discontent, she flipped the blinker and merged back into the center. "You'd have to ask him."

Neal set her phone in the console and clicked his tongue. Another mile passed before he felt the courage to broach the next topic. "I have to tell you, Mirai, I'm astonished you survived that airplane attack. You and your sister. It's just… well, frankly, it's just not the kind of story people live to tell. I can understand your determination to find whoever that was who rescued you."

"It was Kan Thura." She nodded. "I'm positive."

Neal's nod was less certain. "I'm looking forward to meeting him."

Sunlight broke through the storm clouds while the convertible increased speed along the coastal highway. It moved with intention, reflecting the nervous energy of its passengers. There was a palpable sense within the cabin that whatever awaited them at the destination was time sensitive. Like a moving target, the bullseye resided on one man, yet what it would mean to hit it was something neither Mirai nor Neal had fully determined.

The quest for answers propelled them through the lengthy drive. Upon seeing the first interstate sign for Cocoa Beach, Neal withdrew his own phone and placed it on the dashboard. Navigational directions pulsed to life.

"Where are we going?" asked Mirai.

"Someplace I've never been. The PRN America transmitter in Winchel."

The highway exit led them along a series of side roads. Towns with smaller populations guided them inland, until off in the distance was a radio mast anchored to the earth by a fleet of guy-wires. The white-and-red structure pinnacled high into the air, seeming as if it were ready for launch. Various protuberances stuck out from the steel lattices of the broadcast antenna, and at its base was an aluminum shed.

"You can pull over next to that fence," said Neal, pointing.

The patch of off-road land was mostly gravel, with sporadic bushes and plants doing their best to reclaim the territory. When they got out of the vehicle, Mirai directed her eyes straight up, and felt a sudden and frenetic wave of vertigo. "Wow," she said, looking back down, "the stationary mast against the moving clouds really does a number on me."

"One of the many reasons I've never climbed one of these things." Neal laughed. "I have a fear of heights from both top and bottom."

He removed the padlock on the chain-link fence and then proceeded to find the right key for the shed door. "General manager key," he said, holding it up. "Opens almost any door owned by the network."

Mirai widened her eyes sarcastically. "Wow. How many girls has that pickup line landed you?"

"Surprisingly few."

Neal worked the key until he heard a click from the latch. The structure emitted a brief shimmy as they entered. A motion-sensor bulb buzzed to life above their heads. Lining the walls were racks of broadcast equipment, audio monitors, compressors, and indicator lights blinking at random intervals.

"Hard to believe that this is all it takes to transmit a signal across a town, isn't it?" asked Neal.

Mirai let herself wander for a moment before responding. "It's less than you'd imagine until you see all of the fine-tuning and precision that went into the work. Then it seems like there's actually quite a bit to it."

"Just like in a painting."

Mirai turned back to Neal and nodded. "My thoughts exactly."

On a desk in the corner sat a computer and printer. When Neal tapped a random key on the keyboard, the monitor awoke and flashed an askew image before self-correcting. "Man, this computer is a relic."

Mirai looked over Neal's shoulder as he bent forward next to the rolling chair. The screen illuminated their faces as they watched the audio conversion represented through a series of waveform lines. Neal reached his hand out to one of the racks and slowly turned a dial. The sound of the announcer's voice softened the edges of the room.

"… several thousand people a day from the Mesa Revival. The sudden exodus has puzzled some locals, who wonder if the mass gathering has finally run its course…"

"What's he talking about?" asked Mirai.

"… but officials insist they're simply making the encampments safer for emergency vehicles and aid workers to provide much-needed humanitarian services. No statement has yet been released from Alexander or the Preserve."

Neal shook his head as the announcer moved onto other news. "I'm not sure."

Next to the computer lay a binder with considerable heft. Mirai turned the cover and began examining the pages. On each document was a series of readouts, some printed, others handwritten. At the bottom corner of each page was a date and a signature. Neal glanced down and followed the white nail polish on Mirai's forefinger as it tapped the loops of the operator's name.

"Bruce Donovan," they muttered in unison.

"Does that ring a bell?" Neal asked.

Mirai thought for a moment. "I don't believe so. Why?"

"Look at these dates," Neal said, turning pages with increasing speed until he had nearly scanned the whole ream. "These maintenance logs go back to before I was born. Same guy listed throughout as network engineer. Yet I've never heard of a Bruce Donovan."

"Maybe he left the company before you became operations manager."

Neal squinted. "Then why is the most recent entry a week ago?"

Mirai looked over the binder herself and nodded methodically, as if her mind was piecing together something else entirely. "Also, look at the signature itself. It's evolved over time."

"What do you mean?"

Turning from page to page, she said, "The Bruce Donovan in the past is not the same signer as this Bruce Donovan, and the most recent Bruce Donovan signatures don't look like either of the other two. They're all different people."

"How can you be sure?"

"The slants, the loops, the way he stresses the capital letters. It's all consistent for a period of years and then drastically changes. I see three distinct signature traits and none of them could be from the same signer."

Neal chuckled to himself. "Your graphology analysis is pretty good."

Mirai shrugged and snatched a pen out of a tin mug. She signed the name *Bruce Donovan* on a notepad and turned it toward Neal.

"Holy mother of God," he mumbled, "that's a perfect forgery."

Mirai winked. "It's not forgery if it's art."

Neal backed away from the computer and flashed a worried grin. "Thanks for that terrifying lesson, Miss McGarry. Still though, I wonder who this guy is. All network engineers report directly to me. Even people we contract for rotational work. Huh… Bruce Donovan…"

Shaking his head as he dialed, Neal pressed his phone up to his ear and asked the receptionist to transfer him to bookkeeping. Mirai continued thumbing through various folders as Neal said, "Kelsey, it's me. Would you look up paystubs for a Bruce Donovan? What? I'm at the Winchel station. Yes, in beautiful sun-kissed Florida. What do you mean what am I… I'm sweating my balls off inside a makeshift shed— Bruce Donovan, Kelsey. Yes, I'll hold."

Neal rolled his eyes while Mirai withheld a laugh. When Kelsey returned to the line, Neal placed the call on speakerphone. "Yeah, according to the database, Bruce Donovan's been an independent contractor for the southern region for almost forty years."

Neal's gasp left his mouth wide open. He blinked repeatedly while trying to make sense of that which was incongruent. "Are… are you telling me this guy's been on the payroll for four decades as a subcontractor?"

Kelsey paused before confirming Neal's statement. "It would seem so."

"Who hired him?"

"That's a question for HR."

Neal sighed heavily. "Would you mind, Kels?"

"One minute."

Mirai whispered, "Remember, we may not be talking about one man here. Those signatures vary over time."

Neal nodded as the HR manager answered the line. "Mr. Lalonde. Hope you're doing well," the man said, his voice more chipper than the situation warranted. "How can I assist?"

"Bruce Donovan… southern region… independent contractor who apparently has been on the payroll since the first ice age. What can you tell me about him?"

The insistent clicking of keys led to a thoughtful silence as the manager pulled up the records. "Not much, I'm afraid. We don't keep extensive records on nonemployees, vendors, etcetera. All I see here is that Mr. Donovan was kept on a sort of retainer to perform routine maintenance and recordkeeping for the Winchel station, going almost all the way back to the network's founding."

"Manage the… But we already have a chief engineer for all PRN America stations east of the Mississippi River and south of the Mason–Dixon line, plus a local manager for all Florida stations."

"It seems that they wanted some overlap."

"Who did? Who initially contracted him?"

"That would be your father."

Neal sighed again. "Of course it was."

"Also, and forgive me if this is redundant information, but the notes never mention the southern region. It looks like this Mr. Donovan was contracted for the Winchel station only."

The hand holding up the phone sank ever so slightly against the weight. A look of utter bewilderment caused several lines to manifest in Neal's forehead. His blue eyes locked onto Mirai's brown eyes. In his gaze, she could sense that something was troubling him beyond the wasteful spending.

"Is there anything else, Mr. Lalonde?"

"You… wouldn't happen to have a phone number for this guy?"

The HR manager provided the digits and Neal ended the call. Dialing with his thumb, he punched the numbers into the screen as if his phone was personally responsible for his irritation. Several rings passed by before a gruff voice answered.

"Hello?"

"Hi. Is this Bruce Donovan?"

A long hesitation built gradually into an unconvincing reply. "Speaking."

Neal narrowed his eyes at Mirai. "This is Neal Lalonde. I'm the operations manager for Palisades Radio Network."

The man cleared his throat. "Oh, uh, hi there."

"Forgive the interruption, but I'm doing some checkups on the Florida stations, and frankly… I don't believe you and I have had the pleasure of meeting."

"Yeah…" the man droned, "about that. I'm more of what you'd call a seasonal worker. I just fill in whenever the regional engineer gets too much on his plate. You know what I mean?"

Neal squared his jaw. "What I know, is that you've been signing the station logs for forty years but don't sound a day over fifty. Were you some sort of child prodigy in engineering?"

The man chuckled nervously. "No, no. Nothing like that. I'll be honest with you, Mr. Lalonde. My name's not really Bruce Donovan. See, I only started filling in ten or so years ago to do the weekly checks on Winchel. When I was brought on, I was asked to keep using the previous guy's name on the log sheets. I know… it's technically illegal. But this is super part-time for me, and I figured, what's the harm? No one ever even looks at those sheets."

Neal tried to rein in his incredulity as he said, "You're telling me that a decade ago, someone from PRN put you on the payroll to perform the weekly Winchel station checks, and asked you to forge someone else's name and signature?"

"I'm afraid so. Funny thing is, it was only supposed to be a temporary thing. Was told this would help cover a hiring gap without a lot of extra paperwork. But then, no one new was ever hired, and I was never told to stop using the old name. So… months turn into years, and eventually—here we are."

"Who authorized this?"

The engineer let out a shameful sigh. "Look, I couldn't very well say no to the man. He is, after all, *the man*."

Neal blinked in confusion. "What are you talking about?"

"It was your father, Mr. Lalonde. He was the person who set this whole deal up."

The call ended and Neal bit his lower lip. With furrowed brows and a pensive stare, he tore three different log sheets out of the binder and stuffed them into his pocket. "Let's go."

"Go where?"

Neal shut off the computer and shuffled through the keys on his key ring. "City Hall. We can ask about Kan Thura too. But first—the actual Bruce Donovan—I wanna know who this joker was."

"Kan who?"

Mirai and Neal stood opposite a woman who managed the city records office, separated by a faux marble countertop and a computer monitor. The woman was older and had the kind of face that was impervious to surprise. Neal cleared his throat and made a second attempt at the name.

"Kan Thura. I need to know if he's a resident in Brevard County."

A series of thorough, albeit unenthusiastic, searches from the clerk resulted in a blank stare as she delivered the news. "I'm afraid not. Any derivations you'd like to try?"

"We'll come back to him," Neal said, while retrieving his

identification and press card from his wallet. "I'd like to see the licensure for a Bruce Donovan. He's a contract engineer for Palisades Radio Network."

A volley of clicks from the keyboard preceded a momentary pause from the clerk. "I have it here," she said nonchalantly. "Bruce Donovan, formerly of 2824 South Poplar Street, Winchel, Florida. Moved out of state thirty-nine years ago."

"I'm sorry?"

"Yeah, license expired then too. Take a look."

The clerk pivoted the screen toward Mirai and Neal. The image of the engineer appeared on the lower right-hand corner of the document scan. He was once a man in his early thirties, with light blond hair and green eyes. His smile was genuine; his rounded face—content with life as it came. He had worked for the network before Neal was born. A footnote in the saga of a broadcast empire.

"There's no other Bruce Donovans in the area?" Neal asked.

"Not with the credentialing you'd be interested in."

Neal tapped his fingers on the desk and shot a glance at Mirai. It was at that point when the clerk cocked her neck. "Although it does seem like we have a duplicate license for some reason."

"What do you mean?"

The woman pulled up two documents on the screen and arranged them side by side. Both copies of the license had the same name, same address, and same credentials. The dissimilarities began with the issued dates, one a year after the other. The next discrepancy was the signature, vastly different than the original yet identical in nature to the second log sheet Neal had ripped from the binder. The last difference was the photo. A man with blond hair and green eyes stared back at them, but with a much more gaunt face. The jawline was straighter, the forehead more pronounced, and the razor-thin smile caused a flood of childhood memories to come rushing in as a deluge from the recesses of Neal's mind.

"Is that..." began Mirai, her eyes squinting. "It sort of looks like..."

"Dad," Neal said, the muscles in his face seeming to contort around his eye sockets. "That's… that's my… father."

The two gazed at the image for several more seconds as a cavalcade of questions marched across their consciousnesses. Neal blinked repeatedly before moving in closer to the screen. The license was for a chief engineer, living at an address in Winchel, Florida, who at a glance appeared somewhat similar to the original license holder, but who on further inspection was clearly the founder of the network— Howard Lalonde.

"What the hell is this?" Neal asked. He continued absorbing the screen, his vision unable to pull away from the incongruity of his father's face on a stranger's name.

"Is that Howard's handwriting?" Mirai asked, spreading out the second log sheet in front of them. Upon examination, Neal turned away from the clerk and fished out his phone.

"Yeah," he said while dialing, "I realize it now. It's definitely his."

"Who are you calling?"

"Dad?" Neal said into the device. "Dad, can you hear me? It's Neal. I have a question for… What? I… I don't know about… Dad, listen to me for a second. Does the name Bruce Donovan bring anything to mind? Bruce… Donovan. Your signature is on the log sheets down here at the Winchel tower… Yes, I'm down here right now. *Why?* Because you asked me to come down here and find someone named Kan Thura, which I'm sure you…" Neal hesitated, sighed, and rubbed his hand over his face. "Which I'm sure you don't remember."

Mirai watched sympathetically as Neal tried to steer the conversation with Howard. The blank stare on the clerk's face remained unchanged.

"Dad… why were you signing log sheets as Bruce Donovan after the real guy left? Why did you apply for a license to work down in Florida using someone else's credentials, and then later, authorize some yokel to continue the charade for years afterward? I mean, you've essentially been making payments to yourself via this contractor who stopped working for us after year one. All of this is fraud, Dad. The network could get in a lot of trouble for that. You understand what I'm… Dad? Are you still there?"

Mirai could tell from Neal's expression that the call had been ended. When he eventually pulled the phone from his ear, his look of consternation intensified.

"Good goddamn," Neal snapped.

Inside the visage of his outburst, Mirai could see a lifetime of frustration boiling to the surface. She watched as he paced the records office in search of his composure. It was evident that he would not find it there.

"Is there anywhere else you could check for Kan Thura?" Mirai asked the clerk. "It's vital we locate him."

The woman was unconvinced that running the same search again would garner different results, but she acquiesced and performed the rote operations a second time. Her monolithic face gave Mirai the answer.

"No Kan Thura," the clerk said flatly. "Only a Kan Donovan."

Neal instantly stopped pacing. Mirai sensed her lips gradually opening. The clerk pivoted the screen back around and pointed at the residency data. "See? Bruce Donovan, 2824 South Poplar Street, Winchel, Florida; other occupants: Chaw Donovan, Kan Donovan."

The office remained perfectly still for a moment, as if the whole building was taking a steadying breath. Neal tilted his head a bit and shot a glance at Mirai. If it were possible to be grasping on to someone merely by their gaze, the look held between the two was that very phenomenon.

"Chaw… and Kan," Neal whispered. "Are… are those both…"

"Burmese names, yes," said Mirai.

In a methodical, tortured movement back toward the desk, Neal placed his hands on the countertop and asked, "Is there a photo… of these two people, living at *that* address, with this… man?"

Only beginning to piece together what Mirai and Neal had already concluded, the clerk's face finally registered a slight frown. As the woman searched, Mirai stood next to Neal and momentarily contemplated holding his hand. Something about the pained look in his eyes and the rigid way he was maintaining his stance made her ultimately decide against it.

"Nothing in the official records," the clerk said, wielding the mouse with purpose, "however, one search result online brings back a photo that might interest you."

The woman double-clicked on an image and it filled the screen. It was a scan of a local newspaper article from years prior. The top caption stated that the picture had been taken at a festival along Cocoa Beach. Attendees filled a boardwalk, all talking, or laughing, or eating, each face frozen within the confines of a candid moment. It was the center of the image that demanded attention, as a couple stood facing the camera, each holding an ice-cream cone, all smiling the awkward smiles of being ambushed by a street photographer.

The man was standing next to a woman of Asian descent whose white headband barely reached the crest of the man's shoulder. Between them, nestled in the arm of the woman, a baby stared at the camera with a gleeful essence. Below the picture was a caption.

Cocoa Beach Pier: The Donovan Family enjoying the festival— Bruce, Chaw & their son, Kan.

"Oh my God," Neal muttered, appearing as if he was about to become ill. "That's… my father… with another… The… the… *Donovan* family?"

Mirai placed her hand on his arm. "Neal—"

"Don't," he said, jerking away from her, the clerk, and the office, and briskly shoving his way through the exit with a cyclonic fury.

The sidelight glass shook while the last vibrations between the door and the jamb ceased. Mirai stood at the counter uncertain of what to do. When her body language appeared as if she was about to go after Neal, the clerk reached out her hand and gave Mirai's wrist a gentle squeeze.

"I've seen stuff like this happen before," the woman said. "Best to give him a minute alone."

Mirai nodded and forced herself to look anywhere but at the door. Her eyes drifted downward until all she could see was the three pages torn from the binder. She set her fingers on the first log sheet and turned it over; same type of information, different date. The second piece of paper was no different. Only when she reached for the third did a blaring contrast capture her attention.

That doesn't say Bruce Donovan.

The cursive signature was straighter, more diminutive, and had a slash across a letter she assumed was a lowercase *T*. The first name started with an *M*. The surname almost certainly started with an *S*.

"What do you think that says?" Mirai asked, as a slight tremor filled the hand turning the page around.

The clerk took a passing glance and declared, "Perhaps... Mark Stone?"

The oxygen seemed to evaporate from Mirai's lungs, from the office space, and for all she knew, from the rest of planet earth. A bolt of wildly conflicting sensations charged through her slender frame, leaving her lightheaded and chilled. The brightness in the room suddenly seemed blinding, the weight of her body too great for her buckling knees. She gazed at the clerk, feeling extremely exposed. It was in that condition Mirai finally asked, "Can you check... to see if there's a... Mark Stone..."

"There's gonna be a lot, sweetie," the woman protested. "That's a common name. The cross-referencing would take—"

"Not online," Mirai corrected. "Just in the database. As a licensed contractor. For PRN America."

The clerk shrugged and entered the search. Her fingers flew across the keys and then came to an unobstructed halt. "That's unusual. The record is locked."

"Locked? As in..."

"Yeah. I've only ever seen that when it's a high-level official and the search requires additional clearance. This guy isn't a federal government employee, is he?"

Mirai blinked. "Not that I'm aware of."

"Well, maybe..." said the woman, trying something else. "Nope. Whoever this is, his record is above my pay grade. Need a password to access."

"A password." Mirai stated it not as a question, but as an inkling.

The clerk then chuckled. "On that note, I'd say we're done here. Unless you happen to have the luckiest guess in the world…" Her sentence trailed off the instant she caught the piercing radiance in Mirai's eyes. It was a stare of determination. Of suddenly finding oneself on the verge of a breakthrough and savoring the euphoria. Of having faced tremendous obstacles and peril in order to achieve the confidence and the right to state it.

Poising her hands against the faux marble surface, Mirai drew in a steadying breath and uttered the word that made her heart palpitate.

"Osiris."

CHAPTER 11
GIMBAL LOCK

"Omni. Its limits are beyond your imagination."

Carys McGarry pressed her hands together and did a small leap. It was her second consecutive viewing of the advertisement. What emanated from the laptop screen was a radiance and an authority. Her face, her voice, and the state-of-the-art virtual graphics gave the video a gravitas only surpassed by the Omni logo itself.

Carys shut her eyes and ran her fingers through her blonde hair. A buoyant smile refused to be censored. She stood on the balls of her feet and pivoted around to face her parents. "Well? What do you think?"

Jason and Valerie stood behind their daughter in the kitchen. A few seconds of silence ended abruptly when Jason made the first attempt at a reply but was accidentally cut off by Valerie.

"Wow… remarkable," she said, her mouth and her face somehow misaligned. "I'm just… surprised… by the turnaround time. You only recorded it last week."

"Same," interjected Jason. "Absolutely shocked by their speed."

"My agent said they never get an ad campaign together this quickly. I'm the rare exception."

"You certainly are," replied Jason.

Carys embraced them both and turned back around to watch the clip once more. As the scene opened, Carys was jolted awake in her dorm-room bed, suddenly frazzled by her mental to-do list. "Omni—check my calendar, recent messages, and social media alerts, then prioritize everything that needs to be done today."

"Sure thing, Carys. I have it all right here."

"Perfect. Get to it."

The ad continued with her rushing to shower, do her hair and makeup, and choose an outfit for the morning. When she reached for her phone again, the checklist was done. Carys smiled and faced the viewing audience. "All emails sent, all messages and social media comments responded to, all in my style of communication and using the logic of my personality type. Plus, who doesn't despise making phone calls? Omni takes care of that for me. Through speech recognition technology, it mimics my vocal patterns to leave voicemails and make appointments with receptionists, saving me time and anxiety. If there's a task Omni can't do, just tell it to learn how—and presto—the code writes itself. It's the only AI that frees up my time for *actually living*. And speaking of… I'd better get to class."

The features of the program filled the screen, overwhelming the senses with its capabilities. Pulse waves of information appeared and vanished at the speed of thought. It was the application to end all menial tasks. The ultimate delegation tool. A partition between thinking and action.

In the final frames of the ad, Carys's face reentered the image and smiled warmly. "Omni. Its limits are beyond your imagination."

In the McGarry kitchen, her hand gently closed her laptop screen. Carys nodded intently as her mind envisioned the future. Her words came as less of a whisper and more of a prayer. "They said my face will be everywhere. Billboards, television, magazines, online ads, anyplace you've ever seen a promotion, you're going to see me. This is it. My big break." She then turned back to her parents and reached out for another embrace. "I owe it all to you both. Thank you for believing in my crazy modeling dream. I promise… I'll make you proud."

She walked out of the kitchen as if wandering through her own daze. Jason and Valerie said nothing as they stared at the laptop.

Outside the windows, the early evening sunlight was sinking through the tree branches and casting a fragmented orange hue against the McGarrys. They continued their stances, affixed to the floor, speaking not a word to the other nor to themselves. Just when the silence was about to become unbearable, Valerie left the room and sought refuge in the den. Jason moved slowly back to the countertop and continued chopping vegetables in preparation for dinner.

"Hi, Dad," came a sullen voice from the back door.

Jason flinched and turned around to see Mirai standing in the kitchen. He exhaled into a chuckle and said, "Geez, you got the jump on me there, kiddo. Didn't even hear you come in."

Mirai nodded silently.

Jason continued chopping but then hesitated. "Where were you all day?"

The light from the windows seemed harsher than it had been a moment prior. Mirai stood ablaze in the fiery shadow of her own silhouette. "Out," was her solo response.

The sound of the blade snapping against the cutting board matched the pacing of her steps as she approached the dinette set and casually sat down. Her back was to the wall. She spoke to her father's back from the other side of the room.

"Is Mom here?"

"Uh… yeah. She's in the den, I think."

"Carys?"

"Upstairs. In her bedroom. Probably watching that Omni ad for the billionth time."

Jason set down the knife and collected the chopped vegetables in his hands. He tossed them into a giant bowl and then proceeded to chop the next batch. "You hungry? I'm making a chopped chicken salad. Your mom bought way too much produce at the farmer's market with Aunt Allison. We gotta use them or lose them."

Mirai looked down at her hands. They were bathed in the last rays of daylight. In her right hand were the subtle signals of duress. She thought of having been denied the Potion, but at the moment, she had more pressing things on her mind.

"Did you hear me?"

"Hmm?"

Jason smiled and reached for a cucumber. "I asked if you're hungry."

The anxious tension held within the edges of her face was rapidly melting away, leaving behind something akin to sorrow. As she parted her lips to speak, it seemed as if she was trying to savor something beyond the words; a moment, a reality, a version of the truth that would never again be relevant. In the tone of one saying goodbye, she whispered, "Yes, Dad, you know I'm always hungry."

The statement came and went, and with it, closed a chapter in her life that she knew was irrevocable. All sorrow then vanished from her expression. After drawing in a deep breath, Mirai squared her jaw and narrowed her focus in on the man to whose back she was talking.

"I know who you really are."

The rhythm of chopping ceased. Mirai could see the muscle outlines underneath Jason's polo shirt shifting to turn his body around. His eyes wore the mask of amused confusion. His tone was that of the accused.

"I don't get the joke?"

Mirai's face sobered all the more. "I don't think it's funny either."

"What's not funny?"

"That you're Mark Stone."

The name left her lips with a burst of energy. An inner tremor was starting to build. Across the room from her, Jason's reaction was unaltered. He stood appearing perplexed, all the while holding the double-bevel knife in his right hand. "Mark Stone?" he asked, a smirk pushing up his cheeks. "Who's that?"

Mirai crossed her arms against her chest. "Your real name. Before you changed it to Jason McGarry. Back when you were an engineer for PRN America and lived in Cocoa Beach."

"Mirai—what on earth are you talking about?"

Through her focused stare, she could see his consternation. It was brimming to the surface of an otherwise flawless performance. She continued, "Is that really how it's gonna be? After all our years together? All the senseless arguments and precious moments you and I in particular have shared… you're gonna keep lying to me? Isn't two decades of lies more than enough?"

Jason stabbed the knife into what remained of the cucumber and leaned his waist against the counter. A heavy sigh evoked a mild shrug. "Okay, I give up. What's the punch line here?"

Mirai straightened her posture even as she remained sitting. A bolt of fear surged through her body. With a quiet determination she breathed through the discomfort and stated, "Osiris."

For as long as Mirai could remember, her father was a peaceful man. His pacifistic nature had seeped into everything he did, into the words he chose to use, and through his nonconfrontational attitude toward life. De-escalation was his modus operandi. It was a trait she had always valued in him, even during their most tumultuous misunderstandings. Jason brought peace to any situation. He was a loving, kind, funny, and compassionate presence in a world filled with hate.

The instant after uttering the mystifying password, Mirai began to suspect that Mark Stone was none of those things.

A twisted expression transformed his rugged facial features, drawing not from malevolence, but from pain. Mirai was certain it was a pain both lived and dreaded. His lips parted into formless words. It was as if she was expected to comprehend a lifetime of conspiracy through mere telepathy. She eventually broke the silence with, "Let's unlock some doors, shall we?"

"Mirai…"

"Yes, good… let's start there. When you and Mom adopted me, my name wasn't Mirai, was it? Why did you change it? Why did you change your own name and then move down to Miami? Does Mom know? Did she change her name too? Was it because you both were on the run? Who was chasing you? Was it them?"

Jason titled his head. He was braced for something. "Them?" he asked.

Mirai knew why he had tossed the question back. The answer was on the tip of his tongue, but he needed the words to proceed from her mouth instead of his. She began massaging her right wrist and said, "Yes, of course, *them*. The group that's been terrorizing the planet. That's started a countdown clock on mankind. The one that attacked the plane and almost cost me and Carys our lives. The one at war with itself and the one you joined before I was ever born. Yes—I'm talking about Ad Ordinem. The secret society you wrote about in your journal. 'Evermore and evermore.'"

A radiating panic filled Jason's eyes as he straightened himself, seemingly poised to begin a sprint.

"Is Ad Ordinem trying to find you?" she asked.

There was a speed and a dexterity with which Jason sailed across the kitchen that left Mirai stunned. At first, she wondered if he was about to flee the house. But his mad dash toward the family den sent her thoughts spiraling.

"Dad—wait!" she screamed, and bolted from behind.

"Jason… what the hell…"

Valerie's amputated sentence was the last thing Mirai heard before entering the room and witnessing the daggers coming out of Jason's eyes. With his back already turned to the built-in bookcase, he held a large, leather-bound copy of Aristotle's *Poetics*. The book was open in his hands, and between the faded covers, was a hollow space, perfect for hiding a book within a book.

"Where is it?" he demanded.

Mirai exchanged glances with Valerie, who had the look of one realizing that if things had already escalated to this level, then they were all past the point of no return. Her mother's stare was that of unadulterated horror, the horror that Mirai would never again look at her the same way.

"I said where is it?" Jason reiterated.

"The journal? I have it. It's in my room."

"How did you find it? Who told you to go searching for it?"

"Nobody," said Mirai, suddenly discerning that she was the one on the defensive. "I found it in a box over in Julie Laufer's bedroom."

Jason shot a brief glance at Valerie before redirecting his eyes back on Mirai. "Why… in the hell… was it over at the Laufers'?"

Mirai drew in a quick breath. "I don't know, Dad. I wish I could pick up the phone and ask her."

"This is serious, Mirai. That journal was meant to be private. It's dangerous in the wrong hands. The only reason I kept it at all was to maintain a partial record of what I witnessed. A fragmented chronicle of people I should never be tempted to revisit."

"Okay… so?"

"*So*… I need you to tell me why she took it."

"She likes old books!" Mirai exclaimed in anger. "Julie spent more time browsing our shelves than I did! We've loaned stuff to each other since we were kids! How would I know why she chose that one? She found it, borrowed it, and forgot about it. Case closed!"

Jason smacked the decoy book shut, emitting a deep thud. He placed it back on the shelf and patted his hands in the air so as to settle the mood. "Okay, let's everyone just… calm down. There's a lot to unpack here and we don't have a lot of time."

"Time? For what?" challenged Mirai.

Jason glared at her incredulously. "Time to get out of here. To evacuate. Find a new city. A new place to live. Establish new identities. *Goddamn it*—I knew Carys's career would destroy us."

"What are you talking—"

"They know!" Jason screamed, startling both Mirai and Valerie. "If you understand things up to this point, how do you not comprehend that? Ad Ordinem is onto us! We're on a short list somewhere and they're closing in! My God, if you could piece this together in one afternoon… can you imagine…"

"Jason," protested Valerie, standing halfway between her husband and her daughter. "Please… just stop for a moment. Let's… let's think this through. Perhaps it's just a coincidence. It's been months since the jet attack. Maybe they never made the connection and moved on."

"What connection?" asked Mirai.

"Be serious, Valerie," snapped Jason. "You think that measly federal investigator was enough to spook them? We know how this works. They're lying low until the coast is clear enough for them to continue the hunt. And now that the journal has been floating around… God knows where…"

"Wait, what connection?"

"… it's only a matter of time before they follow the same line of investigation Mirai did."

"Will someone please answer me? What connection?"

"The airplane attack!" cried Jason, his voice cracking from the strain. "It had nothing to do with you! They were looking for us! They *are* looking for us! They obviously weren't certain about your connection to us, but they suspected…"

Her father pressed his forehead into his palm and tried to settle his nerves. Mirai looked down at the carpet and felt the neural linkages twisting together. When the picture was complete, the devastation was nearly more than she could handle.

"We were just… bait? To try and lure you and Mom out of hiding? But why? They must know where we all live. Why don't they just come on over and knock on the door?"

"It's not…" Valerie said, trying to construct coherence out of a plethora of thoughts, "it's just not that simple. We… your father and I… we didn't allow it to be that simple."

"Why not? If they know what you look like, why were Carys and I almost burned alive?"

Valerie's shoulders slumped, and with them, something intrinsic to her being. Out of an imbroglio of falsehoods, this seemed to be the primary thing that would crush her upon confession. As tears welled in her eyes, she opened her arms for a hug but then abandoned the motion. "That's… the whole point. They don't know what we look like… anymore."

How is Carys so beautiful?

The memory invaded Mirai's thoughts with a brightness to blind the entire room. She had stood in the same spot, in the den facing the bookcase, while watching Julie sing karaoke to her favorite songs. It was a year before Julie's departure to the Preserve, back when she had not necessarily been happy, but had managed to keep her existential depression in check. The two had invited Carys to join the fun. As each girl took a turn at the microphone, the merciless heckling sent volleys of laughter throughout the house.

"How is Carys so beautiful?" Julie had asked Mirai while Carys left the room to grab a snack.

"What do you mean?"

"Are you really gonna make me say it?" Julie winced.

Mirai laughed, still oblivious to the notion. "Say what?"

Julie's sapphire eyes stole a glance over at a family portrait of the McGarrys. When she was certain Mirai was looking too, she said, "There's not enough genetic mutations in nature to explain how that bombshell came from those two people. Sorry, but you know?"

Mirai recalled shrugging, quasi-agreeing, and moving the conversation onto something else upon her sister's return. Julie never directly broached the topic again, except in passing, to compliment Carys for her remarkable and highly memorable face. Mirai, being conditioned to the way life existed inside her household, and herself being an adoptee of another ethnicity, hardly noticed the disparity.

Yet standing before her parents, with Jason and Valerie teetering on the verge of crazed panic, Mirai shifted her eyes back and forth between the couple, slowly coming to a truth she longed to reject.

"That's why there's no old photos of either of you. The story about the fire, and scars, the loss of everything from before I was adopted… none of that was true. You both… did something, had something— done to yourselves… to alter your appearances. To change your looks. Cosmetic surgery or… something drastic… something…" Mirai suddenly felt sick and reflexively swallowed. "Something—*ugly*, so that no one would ever suspect your real identities."

Jason shook his head, yet Mirai knew it was the power of denial moving his neck. Valerie again tried to make contact. She reached out her hand, but her daughter jerked away.

"Oh my God," Mirai whispered.

"I know this is a lot to take in," pleaded Jason, "but now is not the time to process it. We are all in grave danger if Ad Ordinem finds us."

"What would they do? What do they want?" she asked, combatively.

Jason's face morphed from agony back to a bone-shattering terror. "Trust me, you are not prepared for the answer to either of those questions."

"Trust you? Are you insane?"

"Mirai—"

"No!" she snapped, taking a step backward toward the room's entryway. "You don't get to tell me to trust you *ever again*. Who are you people? What were you involved with before I was adopted?"

"We're your family," Valerie choked, tears overwhelming her eyes. "We love you."

Mirai shook her head and the room began to spin.

"We made a lot of bad choices in our early adult years," added Jason. "We got involved with people who seemed virtuous on the surface yet were nothing but peddlers of bloodshed and death. We are haunted with regrets. We are haunted by our time in Ad Ordinem. We made so many mistakes and we're still living with the consequences."

"You were… terrorists?" she mouthed, the words feeling like razors leaving her lips.

"Not… No, we didn't…" Jason stumbled over his next sentence too. Mirai listened and was suddenly uncertain as to what he had just said. Their voices screeched inside her mind. *Lies… all of it… from the very beginning…*

"… we were disillusioned with everything going on in society…"

"… they had a recruiter who was very persuasive…"

"… assured us that we could leave the group at any time…"

"… became more radicalized without realizing it…"

"… if we only knew then what we know now…"

"We were almost killed because of you," shot back Mirai, her hands trembling with rage. She could feel her blood pressure pounding in her ears. The den was becoming misshapen, with the middle of the room bulging out. As her vision narrowed, she closed her eyes and tried to find a graspable center.

"We never meant to put either of you in harm's way," Valerie pleaded. "It was for your safety we uprooted our life, changed our names, permanently altered our appearance…"

"*You did all that before us,*" spat Mirai. "Carys wasn't born yet and I was just a kid. Barely four years old. Being adopted by two fugitives of justice. Two defectors from a secret society—pursued by people who would do God knows what to you if… But why then? Why adopt me at all? If you were in mortal danger, why drag me into it?"

Her memory threatened to place her back in the playroom, working on a puzzle, chatting with the man who would eventually be her father. *You have to take me home…*

"No," Mirai said, responding vocally to the torrent of emotions skirmishing in her head.

Each passing second left Jason looking increasingly disarmed. Mirai viewed him as a man out of tricks and out of time. That vulnerability made her wonder if one confession was worth another.

"Is that why you adopted me—a little Asian girl—to throw them off? And a four-year-old no less, make it seem like we've been a family for years already. Was I just a smoke screen? A diversion tactic?"

"We loved you the instant we laid eyes on you," Valerie countered. "It was about so much more than just a cover."

"But I *was* a cover. I'm waiting for either of you to be courageous enough to admit that."

Silence filled the room. Mirai nodded. Jason sighed wearily and said, "One of our many faults. We are not courageous people."

At the sudden sensation that the carpet was sliding out from underneath her feet, Mirai took a side step and sat on the arm of the sofa. She planted her face into her hands and leaned forward, peeking through her fingers at nothing but the horror in her mind's eye. It was the memory of being in the Preserve and fearing she may never escape. The scene evolved into a solitary face; it was that of the young woman seated next to a cult leader.

Julie… why aren't you here with me right now? Why did you leave? I can't do this without you… I have no one… absolutely no one…

"Mirai, please believe us…" Valerie begged.

"We can still make this work," added Jason. "After all, we are still a family."

"A family," Mirai breathed, massaging her fingertips against her forehead. "How can we be a family? How could we ever have been a family?"

Jason took a step toward her. "What do you mean?"

Mirai looked up, both to address him and as a warning not to advance further. "What I mean, is that if you both had just recently gotten drastic surgery, changed your identities, moved around until Ad Ordinem lost your trail, and presumably had no references—no employer—no history—that confirmed you were the McGarrys instead of the Stones…" She let out a bitter chuckle and said, "How in the godforsaken hell were you allowed to adopt a child?"

You have to take me home… The playroom emerged yet again. The administrator standing off-center with Jason and Valerie. The young boy in the corner who was smitten by his first crush. Mirai remembered the office-like hallways, florescent lights, cafeteria where she had eaten her meals, the dormitory where she had taken her naps. Something about the environment now seemed contradictory. *Why can't I recall the nights there? My bed, being in pajamas, someone tucking me in. I don't think I ever slept overnight in that place. And why were none of the other children ever adopted? It was always the same faces… the same happy, carefree, nourished, loved, smiling faces…*

With the blast of a floodlight, a series of fragmented images swept past her recollection. "The alphabet on the wall… the floor mats where we napped… snack time, song time, craft time… That wasn't a group home…"

"Mirai—"

"It was just a daycare. A place where I was dropped off each morning. But then… who was dropping me off and picking me up each day? Each day… before the day you two showed up?"

"We have got a lot to deal with right now and not a lot of—"

"Who was it?" Mirai asked, finding the strength in her legs to rise.

"You're getting confused, mixing up memories," Jason said. His statement fell flat, as unconvincing as his burned alias.

"No," Mirai challenged, her eyes reflecting what was rapidly piecing together in her head. "I remember it now—some of it. Enough of it to know that it *was* a daycare. Who was picking me up?"

"*We* picked you up. On the day we brought you home with us to live together as a family."

"I had never seen your faces before, and then afterward I never saw that playroom again. *Who was picking me up each day?*"

Jason's words faltered incoherently, as if he was trying to manifest a new timeline from will. "We met you... we loved you... we signed the adoption paperwork..."

"If that was a daycare..." she surmised.

"... you connected with us immediately..." Jason cried, "you wanted to come home with us..."

"Then it had to have been..."

"... your mother and I only wanted what was best for you..."

"*My mother.*"

Mirai continued to hold the word on her tongue even as she pronounced it. It struck Jason and Valerie with the force of provocation, an incendiary meant to destroy the last vestiges of a claim on their daughter's story. Their reactions confirmed Mirai's suspicion. All at once, she felt both massacred and reborn.

You have to take me home...

"My mother," she whispered, the sound verging on a whimper. Her eyes wandered the room in search of an emotional gimbal. Within the cocooned walls of her childhood home, she found nothing to correct the orientation.

"How could you do that to me? Do that... *to her?*"

"Mirai, you have to understand," Jason said, "their marriage was falling apart. The whole thing was a sham to begin with. It was no environment for a child to grow up in. For God's sake, you would have ended up going back to Myanmar! We did you a favor. We brought you into our family instead. It was a win-win for both of us."

Mirai seethed through a whisper. "You selfish bastard."

"Mirai—please..."

My poor mother... The thought gave birth to an image. Mirai determined she was in no condition to analyze whether the image was a rendering or reality. She imagined, as she always had, a beautiful Burmese woman, with dark brown eyes, the color of cocoa, and long black hair, the color of obsidian. The woman's face was round, with prominent cheekbones and a welcoming smile. It was a picture she could have painted directly onto a canvas, a stabilizing order emerging from a dense chaos.

"My mother's name is Chaw, isn't it?"

Jason's and Valerie's rambling altogether ceased. It was a choke hold beyond which lies were no longer possible. Their silence matched their stares, the last glimmers of hope seeming to drain from their eyes.

After a moment of decompression, Mirai turned away from the McGarrys and began walking out of the den.

"Where are you going?" they asked in unison.

Mirai didn't stop or look back. "To find Chaw Donovan."

The evening breeze rustled through the open cabin of the convertible. Mirai held the steering wheel with both hands. Her fingers gripped the polyurethane covering as if strangling it would increase her precision on the road. Her eyes darted across the visual landscape of the Miami skyline. No traces of sunlight remained behind the buildings. It was only the other side of the road that showcased any natural brightness as the moon hung over the ocean. Mirai gazed upon it and felt no relief from the searing pain of betrayal forming like welts on her soul. She then glanced a bit higher in the sky and felt the inexplicable dread of viewing Brubaker's Comet. The sensation brought her a perverse modicum of peace. For it was within the dread that she remembered she was still alive.

"That was *Danse macabre* by French composer Charles-Camille Saint-Saëns," said the announcer, "heard this evening on Palisades Radio Network. Thank you for joining us during our classical music hour. Now, for tonight's headlines: Attendees of the Mesa Revival continue to be leaving in droves, and there's no clear explanation as to why. Officials claim that the punishing summer heat is a likely factor, along with diminishing resources and deteriorating living conditions on the grounds. However, some gatherers have reported forced evictions by military officials, and a realignment of the event perimeters further away from the Preserve. Neither Alexander nor his press team have issued a statement…"

Chaw Donovan is my mother, thought Mirai. She laughed while a single tear escaped her eye. Placing her phone on the console stand, she tapped the call button and listened as the ringback tone blared through the speaker.

"Hello?"

"Neal—it's Mirai."

A heavy sigh crackled into the wind. "God, what a day."

"Yeah," she replied, all energy having been syphoned from her voice.

"Did you have a chat with your parents?"

"Regrettably."

"Me too. Just got off the phone with Dad. He denied everything. Claims I'm nuts. Also is sundowning about now so who the hell knows, right? Haven't talked with my sister or my mom yet. Honestly, would rather just relocate to Florida at this point and follow in my father's footsteps."

Mirai huffed, nodding into the rearview mirror as an ambulance with lights ablaze passed by. "Well, you're not the only one to unearth some family gems this evening. I found out that I wasn't so much adopted by the McGarrys as I was abducted."

"I'm sorry… what?" Neal asked incredulously.

"Stolen. Repurposed into a new family for the sole purpose of being a backstory for their manufactured identities. As you recall, we saw the name Mark Stone on one of the station logs you tore from the binder. Turns out, Jason McGarry used to be Mark Stone, a man who was once an insurgent with Ad Ordinem. Then he fled and needed a cover, at which point, my fake father went to work for yours. That's how they met. That's how your father found out about the secret society. That's how this disgusting deal was hashed out—likely motivated by a desire to rid a powerful man of an inconvenient woman."

"I can't believe this," Neal mumbled, in the hollow tones of one who believed every word of it.

"Brace yourself for this. You and I might be half siblings."

The silence that followed was short. Neal's truncated laughter had elements of shock along with a thin veneer of coming to terms. "At this moment, I have no reason to doubt you. Does that make this Kan Thura guy our half brother too?"

"Probably. Which… I mean, it explains a lot about when Kan and I first met. Some of the things he said… Well, anyway, the three of us possibly share a father, but for certain—Kan and I—a mother."

"Chaw?"

"Chaw Donovan."

"Holy hell," Neal groaned. Mirai could hear him rubbing his palm against his chin stubble. He took another minute to process the news while Mirai continued driving. Then he asked, "You on your way to a bar? Cuz that's where I am. Winchel Airport's finest."

She pursed her lips and gazed straight ahead. "Nope. I'm just driving for the time being. After that, I'm gonna go see my mother."

"See your… You mean—you know where she is?"

"I do not. But Omni might. Doesn't it know everything?"

"On that topic, I'm actually one step ahead of you. I spent the last hour scouring the web. No one by that name is listed anywhere in the state of Florida, at least not in the last twenty years."

"What about before then?"

Neal sighed. "About what you'd expect. A Bruce and Chaw Donovan living together at that address in Winchel. The only other Chaw Donovan was down in Miami, also a long time back."

"Oh?"

"Yeah. There was almost no info about her, except a mention on this old website that she was once featured in a men's magazine. There were two names side by side: Chaw Donovan and Chaw Khin Thet. Made it seem like one was her real name and one was used professionally."

Mirai blinked. "A magazine? Like, as what? Like she was a model?"

"Maybe. She was listed as the Featured Girl for the month of May. But again, this was almost twenty-five years ago."

"Twenty… *five*… years ago?"

"Uh-huh. Why?"

"What publication?"

"I'm sorry?"

Mirai wheeled the vehicle to the right and began merging lanes until skidding to a stop in the emergency lane below a freeway overpass. She placed the car in park and said, "What's the name of the magazine?"

Neal paused. "I'll check, but, Mirai, I don't even think it's in print anymore."

"*The name*, big brother."

A hearty chuckle radiated through the phone, and for the briefest of instances, Mirai forgot her misery. "Yeah, here it is. *Men's Realm Magazine.*"

Mirai felt the rumble of the freeway through her seat belt. She glanced down at her phone, even though there was nothing to see, and flashed a determined smirk. "Thanks, Neal. I'll be in touch."

Several miles west led to an off-ramp and a deserted exit. Mirai took little notice of the condition of the neighborhoods as she drove through the unfamiliar streets. Amber traffic lamps pierced the darkness along each block. The directions on her phone indicated a right turn up ahead. At the corner, a man lay on a bench below a bus-stop sign. His eyes locked onto Mirai's as she hesitated at the turn. He waved his hand at her slowly, yet it was not the wave of recognition. Mirai shook her head in reply and drove on.

Another few streets led to an aging strip mall flanked by rows of palm trees in the parking lot. Most of the shops it contained were closed for the day. Mirai parked directly in front of the one with a bright neon sign in the window that read *Open 24hrs*.

"Howdy, howdy," a middle-aged man said lackadaisically as the entry door pealed. He stood behind a register that sat atop an acrylic cabinet. Mirai acknowledged him and then granted herself a moment to scan the surroundings. The memorabilia store was old, overpacked with merchandise, and had metal racks of tchotchkes lining the walls. In the center were glass cases filled with costume jewelry, autographed headshots, and props from television and film.

Mirai gave her backpack strap a tug and walked up to the proprietor. She wasn't entirely certain if it was the setting or the information she came to find that was causing her heart to pummel her rib cage. "I called a little while ago about that copy of *Men's Realm Magazine*."

"Right," he said, tapping his fingers against the acrylic. "I have that issue over in the book section."

The man led Mirai through the maze of shelves and abrupt turns in the shop. At the back of the store was a series of bookcases. Between the cases was a pair of double swinging wood doors with a notice to customers.

"*Adults only*," she read.

"Yeah," the man said, sheepishly, before giving Mirai a lengthy once-over. "You're over eighteen, right?"

She was still gazing at the notice on the doors when her head offered a subtle nod. Realizing that the owner was unconvinced, she blinked and said, "I'm not a kid anymore."

The statement was uttered distantly, yet with an undercurrent of defiance. The man's smile was cordial. "Sorry, just had to ask. You look too young to be a fan of the magazine."

"I've… never seen it before."

"It's obscure, I'll admit." He chuckled, pushing through the wooden panels and leading Mirai into a room with a fuchsia tint. "It was popular for about a minute then went bankrupt. I sold some vintage issues for a while, but the public interest dried up pretty quick.

It was a locally produced thing here in Miami. They just didn't have the funds to compete with the big publishers."

A shelf of thin magazine spines seemed to stretch from one end of the room to the other. In the corner was a recliner and a small lamp. On the opposing walls were posters and an assortment of shelves with adult-themed paraphernalia. Mirai took a deep breath of the room's musty air and redirected her curiosity toward the magazine racks.

The owner mumbled as he searched. "Let's see here… *Men's Realm*… Okay, we got… Well—here's the year… January, February, March, April… bingo." With confidence he swiped the plastic-wrapped magazine from the shelf and held it out to Mirai. "May issue. Mint condition."

Mirai's hands made contact with the archival plastic and heard it crinkle when she gave it a gentle squeeze. Through the clear bag was the front cover of the publication. Below the masthead was a depiction of two women, each holding a phone up to their ear connected by the same curly cord. Both their expressions and body language indicated an engagement in salacious conversation.

In the center was block text promoting the topics to be covered in that issue. Mirai skimmed it quickly, hunting for key words and phrases. Upon seeing the name Chaw Khin Thet, her eyes stopped, and stared, and became moist with emotion.

"Could I… have a minute…" she breathed.

"Oh, yeah, yeah, of course," the proprietor said while backing out of the room. "You take all the time you… uh… need."

The double doors finished swinging while a hallowed pause settled over the space. Mirai remained motionless and listened to the silence as if it had cosmic significance. Her memory strained to recall the image she had only briefly seen of Chaw Donovan standing next to Kan and Howard. The facial features were hazy, the build merely an outline, yet there was one thing she remembered for certain.

My mother was so beautiful.

She took an unsteady few steps toward the recliner and sat down, leaning in toward the light that pushed back the shadows on the cover. After carefully removing the magazine from the archival bag, Mirai opened it and saw a table of contents on the second page. She turned each page with reverence. The spine crackled as she progressed, seeming to inhale for the first time in decades. Each section contained topics of general interest to men, followed by full-page advertisements for the latest and greatest thing. When she landed on a page that read *Featured Girl of May*, she stopped.

Chaw Khin Thet…

Mirai saw the face, and in the recognition, believed that she had always known it. The woman in the magazine was the mirror image of the woman holding it.

Oh my God… I can't believe it's her.

Chaw was photographed in a floral bikini, the kind Mirai herself would often wear, the kind she distinctly remembered wearing when Annette Laufer had humiliated her during Julie's birthday party. Chaw was depicted in mid-leap, about to hit a beach ball, the sun behind her casting a shimmering ray against the crest of her flowing hair. The setting was a beach. Overlying the sand was a text box prefacing an interview the publication had conducted with this "radiant up-and-comer."

Mirai turned the page and saw a palm tree stretching out across the spread. Her mother was leaning against it with a relaxed look on her face. The start of the Q&A filled most of the opposing page's space. At the top next to an asterisk, it read: *The editorial team at Men's Realm Magazine conducted this interview with Chaw Khin Thet. Portions of grammar have been edited for reader clarity.*

Tracing the words with her finger, Mirai found the start of the section and drew in a purposeful breath.

MRM: Chaw means "pretty" in the Burmese language of the people of Myanmar. We certainly couldn't agree more. Our Featured Girl for May recently arrived in Florida to start a new life. Just like in her home country, she wanted to live someplace tropical and bustling —good thing her plane wasn't diverted to Montana. Tell us, Chaw, what made you want to come to America?

Chaw: To experience new people, new foods, and new cultures. Also, I wanted more freedom to express myself and explore my fun side.

MRM: We're having fun just talking with you. Are all the women of Southeast Asia as pretty as you?

Chaw: Myanmar is filled with beautiful people inside and out. They work hard, care for each other, and find productive ways to provide for their families. Also, many don't know this, but it's the most generous country in the world!

MRM: Did you grow up in a rural or urban environment?

Chaw: Very urban. I grew up in a large family in the city of Yangon. It has everything: street food, nightlife, tiny shops where you can find just about anything. Each day after school my siblings and I go down to the street vendor who serves mohinga, which is fish soup with rice noodles, some boiled eggs, and spices. It's the main comfort food of Burmese people.

MRM: Probably not as readily available on the streets of Miami, but we'll keep an eye out for it.

Chaw: I found it at one Asian restaurant on the west side. Maybe more will follow.

MRM: Anything from your hometown that you miss?

Chaw: I miss the street food. There's so much and for only small price. We're a country of festivals—like Thingyan, which is our New Year's celebration in April. People go around town dousing each other with water for good luck.

MRM: Wow! I think they'll write you a ticket for that in Miami-Dade.

Chaw: In Yangon it's different. The Burmese water festival is enjoyed by almost everyone. There's singing, live music, dancing, and being generous to neighbors. And you get really, really wet.

MRM: Speaking of getting wet, you moved to a place with some of the most pristine coastal beaches anywhere. What made you relocate to Florida?

Chaw: You seen my bikini body?

MRM: Touché.

Chaw: Miami and Yangon have many things similar. Diversity of cultures, food, activities, plus, the weather is exactly what I'm used to.

Hot. I get to enjoy some of my home city in a brand-new place. And I'm still young enough to enjoy it!

MRM: How young is that?

Chaw: Just turned twenty-four.

MRM: Could have fooled us. You look eighteen.

Chaw: That's what people always say.

Mirai blinked as what she had just read sank in. "She was my age," formed a whisper. "In a new country, trying to start a new life, all alone." Mirai turned the page and followed the paragraph blocks to the continuing interview, all the while trying to avoid eye contact with her mother's photo on the right, in which the palm tree and ocean had stayed but the bikini had not.

MRM: Tell us about your hobbies and interests.

Chaw: I go swimming all the time. I also try Jet Skiing for the first time. So much fun. But then there's the homebody side of me. I enjoy cooking, reading good book, and watching American movies.

MRM: You haven't been in the States very long. Have you developed some friends in your short time here?

Chaw: There are some girls my age who live in apartment complex. We get together on weekends, but we all have the full-time jobs too, so very busy. We not all work nine-to-five.

MRM: Is modeling your career now?

Chaw: I wish! I've been waitressing a few months at tiki lounge. Hoping this interview leads to other modeling opportunities for me.

MRM: How did we come to discover you?

Chaw: Something difference of opinion on that. I come across your magazine on newsstand and called the hotline on back cover. But I get no answer. A few weeks later one of your talent scouts approach me while I was jogging on the South Beach. I said, "I've been waiting to hear from you guys!"

MRM: Either way, we're thrilled to have you gracing the pages of the magazine. You're our very first Asian Featured Girl of the Month.

Chaw: What do I win?

MRM: You've won our hearts.

Chaw: I accept.

MRM: Related to that topic, we're just dying to know, what made you want to pose for Men's Realm?

Chaw: The chance to do something like this would have been culturally not acceptable back home. I respect my family and friends too much to cause them any embarrassment, so instead I follow my modeling dreams here where no one knows me. I love that I now have the freedom to do something like this—bring beauty into the world in my own small way. If someone's day is brighter just a little by seeing my photos, it will make me very happy.

Mirai reached the end of the column and turned to the final section of the Q&A. More of Chaw's pictorials filled the left page, some striking a pose, others seeming more candid. The pictures were too dazzling to ignore. They were shot with a masterful use of natural light and a keen sense of angle. An almost milky softness cradled the images within the frame. The woman was delightful, mesmerizing, and had an expression that refused to release the viewer. Only after another moment of admiration did Mirai notice the lone dimple on her mother's left cheek. Mirai then touched her own, and felt flushed with an indescribable warmth.

MRM: Okay, time for the lightning round. You ready?

Chaw: Always ready.

MRM: Favorite color?

Chaw: Magenta.

MRM: Favorite food?

Chaw: Mohinga if I'm in Yangon and ropa vieja if I'm in Miami.

MRM: Hot weather or cold?

Chaw: Duh.

MRM: Morning person or night owl?

Chaw: Can I say both?

MRM: Favorite movie?

Chaw: The Wizard of Oz.

MRM: Really…?

Chaw: Yeah.

MRM: Out of all the great American cinema—you know what, never mind. Favorite type of music?

Chaw: Bossa nova.

MRM: A person from history you'd like to meet?

Chaw: Confucius.

MRM: A person from history you'd like to sleep with?

Chaw: Also Confucius.

MRM: Ideal type of man?

Chaw: Someone kind, funny, considerate, who provides for the family, wants a few children, and enjoys spending time with me. Someone honest, with a good heart, who will love me for my body, my mind, and my soul.

MRM: Have you found anyone like that yet?

Chaw: Before I leave Myanmar, the fortune-teller say not to worry.

MRM: Oh?

Chaw: Yes. I believe when the time is right, that man will find me.

The network portrait of Howard Lalonde manifested centrally in Mirai's mind. She imagined him stumbling across the magazine one day, perhaps while on a routine inspection tour of the Florida radio stations. Eyes overwhelmed by Chaw's beauty, ethics weakened by years of empire-building, he entertained an idea too outlandish to ever work. Yet the idea persisted in its infection. He would find this young Burmese woman, introduce himself as the persona of his recently departed former employee—Bruce Donovan—a man who could have been his identical twin, and see if any concupiscence would emerge from their meeting.

Mirai gripped the magazine a little more tightly as the storyline played itself out. The polished, gentlemanly, and down-to-earth essence of this Bruce Donovan would no doubt have been alluring to the lonely, searching, and cash-strapped migrant trying to fulfill her dreams in a new country. Howard had probably made it seem like his bumping into her was pure happenstance. Pure fate. Chaw would have been cautious at first but hopelessly swooned thereafter. Between his financial stability and his generosity toward her, their courtship was probably quite short. As ambitious, intelligent, and conscientious as Chaw was, the barriers of a newly acquired second language and the complexities of municipal government would have made verifying anything about Bruce Donovan beyond her capability.

Howard Lalonde would have known that. Feeding off of her trust and possible desperation, he took full advantage of her firm belief in the prophecy of the fortune-teller and paved the way for his own alternate life. His second family. A chance to begin anew without ever having to give up the old.

And Chaw would have believed it. She would have believed it through the courthouse wedding—complete with counterfeit marriage documents so as to assure that Lalonde's greatest crime was fraud and not bigamy. She would have believed it during her husband's lengthy departures and frequent cross-country work trips, when he would call her claiming to be stationed on the back roads of some Iowa radio tower but was actually sitting in the executive suite at PRN America. She would have even believed it listening to Howard Lalonde on the radio. A mild alteration to his voice, an EQ adjustment here, some compression there, and so long as she never looked up Lalonde's picture online, Chaw would have never been the wiser.

It had been a perfect con, at least, until Chaw announced that a baby was on the way. Suddenly confronted with an unalterable consequence of his affair, Lalonde would have panicked, imagining the scandal brought on by his charade being broadcast for his listening audience, and both of his families, to hear. His reputation destroyed. His achievements forever marred by an asterisk.

He must have sent her back to Myanmar... with baby Kan... but without me.

Mirai sensed a wave of emotion sweeping over her. Suddenly the words were becoming difficult to read, filtered through tears that refused to fall. When she turned the final page in the section, a full layout photo of her mother was displayed without commentary. The woman stood facing the viewer, wearing nothing but a smile that projected a genuine love for living. Behind her was a melting sunlight that shimmered off the ocean waves. Soft shadows caressed parts of Chaw's body. Her eyes twinkled with hope.

It was due only to the withholding of a blink that Mirai noticed something in the background. A slightly blurred promotional banner billowed across the side of a beachfront tiki shack. It was on the right-hand edge of the photo and partially cut off. Yet Mirai could easily recognize the logo and make out the first few words.

"*Annual WaterSplash Festival Today*," she read. "*September…*"

Mirai hesitated while working some math out in her head. "September… That means these photos were shot at the event, then published in the May issue of the following year." She flipped back to the cover and nodded at the date. "The same month and year I was born."

A tingling began to saturate her muscles as she turned back to the photo. Her eyes darted across the page as she tried to find fault with her math, with her logic, or with anything else that could come back to cruelly mock her.

"Photo taken in September… published the May I was born…"

All at once, the tears that had refused to fall broke through the emotional levee, as a wellspring of tension gave way in her chest. "Oh my God," she whispered.

Her eyes and her finger met in the middle of the page and stopped just below Chaw's sun-kissed navel. Mirai's finger trembled as she touched it. "You were pregnant with me in this photo."

The rest of the words stalled at the tip of her tongue as a cascade of grief overtook her. Mirai pressed her hand to her face and slowly slid down the front of the chair. She collapsed onto the carpeted floor in a torrent of sobs, her shoulders and abdomen heaving in unison. The magazine fell with her but stayed open. The image on the page gazed back. Mirai stared at it through her muffled weeping, all the while trying to utter what remained in her heart. Finally, after a few minutes of gasping sorrow did she assemble the means to speak it.

"These are our only photos together."

The weight of the statement crushed her for several more hours. Thoughts of Jason and Valerie, of David, of Julie, of Kan, and of Chaw Khin Thet, pulsed through her veins like acid. The darkness overshadowed her and wound her in its black hole. There was nothing else to do but weep, and trust that soon, the tears would drain her body of the poison.

Mirai eventually fell asleep. Leaning against the base of the recliner, she rested her head on her arm and dreamt of a restless nothing. The fitful state offered little in rejuvenation, and she awoke feeling hungover. The time on her phone indicated that it was nearly six in the morning. Her inner clock was certain it was still midnight.

"I'll take it," she said drowsily, slapping the magazine down on the acrylic surface at the register.

The proprietor gazed at her for a moment and then flashed a weary, almost paternal smile. "No charge. I have a funny feeling it somehow belongs to you anyway."

Mirai thanked him and heard the door peal as she exited the shop. A film of humidity wrapped around her body as she entered the parking lot. She took a deep breath while surveying the daybreak light cresting over the faded, Spanish-tiled roofs of the neighborhood. Beyond the terra-cotta sky was a purple hue predestined to turn azure. She gazed at it while feeling the oppressive morning air nip at her skin.

Her eyes then shifted down to the white slanted lines of the strip mall's parking lot. It took her fatigued brain a moment to ascertain what she was seeing, which was a completely vacant space. She turned to the left and back to the right. Not a single car was present in the lot. Her beloved convertible was gone.

"Freakin' eight ball," she said flatly.

Rolling the magazine and fitting it mostly into her small purse, Mirai shook her head and ejected a derisive laugh. A few steps forward brought her into the center of the lot. She did a final twirl to be certain her eyes weren't deceiving her and started for the sidewalk. The direction from which she came was laid out before her in all of its dereliction. A heavily graffitied bus shelter stood at the far corner, demarcating the intersection at which she would turn to head home.

Home? she wondered, her thoughts filtered through a dense haze. *There's no home anymore.*

She stood listlessly, caught in her own inertia, weighing a series of options that were not actual choices at all. In her mind, she pictured spending the night at Julie's house while blowing off the steam of a family squabble. Once the new day dawned, all would be forgiven, all would be set right. The image evaporated into the heat. There was no more a Laufer house than there was a McGarry family. They were now both relics of the past. Memories of a distant planet that had spun out of orbit.

Mirai frowned and felt the impulse to cry. Not a single tear remained to be shed. Instead, she pivoted on her flip-flops and faced the opposite side of the street. The residential properties thinned out leading to a more commercial area. On the right-hand side was a small sign with the logo of an airplane. A few blocks behind it was a much larger sign: a billboard printed in black and white. Mirai felt her jaw muscles tighten as she read it.

Is This the End of the World?

A nascent breeze suddenly rustled her hair. The wind felt unnatural and was connected to a low rumble that steadily grew in pitch. She looked back and saw a commercial airliner flying overhead, its approach slow and targeted as it descended toward the airport. Its glide path brought it directly over Mirai while the tree fronds on the street bounced against the atmospheric disturbance. The plane vanished behind the billboard as the piercing noise settled.

Mirai pulled a strand of black hair from her face. Her focus narrowed in on the airport sign. It was pointed toward the billboard. Even as her eyes stared straight ahead, her periphery could still make out the bold white font ending with that imposing question mark.

Is This the End of the World?

Mirai shrugged and began walking toward the sign.

"If it is," she answered resolutely, "then it's going to end on *my* terms, with *my* birth mother…"

Her jaw then tightened.

"In Myanmar."

CHAPTER 12
YANGON

"Name?"

"Chaw Khin Thet," said Mirai to the Consulate administrator, a burly expatriate with a pair of heavyset jowls. His short-sleeved dress shirt had a stain in the pocket where a pen had previously leaked ink. The splotch made it appear as if the man had been shot in the heart and had proceeded to bleed black instead of crimson.

"Age?"

"Late forties."

"Ethnicity?"

Mirai hesitated, twisting uncomfortably in her wooden chair. "Well… Burmese, I suppose."

The man grunted. "You're in Myanmar now. There are 135 ethnic groups here, comprising eight different national races. I need to know if she's Rakhine, Shan, Mon, Kachin… You get the idea?"

Mirai nodded apologetically. The man glanced at the computer screen on his metal desk and continued, "When would she have arrived back in Yangon?"

"I'm guessing between fifteen and twenty years ago."

"That's a big span. Can you narrow it down for me any more than that?"

"Not confidently."

The man took a sip from his coffee mug and then went back to attacking his keyboard. "Any relatives we can trace? Cross-reference any employment history? Birth records from before she emigrated or visas from when she supposedly returned?"

Mirai's shoulders sank just a little. "I'm afraid not. Look, can't you just run a database search for her name and see what comes up?"

"Oh, I typed that in the second you gave it to me. The initial search listed 580 residents attached to either that name or moniker, all currently residing right here in Yangon, a metropolitan city of millions of upon millions of upon millions of people. So, if you'd like for me to print off that unrefined list, you can go start knocking on tenement doors right now."

The contrast between the man's insouciant grin and Mirai's careworn jet lag was stark in that instant. The young woman was beginning to understand the process, and her time zone induced fatigue would garner little sympathy from the overworked bureaucrat.

"Shall we continue?" he asked. "Does she have any identifying marks, tattoos, piercings, scars, any characteristics we can use to help identify her?"

"I have some photos of her."

"Super thrilled you didn't keep that to yourself."

Mirai withdrew the magazine from her purse and pressed it down firmly against the man's desk. He stared at the cover for a moment before returning his quizzical glare to Mirai. "You must be joking."

"Not at all," she countered. "My mother was a model. This came out the same time I was born. You'll see everything you need to in there."

"I'm sure of that. Don't you have any *other* pictures? Birthday parties, holidays, something along those lines?"

Mirai tapped on the magazine cover and flashed a haggard smile. "Our only photos together."

The man peered around the immediate walking area of the open office. After a heavy sigh he flipped through the magazine until coming across the full-page layout of Chaw. Mirai watched as his eyes examined the photo. When he set the magazine back down on his desk, something in his visage had changed. Where once had been streaks of hostility in his face, were now a few wrinkles of compassion.

"I doubt she even knew she was pregnant with you yet."

Mirai tilted her head. "Perhaps. Or maybe she did and that was why she took the job."

The man drummed his fingers on the desk. He stole another look at the computer screen before saying, "Miss McGarry…"

"Mirai—is my name… if you don't mind."

The man nodded. "Okay, Mirai, let me see if I have this straight. You just found out this woman is your birth mother, couldn't find any current residents in Florida with a matching name, and impulsively hopped on the next flight to Yangon in hopes of finding her, with little more to go on than a name, an age, and an old pinup? Do I have that right?"

A few locks of hair fell forward as Mirai glanced down at her lap. The hesitation in answering his question lingered for a moment, yet the man could sense that it was something other than evasion passing the time.

"Intuition," Mirai said, still looking down.

"Pardon?"

She swallowed and forced her head back up to meet his gaze. "You said I came to Yangon impulsively. I did not. It was intuition that made me come here. This wasn't the result of some tantrum. As sure as I am that we're sitting in this office right now, I know that Chaw Khin Thet returned to Myanmar. And once I find her…" Mirai reached for the magazine, cast her eyes on her mother's smile, and then rolled the issue back in her purse. "All of my questions will finally be answered."

The man again reached for his coffee mug but found it empty. He set it back down and folded his hands on the desk. "I'm gonna level with you here, Mirai. We are not well suited for this kind of investigation. I'm working with limited staff and diminishing budgets on high-priority needs for the State Department and local officials here in Yangon. I've been in this country now five years. It's a gorgeous place with amazing food, and some of the most generous people you will ever meet. However, it's also a place of transients, political strife, socioeconomic turmoil, and a wildly varying infrastructure. It's still considered to be a developing nation. The people here have good hearts and productive minds, yet a lot has worked against them over their history. I say all of this to paint a mental picture of what you're walking into. This isn't gonna be picking up the phone or asking Omni for directions to your mother's house. Things here are different than what you're used to. I need to know you understand that."

Mirai had begun nodding before he had finished his statement. "I do understand. Trust me, I'm resilient. I'll do whatever it takes."

"I don't doubt your resilience, Miss—Mirai, but for instance… do you speak Burmese?"

"No."

"Any of the other major languages of Myanmar?"

"I only speak English."

"Some of the population is fluent in English, some only know a little, and others can't speak it at all. As for money, do you have access to your accounts while abroad?"

"Yes."

"Good. Currency conversion can be done here at the Consulate. You'll mostly be using this." The man laid down a multicolored note in front of Mirai. "Spelled *K-Y-A-T*, pronounced *chet*. You can also pay with small denominations of US dollars if you have them. When you rent a hotel room or hostel, there will be a higher price charged due to you being a foreigner. Don't take it personally, it's just the way it is here."

"Got it."

"*Mingalaba* is the standard greeting by many Burmese. *Tat tar* is goodbye. You can use the translator on your phone for the rest."

"That's how I hailed a taxi and got from the airport to here."

"Well done. But a taxi will only get you so far in the search for your mother. Best bet is to hit the streets and talk to the locals. Find out what you can from whom you can. This is a city of street vendors. Food, clothing, trinkets, knickknacks, anything you can imagine is sold outside these doors. There are also luxury shopping plazas and upscale areas if you need them, like Times City on the south end."

"Understood."

"I'll spend another hour or so refining this list and then send it to you over email. After that, the rest is up to you. I wish you the best of luck."

"Thank you."

The man nodded intensely. "You're gonna need it."

Organized chaos, Mirai thought to herself, as she took her first few steps out into the crowded streets of Yangon. Tenement buildings flanked both sides of the road, towering high above the area where pedestrians and vehicles wove around each other in a beehive motion. Mirai followed the flow of foot traffic and stayed near the merchants along the curbs. Men standing next to carts shouted things in Burmese that she suspected were invitations to sample cuisine. Women sat atop weatherworn stools while pointing at an array of durians in giant metal bowls. The armored green fruit glistened in the sunlight as Mirai passed by. Her eyes darted rapidly across the panorama of activity. It was difficult to absorb in the span of a single blink.

"*Sar kyi ma lar?*" a woman asked her, gently touching her wrist with one hand while showcasing a yellow mango with the other.

Mirai smiled and shook her head. A moment later she regretted that decision, as the pangs of hunger mingled with lassitude. She considered turning back against the traffic, but soon spotted another assortment of fresh fruits only a few steps further. A teenage girl stood next to her mother while shouting out the same words in perpetuity toward the crowds. The merchants spotted Mirai eyeing their produce. The teenager took a step toward her.

"You eat mango?"

Mirai nodded and handed the girl some kyat. "Is this enough?" Mirai asked.

The girl smiled and walked back to her mother with the money and the fruit. She then took a large knife and peeled back much of the skin to expose the sweet yellow goodness underneath. When the teenager handed the mango back to Mirai, it looked like a blossoming flower. "You look hungry," the girl said, and handed her a thin wooden skewer. "You eat now; you don't faint."

Mirai barely had time to thank her before the girl retreated back behind the table to help more customers. The endless flow of people in front of and behind Mirai pushed her onward, all as she stayed mindful of passing trishaw drivers bicycling throughout the crowd. Chewing as she walked, Mirai savored the ambrosia as it melted in her mouth. The momentary satisfaction hinted that more sustenance would soon be required. Her eyes wandered over to a meat-skewer stand on the street corner with a samosa cart stationed right beside. Beyond it was a row of restaurants lined up sequentially along the road. The aromas from the open-faced eateries wafted into the seating areas nestled next to the curbs. There, patrons sat on small, plastic lawn furniture of assorted colors while eating their meals. Mirai was naturally drawn to the colors first, observing pink furniture, followed by green, yellow, blue, purple. The palette gave her a visual grounding amongst the perpetual movement of the street. Her gnawing hunger then redirected her eyes toward the restaurant signs, some emboldened by neon, others painted by hand.

"*Mohinga*," she read softly.

The crowds wove around her stationary indecision. Upon realizing that she had little energy left to give, she settled on the restaurant and walked up to the metal window.

"*Nyimalay bar sar chin le?*" the man asked.

Mirai cocked her neck and hoped the answer matched the question. "Umm… mohinga?"

The man nodded and pointed at the price on the board. Mirai handed him the money and then proceeded to find a seat along the curb. When it was delivered to her tiny table, steam from the bowl hinted at some of its ingredients.

Fish soup, rice noodles, ginger, garlic, lemongrass… Oh my God this smells good…

The metal Burmese spoon filled with broth and noodles, along with crispy fritters sprinkled on top. As the savoriness embraced her tongue, Mirai wondered how she had ever lived without the culinary staple.

"Good?" asked a fellow patron, a heavyset woman with two young children seated next to her.

Mirai smiled as she nodded and chewed. "Incredible."

"They make it best of all place in here," she said. "You make good choice."

"Is this a popular dish in Myanmar?"

"Oh yes, yes," the woman said while wrangling her son's wandering attention back to his bowl. "It is the comfort food of Burmese people."

The comfort food my mother would have made for me.

The warmth filled her stomach and made her feel both rejuvenated and like she was ready to sleep. She knew that lodging should be her next goal despite an almost irresistible urge to begin searching for her mother. After a slight hesitation, she asked the woman, "Excuse me, but I'm trying to find someone. Her name is Chaw Khin Thet. She's in her late forties and—I believe—lives in Yangon. You wouldn't happen to know her?"

"Chaw Ei Thinzar? She live in building next to me. Good person. Make me tea leaf salad whenever I go to house. But she much older than fifty."

Mirai tilted her head graciously. "Probably not the Chaw I'm looking for. But thanks just the same."

"She your friend?"

"I'd like to think so."

"Lost then. Too many people lost these days. You both come from America?"

"Well, I was born there. My… *friend* was born in Yangon. She moved to Florida and then returned to Myanmar sometime later."

"Ohhh… Florida," the woman said as her eyes lit up. "I've seen pictures online. Look very much like Burma. Hot too, just like today. Are there many like you there?"

Mirai laughed more than intended. "I'm literally the only Burmese person I know."

"That's why you come here? To find friend and meet more Burmese?"

The question tethered them for a moment while Mirai constructed a response. To say that she was only here to find her mother would be dishonest. Yet what the other task actually was eluded the young woman as much as the Burmese lettering on the restaurant signs. Defeated and jet-lagged, Mirai lazily shrugged and said, "To find… some desperately needed answers."

The woman smiled, and nodded, and then reached into her purse to retrieve a small plastic container. When she unscrewed the cap, she stretched her arm out to place it within Mirai's reach. "Thanaka," she said, motioning that Mirai should dip her fingers in to take some.

The paste was smooth and smelled of sandalwood. Mirai wasn't certain what it was or how to go about respectfully declining. Without showing her apprehension, she grazed a small dollop onto her forefinger and middle and brought it up to her nose.

"Smells wonderful," she said, nervously.

"Try."

The weight of fatigue bore down on her as she vacillated between actions. With few defenses left, she took a laissez-faire exhale and plopped the dollop into her mouth.

"No, no!" exclaimed the woman, her face bulging from concern and hilarity. "Not food! Not food! Thanaka for your skin."

Mirai immediately scraped the paste from off her tongue. "Gotcha," she muttered.

"To protect you from sun. Keep skin soft."

"That's a relief," Mirai said, spitting the remainder onto the ground.

The woman burst out into an elevated guffaw. The infectious laugh made its way to Mirai, and they both shared in the levity. The woman then pointed around the street. "You see? On the cheeks."

As if noticing for the first time, she saw the beige-colored paste on the faces of many of the women and young girls walking by. She then watched as the woman applied a generous dose to her own face and onto the cheeks of her two children.

"Smell good and keep the sun away."

Mirai reached forward and took another dollop. "When in Rome…"

"In Rome?"

"Nothing. Thank you for this. Very kind."

Mirai dabbed some onto her cheeks and forehead, rubbing the paste into a small circle in each section. The scent was enveloping. It reminded her of a home she never had.

"After mohinga," the woman said, "you go to the other place. It serve falooda, my favorite dessert. Rose syrup, pudding, sweet milk, and sago. Or, you go over there and have *mont lin maya*—it means 'husband and wife snack.'"

"Cute name. Looks like I'll have to work up more of an appetite. Thanks for the recommendations."

"You go now?"

Mirai nodded. "Yes, I go now."

"Hotel that way. Don't stay in hostel. No good for a pretty young girl. If man tell you he needs your help and to follow him to his room… just say: 'you go away.'"

Mirai suppressed her amusement. "Sage advice. I also appreciate the… Sorry, what is it called?"

"Thanaka. You get some from the shop. It's too sunny in here. Like Florida."

"Yes… just like Florida."

Mirai waved goodbye to the woman and her two children before venturing back out onto the street. Several more blocks led her to a wider intersection that reminded her of the roads of Miami. It seemed like she had suddenly entered a new city. The tenements were replaced by high-rises along with commercial buildings, some in Colonial-style architecture, others with aged edifices and modern façades. Mirai skirted around a logjam of traffic and cut across the road to where a hotel stood in its own realm. There was valet parking, doormen greeting people in the lobby, and a gold-colored placard over the entryway written in Burmese and English: *Hotel Ruby Oasis.*

"Mingalaba, how's your day?" said the attendant behind the front desk. His black dress shirt was unbuttoned at the top, and his punchy mannerisms gave the impression he would soon be off work and ready to party with guests in the hotel nightclub. "How long your stay?"

Mirai sucked in her lower lip in curiosity. "Tell me, how did you know I was a foreigner?"

"I can tell," he answered slyly. "You American. You want suite?"

"No, just a single room would be fine."

"How many night?"

The question stumped her. Without a starting place, it was impossible to know how long her search would take. Maybe only a few days, but possibly more than a week. She rested her arm on the marble counter and said, "Four nights, with the option to extend if I need?"

"Okay," he said. "You need help with luggage?"

"I… have no luggage. So I'll need some essentials."

"Toiletries in room."

"I'll also need a change of clothes."

"Laundry service on site."

Mirai smirked and handed him her credit card. "How do you say, 'you thought of everything' in Burmese?"

"Huh?"

"Nothing. Thanks for the help."

"*Ya par tae*—not a problem."

With the key card in hand, Mirai shuffled through the grand lobby and up the elevator to her room on the ninth floor. The space was cozy, with amenities she was accustomed to expect in the States. She exhaled and stood still in the center of the room. Her eyelids gradually fell forward as her frame decompressed. Not wanting to doze off on her feet, she tossed her purse onto the dresser, dropped her clothes into the laundry bag in the service door slot, and entered the spacious bathroom encased with travertine tile. A step into the shower stall momentarily transported her out of her head, as the warm water caressed her body and gave her a sense that she was rinsing off a film that had been coating her skin ever since leaving the McGarry house. The steam enveloped her face. The stone beneath her feet reminded her that she was someplace other than home. It took all she had left within her to finish showering and towel off.

Tomorrow… somewhere in Yangon… I'll find my mother.

Mirai then collapsed into the bed and fell asleep. She awoke eight hours later to discover she hadn't moved an inch.

The laundry had been returned before dawn. Mirai stood in amusement while laying out the jean shorts, ribbed tank top, panties, and bra, all of which seemed to have been not only washed but ironed with care. She got dressed, fixed her hair into a messy bun, and marched over to the dresser to snatch her purse.

Out the door and down to the main lobby, she found herself eating a breakfast of hard-boiled eggs, granola mixed with yogurt, a bowl of soup, and a side of freshly cut melon slices. Mirai tried her best to finish the meal but also had to acknowledge her stomach's temperament toward the disruption of her usual routine. When the waitress came by to collect the plates, she appeared concerned about the remaining food.

"It was delicious," Mirai preempted, "I'm just not used to eating this much in the morning." The waitress smiled the smile of one who did not fully understand. Mirai paid the bill and left.

Stepping out onto the bustling sidewalk that moved like an assembly line beneath an overcast sky, Mirai suddenly felt her phone vibrate. She took a few steps forward to clear the walkway and unlock her device. A message notification appeared on the screen.

HELLO MIRAI. WELCOME TO YANGON.

Despite the humid air, Mirai felt her blood run cold. A bolt of anger rose up from her core, sending her heart racing.

"Son of a bitch," she snapped, and looked to see if she could block the sender. As usual, the number of origin was unavailable.

I know who you really are! she typed with fury.

THEN YOU KNOW WHY I'M HERE.

The message halted her with the force of a stranglehold. With a panic-stricken look, she took a step back and glanced around the masses surrounding her. An ocean of unfamiliar faces converged upon her from every angle. There were too many to count. Too many to mentally screen. An unnerving sense of claustrophobia began coiling her senses. She blinked and returned to her phone.

I will not be intimidated by you… You have no idea where I am… Ignoring you seems to work pretty well, so that's what I'm going to do.

Mirai locked her phone and slid it back into her pocket. She pressed on into the crowds with a purposeful stride, yet it was not the walk of trying to get somewhere, only of trying to escape. She turned a corner and ended up on a thoroughfare of clothing merchants. Against her leg, she felt her phone vibrate again.

"Longyi?" asked a woman holding out a garment.

Mirai ignored her and kept walking.

"This… very pretty… on you," said a man wielding a pair of gemstone necklaces in each hand.

More vibrations buzzed along her thigh. Emloch was sending messages with increasing frequency. Mirai moved deeper into the bazaar, where the proliferation of awnings and giant parasols littered the tops of street carts. The coverage, however vertical, gave her a momentary sense of protection. After catching her breath, she backed herself into a corner and withdrew the phone from her pocket. Her dark eyes summarized the texts in rapid succession.

… NEED TO CONTINUE THE SEARCH FOR OSIRIS…

… VERY LITTLE TIME LEFT, AND YOU ARE WASTING IT…

… IGNORING ME ONLY MAKES THINGS WORSE…

Her hand tightened as she replied, *I don't work for you anymore! DO NOT MESSAGE ME EVER AGAIN!*

No ellipsis appeared for a rebuttal. The thread was silent and remained silent. Mirai hesitated. She waited a full minute and then a full minute after that. More pedestrians wove by her, offering only a passing glance at yet another face. Mirai looked up from her phone, and then back down. She closed out of the messaging window and felt a sigh of relief. She had nearly slid the device back into her shorts before another vibration tightened her wrist.

This vibration didn't stop.

Her mouth was partially open when her eyes read the screen. It was not a message. It was an incoming phone call.

Caller Unknown.

Two sensations converged within Mirai. One had to do with slamming the phone to the ground and stomping it until she was certain it was shrapnel, and the other had to do with what her first words to the Emloch persona should be in light of the fact she now knew it was David. In the end, the feeling of retribution won out and she tapped on the answer button to greet the caller.

"Hello, David," she said.

"Hello, Mirai," came the response.

It was unarguably his voice. Mirai nodded with a scowl that hid behind a thin veneer of sadness. It was the aching disappointment in having been right. "I figured out you were Emloch."

"So you did," he said.

"What do I win?"

"Win?"

"Wasn't this all a game? Some sort of twisted invention to break me while setting you up as my rescuer?"

"Is that what you think this was?"

"No," Mirai said, her voice growing solemn. "I think this was something more horrible than that. I think someone at the Preserve put you up to this—a backup plan in case I refused to join after the orientation. I think you created Emloch to manipulate me into manipulating others. I think you caused the area code disasters and the terror those incidents incited. I think you were the only other one who knew Carys would be at the airport photoshoot because you had access to our home calendars. And I think you sent me into that plane to be traumatized just enough to be *pliable*. To be vulnerable. Willing to fully trust you. Willing to…" Mirai sensed a crack in her voice coming and took a moment to swallow. "Fall in love with you…"

"Yes…" was the only reply.

"The whys… why to any of it… why to all of it… I didn't have a clue until this very second. I suspect it's because you really are looking for Osiris. Is that right? Is that the correct answer to this multiple choice?"

"As always, Mirai, you're right on target."

"Very well then, Emloch. If it's the god of the afterlife you want, it's the god of the afterlife you'll get."

"Oh?"

Mirai hesitated, and as she did, absorbed the thrill of its fleeting power on her lips. *"I can tell you who Osiris is."*

Even without the ability to see him, Mirai could feel his bracing interest from over the transmission. That assurance clouded everything else.

The voice then asked, "And the name… of this Osiris? You have it?"

Mirai felt a sudden chill in the air incongruous to the climate. She further stepped back into the shadowy corner and said, "I do. And once I give it to you, I'll never hear from you again. Correct?"

"You have my word."

Passing by the street was a young Burmese girl with her parents. Mirai saw her and estimated that she couldn't have been more than four years old. The girl walked along haphazardly as children sometimes do, distracted by the myriad of things to look at and people to see inside the bazaar. Her young parents slowed their pace to help her keep up. They gazed down at her adoringly, seeming to never wane of seeing the black locks of her hair, or her inquisitive nature. The family passed by the corner where Mirai was hunched without noticing her. The pair of doe eyes staring back at them never wavered.

Mirai continued gazing even after they vanished into the masses. Her vision could somehow still see them. She saw the young girl age rapidly, from a child to a teen to an adult. The parents had aged too, shedding the plasticity of youth to reveal the wizened wisdom of their emeritus years. The individuals changed yet the family remained as a portrait—unaltered by time. The colors, albeit less vibrant, remained, and created a contrast to the hardships and needless pain of daily living. Love was their bond, a bond built on shared history, a hope for the future, and atop a foundation of objective truth.

The sentiment weighed heavy on Mirai's chest as she held the phone to her ear. Something in the back of her mind was setting off a warning flare. An exhortation to reconsider what she was about to do. Yet the hesitation fizzled as quickly as the last pops of light from a firework. Replacing it was the molten sizzle that had been boiling since slamming her parents' front door. It was rage disguised as righteous anger. It was the refusal to ever again be a victim. It was her one chance at freedom from David, Emloch, Ad Ordinem, and the volley of lies that had been assaulting her since the age of four.

Mirai's mouth was the barrel. Her lips were the trigger. The name was the bullet.

"If you want Osiris…" she said, gravely, "you'll find him in the same house where you first told me you loved me."

The sound of a breath crackled in the speaker. It was not from an inhale, but from an unwitting gasp. "You mean…"

"Oh, yes," said Mirai. "Osiris is Jason McGarry."

The sudden lack of words morphed into a total vacuum of sound. Mirai waited for a response before becoming curious and pulling the device away from her ear.

Call Ended.

All at once she felt an adrenaline rush to her head. The last vestiges of wrath scattered like vermin, leaving behind a chilling clarity. It was the act of writing the sum before finishing the equation. Of declaring checkmate while the opponent still has a final move.

The alignment of her decisions formed into a straight line, allowing her mind's eye to view them at a glance. It was that terrifying instant in which Mirai recognized her crucial mistake.

He doesn't need me anymore..

She backed away from the corner and moved into the street. The action made her feel in control and exposed simultaneously. The dichotomy wrestled within as her eyes scanned the area. A gnawing sense of paranoia flooded her abdomen.

That was when the hand reached out to grab her.

"No!" she screamed, trying to lurch away but finding herself already in the man's clutches.

He was Burmese, middle aged, and stood with imposing height over Mirai. In his right hand was her upper arm. In his left was a serrated blade.

"You come… now… or won't be good for you," he said, working Mirai back into the darkened corner.

The man appeared to be saying more, but Mirai never heard it as she instinctively wielded her left fist toward his mouth and hit him with every spasm of power her muscles contained.

They both stood idle for a moment: her—stunned at the reflexiveness of her own action—and him—spitting a red globule from his mouth and sending with it one of his teeth.

"Oh, crap," Mirai muttered, before twisting her arm out of his grasp and breaking into the crowd.

"*Tha khoe!*" she heard from behind, and noticed several heads turning her direction.

"Thief!" an indignant tourist repeated.

Mirai clenched her jaw and felt a hundred eyes forming into one. Without looking back, she bolted from the spot and began a frightened dash down the street, weaving around people, carts, and the frenzied notion that the assailant was just steps behind. She ran and felt each slap of her flip-flops smacking up against her heels. Fearing they would cause her to slip, she kicked off one and then the other, wincing as her bare feet absorbed the merciless impact of the road.

The shops gyrated within her field of vision as she ran. The crowds thinned, then grew, then seemed to disperse altogether as the bazaar came to a dead end. Mirai spun around and saw the Burmese man approaching—the blade in his hand matching the daggers in his eyes.

Her only option for escape seemed to be the least advisable. A tenement door stood open with a dimly lit stairwell leading into the building. Mirai looked up and saw the eight-storied structure towering high above the street. Her muscles tensed in rebellion to the idea. A command from her mind overrode them.

Very stupid, she thought to herself while ascending the inner stairwell. *Very, very stupid idea.*

Her feet pounded the wooden steps for as much speed as they could offer. She frantically turned the corner and bounded up the next flight —all the while certain that in her periphery, a human shadow had just formed along the lower wall. The stairwell was cavernous and echoed with each smack of her steps. When she reached the second landing, Mirai considered knocking on any of the apartment doors and pleading for help. Even as she decided to do it, her legs propelled her upward and away from the panting sounds of the oncoming pursuer.

Where am I going? she chastised, as yet another landing approached.

The hallway stretched deep into the building, with only two doors on either side. Both options seemed too far down the corridor and too risky a gamble, so Mirai turned yet another corner and bounded up the next flight. It was not until she reached the top floor that an apartment door stood within easy reach. She winced upon realizing how much her left hand still hurt from punching the assailant. Using her right fist, she pounded the door and called out for anyone to assist. The knocking sounded as hollow as it felt. Either no one was home or no one wanted to get involved.

In frustration she gave the door one last fisted bang, as if hammering the final nail into her own coffin. The barrier stood indifferent to her plight. All that was left to do was to keep running. Mirai grabbed ahold of the railing and started up the last half flight of stairs toward a metal door at the top. When she burst through it, the blinding light of the sun forced her to shield her eyes. It was that action that prevented her from seeing a man's arm coil her into a choke hold.

"You take it easy, yes?" the man said in English but laced with an eastern European accent.

Mirai gritted her teeth as the man's elbow crease tightened around her neck. Her hands clutched his tensing forearm. Her back stayed pinned against his torso. When the rooftop door flew open a second time, Mirai heard two clicks in order: the first was from a gun being aimed directly at the Burmese man who arrived breathlessly spent; the second was from the sound of his blade dropping onto the cement roof.

"No problem, no problem," the Burmese man said, his hands raised, his bloodied lips assuring that there was no reason to shoot.

The man holding Mirai nodded. "Good. Be calm. I've got vhat I came for. Stay put and let me be on my way."

Mirai's eyes widened as the situation crystalized in her mind. *One of them is Ad Ordinem... The other is Emblem.*

The echo of leather scraping against wood had the rhythm of footsteps. When yet another man made his appearance from the stairwell, both the Burmese man and the man holding Mirai took a step backward.

"Hold on there, mate," the newcomer said calmly, "don't do anything bloody foolish."

The barrel of the gun turned toward Mirai, and at varying intervals she could even feel its cold metal against her temple. The man said, "You don't move. Don't come closer, yes?"

The Aussie smiled and took a step forward. "Well, you're a fresh face, aren't yah? They just running out of recruits over there or did you get a promotion?"

"I vill kill her!" The man seethed, flexing his arm tighter around her neck.

"No worries, luv. He won't shoot you. Wouldn't make any bloody sense."

The man did not respond. He simply exchanged worried glances between the other two men and tried to show his sincerity in the threat to put a bullet in Mirai's head. "You... I... vill do vhat I must. A joking matter this is not!"

"What is that?" the Aussie asked curiously. "You're really biting hard into those *V*s. Somewhere from the Balkans, is it?"

"Shut up!"

"So, what's your plan here, mate? Take this little sheila and lock her up somewhere? That won't get you no place. Listen, take my advice and use your head. Wouldn't it make a whole helluva lot more sense to just shoot me instead?"

The man holding Mirai smiled. She could sense his body bracing for something. When he pulled the gun away from her face, the light cast an amber glint across the steel. "Agreed," the man said. "I shoot you instead."

Mirai shut her eyes and waited to hear the deafening roar of the bullet slicing the air. What she heard instead was the ghastly sound of a knife tearing into human flesh, and the guttural reaction evoked from it. The gun fell from the man's seizing hand and clattered to the ground. His arms fell limp and freed Mirai from the choke hold. As he collapsed backward, Mirai took a step away from the scene and turned to see Kan Thura cradling the man he had just fatally stabbed.

"Be at peace. Be at rest." Kan spoke the words with a pious reverence before laying the man down flat on his back. A puddle of crimson was forming along the cracks in the cement. Mirai watched in horror as the man struggled to hold on to life.

Kan knelt down next to him and placed his palm on the man's forehead. For an instant, the two locked eyes, conversing in a language known only to the dying and the angel of death. Then, in a soft whisper, Kan said, "Let it go."

The man wheezed, and choked, and tried to draw another breath. Discovering there was no oxygen left in his world, he gave up the fight and blinked for the last time.

Kan bowed his head and muttered something only he could hear. When he was finished, he stood up quickly and seemed to switch gears with an attitude of the expedient. "Are you unharmed?" he asked Mirai, who stood trembling in a halo of sunlight. "I would say I'm sorry you had to see someone die, but as I now recall, this isn't your first witnessing of it."

Her focus reeled from Kan to the Burmese man disposing of the blade and gun, to the Aussie walking over to Kan to help search for the dead man's phone and identification. The three men worked swiftly and efficiently. In a matter of minutes, the body was hidden behind an outdoor vent shaft and the pool of blood was a faded stain.

"We're on the top-floor apartment at the rear," Kan said, extending his hand as an invitation for her to follow them back down the stairs.

Mirai continued to let her gaze wander. Her emotions fluctuated through each successive second, from terror to relief to crushing guilt and back again. As the thought imprinted itself against her will, stating the obvious seemed to be the only actionable step.

"I just watched that man die."

It was within the statement that she discovered an incremental reprieve. Mirai left Kan's invitation lingering and walked past him toward the corner of the spacious roof. Off in the distance, a golden structure rose high over the city of Yangon. It shimmered against a pale blue sky and cut through the mountainous white clouds on the horizon. Its shape was that of a massive golden bell. The terraces at the base gave way to various narrowing levels until, at its pinnacle, rested an embellished crown. The structure stood in marked contrast to its metropolitan surroundings, yet as Mirai drank in its visual splendor, she determined that something about its ancient beauty seemed perfectly suited to the country.

"What is that?" she whispered into the wind.

Kan joined Mirai at the railing. He cast his eyes downward, describing the picturesque vista from memory. "The Shwedagon Pagoda—the symbol of the city. Constructed thousands of years ago. Covered in gold, precious gemstones, diamonds…"

Mirai's face softened as she studied the wonder. Kan's face tightened as he flashed a conflicted look back at the other two men. Mirai said, "It's one of the most beautiful things I've ever seen." After another purposeful reflection, she added, "I'll need to paint it."

Kan nodded thoughtfully. "I'm certain it will be stunning. But for now, we really should be getting downstairs."

It was with the kind of reluctance displayed at a funeral when a mourner departs the casket after paying final respects, that Mirai broke away from the view and followed the motley team back down the stairwell. The apartment they entered was an underfurnished loft. It appeared makeshift, like it was set up to be torn down at a moment's notice. Rows of folding tables lined the walls, over which pushpin boards with drawings, notes, and various schematics littered the panorama. Metal chairs were scattered about. In the foreground was a kitchenette with a countertop space being used for anything but food preparation. The tall windows of the loft were covered with bars. Natural light cascaded through them anyway.

"Is that your blood?" Kan asked.

Mirai looked back and realized the question was being directed at her. On the floorboards were partial crimson imprints leading up to where she was standing. When she lifted her right foot, a thin red glaze caught her by surprise.

"I must have cut myself while running."

"It happens," Kan said, dismissively. He hustled over to a cabinet and returned with a first aid kit. Mirai sat in one of the chairs as Kan knelt down, cleaned the wound, and then dabbed it with antiseptic. "This might sting."

"No worries. Pain seems to be my forte in life."

Kan seemed poised to ask a follow-up to her statement but ignored the comment and continued treating the cut. "Small laceration. No big deal. Keep it clean and bandaged for the next few days. And of course, watch for signs of infection."

He finished wrapping the gauze under and around her arch and then secured it with tape. As he placed the supplies back in the box, he noticed Mirai staring at him with curious eyes.

"Are you my brother?" she asked, softly.

Kan snapped the kit shut and walked it over to the cabinet. "Half brother, actually. Same mother, different fathers. But then again you must have already figured that out or you wouldn't be in Yangon." He hesitated in the middle of the room and turned back toward the door. "Why is he still here?" Kan asked the Aussie, pointing toward the Burmese man. "Just pay him so he can go."

"Already did. Says he'll be wantin' something extra for the tooth she knocked out."

Kan laughed and lit a cigarette. Crushing the match between his fingers, he replied, "Tell him I don't pay extra for incompetence. I wanted Mirai brought in safe and sound, not like she was being abducted into slavery."

The Aussie communicated the sentiment to the Burmese man, the latter of which took the news with a look of genuine disappointment. Mirai watched as he turned toward the door, all the while shifting his tongue in the cavity of where his tooth had been. Something about the arrangement made her certain that the reward money wouldn't cover the procedure, his smile being forever altered as a result.

"I… didn't know he was part of your team," she confessed.

"Only occasionally," Kan emphasized.

"I'm sorry. I hit him so hard cuz I was freaked out."

"And bloody hell—what a punch it must have been!" said the Aussie with exuberance.

"Couldn't I just throw in some extra for him to get it fixed?" Mirai asked Kan. "I'm sure it will bother him otherwise."

The atmosphere in the loft seemed directly tethered to the mood Kan happened to be in at any given moment. As Mirai's question hung in the air, everyone could sense the mood turning sentimental.

"Oh, for God's sake." Kan exhaled a puff of smoke and walked over to one of the tables. He jotted a note down on a piece of paper and handed it to the Aussie. "A dentist in Kamayut Township owes me a favor. Tell him he can cash it in by proxy."

The Burmese man read the note and raised it at Kan in thankful acknowledgment. He turned to leave, nodding toward Mirai ever so briefly. When the door closed, Kan brought up another chair and sat in front of his half sister. He crossed his ankle over his knee and continued smoking.

Even in his voxhall office, Mirai had never witnessed him so relaxed.

"I'll need to be heading out shortly. Don't really have a ton of time. But I wanted to give you at least a few minutes to ask the questions you undoubtedly have for me. So… shoot."

The Aussie reverted his attention to other things over in the corner. Mirai watched him without interest. Her mind was preoccupied with filtering a thousand questions down to just the imperative. As she pondered them, her eyes drifted down to the white gauze wrapping part of her foot. Sticking out from the top were toenails painted in violet. The color reminded her of a palette, and the gauze, of a newly stretched canvas.

I need to paint that pagoda...

"Mirai?"

Her vision darted back up.

"Under a serious time crunch here. Questions?"

"Yes," she blurted, "who was the man you killed?"

The cigarette hung from the edge of Kan's lips as he casually rubbed his thumb over the knuckles of his other hand. "He was… a trespasser… who would have shot you for nothing more than the pleasure of watching you bleed."

"He was with Ad Ordinem, right?"

Kan stared at Mirai while a thin vapor exited his mouth. Finally removing the cigarette so he could fully exhale, he said, "Yeah."

"And you are also part of Ad Ordinem—a subversive team within the organization called Emblem, sure—but ultimately still under their umbrella. Correct?"

"Correct."

Mirai composed herself and said, "So the parent group is trying to bring the world to an end, and your group is attempting to stop them?"

"That's an oversimplification. I'm afraid. Our motives are more attuned to one particular area of disagreement, a fundamental tenet which the leadership of Ad Ordinem has perverted into a course of action. It's a course Emblem intends to channel back to its proper trajectory."

"Can you humor me with specifics?"

"I cannot."

Mirai pursed her lips but decided to move on. "How did you know I was in Myanmar?"

"The same way I knew you were on that plane. I've been tracking your phone."

Mirai's heart skipped a beat. "Tracking my… Why?"

"To protect you."

"Protect me from what?" Kan pointed toward the ceiling. Mirai sighed heavily. "What do these people want with me? I'm not Osiris!"

"You being Osiris was never in question."

"What do you mean?"

"First, a question for you, Mirai. How do you know, I mean really *truly* know, that Jason McGarry is Osiris? How *exactly* did you come to that conclusion?"

"He told me."

For a split second, Kan's face was almost nonplussed. He reeled in his surprise before it could fully take form. "Jason McGarry… told you so?"

"Yeah, two days ago in our family den. In front of his wife. After I confronted him about his time living in Cocoa Beach, working as an engineer for PRN America, under his real name… Mark Stone."

Kan nodded, and in his nod was a sliver of contempt. "I'm impressed. Back when I started digging into our past, it took a lot longer to piece all that together. You're a clever one."

"Good for me. Now getting back to my question: Protect me from what?"

Kan took a long drag from the cigarette and then crushed it underneath his boot. He stood up to pace and to find words within the motions of movement. "Everyone gets Ad Ordinem wrong. They whisper, they theorize, they offer conjecture on what little is known about the society through its veiled history… Many of their conclusions are inaccurate. The only person who came close was George Domínguez in that worst seller he penned. Some of his analysis was spot on, and for a brief time, several people within the organization assumed that he gained this info from an insider, a Paragon informant, and wanted Domínguez eliminated. When they saw that the general public didn't really care about the inner workings of an ancient—mostly defunct—secret society, a vote was cast and they spared his life."

Kan gesticulated while trying to form a concrete from the abstraction in his mind. "It's difficult for those outside the society to truly grasp its mystical underpinnings."

"Mystical?"

"Spiritual. Supernatural. Whatever you wish to call it. Their actions are driven by a philosophy. A belief. One as all-powerful and encompassing as any religion. It's this precept that motivates men to… for instance, slaughter innocent people and hijack an airliner, or derail trains in Kentucky, cause power grid failures in New York, or threaten meltdowns in Texas. This conviction is so strong, that even if it starts off as mythology… the power of *belief* and the belief systems that implement it, begin to make it real. Does that make sense?"

Kan didn't wait for a reply and continued pacing. "It's that sense of calling which motivates us. The faith that providence has sanctioned our cause. As a result, we work tirelessly to bring about that which God has prophesied, and which nature has failed to do."

Mirai furrowed her brows. "To bring about the end of time?"

"The end of *time*—yes—not the end of humanity." Kan said it with his forefinger outstretched, as a preempt to further protest. "It's about eras, not annihilation. And therein lies the splinter between our two factions. For as Ad Ordinem wishes for the destruction of mankind and a restoration to the supremacy of nature, Emblem understands that the original command was for an *evolution* to take place. The next phase of a new and improved human. Death, suffering, destruction will all be precursors to this rebirth, that is a true and unfortunate consequence to societal transformation. But once completed, a new generation will shape a new world. This is the promise, the progress, and the purpose of what we… and yes, what I—am trying to accomplish."

"You used the word *prophesied*," inserted Mirai. "I'm confused. When I met you in the voxhall, you said you didn't believe in any of that."

"What I said was that I don't believe in the pretentious piety and repetitive rituals of those who bottle up the Love of God like it was some sort of top-shelf liquor. I have no use for their demands of allegiance, nor their mantra of waiting on God to bring about the change we seek. I used my position there only as a cover, as a means to an end."

"What end?"

Kan sighed sympathetically. "As with so much, I cannot tell you, Mirai. But just know that it was with the most righteous intentions that I played the role and played it well. God will forgive me for my deceptions…" His eyes wandered without blinking for a moment. "Just as he will forgive me for so much else."

Mirai ran her hand over her arm and shook her head. "Secrets known only by the elites, prophecies given and misinterpreted, sacred passphrases, vague plans for the future dictated by inaccessible figures… I don't know, Kan. The voxhalls and Ad Ordinem don't sound all that different."

Kan smiled. "I know it's difficult for you to understand. But I assure you, if you'd see what I've seen, you'd believe it too."

Mirai met his intense gaze. "Stop proving my point."

The two held each other's stare before a cough from the Aussie broke Kan's concentration. The man in the corner tapped on his wristwatch. Kan nodded dismissively.

"So is Ad Ordinem also behind the billboards?" Mirai asked.

"The what?"

"'Is This the End of the World?'"

Kan chuckled. "Oh, no, that's not us. Have no idea where those came from."

The answer seemed to perplex Mirai all the more. "Well, if you can't tell me what Ad Ordinem really has planned, can you at least share what's going to happen to Osiris?"

Kan's face registered an instant of shock. "Sorry, it keeps throwing me that you're aware of him. What do you wish to know?"

This time it was Mirai's face projecting surprise. "What do I… *Kan*, I just handed my parents over to God knows who… for God knows what purpose. Doesn't that strike you as a bit strange?"

"Not at all. I know why you did it and I know the rotting, radioactive, molten rage that made you do it. I know it because it's the same cesspool of hate that fuels what I do every day. Trust me, you'll learn to live with it, to channel it productively, in a way that prevents it from eating you alive."

Mirai dropped her face into her hands and pressed her fingers hard against the pounding in her forehead. "It's not hate. It's not pain. I could manage those if I had to. No… What I feel toward them is worse than that. It's the thing I fear the most, actually."

Kan withdrew another cigarette but didn't light it. He squared his jaw and responded, "What you feel toward them… is nothing. Right? A shocking, frightening, vacuum of space sort of nothing when you think of them. When you recall previously happy memories. When you imagine their embrace, their smiles. When you think of sitting down to dinner, watching a movie, going on a family trip, all of it is now contaminated through a comprehensive lens of absolute numbness."

Mirai let her hands fall to her lap. She looked at Kan as she once had in the voxhall, when she believed him to have all the answers. "Am I that obvious?"

"Not really. I just know that you and I have chosen to take different paths based on the cards life dealt us. You must go on bringing beauty to the world, and I must kick it into its next phase of evolution."

"Through violence and terror?"

"Temporary tools, long-lasting results. Again, God will forgive me."

"But will you?"

Kan struck a match and the amber tip of his cigarette pulsed to life. Mirai saw him pace again but knew he was about to cut their conversation short. She cleared her throat and decided to pivot. "What will David do to them? To… Jason and Valerie?"

"David?" Kan said through a puff. "Oh for… That wasn't David on the phone, Mirai. That was…" Kan fully exhaled and pressed his fingers against his central forehead. He massaged the spot in a circular motion while seeming to organize his thoughts. Calming what seemed to be a surge of self-directed irritation, he said, "That wasn't David on the call. That was someone from Ad Ordinem manipulating you via Omni."

Mirai blinked. "Via… Wait, what?"

"I assume you're aware of the application's capabilities?"

"Umm… I guess."

"Then you must know that it can write messages on your behalf, texts, emails, leave voicemails, hold basic conversations for the tedium of life's tasks, all with your voice and cadence and using your personality profile as its framework."

"I'm aware of what Omni can do. I didn't want it utilizing those features. That's why I toggled those preferences off on my phone."

"*You* may have," Kan said as he brought the cigarette back to his lips, "but others can still use their Omni to interface with you and you'd never be the wiser. Emloch easily exploited that vulnerability in the application."

"I'm still confused. How do you know it wasn't David behind the call?"

Kan began pacing again. His tension was suddenly palpable. In the corner, the Aussie also seemed on edge; his eyes followed Kan's movements as if concerned that he would fall into a sinkhole. "I gotta be real careful what I share here, *ma kyi*. You're my big sister, and I love you, and I trust you, but for your own protection—"

"Is David Eban the Emloch persona? Yes or no?"

Her inquiry had an urgency behind it. There was a flammability to her words. The demand in her eyes was the admittance of the truth. Kan gazed at her with a pleading that she not require more of him than he could offer. "David… accidentally got caught between the crosshairs of something very complicated. You misinterpreted it and he got blamed. Blamed for something he didn't do. Blamed for something I did."

"You?" she blurted. "Are you telling me… you're Emloch?"

Kan shot a glance back at the nervous Aussie. After shaking his head in reply, Kan turned back to Mirai and said, "My dear, no one is Emloch. Not really. At least, no one physical. Emloch is just the manifestation of a computer program I wrote. It's not real. It's a generative artificial intelligence. A large language model. I created it over a year ago to assist Emblem in their subversive efforts against Ad Ordinem."

"*Kan…*" protested the Aussie.

"Shut up," Kan grumbled. "Mirai, Emloch was a persona that emerged from the program with the specific purpose of helping us locate Osiris. We needed an advantage over Ad Ordinem as they were looking for Osiris too. Our side was outnumbered and falling behind. So, I crafted Emloch with everything it would need to conduct wide-scale outreach, to help us find Osiris before Ad Ordinem did. During the fine-tuning stage, it produced countless false leads and led us down many blind alleys. But every now and then, it offered a prime candidate."

Mirai listened in a dazed state of wonder. Her words formed as if from somewhere beyond her conscious mind. "People like Leighton Russo... and George Domínguez..."

"Yes," Kan said tenderly, "also many others. Sifting through them took time, resources, energy we barely had. Emloch was a highly effective tool. Extremely convincing."

"Too convincing," she muttered.

Kan squared his jaw. "Emloch reaching out to you was a mistake, Mirai. A massive oversight. I didn't catch it until it was too late. You must understand that an AI is capable of countless interactions simultaneously. Emloch was talking with you alongside hundreds of others. Yet for some reason, several conversations it carried out never made it into my report. I didn't know you two were communicating until I conducted an audit on the wire transfers Emloch was sending to people like you via the Emblem bank accounts. I saw your name on the statements and realized we had a problem. Had I known Emloch was working you for information, I would have removed you from the sequence immediately. I guess you could say that briefly, the creation surpassed the creator."

"That doesn't make any sense," Mirai shot back.

"What do you mean?"

"You had all of the info on Jason McGarry before I did. You knew his history and background. You must have known he was Osiris."

"I knew he was a strong candidate. But there were dozens of leads who could also fit the profile. I didn't know for sure until Ad Ordinem called you today."

"Profile? You knew his real name. You knew he used to belong to Ad Ordinem. You knew about his time with PRN. You knew how he came to obtain me. You knew that he got cosmetic surgery to alter his appearance out of fear of being discovered by his old comrades. You knew all of it! You knew everything! What else could there possibly be?"

Kan appeared puzzled, yet not in the way one would be if they were entirely oblivious to a situation. He shifted his eyes back toward the Aussie. For the first time in several minutes, they appeared to be on the same page. Kan answered in a steady tone, "A bit more, I'm afraid."

The tension in the giant room slowly began to wane. It took Mirai a moment to understand why, and when she did, her frame slouched. Kan was out of time and wrapping up the conversation. There would be no more facts unearthed. Questions still abounded, yet one thing had become abundantly clear.

Mirai winced as her face formed into a singular thought. "Oh my God," she said through her breath. "David."

"Yes," Kan said, "I'm so sorry that happened. Call it collateral damage. All I can do is apologize and assure you that David is entirely trustworthy."

"You know him?"

"I know everyone in your life. Through my various operatives, I've been keeping a protective eye on you for some time. You're my sister, after all."

Mirai's vision sank to the floor. Her eyes were lost in a series of fragmented memories. Kan circled the loft for a minute before stopping at the table and jotting something down on paper. He tore the sheet from the pad, folded it, and returned to where Mirai was reflecting.

"Hey," Kan said, kneeling down next to the chair, "try to believe me when I tell you there is nothing to worry about. I have a plan, and it seems to be working. The McGarrys will get what they've always had coming. My father will continue to be tormented by his past thanks to the madness now afflicting him. The leadership of Ad Ordinem will be overthrown, and humanity will not come to an end—only a new beginning. Soon, all that has been weighing down your talented, superlative mind will be rendered meaningless. You and David can continue your love story. And your artwork will hang in places of prominence around the world." With that, Kan gently opened Mirai's hand and placed the folded paper inside it.

"What's this?" she asked, dejectedly.

Kan's expression was a mixture of love and pain. He arose off the floor and kissed Mirai on the top of her head. "What you came to Yangon to find."

CHAPTER 13
ANGEL OF WHISPERS

Her mother wore purple.

Chaw Khin Thet stood outside her home that was nestled along a curved street. The house was a two-story single-family style, with enough breathing room between the neighboring homes to have a small garden. Inside the garden were magnolia bushes, accompanied by clusters of golden-yellow padauk flowers. The woman was standing amongst the shrubs with a ceramic watering pot. She appeared to be blossoming from within a bouquet.

Mirai watched her from afar while feeling faint from the punishing midday heat. She had been following her mother for over an hour, starting at the house, then to a nearby mall, then to the fresh market, and finally back to the house. Mirai had made no attempts to approach her. She had trailed from behind like a stalker, unable to summon the thing within herself that would overcome her trepidation.

Exposed to the oppressive heat, and without sufficient hydration, Mirai was now paying the physical price for her hesitancy.

You can't keep doing this… Just go talk to her. Maybe the words will come if you start speaking…

The sandals she had purchased in the bazaar took a loud scrape across the gravelly road. After her first few steps of intent, however,

Mirai circled back around to where she had begun and cursed the timidity shackling her soul. She leaned against the trunk of a tree. The edges of reality were losing their sharpness. Her vision began to swim.

Stress and excessive heat can trigger MS episodes. You need to be careful...

Nausea drove her forward as much as it threatened to hold her back. Mirai took deep breaths as the details of the house came into view. The exterior was mostly white-painted wood with a barrel-tile roof. A cherry-mahogany door stood partially open, allowing for a cat to peek its head around the base of the jamb.

The woman in the garden wore a short-sleeve blouse and a longyi tied at her waist. Mirai saw the face and felt a strange sense of nostalgia, coming not from what she recalled of the magazine, but from a memory going back much farther. Her mother's shoulder-length black hair now had a few streaks of silver, and her cherubic face looked upon the flower petals with the grace of a matured beauty.

I know her.

When Chaw was finished with her pruning, she retreated back into her house only to return a moment later with a small purse dangling from her wrist and some freshly applied Thanaka on her cheeks. She started off into the neighborhood much to Mirai's chagrin.

This is my own damn fault...

The neighborhood lasted only a few blocks until the main road reappeared. Pedestrians gathered near an intersection where a sign was posted in Burmese lettering. Mirai blended into the crowd and within reach of her mother. She kept an eye on her while waiting, and in doing so, chastised herself for succumbing to the temptation of delay.

A bus pulled up to the stop and several passengers disembarked while new riders wove around them to climb aboard. Mirai did her best to keep Chaw in view amid the shuffle. Her mother found what appeared to be the last available seat. Mirai snatched ahold of a strap hanger and struggled to balance herself as the bus maneuvered away from the stop and gradually picked up speed.

The bus driver called out something in Burmese. Mirai was unable to determine if it was directed at her, route information for the passengers, or something else to which she as a foreigner would be oblivious. The streets began passing in waves. The roar of the engine matched the pressure of acceleration. Mirai gripped the strap tighter and tried to fend off the sensation of wooziness.

I can't believe I'm here right now. I can't believe I'm doing this.

Through the rectangular windows, Mirai witnessed a sudden break in the cityscape. Sunlight shimmered off a body of water that was enveloped by scenic walkways. In the center of the lake was a two-story palace connected to the land by a barge. Its golden pyatthat roof pierced the open air and captivated Mirai's attention as she passed by. Before it was out of view, a decorative sign planted along the street answered her immediate question.

Kandawgyi Lake Park—Karaweik Hall.

"I'll need to paint that," she said under her breath, gazing until the very last peaks of gold vanished behind the oncoming buildings.

The bus slowed to make a left turn, and the city shifted along with it through the panorama. The driver once again yelled out what sounded like a command. Mirai took a quick survey of the riders in her vicinity. No one seemed phased by the statement. They all were absorbed within the spheres of their own lives.

An older man gazed out his window and seemed to be reflecting on a scenario playing out in his mind. A young couple with a squirming toddler sat huddled together while trying to maintain grasp of their multiple grocery bags. Back a few rows, a woman slightly younger than Mirai listened to music in her earbuds—the bopping of her head causing her topknot hair bun to bounce in unison. There was a mix of ages, professions, and personalities represented within the microcosm of civilization on display. It was not much different than any sample Mirai could envision back in Miami… save for one dissimilarity.

Wow… came a dawning thought, the thought forming into a half smile, *for once… all of these people look like me.*

The truth redirected her sights toward her mother. The woman sat with a contented expression, and the eyes of a person unafraid to observe the world. Mirai watched her for a moment, and in doing so, hoped that the act of watching would grant her courage.

A few more streets passed before the bus shimmied to a halt next to a crowded sidewalk. Chaw arose from her seat and prepared to disembark. Mirai positioned herself accordingly. The heat of a blast furnace greeted them as they left the transit system behind and started along the road. Chaw marshaled herself ahead, seemingly impervious to the temperature. Mirai kept a few paces behind, feeling borderline faint.

It was only the blinding glint from a towering object that stole Mirai's attention away from her target. Off in the distance, a bell-shaped structure radiated in golden shimmer, tearing through the cerulean sky from its base all the way to its pinnacle. Mirai squinted while trying to make out the image. As she continued walking toward it, the shifting light created a recognizable outline.

The Shwedagon Pagoda stood hundreds of feet above anything else in view. Its enormity refused to be dwarfed by the massively wide entrance stairways or the colonnade-flanked atriums leading up to its marble platform. Mirai could scarcely take her eyes from it, even to track her mother's movements. The marvel was unlike anything she had seen. It was unlike anything typical of Western architecture. The shape, style, majesty, and grandeur were from a different culture, transcending from a different time. There was something mystical about it, otherworldly, and altogether incongruous with modernity.

Mirai gasped. For the first time in her career, the young artist felt no certainty that she could re-create reality better on canvas.

Still though, I'll need to try...

Her eyes wandered for a moment. Chaw was nearly to the base of the megastructure. Mirai refocused her attention and crossed the street. She watched as her mother removed her sandals before taking the first step onto the lavishly ornamented stairs. Mirai copied her actions and began the ascent. Above her, two giant Chinthe statues guarded the entrance. The carved lions stood forever with their mouths open—incisors showing—and their eyes punctuated by a seemingly omnipresent gaze.

Mirai felt incredibly small as she climbed the stairwell. Each landing led to another row of steps, a pattern repeated well after she entered the pagoda's main atrium. Inside, the red-and-gold ceiling towered overhead. Support columns etched with intricate designs and symbols conjoined the floor with outstretched rafters also bedecked with meaning.

The grand hall commanded reverence. Yet with each successive landing and set of stairs, Mirai could not help but muse at the sudden appearance of vendor displays lining both walls of the pagoda. The clusters of merchants ascended along with the stairwell. Clothing, golden figurines, colorful trays filled to the brim with beads, charms, and pendants; the items for sale would have been hard to ignore if offered anywhere else. Yet Mirai could not be distracted.

Her eyes looked straight ahead, up the next flight of steps that tunneled through the majestic gateway. At the end of the tunnel was a light source. It shined in dazzling brilliance at the top of the stairwell. There was a clarity to it, as if its properties had bypassed the atmosphere entirely, leaving behind nothing but pure sunlight. It grew in radiance the higher Mirai climbed and shifted in appearance between gold and white. The translucent orb mesmerized her. She no longer watched the steps drawing her upward, for her eyes refused to gaze anywhere but directly into the halo. Not even the need to blink interrupted her unobstructed view of the celestial vision. It was only the silhouette of a human form that caused her entrancement to crack.

It was her mother. Chaw was now walking directly into the glowing sphere. For a moment, she was ablaze in light covering even the black strands of her hairline in aura. Mirai blinked and then watched as the last vestiges of the woman's purple clothing was absorbed into the light.

Mirai quickened her steps as a mild jolt of fear caused her to wonder if she would ever see Chaw again. The soft slapping sounds of her feet hitting the tiles followed all the way up to the final landing. It was just past the blinding light that Mirai could finally see what was directly ahead of her—the marble platform of the pagoda, and the open air of the outside world that seemed to have prematurely circled the sundial and begun the day anew.

"Oh wow," Mirai whispered, gazing up at the golden stupa. It seemed poised to launch into the sky. Surrounding it were stations set up for prayer or meditation. Onlookers perambulated clockwise around the structure. Some spread out mats or simply knelt on their knees. Others lit a series of candles while whispering silent thoughts from their lips. Mirai meandered in the general direction of her mother. She continued following from behind as Chaw stepped atop a dais and reached for a small cup. After dipping the cup into a basin, she proceeded to pour the water over what appeared to be an ivory statue. The carving had been bestowed with flowers throughout the day. The blossoming petals bounced with each droplet of water.

Chaw repeated the ritual several times before offering a final whisper and returning to the marble platform. She then joined several others in kneeling and praying. Once her offerings were completed, the woman simply remained kneeling, too serene to immediately return to a standing position.

Mirai stood only a few short steps from her mother. She felt like walking up and gently tapping Chaw's shoulder. Or perhaps addressing her congenially with the common Burmese greeting of *mingalaba*. The scenarios pulsed through her mind. None of them gave Mirai the courage to close the remaining distance. The hesitation shackled her legs in place. The inertia drew ire within herself. Without the proper words, there would be no introduction. The journey to Myanmar would be incomplete. She would return home with no resolutions, no deeper knowledge, and no insight into how her past would affect her future.

Her eyes welled with tears of despair. She clasped her hands together and looked down at the marble. Her vision swam from emotion. Her vision swam from lightheadedness. Whether from the heat or the dehydration or the constant feeling that the world was teetering off its axis, Mirai could not discern. The ache in her right shoulder was steadily working its way down her arm. Pins and needles were forming in her hand.

I just need some water...
I just need some shade...
I wonder if the Potion is available in Yangon...
Maybe I can get it without...

A twisting pain sliced into her wrist. Mirai groaned and felt her knees begin to buckle underneath the weight of her wilting frame.

It's not just lack of water…

It's not just lack of shade…

The Potion isn't a long-term solution. . not for what I have.

A ring of sweat tugged at her collar. Her eyes darted about trying to determine if the area had suddenly gotten brighter. A few feet out of reach was her mother, still kneeling contentedly and taking in the peace of the moment.

Mirai placed one foot unsteadily in front of the other. In a languished breath she muttered out in Chaw's direction, "I…"

Her voice trailed off into the ether. Her lips continued to try to formulate words. Nothing emerged. Suddenly struck mute, Mirai saw the marble tiles of the platform shifting beneath her feet. She shut her eyes in an effort to find a stable center. Even from behind her eyelids, she could still see the inescapable light.

Say something to her… Anything…

Mirai could no longer hear her own thoughts. All she could do was picture her mother—and in viewing her through partially opened eyes —discover that she was just as inaccessible as the imagined image. The Shwedagon Pagoda tilted sideways against the skyline. The knowledge that she was falling came too late to prevent it. Her left shoulder hit the ground a split second before her face did. As her cheekbone smacked the unforgiving tile, streaks of pain surged across her face.

It's too late… I'm too late…

Mirai stared at the slanted world through a daze. After a slow blink, she was on her back looking straight up at a puffy cloud passing overhead. Her throat felt significantly more parched than it had been earlier. A small crowd had gathered in a semicircular cluster. The natural progression of time seemed to have been altered. Seconds had passed, possibly minutes. The only thing she knew for certain was that a woman was kneeling next to her head, and a hand was gently rubbing her hair.

It took Mirai by surprise when she realized that the woman was already looking at her. The eyes held Mirai in a curious sort of trance. It was the kind of greeting obtained when an introduction seemed superfluous.

"It's okay," the woman said. "You need water. We get some in here."

Mirai experienced the woman's invitation through two visions: the first, from within her own desaturated awareness, and the second, from an extrasensory perspective located just outside her body. The duality jarred her as she felt the rim of a cup being placed at her lips.

Mirai swallowed some water, hesitated, and then went back for another sip. The woman caring for her said something to another person and they hoisted Mirai up to a seated position.

"You become faint," the woman said, her voice oddly cheerful. "Too hot out. That's why I water plants. Otherwise, they faint too."

Mirai felt like her mouth was smiling even as her eyebrows were furrowed. She took another lengthy sip from the mug. The stagnant heat in her core was quickly dissipating. The fog in her mind was not. "Thank you… I… I was just trying to…"

A fatigue not associated with the heat rapidly overwhelmed her. It stemmed from a place in her body to which Mirai felt inadequately introduced. The force and the speed by which it drained her of energy terrified her. It felt like she was bleeding out, not of blood, but of that which made blood so imperatively vital.

What's… happening to me?

Her head became too heavy. The muscles in her neck began to relent. As her vision aimed upward again, the lovely face of her mother and the towering peak of the golden shrine served as the final images Mirai saw before a shroud of darkness absorbed the world.

"You rest. Everything okay."

The voice drifted into Mirai's semiconsciousness. As she awakened, the last vestiges of a dream lingered at the precipice of her lucidity. There had been an easel. Paintbrushes in both hands and between multiple fingers. A studio not unlike her own, but also not exactly. There had been a painting. She recalled trying to apply color to various parts of the canvas and them shifting indiscriminately from where she wanted them to go. Instead of staying in place, the colors moved like a kaleidoscope, leaving Mirai in a state of maddened vexation at her inability to settle the image. The more she applied the brushstrokes, the farther away she chased the colors. Before long, the entirety of the painting was nothing but a muddied collage.

Mirai let go of the dream even as the tightness in her chest remained. She opened her eyes and saw a blurry reality. She was inside a house, lying flat on her back atop a well-cushioned sofa. The blades of a ceiling fan whirled slowly. The plants outside a window rustled gently in the sweltering breeze.

I think that woman was my mother… I think this is her house…

"Please say if you need anything," came a voice from somewhere just beyond Mirai's periphery. "Air-conditioning is back on. Power was not too much out."

Mirai listened to Chaw speak. Her eyes then wandered to the interior of the home, where the attention to detail given to the furnishings stood in dramatic contrast to the aged walls behind them. She thought of the house as a perfect summary of the country of Myanmar itself, a retrofitted blend of new and old, modern and ancient, a clockwork of life in a timeline—from one generation to the next.

Mirai blinked. Everything she saw remained slightly out of focus.

"Jasmine tea," Chaw said, returning with a small white cup on a saucer. "And here's some spoon."

"Thank you," Mirai murmured.

"You sick? Maybe coming down with fever?"

"No, I don't think so."

Chaw set the tea down on the end table and placed the back of her hand against Mirai's forehead. "Maybe you have infection?"

Mirai opened her eyes wider and saw her mother pointing over at the gauze wrapping on her foot. "No. It's… just a cut. It was disinfected."

"You need doctor? If so, you just tell me and I take you."

A heavy sigh filled the living room. "I'm afraid a doctor can't help with this."

Chaw sat down in the chair opposite the sofa and gazed contemplatively at Mirai. In her eyes was an even mixture of concern and curiosity. She rubbed her hands together in a fidgety motion. Her words were spoken with tremendous delicacy.

"I brought you here quickly in taxicab, after you faint at the pagoda. I remember seeing you from earlier today, outside the house, and then again near the market. I thought… maybe she is looking for me."

Using her hands, Mirai pushed herself up into a seated position on the sofa and was astonished at the demand that the simple action required. There was an intensity to her fatigue. It radiated throughout her body and nearly left her breathless.

"Thank you," she answered, reaching for a glass of cold water and then alternating with the teacup. "It was very kind of you to bring me here."

"You look so young," Chaw said cautiously. "How old are you?"

Mirai took a sip of tea and set the saucer down on the end table. "I'm twenty-five as of this month."

"I see, I see. And where you came from?"

Mirai spoke the words while watching for her mother's reaction. "The United States. I live in Florida, in a place called Miami." Chaw was already sitting perfectly still, yet from Mirai's perspective, she grew even more so. "Ever been there?"

"To Miami? Yes. I live there fo' years." Chaw spoke with the same watchful glare toward Mirai. The two women stayed silent for a moment. It appeared as if Chaw was searching for permission to broach the topic.

Mirai softened her gaze as the lassitude wore down her defenses. "Did you… Do you… have any children?"

Chaw smiled brightly. "My son—he is wild one, travels the world.

Never sure what is he up to? He writes and calls sometime. I wish I see him more."

Mirai pulled a strand of hair away from her face. "Any other children?"

"Yes… well, from many years ago. A daughter. Very beautiful. Very much like you."

Mirai smiled, exposing her lone dimple. "I'm sure she doesn't come close to your beauty."

"Oh, that long gone," Chaw laughed. "My face look like the mashed potato."

Mirai observed Chaw's jovial animation while trying to hold herself together. The torrent of emotion was rising to the surface of what Mirai could bear. Yet the question that would free her remained dammed up beneath a barricade of fear. Fear of both the answer and of whatever a proper response would look like.

She parted her lips to speak when Chaw interjected, "What you do in United States? You work?"

"One could call it that."

"You very pretty. Must be actress or model."

Mirai mused to herself at the irony. "No, not me. My sister is a model, though. She's the new face for Omni."

"For what?"

"You know, the application that basically runs the world." Mirai removed her phone and pulled up a static image of Carys's advertisement. "This is the new promotional campaign. That's her."

Chaw stared intently at the photo and then glanced up at Mirai. "She's… your sister…"

The meaning of the statement softened whatever vestiges of tension remained in Mirai's face. She slipped the phone back into her pocket and then rubbed her hands over her legs. "Yes. My sister… from my adoptive family."

"Oh…" came Chaw's incomplete response. "Nice family?"

Mirai's ready-made answer, the one that had sufficed all her life in extolling the virtues of the McGarrys, came to a grinding halt inside her mouth. Her tongue atrophied. Her mind drew an exhaustive blank.

There were no words in her vocabulary up to the monumental challenge of answering Chaw's question. A helpless stare was all she could reply.

"Well then… what kind of work you do in Miami?"

"I'm an artist."

"Artist?" Chaw reiterated. "Oh… you paint… on canvas…"

Mirai noticed a subtle change in Chaw's expression. "That's right. I developed my own style over many years. I've been selling my artwork since I was a teenager."

"Describe, please."

The question caught Mirai off guard. She sat for a moment in embarrassment while trying to garner the necessary descriptors. "Umm… well, they all… My technique is essentially…" She stopped and drew in a breath. "I paint order coming out of chaos."

The woman pondered the words carefully. "Order… chaos…"

"The background is disordered beauty, whether it be natural, abstract, whatever… with the center focus being a portrait of a human face. The face then brings order to the chaos. That's it. That's my trademark. Signed at the bottom with my first name as my moniker."

Chaw tilted her head with graceful ease. In her eyes was the re-creation of a mental image. "What name is that?"

The young woman felt a tug at her chest as she said it. "Mirai, with a heart for the *M*."

"*Mirai*…" Chaw whispered. She said it with a tender searching. The lack of recognition left a sadness on her face. "But…"

With a determined swiftness, Chaw rose up from her chair and marshaled herself across the room. It took a moment for Mirai to understand what she was doing. Once she did, the living room seemed to close in on them both.

"Oh my God," Mirai said.

Staring back at her from between her mother's hands was one of Mirai's earliest paintings. She blinked madly in an effort to see through the blurriness. The piece was so old that Mirai second-guessed herself as to if it truly was her work or that of an impersonator. The signature on the lower left put all doubts to rest.

"How… did you obtain this?" Mirai asked.

Chaw gently set the painting down between the two arms of an upholstered chair. "My son give to me many years ago. He bought online and mail to me. I hang it in all these room, but the light in here best. I see it every day. Every day… I think of you."

Mirai felt something within her decompress. "Think of me?"

Chaw nodded, and as she did, the moisture in her eyes reflected the recessed ceiling lights. "Isn't that you?" Her face was asking the question, but her finger was aimed at the painting.

There was still a churning part of Mirai that wanted to leap from the sofa and bolt out the front door. She inwardly laughed at the absurdity, knowing that she could barely lift her arms. "Yes… that's me."

Chaw appeared to be vacillating. "So many year ago, I watch my daughter write her name with a heart-shaped *M*, just like yours. But how can that be? Mirai is not what I name my daughter. I name her after her birth month."

Birth month…

The words felt like a knife, slicing off a part of her body that no longer belonged. A pain welted into Mirai's chest. It became difficult to gain a deep breath. A single tear escaped from one eye, then the other. Through her rich mocha irises, she gazed at her painting as if witnessing it for the first time. Nothing about it seemed familiar, least of all—the signature.

"My name is May?"

"May La Yaung Chae," said Chaw, through a quivering lower lip. "You see, when I live in Miami, I watch all these cargo ship on the ocean each night. They have lights that twinkle underneath the moonlight. Look like beacon. So beautiful. It was that beauty that make me think you too could one day be beacon of beauty and color to the world. That hope give me belief that I could raise you on my own. That why I name you May La Yaung Chae. It means, painting with moonlight in May."

Mirai's wilting frame trembled as she reached out to embrace her mother. Chaw bent forward and the two held each other tightly in front of the artwork depicting chaos—their faces now creating the order. From the torrent of didactic events leading up to the moment of reunion, Mirai felt a woven thread leading back to a solitary question. *Why is my name Mirai?* The answer was the sensation of a hand touching skin. *My name is May.*

She sobbed. Down her cheeks fell the tears of a lifetime spent wondering. The composite mental pictures of the woman who had given her up failed in every meaningful way against the reality set before her. Frailty, poverty, abuse, unbearable circumstances, or just simply a lack of interest, had all stood in as reasons to explain her mother's abandonment. As she hugged the woman tighter, the stark truth eliminated the revisionist history.

I was never abandoned. I was stolen.

"I'm so sorry… so sorry," Chaw whimpered. "I look so long for you…"

"No…"

"… I should have never believe him…"

"Stop—"

"… I never forgive myself for letting this happen to you…"

"I said stop!"

Mirai pulled away from Chaw and forcibly wiped the tears from her own cheeks. "Don't ever say that. Don't ever apologize… not for what that man and that couple did to us. It's not your fault. It was never your fault. They set you up to bear the burden of their crime. They knew what kind of power maternal guilt can be and they used it against you. Used it to keep you devastated, tethered to that man, and eventually hopeless enough to agree to return to Myanmar."

Chaw pressed her hands together in front of her chest. "May La will believe me when I say, I did not know he was married, had family, children, home on the other side of the country. I never hear his voice on the radio and know is that him? He says his name is Bruce, not Howard. He says he is engineer… works for big network. When we meet, you were tiny. I never know until too late that he is boss of big network. He married man, husband, father, but he never tell me. Otherwise, I would not date this man. I would not agree to marry him and allow you to call him your *hpay*. Then, when he find out I'm with his own baby, he change. Become not so much kind. Later, after I have your baby brother, I very weak and unwell. So he send me and Kan Thura back to my parents' home in Yangon. Says for me to rest. Says he will care for you in here so you don't have to leave America. Only then I discover that marriage was never real. He already have wife. Our marriage papers fake. Now I stuck in Myanmar with new baby but no May La. I try to arrange to bring you here, but find out you no longer where I thought. Someone at daycare call me months later to confess that my husband let strangers take you away… to be with good family—yes—but no more with me. They would not tell me more. They fear being in trouble."

Mirai ran her palm across her forehead and let out a weary sigh. "The McGarrys told me it was a closed adoption. That I would never know why my birth parents didn't want me anymore. I remember being so confused and so heartbroken. It took me so long to be conditioned into accepting this new reality. But after a while… I mean, what else could I do? They were my new family, and eventually, you were nothing more than a hazy memory."

Chaw nodded remorsefully. "I try. Every day I try. How am I supposed to find my daughter from across the world? Bruce no more takes my call or answers my email. I go crazy with worry about what happened to you. Nothing worked. Now I know why." Chaw reluctantly glanced over at the M-shaped heart on the painting. "I tell everyone your name is May."

The story rattled inside Mirai's brain, unable to find a cogent place to land. She pictured the young mother devastated at the inexplicable loss of her beloved daughter—mad with worry over her condition and fate, heartbroken at the crumbling of a fake marriage, destitute with an infant, exiled back to her home country to cover up a crime beyond her comprehension.

The weight of the thought pressed down against her eyelids. The emotional upheaval left her energy reserve in the negative. Mirai knew that there was so much more to ask, to hear, to ponder, and to learn from the enigma standing before her. A pulse of anger flooded her senses even as she felt herself retreating from consciousness.

Not now damn it! I want to keep talking... keep listening...

Chaw leaned in to touch the side of Mirai's face. "You look very tired, yes?"

Mirai shifted her eyes apologetically. "I just need… a minute…"

"Come with me in here."

Helping Mirai with each step, Chaw guided her slowly into a side bedroom. The space was small and quaint. A bed and table were nestled against a solitary window. On the wall was a tapestry with several lines of embroidered text woven into it. Mirai squinted as she entered the room but could not make out the words.

"You rest as long as you need," Chaw said.

Mirai had no gumption to argue. She would accept this opportunity to regain her strength and be back to conversing with her reclaimed mother by dinnertime.

I just need to sleep this off... this fatigue. This awful... horrible fatigue...

I can tell you who Osiris is...

Mirai gasped awake while her heart slammed against her rib cage.

Her eyes opened to darkness. The bedroom had been sucked into a black hole. Outlines of walls and furniture, the hallway door and the lone window, all existed through the lens of a blurred shadow. Her mind started to race, wondering if her vision had been completely lost —or at least diminished—to the point of one groping into a void.

As her eyes wandered the tiny room, the answer was found upon her hand making contact with her phone. The screen lit up. Numbers establishing the current time were awash in blinding backlight. Mirai squinted, and to her dismay, discovered that it was nearly midnight.

God... she groaned to herself, while letting the phone drop back down to the bed. The time distortion was never gentle on her psyche.

Minutes, hours, sometimes days, fluctuated within the sequence of events that was her daily life. How certain memories linked to various actions was a chain too broken to ever fully trust.

Mirai sighed heavily and ran her right hand over her abdomen. Pins and needles danced across the skin of her arm. Her wrist was steadily tightening. Three of her fingers were numb.

Not again... she pleaded.

Using her elbows, Mirai propped herself up slightly off the pillow and wondered why her lower body felt like cement. She tossed off the bedsheet and could scarcely discern the outlines of her legs and feet. In her left leg she sensed a mild cramp, due mostly to the odd angle it had been twisted during her nap. As she reached her left hand down to massage it, a new realization slowly dawned.

My right leg is completely asleep... isn't it?

She moved her hand from one thigh to the other. Her hand felt the leg just fine; her leg felt nothing at all.

Oh my God...

Under what felt like the weight of another human being atop her chest, Mirai maneuvered herself until she was sitting upright on the mattress. She exhaled and reached for her phone. The screen light illuminated the bed, the wall, and her numb appendage. Nothing visually appeared to be wrong. Mirai gritted her teeth in the knowledge that her enemy was invisible.

"Come on..." she prodded, rubbing the muscles of her right leg with a trembling left hand, "come on back... *please...* you can do it..."

The rough massaging left her hand feeling warm. In contrast, her leg wouldn't have even sensed if it was on fire. Mirai smacked her hip, her kneecap, her shin, and stretched as far as she could to reach her bandaged foot. The internal disconnect between that which she used to touch and what she was touching rattled her mind. With widened eyes, she gazed down at her right leg and tried desperately to move it.

The limb remained still.

"Mom!" she yelled out.

Two competing expressions battled on Mirai's face the second

Chaw entered the bedroom. The first was that of surprise; the second was a chastisement for having been surprised.

Of course it's her. Who were you expecting?

"You okay?" Chaw asked, appearing as if she hadn't yet been asleep.

"I… I just…" Mirai faltered.

All of Mirai's attention seemed to be focused on her right leg, so Chaw naturally went to analyze the gauze around her foot. "Probably infection," she said. "It look all right, but definitely not."

"No… it's not—"

"It's okay," Chaw assured. "I know doctor. Practice excellent medicine. He come in here and treat you."

"It's not the cut," Mirai said, her tone seesawing between frustration and hopelessness. "I'm sorry for waking you. I just wanted… I… I just wanted to have you… by my side for a minute."

Chaw appeared confused as Mirai burst into tears. She whimpered, "I'm just a little scared…"

Mirai dropped her forehead into her palm. Chaw sat down on the edge of the bed and pulled her daughter into a side embrace. "You not feeling well because of infection. Let me call the doctor. He give you the antibiotics."

Mirai felt herself melt a little. There was something about Chaw's presence that granted her an iota's worth of clarity to think. She watched as the woman's terry cloth sleeve brushed along the side of her right arm. Mirai was certain that before too long, the skin on the right side of her body would no longer be able to sense the fabric.

"What you say?" asked Chaw. "I go call him now?"

Mirai drew in a slow, steadying breath, and casually wiped the lines of moisture from her cheeks. For the first time since the new year, since the conversation in the doctor's office, since the subconscious decision to never acknowledge this particular reality, Mirai felt her defenses crumble to the point that they would never again be rebuilt. The reasons for their original need vanished along with the sensations in her nerve endings. The numbness spread to her heart. She no longer feared the words, only the outcome if she didn't utter them. If she didn't state the truth.

If she didn't ask for help.

"There's no need to call a doctor," Mirai answered. "I don't have an infection. I have MS."

Chaw hesitated, and in the hesitation Mirai witnessed a mind at work. "M… S…" the woman enunciated. Her eyes locked onto her daughter's. "Multiple sclerosis?"

Mirai nodded. "Yeah."

"Oh…" Chaw replied, holding back. "You… have it long time?"

"I've had symptoms for years. Was finally diagnosed last December. My doctor said it's the relapsing-remitting kind. Good times interrupted by tough ones—episodes—which is what I'm having right now."

Chaw placed her hand on Mirai's back. "You in pain?"

"A little, but mostly it's numbness. I hate numbness. I'd rather feel the pain."

"Why?"

Mirai's head shook slowly as an antecedent to her next sentence. "Because at least with the pain I can still feel like I have some control. I can work through it. Manage it. Try to ignore it or just deal with it. But if I can't feel anything, if my leg, or my arm… or my hand… is inoperable, I'm trapped. There's nowhere to go from there. I'm completely at its mercy… at its mercilessness. No negotiation. Just completely cut off from my life whenever it decides. Doesn't matter if I'm in the middle of something important, like enjoying a conversation with a friend, or making love, or putting the finishing touches on a new painting, the disease doesn't give a damn. It will disrupt my life as much as it likes— take what it wants and leave me with the scraps. It's a degenerative illness. And as it slowly wears me down, physically, emotionally, mentally, I'll become more frustrated with myself, which in turn will make me lash out at other people. I'll morph into that sort of person I pity, and as a result, my resentment toward the world will grow. Before too long, I'll be nothing but a shell of my former self—my former life—when I was on the cusp of being known as a great artist, a passionate lover, the most loyal of friends.

There will be nothing left of who I was. The old Mirai will become the new Mirai, and I know with absolute certainty… *I'm going to hate her.*"

The darkened room fell silent for a moment. Neither moved, remaining as still as Mirai's right leg. The words permeated the air. There was almost an odor to them. Mirai felt some relief after her diatribe, yet she also sensed a continuing presence, like the freeing of a body from possession only to have the end result be a lingering poltergeist.

Chaw's eyebrows were furrowed. Her lips were on the verge of expressing the formulated thought in her mind. Yet as she drew in a breath to speak, Mirai slowly turned onto her side and pulled the covers up to her neck. All at once the conversation was over, silenced by the ever-moving second hand of the wall clock.

"How you find me?"

Mirai awoke to blazing sunlight in her small room and the feeling that someone was sitting at the foot of the bed. She turned over and made out Chaw's delicate features through blurry eyes. The smell of soup gently wafted from the nightstand. Mirai assumed it was already midmorning.

"What did you say?" she asked, groggily.

"How you find me in Burma?"

"Oh," Mirai said through a yawn, "Kan gave me your address."

Chaw seemed stunned. "You know Kan Thura?"

Mirai nodded from her pillow. "*Know* is a strong word. I met him for the first time back in Miami… and then again here in Yangon."

"How did he know you are his sister? And if he knew… why he not tell me sooner?"

Mirai smirked. "Who knows why Kan does anything."

The retort evoked a moderate laugh from Chaw. It was within the laughter that Mirai caught the hazy reflection of her own face. The similarity was a spark that appeared and vanished. It left her wondering where the other half of her features had originated. Sitting up gradually, she leaned back against the headboard and tried to exhale the enormous weight sitting atop her chest.

"How you feeling?"

"Like I was hit by a truck, backed over by the truck, and then dragged through the streets of Yangon… by the same truck."

"I bring you some breakfast. A few different things to see what you like."

"I see that. You're sweet."

"And your leg? You feel anything?"

Mirai didn't bother touching it. She knew the answer by omission. "No, but my arm and hand are tingling so badly I wanna cut them both off. So, I suppose that's a win?"

Chaw smiled and moved the breakfast tray onto Mirai's lap. "You eat. Get strength back. I'll care for you. You can stay with me here until you feeling better."

Pack some patience… It might be a while.

"Thank you."

Mirai gazed down at the food, hesitated, and then looked back up at her mother. "I know Howard Lalonde is Kan's father," she said, "but I still have no idea about my own."

The last remnants of Chaw's smile dissipated from her lips. She glanced down at the floor and shook her head. "I wish I could tell you more. I did not know him well. He was brother of my roommate when I first come to Miami. She and him both Burmese like me. He stop by a few time. We all talk and laugh. We stay up late and drink too much. Then one night my roommate get called back to work, so just me and her brother at apartment. He was nice to me… so I was nice to him. A few week later my girlfriend says her brother land big new job out of state. I don't hear about him again. Sometime after that, I find out there was little you on the way."

Mirai rubbed her hand while thinking. "What was his name?"

"Kyaw. He very handsome. Hard for me to resist."

The two shared a laugh. "Yeah… I… know the type," Mirai replied.

"Sad to say I don't have photo of him. But he good man. I never tell him about you because he move far away—across the country for job—and I didn't want him to feel like he need to stay with me. I could take care of myself."

Mirai swallowed some soup and asked, "After Kyaw, then much later after Lalonde, did you… I mean, were you ever again in love?"

"Oh, I give up on love for long time. Men say this and say that to me. But I ignore. Not until Kan Thura grown did I go on date. I find nice man now. He's Burmese. Very honest, kind, has good heart. He live in Singapore for job. He come here to visit and I go there sometime. What you call it? Long-distance relationship? We make it work."

"I'm so relieved to hear that," Mirai said. "You deserve all the love in the world."

"He's faithful, hardworking man. We meet at my shop in the bazaar."

"You have a shop?"

"Oh, yes. Photography shop. You have studio and I have studio. Only mine is for shooting the photo."

Mirai laughed in surprise. "You're a photographer?"

"That what my customers tell me." Chaw smiled. "I take photo of weddings, and big event, sometimes just for one person who need pictures of product for website. I enjoy being behind camera."

Mirai grinned while eating a slice of fruit. "You ever enjoy working in front of the camera?"

"What you mean?"

A full smile warmed the corners of her face as she asked, "Did you know you were pregnant with me when you did that photoshoot?"

"Photo… shoot?"

Letting her hand slide off the edge of the bed, Mirai shifted her arm until her fingers came in contact with her bag. She slowly retrieved the magazine and then extended it in Chaw's general direction. "Blast from the past."

Mirai could not clearly see her mother's reaction. All she could ascertain through the blurry shroud was a hesitation, followed by a gradual slump of Chaw's shoulders. At first, Mirai was worried that she had embarrassed her mother, that perhaps Chaw would have preferred to leave this particular relic in the forgotten corridors of her own history. Mirai began retracting the magazine when she felt it slip from her fingertips.

"How… did you find?" came Chaw's voice.

The question was posed through a tone of nostalgia. Mirai continued eating while listening to the crinkling of the pages as they turned. "Oh… just connected some old dots… which eventually led to this. It was in the dusty back room of a memorabilia store in Miami."

"Easy to find?"

"Not at all."

"Oh, good," Chaw responded with a chuckle. "I was a different person when I did this, in a different place. I have good memories of the experience, but I never mention it here. Family would be ashamed. Still though, don't I look like the *mama hlahla*?"

Mirai took a bite of mango and nodded in agreement at what she suspected was the meaning of the colloquialism. "I learned a lot about you from that Q&A. Was it all true?"

Chaw shimmied her shoulders. "I exaggerate a few thing and editor change a few of my words later. But it mostly me. I just did it for fun, for some money, and to add some beauty to the world. Can you understand?"

Mirai felt her cheeks randomly flush. It seemed like her internal temperature was fluctuating wildly, with an oncoming fever one minute and borderline chills the next. She redirected her eyes down toward her hands. They were clammy and tense. The pain from her fingers radiated into her joints, through her elbow, and eventually up to her shoulder. It burned and twisted, demanding to be acknowledged. She slowly flipped her right hand over and gazed contemplatively at her palm.

"Can you understand?" Chaw repeated.

"Yes," Mirai said through a half smile. "I know exactly what you mean."

Chaw cleared the tray after Mirai finished eating. Providing a torso to lean on, Chaw then assisted Mirai to the bathroom door and then back to bed for more sleep. As exhaustion overwhelmed Mirai's faculties, her eyes wandered the room in a last-ditch effort to remain in the conscious world. She again spotted the tapestry on the wall but could not make out the lines of writing.

Gotta ask her about that… about what… those words… say…

An hour-long nap left Mirai feeling listless—too tired to attempt anything yet too antsy to stay in bed. She couldn't tell if it was before or after noon. All she knew for certain was that her clothes felt like they were stuck to her body. A shower was beyond necessary. It also seemed beyond reach.

Get up… Just get up and do it.

Mirai ordered herself to move a little at a time. The edge of the mattress creaked as she slid off and landed on her left leg. Her arms reached out to steady against the wall. With a series of hops and hobbles, she inched her way toward the bathroom. The weight of her slender frame felt massive, and the pull of gravity from below made it seem as if Myanmar was located on another planet.

What is wrong with me?

Her hand snatched ahold of the door handle for support. She breathed through each motion, trying desperately to stay vertical. The bathroom was directly in front of her. Only a few more steps would complete her excursion. Yet the distance appeared not only elongated but misaligned from the rest of the house. Mirai blinked repeatedly and the hallway corrected itself.

Come on… Just walk damn you… Just do it normally.

She hobbled a few more times and reached out with both hands to secure her positioning between the doorjambs. An exhale led to a sigh. The sigh led to an instant of vertigo. Another hop and she was inside the bathroom. Her torso collapsed forward, and she leaned against the vanity in relief. Her muscles felt like they were hanging from her skeleton by tenterhooks. Her slanted body shifted awkwardly toward the shower stall.

She had no idea how much time had elapsed when she exited the shower and began toweling off. All she knew for sure was that it had taken every ounce of energy she had to stand under the water, and most of her routine had been skipped. Droplets fell from her strands of greasy hair that she had not had the strength to fully wash. Goose bumps traveled down her arms by skin unable to decide if it was freezing or overheated.

The wet towel slid to the floor. Mirai glanced at herself in the mirror, hesitated, and then looked away. A linen robe, with the picture of a white elephant, dangled from the corner of a small closet. Mirai donned it and shuffled out of the bathroom, leaving behind a trail of waterdrops. In the hallway, perched below the handle of her bedroom door, was a handcrafted teakwood cane.

"Is this for me?"

"Yes. For you."

Mirai stood slightly askew in the kitchen of Chaw's house while leaning heavily against the cane. The curved handle helped Mirai keep hold of it, even with some of her fingers still numb. The pins and needles in her arm had transformed into moderate pain. Her leg remained an accessory.

"Very kind," she said, hobbling toward the table and chairs. "Did you make this?"

"No, no. My friend Thet Htar, she bring cane for me when I sprain ankle last year. I use and then put away in closet. This morning, I remember for you."

Mirai sat down slowly and adjusted the hem of the linen robe over her knees. In the background was the soft lull of symphonic music, making her wish that she felt as pleasant as it sounded. Inwardly she was fuming.

"Tea?" asked Chaw, joining her daughter at the table.

"No, thank you."

"You feel better? Shower all by yourself?"

"Not really, no."

"Oh?"

Mirai rested her right hand on the table and glared at it with contempt. "I didn't even wash myself completely, and I'm absolutely exhausted." Chaw began to speak but Mirai bulldozed on. "I'm still hoping to wake up from this nightmare. Discover that my brain isn't shredding itself. That my muscles aren't rotting. That my future is still bright and I'll be a world-renowned artist." She lifted up her right hand and tried to form a fist. "Right now, I couldn't hold a paintbrush if my life was on the line. I hate that feeling. I hate thinking about it. I hate seeing its effects. I hate looking at myself. I've always had a positive attitude about my body. But just now, when I saw my reflection in the mirror…"

A wave of emotion nearly captured Mirai's voice. She quickly suppressed it and continued, "Anyway… I hate what this disease is doing—what it has the power to do. I hate that I can't paint when I want to. That I'm not over at the pagoda right now working on an outline. I hate so much right now. I'm so frustrated. I want to scream in anger but I don't have the energy. Isn't that just hilarious? I don't even have the energy to be angry the way I want. So, I just sit here, stewing in a rage I can't expel… waiting for however this disease decides to torment me next."

Chaw glanced down at her tea as Mirai grimaced through eyes that refused to cry. "No," she said derisively, "I did not shower all by myself."

The music in the background swelled and then settled into a gentle refrain. Mirai could not recognize the song, but something about it made her think of a harp. The image naturally caused her to then think about David.

"Well," Chaw said, as if responding to a counterargument in her own mind, "you have two choice then. If you can't do full wash all at once like you used to, you'll have to split shower time in half. Do what you can in one session, do the rest when you have more strength. Same with cooking. Same with laundry. Same with any work you used to do at one time. You can still do it… just make allowance for yourself."

Mirai bristled as the simplicity of the idea softened her antagonism.

The thought of having to make any allowances for herself when testing her capabilities sat tensely along her jawline. She stared at the wood grain of the table and nodded disagreeably. "And what's the second choice?"

Chaw's smile had the sudden warmth of maternal wisdom. "You could ask me to wash your hair for you. I happily do it."

The way in which she had said it, or perhaps just the offer in and of itself, forced Mirai's vision straight up toward the ceiling. Her cheeks flushed as she sensed moisture flooding her eyes. She quickly swallowed while resisting the surge of emotion. The words had broken her. They had unleashed something that was now free to leave. She breathed in deeply, hoping to assuage the buildup of warmth, but was too late to stop the tears from spilling over and running down both sides of her face.

"It's okay, *thameelay*," said Chaw. "What you facing is tough. No one saying it's not. You have to be strong. But it okay also to ask for help. What can I do? How can I help you right now?"

Mirai lowered her head and wiped her eyes with her right hand. She blinked in surprise upon realizing that she could now sense four out of five fingers. Within the spaces, she suddenly visualized David's hand enveloping hers, the same hand that had plucked the strings of his harp so delicately, that had held her face so tenderly, and that had drawn such immense pleasure from her innermost being.

David...

The next thought emerged from his voice, as if spoken wistfully into her ear.

Courage creates courage...

Mirai gradually nodded. "Okay," she whispered back, and then locked eyes with her mother. "Would you, then? Would you wash my hair?"

Chaw pursed her lips to hold back a burgeoning smile. Within minutes, Mirai was again staring upward at the ceiling, her sable hair cascading into a basin situated in the kitchen sink. As she leaned back in her chair, she chatted with her mother, asking questions about life in Yangon, and answering some about her work as an artist.

The conversation flowed with ease. Chaw massaged Mirai's scalp, worked the shampoo against the grime and sweat, and repeatedly rinsed the thick locks of hair, until all that remained were long strands of sheen ready to be blow-dried. When Chaw finished, Mirai curled some hair between her fingers and touched it to her face. She was certainly still reeling from an MS attack, crushed by betrayal, and filled to the brim with more hatred than she could possibly bear, yet the sensation and smell of freshly washed hair gave her a moment's peace.

Mirai leaned her head in toward Chaw's shoulder in gratitude. "Thank you."

Nothing more was spoken as they listened to music, which drowned out both the ancillary thoughts in Mirai's mind and the vibrating notifications from across the room, as a sudden inundation of text messages overwhelmed her phone.

CHAPTER 14
THE THREE GIFTS

The nightclub was a step back in time. Unlike most of the discotheques of Yangon—characterized by uproarious music and pulsating strobes—this setting was one of recessed halos, a live jazz band, and the omnipresence of wafting smoke coming from the dining tables and bar. The fixtures were lavish and often twinkled against the soft light. Patrons sat, or stood at the bar, or danced rhythmically to the crooning musicians. All were dressed formally. All appeared to be reminiscing about a time they remembered or wished they could. In the center of the club stood a young man.

"Freshen up?" the bartender asked him, first in Burmese, then again in English, while pointing to the tumbler in his hand.

"No, thank you," the man said with a smile.

What remained of the ice jangled within his glass as David Eban turned to scan the room. His eyes zeroed in on the front entrance, a semicircular foyer with a red velvet carpet that followed three steps down into the club. A couple entered arm-in-arm. They were already tipsy as they approached the bar and asked for a tab. David glanced at his wristwatch and sighed. He finished his drink and set it down on an empty table. His hands then pressed against the wool of his navy-blue vest before running both sleeves of his white dress shirt up past his wrists. He stood aimlessly while watching and waiting.

It was nearly ten in the evening.

"Looking for a pickup or hoping to be picked up yourself?" came a voice from behind.

David turned to see a woman in a cocktail dress standing beside him. She had the sort of pale blue eyes that told a story. It would take time and patience to determine whether the story was a romance or a tragedy. The drink in her hand was being nursed slowly. Her smile was warm, albeit with a trace of caution.

David flashed a weary smile in return. "I'm sorry?"

"Don't worry about it. Just a joke. I'm terrible at the approach tactic. Almost as terrible as all the men seem to be at it. You… waiting for someone?"

David clasped his hands behind his back and nodded. "I am. She should be here any minute."

"Lucky girl," the woman said, completing a visual once-over. "You live here? In Yangon?"

"No. I live in the States."

"Same. Well, occasionally. I travel all around. Been searching for something my whole life. Haven't found it yet."

"Oh?"

The woman's smile somehow seemed like a frown. "I suppose it would help if I knew what I was looking for."

They stood in silence for a moment while a new cluster of patrons entered the premises. The club momentarily got louder as an eruption of laughter swept across three tables. Too late to interpret the punch line, David studied the front doors before turning back toward the woman.

She said, "You look tired."

"Mhmm."

"Jet-lag tired."

"Yeah."

"Did you just fly into Yangon from America?"

"I did."

"Geez. Long flight."

A waitress maneuvered past them while balancing a tray of martinis. The woman effortlessly snatched an olive skewer from one of the glasses as it drifted by. She smirked mischievously at David while sliding the olive into her mouth. "I gotta get my kicks where I can find them."

"Impressive."

"That's not the only thing I do that's impressive."

David offered a gracious nod. "Flattered, but as I said, I'm waiting for someone."

"Fair enough," the woman answered softly. "I won't ask again. You can't blame a girl for trying."

"I'm sure with your persistence you won't leave here alone tonight."

She laughed. David had never heard a laugh so hollow. "You'd be surprised. For how many people there are on this planet, it sure is a lonely rock."

David looked back at the door, his mind still tethered to her statement. "Yeah."

"I'll leave you be. Thanks for chatting with me."

"Miss?"

She turned back toward him, hesitantly. "Uh-huh?"

David felt his shoulders relax. "Please don't think me unkind. I wish you all the best."

The woman stole a glance at her drink. Her body shifted slightly as she said, "Thanks. For some reason, I believe you actually mean that. I say that never knowing who or what to believe anymore. It's all so confusing. So chaotic. I never know what's true. Not even sure I *can* know. You ever listen to Alexander?"

David blinked at her sudden change in topic. "In all honesty, I try not to."

The woman shrugged. "He's not for everyone. I connect with a lot of what he says, certainly not everything, but a lot. I was gonna go visit the Mesa Revival. Just haven't made it yet. But I should go. I really should. Maybe there I'll find what I'm searching for. Even if not, I just wanna see it, you know? See the whole damn circus before it folds up and leaves town forever."

David bit his lower lip. "I'm afraid I have seen it. Up close."

"And?"

"Unless you're hunting for fool's gold, I'd search elsewhere."

The woman's face crinkled at his response. "It can't all be phony. It just can't. Why would a hundred thousand or a million or however many people stay in the desert for so long if the whole thing was a scam? Even this stuff," she said, punctuating her statement with the removal of a small white container from her purse, "the Salve—it's amazing, really works wonders for anxiety and depression—most of the time that is. There must be some truth to it, to the healing, the miracles, the illumination, the community. There *has* to be. I've got to go see it before the Feds shut it down."

David blinked. "Shut it down?"

"Haven't you been staying on top of the news? The military keeps shifting the perimeter fences farther away from the Preserve. The disruptions are displacing a thousand people a day. They're obviously trying to shut down the Mesa Revival. At this rate, it won't last another month."

The look on David's face made the woman tip her glass to him. "See? Sometimes I know a thing or two." She then took another sip and patted David on the arm. "I better go. Thanks again for the conversation. And by the way… she's absolutely lovely."

David furrowed his brows as the woman walked away. Only when he turned back toward the entryway did he see what the woman had known by intuition.

"Mirai."

She stood at the top step filtered through a haze of dimly lit smoke. Her hair was pulled back into a curled ponytail. On her lips was the lightest touch of cerise lipstick. She scanned the room for a moment, as if from a crow's nest looking for land. Her left hand ran the length of her formfitting, cotton lace blouse—the color of tangerine—while seemingly holding her upright; a terra-cotta longyi traced her hipline and legs down to a pair of white heels. The outfit was unlike anything David had ever seen her wear. Yet it was the accessory underneath her right hand that more severely captured his gaze.

Descending the stairs carefully, she met each step with a limp and with the support of her teakwood cane.

Mirai, David repeated silently.

Their eyes met the instant she reached the club-level floor. David took a step toward her, momentarily seeming as unsteady as Mirai looked. She further closed the distance, passing through a plume of cigarette smoke that vaporized into her hair. When they met in the center of the room, neither addressed the other. They stood silently in disoriented confusion, the way one would if confronted by a hologram.

Patrons moved around them. The bustle of the club refused to cease. Yet within their tiny sphere, they lost all contact with the present. It was inside the isolation that Mirai saw David's face, his hazel-green eyes, the slight curliness of his hair, the stubble from not having shaved in several days, and that indescribable element missing from his countenance. It was the expression of someone who had been mourning a loss. Simmering under the surface was the hope of resurrection.

Mirai blinked and then let her eyelids shut out her vision completely. The moment was beginning to crush her beyond the weight that even the cane could bear. A lock of wavy hair fell to one side of her face as she sighed. "David..." she whispered, "I am so sorry..."

Her eyes reopened to see him pulling her into a full-bodied embrace. All at once she was transported back to their last moment together. The feel of his chest against her cheek, of his hand on her shoulder, the scent of his rustic cologne, the sound of his breathing, the sensation of his heartbeat. It was instantaneous, a reenactment of their timeline woven through the span of a single exhale.

Mirai gazed up at him. Their eyes locked in fierce recognition of each other. She said, "When you sent me those texts from the airport, I was in shock. I can't believe you flew all the way to Yangon. How did you know I was here? And why come at all? After what I did... to us..."

"It doesn't matter," he assured. "The urgency was that I made sure you were safe."

"Safe?"

"I'll explain. Shall we sit?"

Mirai didn't budge. She was still processing the reality of his touch. "I misjudged you. Misinterpreted the situation. Everything I was led to believe about you was wrong. I fell for it and I'm so sorry. Do you…" Her voice trailed, yet she still tried to enunciate clearly. "Do you still love me?"

Even as she posed the question, she could see that his eyes had wandered down to her lips. Without waiting for him to reach her, she gripped the back of his hair and pulled him into a kiss that eliminated all need for further inquiry. David's hands pressed her torso against his. Mirai wrapped her arms over his shoulders. For an effervescent moment, they both forgot whose lips belonged to whom. Their act was a statement of faith. A belief in that which had brought them together, and what would keep them united moving forward.

"Mirai," David said, his fingers cupping the sides of her face, "of course I still love you. How could I despise my own soul?"

Her gaze flickered with light. She slid her hands down the back of his navy vest, sensing the fabric, all while succumbing to his disarming stare. Mirai's lips formed around words that she knew were long overdue. "The first time we made love, I felt like you had already seen me naked. Now I realize why. The moment we came back from the Preserve, and you walked into my studio, saw the process for how I created my artwork, my unfinished paintings, my life motto on the wooden plaque, I remember feeling very exposed. It was the kind of vulnerability that leads to either a sense of violation or exhilaration. You turned it into the latter. Having you in my sacred space felt wildly intimate. It also felt incredibly safe. In that instant, I knew I loved you. I *do* love you, David."

They held each other as if perfectly formed out of a block of marble. The rough edges having been smoothed away, the carving stood under waxing lights highlighting only their virtues. A gossamer glint in her eyes projected a relief in having spoken the truth. Her hands tightened around his waist, and in doing so, she formed a realization that her cane was no longer underneath her hand.

They glanced at the floor in unison and ejected a small laugh. David bent over and picked up the cane. "Shall we?"

Mirai nodded and the two found a dimly lit, semicircular booth hugging a corner of the club. After the waitress brought them a pair of mai tai cocktails, David raised his glass to Mirai. He said soberly, "To your health."

She smiled and the two clinked their glasses together. The big band arrangement of the previous song mellowed into a crooning instrumental. Several people got up to slow-dance to the tune. David eyed the crowd for a moment before redirecting his attention to Mirai.

"How long—"

"How did—"

They shook their heads in amusement at the mutual interruption. "You go first," said Mirai.

"How long have you been here? In Yangon, I mean."

"A little over a week, I think. Or maybe closer to two. I'm not really sure. My brain has been a bit foggy."

"Understandable," said David. He then pointed at her cane. "Are you in the middle of a relapse?"

"Hopefully nearing the end of it."

"Looks like it's been a rough one."

Mirai nodded slowly. "Yeah."

The white of her fingernail polish bounced rhythmically as she tapped her glass. David reflexively moved to take another drink but decided against it as his fatigue wore on. "How did I know you were here, you were about to ask?"

Mirai shifted in her booth. "I suspect my guardian angel tipped you off."

"He seems like an interesting fellow."

"That's certainly one way to put it."

David chuckled, hesitated, and then grew more serious. "Before I connected with Kan, your parents reached out. Last week. They were worried sick about you but also seemed frantic about something else.

They wouldn't give me specifics. All I could ascertain was that they were leaving town and taking Carys with them. They asked that I find you and keep you safe."

Mirai's stone-faced reaction to the news found hints of acknowledgment in David's eyes. He added, "So, I texted you, numerous times."

"You did? I never received anything."

"I know. Because Omni intercepted them and then replied on your behalf."

David slid his phone across the table with the message window already open. Mirai gazed down at the screen in horror.

"Oh my God," she gasped. "David… I… would never write… *say*… any of those things to you…"

"Oh, but you did."

David pressed a button and a recorded message began to play. The voice that emerged was unarguably Mirai's, yet something about its essence was unnervingly misaligned.

"I can't believe I even have to do this. I can't believe you're texting me when I told you to leave me alone. How dare you violate that boundary. By contacting me at all, you are threatening my safety. Your words are literally violence to me. Do you understand that? Just having to see your name on my phone causes me indescribable trauma. This abuse must stop! I don't care that you're worried about my well-being. At this moment, you are the threat. Never, ever reach out to me again."

The voicemail ended. David looked at Mirai even as Mirai gazed down at the screen. In her eyes were a pair of daggers that wished to stab something much deeper than the device.

"Omni. *Damn it to hell.* David, that wasn't me…" she muttered through clenched teeth.

"I know," he reassured. "I knew it instantly."

"They did it to you too. Making me think you were Emloch. Then having you call me while I was in the bazaar. It was the same thing. Your voice, your tonality, but the words… The words were not the way

you speak to me. They were heartless, and menacing, and sinister…
and…"

"Made me sound like a monster?"

Mirai finally blinked. Her brown eyes latched on to David's stare.
"Yes—like a monster."

David gently took Mirai's hand in his and gave it a squeeze. "As if
someone was tasked with re-creating a human being, only to extrapolate
the worst characteristics from the cesspool of history. A human form
without a soul. An intelligence without that spark of divinity."

"Without that spark of *love*."

David nodded while leaning in toward Mirai. "I promise, I never
thought it was you for a second."

"I wish I could say the same."

"It doesn't matter. Not anymore. The only thing that matters is
what Kan told me we needed to do."

"Which is?"

"Get you out of Yangon."

Mirai huffed incredulously. "But why? I have nothing to go
back to."

"I know that as well. Kan told me. He filled me in on everything.
I'm so sorry for what you've gone through, Mirai. Learning what you
did about your parents—"

"Those people are *not* my parents."

A simple tilt of his head conceded her point. "Understood."

"And anyway, why should I go back? My birth mother lives here.
She's wonderful. And this country is gorgeous. I could spend the rest
of my life putting its beauty on canvas. I don't need anything back
home."

"Kan said that the situation had changed, and he could no longer
guarantee your safety if you stayed here. He didn't think you'd leave
without convincing, so here I am."

Her sizzling retort melted on her tongue as she saw the corner of
David's lip curl into a boyish grin. "I guess I was recruited into
Emblem," he added facetiously.

Her shoulders tugged at her chest as she withheld a laugh. The absurdity of the whole thing settled into the lines of her face. "How do you know it was really Kan on the phone? Maybe someone was using Omni to manipulate his voice too."

"He came to meet me in person. I shook his hand."

Mirai arched an eyebrow and took another sip from her drink. "Human-to-human contact. I guess that's one way to outsmart artificial intelligence."

"At the moment, I'm afraid it's the only way."

They held each other in thoughtful gazes. The rest of the club faded from view. Mirai lost track of the conversation as David caressed her hand in his. His touch had a calming effect, smoothing the rough edges of recent memories and granting her a moment's reprieve from the phantom pains in her body.

Mirai felt her face flush and wondered if David could see it. She wondered if David could sense her happiness to once again be in his presence. Her thoughts led like a train track back to their first time in his apartment, when she had discovered his harp and had entreated him to play it. The first few notes emerged from her mind as if from a recording.

Clair de lune…

She remembered the movement of his fingers. The plucking of the strings. The vibrations both heard and felt. At the conclusion of the piece, he had knelt down on the carpet next to her and had drawn her into a kiss, then a caress, then a series of intertwined ticks of his wristwatch spanning moments she didn't dare recall lest to make her current situation wonderfully unbearable.

Back at the table in the dimly lit club, Mirai squeezed David's hand in reply.

"You look beautiful," he said, eyeing her outfit. "I've never seen you in anything like that."

"I've never worn anything like this. My mom had it in her closet. Said I should wear it tonight. Suits me, right?"

David grinned. "Very much so. I wanna say it's a cheongsam?"

"That's a Chinese dress."

"Kimono?"

"That's Japanese."

"'Twas the extent of my guesses."

Mirai shifted her torso as if modeling the garment. "It's called a *longyi*."

"I will add that word to my vocabulary."

Mirai smiled and tried to lose herself within its protective emotion. As she tried, however, a burning question encroached on both the smile and the moment. The upturned corners of her lips wilted into a grimace.

"How did… everyone seem?" she asked, hesitantly.

"You mean your fam—the McGarrys? Frightened. Terrified, honestly. Your sister most of all. Jason and Valerie were packed as if never returning to that house. Just the basics and a few sentimentals. They called me over to relay that one message, then they left."

"What message, exactly?"

David again scanned the room before answering. "Only that I needed to find you and protect you from Ad Ordinem—"

"Protect me?"

"—and that they were taking Carys someplace safe. Someplace no one would be able to reach her."

Mirai's attention drifted away from the table. *Someplace safe…*

"That was it. They refused to tell me any more. I was fortunate that your brother reached out soon afterward."

"Half brother. And yes, he has impeccable timing."

"He told me where to find you. Told me the story of why you were here. And then he said you were no longer safe at your mother's home. That they would find you there. That I needed to get you out of Myanmar as fast as I could, but not to return to Miami until he gave us the all clear."

"*They?*" she emphasized. "Is he talking about Ad Ordinem? Why would they be after me? I'm not Osiris. I gave them Osiris. I handed him over. That should have been the end of it. So why is Carys in danger? Why was she and I *ever* in danger? I don't understand this, David."

His face suddenly looked more haggard as the jet lag settled in. "I wish I knew. You and Carys… an artist and a model… What that has to do with any of this… I mean for God's sake; Carys isn't even an adult yet…"

Mirai's wandering eyes zigzagged across the tablecloth in search of a place to concentrate. A singular blink separated the instant before the realization, and the dawning glimmer in her irises afterward. "She's… seventeen," Mirai said, already constructing her next sentence.

"Yeah. Seventeen."

The club filled Mirai's vision only to vanish a second later as she turned back to David. "Leighton Russo and George Domínguez."

"What about them?"

"When we were on the ferry in Seattle, and Russo was holding us at gunpoint, he said that some Paragons had already been harassing him and his family. Remember? That… that they had taken some files off his computer, knew his wife's place of work… where his daughter went to school…"

David nodded in confusion. "Yeah?"

"Russo specifically mentioned—God, I remember this now—that his daughter was seventeen. And Domínguez said the same. I can see him saying it when we were all sitting in the voxhall. He said he could relate to my fear for Carys's well-being since he too had a daughter her age—*seventeen*. Russo, Domínguez, McGarry. The three prime candidates for Osiris that I investigated, all have seventeen-year-old daughters. That can't be nothing, David."

Even as he slid closer to her, his body language stated that he still felt too far away. "A curious common denominator, I'll give you that. But what does that mean for us?"

Mirai thought, and in her thinking brought to mind many conversations that had seemingly led nowhere. Her hand slipped from David's grasp. She withdrew her phone without explanation. A few taps on the screen sent an outgoing call. As she placed the device down on the table, David could see the name displayed upside down.

"He-hello?" came a groggy greeting.

"Oh my God," she gasped, covering her mouth in embarrassment.

"Dr. Domínguez, it's Mirai. I'm so sorry. I completely forgot about the time difference."

A yawn preceded his next reply. "Oh… not… uh… not a problem. It's actually midmorning in Miami; I was just up too late working on my new book. Went to bed at the crack of dawn. What's the old saying? I'll get all the sleep I need when I'm dead. Anyway, where are you?"

Mirai parted her lips but hesitated upon seeing David's cautionary glare. "Umm… just, overseas. Taking some time away from work. You know how it is."

"Mhmm," he said, yawning again.

"Again, super sorry about waking you. I was just—well, a thought came to mind and I wondered if…"

The words dammed up at her tongue. It was the look of someone trying to ask something without having to explicitly ask it. After a second of contemplation, common sense won out. "Dr. Domínguez, I'm just gonna be direct with you. There's no other way. Remember how I told you that this mysterious persona named Emloch was having me check on certain people to see if they were Osiris?"

"God of the afterlife. Yes, I recall."

Mirai took a deep breath. "Well, there's something that you and the other two men in question all share—daughters who are seventeen years of age. I can't help but think that's an important factor in all of this. Now, what I'm wondering is: Based on your knowledge of Ad Ordinem, Emblem, the countdown clock on humanity, is there any reason to suspect that what this secret society is truly after goes beyond Osiris himself?"

"You mean, like a daughter?"

Mirai shot a glance at David. David nodded as if to empower her onward.

"Yes," she stated.

Silence filled the phone call. Mirai listened for the sound of Domínguez's breathing. She knew he was thinking but desperately wished that she had initiated a video call instead. To see his face. To watch him ponder.

"Interesting," he finally mused.

"What's that?"

"Well, I agree with you. All three prospects for Osiris having seventeen-year-old daughters is a noteworthy element to all of this. Or more specifically, the fact that they have yet to reach adulthood. As I shared with you, there is a mystical, spiritual component to their enigmatic belief system. And much like the belief systems of other faiths, there are splinter groups, denominations, sects within Ad Ordinem that interpret things differently from one another."

"No doubt," said Mirai.

"Do you remember the prophecy?"

Her eyes widened, suddenly feeling put on the spot. "The… prophecy?"

"The poem. I showed it to you at the diner last time we met."

Mirai nodded toward the phone. "Of course. It's coming back to me. Sorry, my memory is a little spotty."

"Mine's a lot spotty, which is why I write everything down. As a refresher, it goes: *Come back O man of wistful wiles, And restore your place in sacred isles, Standing firmly neath Agamemnon's gaze, To recompense a wandering vision's loss, And for her virtue, cleanse the end of days.* Ring a bell?"

"Yes, this is the prophecy Paragons think predicts the end of time."

"*Some* Paragons," stressed Domínguez. "We're talking about a tiny subset of the organization here, but apparently large enough to coordinate the countdown clock in Times Square, or the area code attacks, including the one involving you and your sister. Anyway, the reason it came to mind was that last line, *and for her virtue, cleanse the end of days.*"

"Yes?"

Domínguez hesitated and then sighed. "Well, a few scholars over the years have surmised that the *her* is not a diminutive statement nor a reference back to the *man of wistful wiles*, but a secondary person altogether. Perhaps a relative of the wandering man. It mentions her virtue and indicates that in exchange of it, one could cleanse the end of days. If it's speaking of virtue here in the maturity sense—as in a virgin—it would stand to reason that the last line is talking about a young woman. Now, it doesn't have to mean a literal virgin, mind you, but rather someone not yet at the stage of adulthood. This *her*, if believed, could be the key in halting an apocalyptic event."

"Her…" Mirai repeated in a hushed tone, "Osiris's daughter…"

"A curious parallel to the story I told you about Agamemnon's daughter, Iphigenia. The one whose blood the goddess Artemis demanded."

"I don't quite get it. What would they want with her, exactly?"

"How do you mean?"

Mirai locked eyes with David as she said, "These people believe that Osiris could either expedite or prevent the end of time, depending on which side you're on. *How* he would do so has remained a mystery. If, however, they were actually after Osiris's daughter… her presence… her virtue… practically speaking—what would they actually do to her if they ever found her?"

More silence filled the line. Mirai shifted her jaw impatiently as she waited. Yet something about this silence suggested that it was less about buying time to think, and more about how to break complicated news.

"What I'm about to say is definitely not canon," began Domínguez, tempering his voice. "This is only a theory based on the information you've given me. But ever since that night at the diner, when you told me the name of the mysterious sender—Emloch—something about it has been bothering me."

"Something about the name?"

"*E-M-L-O-C-H*. Is that how it's spelled?"

"Yes."

"Huh," he grunted. "It may just be a coincidence, but much like how Mark Stone wove his name into an acrostic in that sentence in his journal, Emloch may be using another type of cryptic—the anagram, the kind where rearranging the letters makes a new word."

"An anagram? What word does Emloch make?"

The conversational softness of Domínguez's tone momentarily vanished. What replaced it was a dark hesitance, as if having to utter a blasphemy under threat of execution. "*E-M-L-O-C-H* reconfigures into *M-O-L-E-C-H*. That's what has been troubling me. You've been communicating with someone whose name may actually be Molech."

All at once, Mirai's blood ran cold. She swallowed the bile that had suddenly permeated the back of her throat. David was already gazing at her through the expression of one about to witness a disaster. They both mouthed the name to each other in stunned silence. As she pictured the letters in her mind, a wave of nausea settled in her stomach.

"Molech," she finally vocalized.

"Historically speaking, do you know who that was?"

"No one good."

Domínguez huffed into the mouthpiece. "Molech was said to have been the pagan god of the Canaanites, a people of the Bronze Age. They worshipped him in order to improve their standing on earth. The way in which they worshipped… involved… human sacrifices."

Mirai already knew the operative word Domínguez had left out. "*Human* sacrifices?"

For an instant, it sounded like the line went dead. Only when Domínguez's voice reemerged did she know for certain that he was gathering the courage to complete the sentence. "*Child* sacrifices, Mirai. Molech was the god of child sacrifice."

Mirai raised her right hand from the phone and realized that it was trembling. She knew instantly that it had nothing to do with MS. "They… they would actually… do that? Ad Ordinem would… sacrifice—"

"Not Ad Ordinem," corrected Domínguez. "Emblem. Remember, the former wants the world to end. In their own misguided way, Emblem is trying to save it. If a child sacrifice is required to cleanse the end of days, so be it. If this prophecy is to be taken literally, then both groups are searching for the same thing: Osiris's daughter. Talk about a rock in a hard place. If Ad Ordinem captures her first, they'll keep her alive, but she'll never see the light of day again. If Emblem gets to her first…"

"Dear God…"

"Also, if this is all accurate, you can forget about that countdown clock for the end of time."

Mirai struggled to reel in her frantic thoughts. "Wh—wait… what?"

"365 days until the end of time? That timeframe was clearly not chosen arbitrarily. It was based on finding the child before she turns eighteen. If the applicant pool for Osiris was whittled down to me and a handful of others, I suspect their original deadline was on the last child's birthday, which would undoubtedly be my daughter's, since she turns eighteen on December 31st. Only I don't think that they think that I'm Osiris anymore."

Starting with her legs and working through her torso and up to her jaw, Mirai felt every muscle she could identity tense in rebellion to a sickening premonition. "I can absolutely guarantee that they do not."

"Well… whoever is left, *that* girl's eighteenth birthday… That's the real end of time. If I were you, I'd open the calendar and start counting."

With a hand shaking so fervently that she could barely tap her phone screen, Mirai said, "Thank you for all of this, Dr. Domínguez. You were beyond helpful."

"Keep in touch and stay safe."

Mirai ended the call and looked up at David. Through lips that had lost their lustrous sheen, she asked a question that was already on David's mind, and to which she already knew the dreadful answer.

"Kan Thura… He wouldn't, would he?"

David glanced at his wristwatch and shook a head flustered with uncertainty. "Unless we get to Carys first, I think he absolutely will."

Mirai recoiled in horror.

"How much time do we have?" David asked while placing some Burmese kyat on a coaster. Mirai was struggling to catch up to his meaning. David clarified, "When is Carys's birthday?"

The sudden glazed-over look of her eyes confirmed his fears. "June 3rd."

David's hands fell back down to the table. "Oh my God."

Mirai nodded, her vision light-years away. "Forget New Year's Eve. We have three days until the end of time."

The bedroom was dark when they entered. A small pile of clothes, which Mirai had borrowed from Chaw, were strewn across the bedspread as if someone had been unable to decide what to wear prior to leaving the house. On the dresser was a neatly folded pair of denim shorts and a ribbed tank top—freshly washed by her mother. They were the clothes in which Mirai had arrived to Yangon. Something about knowing she had to wear them again made her bristle.

"Home away from home," said David, turning on a lamplight.

"Something like that." Mirai sighed.

They spoke in hushed tones so as not to awaken Chaw in the late hour. Yet when her mother appeared at the doorway still dressed in the day's outfit, Mirai realized that they both shared the same nocturnal genetics.

"Careful, this how I end up with baby you," Chaw said with a knowing smirk.

Mirai forced a smile while transferring slightly more weight onto her cane. "This is David. David, my mother, Chaw."

"A pleasure to meet you," he said, still speaking softly. "And thank you for taking in Mirai during her episode. I can see clearly how well you've cared for her."

Chaw leaned against the doorjamb. "You come a long way to see her. I told her that a sign of true love. But how come you not look happy? You both seem like something bad happen."

Cursing her mother's perception, Mirai turned to David having no idea how much to explain. "It's… terribly complicated," he said. "I'm afraid we'll have to be going back to the States immediately. I've scheduled a cab to come pick us up and drive us to the airport. From there we can figure out a route back to the States."

"Oh," Chaw replied, the news registering in her face. "Anything I can do to help?"

"You've done so much already. Unfortunately, this is something we must handle alone."

"I see, I see."

They all stared expectantly at one another, as if waiting on anyone else to grant them exemption from having to begin the next sentence. On Chaw's face was the look of unfinished business, that there was something more she had hoped to share with her newly found daughter. David's visage was saddled under the weight of urgency, that there was much emotional baggage to process but now was not the time to do it. Mirai's countenance was a world separated from the other two.

As if suddenly transported into another realm outside the bedroom in Yangon, she turned away from David and Chaw and walked over to a chair in the corner. She sat down and laid the cane on the floor beside her. Woven into the very essence of her facial features was the expression of one hanging on for dear life. It was the look of resistance, not just to a plan or a course of action, but to a concept. Her jaw shifted as if at war with itself. Her eyes darted across the room in search of an escape. What the other two observers would naturally assume to be fear, Mirai knew to be infinitely more consuming.

Rage.

"I'm not going back there," she stated, in a tone as clear as it was firm. When she said it, her eyes were affixed to David. Yet David knew the words were directed at Chaw. "I won't do it. I won't be the sacrificial animal. They did this. Them. It was their cowardice and lies and manipulation that led to them having to flee, *not my uncovering of it*. It's their crimes against me and against Mom that are coming back to haunt them. Why do I need to intervene? I have nothing to go back to. I'm happy here. And now that you're here, David, I have everything I need. Who says I need to be the rescuer? Let those people figure it out. Let them endure the suffering they so value, the virtue they so admire in others. Let's see them embrace it instead of having to face the contradiction in their belief system. Their world is now spiraling out of control, and I don't wish to be in that orbit. They brought about this chaos. I, for one, choose order."

David stood rigidly against the backlight of the lamp. His hands slid halfway into each pants pocket. His chest bulged as he inhaled both a deep breath and a series of counterarguments. All that exited a second later were two words.

"But, Carys…"

The words instantly crushed the defenses in Mirai's face. In the span of a single blink, rage turned to anguish, and then to utter hopelessness. Her cheeks fell forward into her palms. The whites of her nails pressed against her forehead as if to dig the image of her sister's predicament out of her psyche. Her frame shook in retaliation to the moment. Her shoulders heaved beneath the weight. Without warning and without remorse, Mirai drew in a terminal breath and screamed, *"GODDAMN IT!"*

The lament ricocheted out of the room and out of the house. Mirai sat hunched forward, breathing through her mouth. Her body seemed haggard from the outburst. It had been sudden, yet something about its wail sounded like a scream erupting from a childhood trauma, one lying dormant for decades until finally summoning the courage to detonate in its own time and its own way.

Mirai dropped her hands to her lap and looked up at David. Speaking more through her eyes than through her lips, she whispered, "I hate them so much."

David nodded slowly while suppressing his own churning anger. "I know. And you have every right to. But if you love Carys and wish to save her, you'll have to channel that anger into a course of action."

"I can't," Mirai pleaded, her mocha irises shifting between David and Chaw, "I know that's what I'm supposed to do… make my anger work for me… but as honest as I've ever been… I'm telling you that I don't know how to do that. All I want to do is explode. All I want to do is retaliate. Whenever I think of my sister… I think of *them*, and in that moment my compassion turns to rage. Instead of thinking about how to rescue something I cherish, I fantasize about letting what they adore get destroyed. It's not what I want. Please believe me. I don't want any harm to come to Carys. But when I think about the looks of pain on Jason and Valerie's faces, the cries of torment, the strangulating loss of having their only child murdered because of someone else's nonsensical belief…"

Mirai's unblinking vision drifted, making David and Chaw wonder if she had lost her train of thought. When it returned, she was looking at neither of them. "It's almost poetic."

The room fell quiet as David and Chaw exchanged furtive glances at each other. The available air around them felt sparse. The light from the lamp now seemed dimmer. An intangible had been syphoned out of the space. No one could pinpoint what it had been exactly, but two of the three beating hearts could sense its absence.

"Your sister… Carys…" Chaw began, walking a verbal tightrope, "she in danger? Because of something your parents did? Someone want to do her harm?"

When Mirai didn't respond, Chaw looked at David who nodded in the affirmative. She continued, "*Can* you help her? There is something you can do to prevent this?" David again nodded but this time added a shrug. "And you love your sister, yes?"

"Mom, please," Mirai said through closed eyes and gritted teeth.

"Then why you confused? You must go help your sister. She your *nyimalay*. If you love her, you both share a soul. Hate will only destroy both of you. It eat you alive."

"I just told you, I don't know how to get rid of it. I'm powerless against it. You have no idea what this is like. It just sits there day and night. If I could overcome it, I would. But I can't. I *want* them to suffer. I want them to get what they deserve. I want them to die."

David blinked and glanced down at the floor, clearly stunned by Mirai's admission. Chaw, however, didn't flinch. "You say I have no idea? No idea what it like to feel hate? Are you joking? I lose my only daughter. She taken and no one tell me where did she go? Me? Your mother? Who search for such a long time and then find out man I love take you away from me? Give you to some strange couple to help them hide from bad people. Take away from new life in America and send me back to Burma with little Kan Thura. No money. No support. No love. You say I don't know hate? Oh, *thameelay*. I burn with hate for so long. All I think of is hate. It almost consume me. How could it not? I miss you…" Chaw's eyes welled with tears as she hesitated. "For so long."

Mirai sat up a bit in her chair. "Then how did you survive? How did you rid yourself of it?"

Chaw smiled and placed her hands against her chest. "There's only one antidote to hate. The Love of God."

The momentary spark of hope in Mirai's face was instantly extinguished. The statement fell flat, incongruent to the problem at hand and irrelevant to any further study. Mirai exhaled a half sigh that ended as a grunt. "The Love of God," she repeated. "I've already tried it. The people at the voxhall took it away from me after I refused to sign their oath. After I confessed my unbelief. Whatever short-term benefits I was receiving from it were a placebo effect. It doesn't actually work for me."

"No," said Chaw, "not that. The Love of God does not sit in some container waiting to be dispensed to chosen few. It does not belong to voxroy, and is not trapped inside voxhall. It is everywhere, all the time, and available to anyone."

"If you're talking about the Noble Book, I grew up on it, I've read it. Then we switched to the Worthy Book. The McGarrys were big on sacred texts. I was not. I never liked that someone could place any absurdity imaginable within the covers of what is considered a sacred book, and merely because of that distinction, it would be believed. I never got past the contradictions, the questionable historical veracity, the fact that much of the authorship couldn't be proven, and that everyone demanded I take the book's stories literally when I could clearly see that they were written to be understood figuratively."

"We see so much the same, May La. I went to many voxhall. Read so many book. Talk to many people who tell me this and tell me that. None of it work for me. I still have fire in my chest, burning all the time. It not until I discover the power of the Love of God. It dissolved the anger, the rage, the hatred, as if it was never there."

Mirai tilted her head. The muscles around her eyes tightened as if trying to more clearly see what was right in front of her. "Wait a minute, are you trying to tell me that you've… *forgiven* them? After what they did to you?" Her voice tensed as she continued, "Jason and Valerie McGarry. Howard Lalonde. Whoever else at that daycare who was involved in the cover-up… You just .. let them all off the hook?"

Chaw smiled in response. The expression on her face was suddenly the most disarming thing in the room. "Who to say what forgiveness really is? Do I know? Do you? Do they? All I know is that my hate was killing me, not them. Why should I have to suffer for what they did? I cannot hold love and hate in same hand. Not possible. So I try to let the hate go, but it won't leave. Only the Love of God remove it. Remove it instantly. Free me from torment. Free me from *them*. I never forget what they did. I never forget you. I never stop hoping to see you again one day. But I don't give them one more second of my life. Instead, I use my life for good. Good for myself. Good for others. *That* is true revenge."

"It all sounds lovely," Mirai said, arching an eyebrow, "but as I keep telling you, I couldn't let this go if I tried… and believe me, I have tried. So, unless you have a magic pill for me to swallow, I have no idea how to obtain the Love of God."

Chaw turned to David. Outstretching her hands toward him, she asked, "I see in your eyes such love. You are a good man. Tell me, have you ever seen a miracle?"

David exchanged glances with Mirai who gave an apologetic grin. He paused to give the question some thought. Graciously, he smiled at Chaw whose face was full of anticipation. "In all honesty, no. I have not."

"Me either," she said. "I do not believe in random miracles. I only believe in what God has already given us. At the beginning. The Three Gifts."

"The Three Gifts?" asked Mirai. "I've never heard of that."

"I have," David interjected. "My old concertmaster believed in that. He shared it with me once… many years ago."

"You see? I not crazy. You tell her. She in love with you."

David laughed while shifting his stance. "Well, from what I recall, the first gift—reason. We are conscious, and we can know about the world because of volitional thought. For instance, you say the Noble Book is filled with things hard to take literally. That's an intellectually honest observation. God would not ask us to deny our own reason, to deny our very tool for understanding the world. Therefore, we should use reason on everything, not just the physical, but also the spiritual. To do otherwise is to misuse the gift. There are many examples, but the most dramatic one is eternal damnation. To think of God torturing someone forever is not only heinous—no matter their actions on earth—but also *unreasonable*. The very concept does not stand the test of the first of God's gifts to humankind."

After a quick peek at Chaw to be sure he was on the right track, David continued, "The second gift—nature, or more specifically, objective reality. Nature is tangible proof of a creative force in the universe outside of our capacity. However it came to be, and however long that process took, we find ourselves here in a realm that can be adjusted, molded, enhanced, improved, diminished, or destroyed. It's up to us. The consequences of reality are observed and interacted with every day, each moment. Whether we choose to use that immense power positively or negatively is entirely up to the individual. Nature is our witness of the divine. That creative spark that lit the universe."

Chaw nodded, seemingly pleased with his rendering of the philosophy. "And the third?"

David pursed his lips as he stared at Mirai. "The third gift—the Love of God. The Love of God is the expression of undeserved and unconditional human love toward one another. It is the uniquely human ability to take trauma, tragedy, atrocities, and needless pain, and transform it into a conduit of good toward others. It is the grounding realization that to wish someone an eternity in hell—even our most devoted tormentor—would turn us into them. The Love of God is what allows us to be divine in a world filled with suffering. It transcends rituals and denominations, religious allegiances and personal dogmas, and has been observed throughout history from diverse people, cultures, faiths, and nonfaiths around the world. We are the literal hands and feet of God on this planet." David then nodded as if remembering one more thing. "The Love of God is the desire within us to create beauty… and hesitate when we could justifiably create horror."

Mirai sat silently as David spoke. She did not interrupt or seem as if she was preparing a series of rebuttals. There was only one question loaded on the edge of her lips as he concluded his explanation. Once again she looked at David even while directing her statement to Chaw. "If God was able to set off the creation of the universe, and then gave humanity three gifts as a means of living on earth, why has there been zero intervention in the indescribable suffering our species has endured since our inception? After all, I grew up hearing people thank God for the good things in their lives, but never offer condemnation for the senseless tragedies. And I'm not talking about natural disasters here. I know the difference between an earthquake and a war. Between a famine and a rape. Between a car accident or a disease or being struck by lightning, and the cries of those locked in the merciless hellholes of this world. There's natural misery and then there's the kind cooked up by humans. I'm talking about the latter. How is God not culpable for the suffering of the world since the dawn of time? If there's power, where's the responsibility? And if there's indifference, how can there be hope?"

"You think of God the way everyone always teach," Chaw began. "So did I in the beginning. I was so confuse for so long. Why does God let May La be taken away? Why no compassion for my suffering? Why no miracle I pray for night and day? Then I take honest look at the world. I realize something: God is not who I was taught. God does not intervene in actions of man and woman. God create universe and then step away. It's only way this world make any sense. It can seem scary to think about. But thanks to the Three Gifts, we have everything we need to live on earth—if we all use them. Many time we do not. That cause suffering. It cause hell. When we do use the gifts, we experience paradise. No need to find it. It like air… everyplace. Just breathe it in whenever you need."

"Mom," Mirai said, raising her hand in a manner expressing that she had heard enough, "I appreciate you sharing your story. I do. But I'm… just not there."

Chaw maintained her smile, which had evolved from enthusiasm into gratitude. Without another word, she reached down to embrace her daughter and imbue her with all the emotion of the last few minutes. Mirai returned the embrace wholeheartedly. As she did, her right hand felt the soft fabric of her mother's blouse and tried to record the feeling to memory.

David ran his fingers through his hair. "The cab will be here soon. We should probably…"

"Yeah," Mirai said, suddenly feeling anxious as Chaw pulled away.

"Your clothes are here," Chaw said, wiping a tear from her face. "Please keep the longyi. It fit you so well. And here, keep the cane too. Use it until you don't need it anymore."

"Mom… how can I ever thank you…"

"No need. You my daughter again. We can build relationship now. Even from overseas. You come back here with David someday for visit. I just ask that you bring me another painting when you come. I need another one in here."

A heavy weight on her chest made Mirai feel as if she was about to begin sobbing, and that if she did, it would never stop. She darted her eyes away from her mother and nodded. "Absolutely. We'll be back again soon. I give you my word."

It only took a moment to collect her belongings. As she stood next to David with her backpack purse secured around her shoulders, Mirai scanned the bedroom that had been her sanctuary. Her vision had improved considerably in recent days. With it, she hoped to memorize the layout of the simple space. When her eyes once again landed on the tapestry, she blinked and took a step forward.

"I kept meaning to ask you about this. I would stare at it some nights even though my vision was blurry. Now I see why I couldn't read it; it's all in Burmese."

Chaw took a cautious step toward the wall. She touched the tapestry with care, running her fingers along the embroidered lettering. "I buy this not here, but in Miami. A shopkeeper make it. I ask her:

Where you came from? She tell me from Burma, so I get all excited and buy it. Then later, I really read it and think about it. Much later, after you born, I share with you. I share with you the words because you seem to like them so much."

Mirai narrowed her eyes at the lettering, following the loops and curls as if she could decipher it. "I liked these words? I don't remember…"

"Oh yes." Chaw smiled. "Something about them made you happy. I read it to you every day. Even at your young age, I could see in your eyes, you believed it."

The same eyes were gazing back expectantly at Chaw. "Believed what?"

"That an act of beauty will save the world."

A sense of wonder pumped through her veins. It coursed from a mainspring of both memory and intuition. The feeling tingled down to her hands. It was the effervescent relief of finding the sum to an equation. Mirai curled her fingers and found David's hand already intertwined in hers. A gentle squeeze confirmed that he too remembered her life's credo.

"Beauty will save the world…" she said under her breath.

"An *act* of beauty," corrected Chaw.

Mirai linked the two thoughts together and nodded slowly. Her mind's eye was envisioning something daunting. "Yes, an act of beauty…"

Her arm muscle braced as if uncertain which direction to pull. She shifted her hip slightly away from her backpack. In one sense she was desperately trying to hold on to a mental image, and in another sense, the vibration from her purse was returning her to reality.

"I think someone's calling you," said David.

Mirai blinked and shook her head in vexation. When her eyes landed on the screen, the name staring back left her expressionless. She silenced the notification and turned back to her mother. "We should probably go."

"Go." Chaw smiled, taking her daughter's face in her hands. "I always love you. The Love of God always accessible. So much love available to you whenever you need. No matter where you go, you never without it."

Mirai forced herself toward the door. Another second in Chaw's presence would result in her decision to stay. She swallowed the tightness in her throat and shuffled through the main area and out the front door. As she inhaled the evening air, David's arm wrapped around her torso.

"It'll be all right," he assured.

Mirai curved herself into his body and drew him into a kiss. Their lips lingered, having nothing else left to say. She gathered from him the strength she needed to look away from her mother's house and walk toward the cab parked along the curb. Once in the back seats, Mirai and David held each other as the winding residential street turned into a bustling Yangon road.

Through an anguished face, Mirai said, "I keep feeling like I'm forgetting something. Like I've left something behind."

David firmly kissed the top of Mirai's head. His hand rubbed along her back, shoulder, and hair. As the cab accelerated down an interstate on-ramp, he said, "And that's okay."

Yes… it is.

Mirai was about to close her eyes and rest her head on David's shoulder when her phone demanded attention yet again. This time, they both saw the caller.

"It's Kan," Mirai said, her muscles bracing for something intangible.

"Wait, maybe—" David said, but she had already pressed the speakerphone button to answer the call.

"Kan?"

"Mirai! Thank God you picked up," he said, his voice sounding winded. "It sounds like you're driving. Did David come get you? Are you on your way to the airport?"

"Yes, we're on our way now. You said I was in danger? That I shouldn't stay in Yangon? Why?"

"Isn't it obvious?" He stressed, "*They* are hunting you down in order to find Osiris. Your parents vanished from the house. Ad

Ordinem wants them desperately and there's not a lot of time left to find them."

Mirai tightened her grasp of the phone even as she leaned in closer to the mouthpiece. "Osiris?" After a pensive glance at David, Mirai added, "Don't you mean… Carys?"

The silence on the other end was interrupted by traffic noise. It was clear that the caller was traveling too. "Well, yes," he said, "your parents, Carys, everyone. They're all in danger. That's why I'm here. I need to find them first so I can bring them to a safe house."

"Is that what you'll do with them?" Mirai asked, no longer concealing the edge in her voice. "Bring them to a safe house? Is that why you want me to tell you where they are? Is that the full and honest truth, Kan?"

Something in his tone was also beginning to change. "Mirai… do you know where they are?"

Mirai could feel David's piercing gaze through her hairline. She steadied her thoughts and said, "Depends on who's asking: Ad Ordinem—who wants Carys contained—or Emblem—who wants Carys sacrificed."

A subtle clearing of his throat preceded a lengthy hesitation. "Mirai, come on now, you know me. I don't wish for any harm to come to your sister. I'm the one who rescued you both from that plane attack. I'm the one orchestrating a global resistance to these terrorists and their methods. Do you honestly think I would bring any harm to any member of your family? Mirai, you're my sister… Your family is my family too."

Mirai parted her lips in rebuttal but then stopped. Her eyes widened. All color drained from her face. The hand clutching the phone began to tremble. David noticed and quickly reinforced it with his own.

She mouthed inaudibly, "Oh my God."

"Mirai?" said the voice. "You still there?"

She squared her jaw in both realization and personal rebuke. As if scolding herself for forgetting something that should have been fresh on her mind. After a few seconds of poise, she smiled and even ejected a telling laugh. "Wow, you almost had me there. You really can mimic us, can't you—Emloch?"

David exchanged glances between Mirai and the phone. They both tilted their heads as the screen morphed from a standard call into a new notification.

Incoming Video Chat From Kan Thura.

The two words underneath it encompassed more than the questions.

Accept? Reject?

Mirai looked at David. His expression stated that the answer should be obvious, yet also acknowledged that, armed with knowledge, curiosity could be pursued without too much peril. Mirai watched her thumb vacillate over the two buttons. When she finally hit *Accept?* the image on the phone widened to fill the perimeters of the screen. Inside the image was the face of a man she did not recognize. Behind him was someone standing in the shadows of a dark room. Just off camera was the partial outline of a third person.

"Hello, Mirai," said the man in the foreground.

Mirai didn't answer. She simply stared, examining the speaker's face and wondering why—if he was in fact an artificial simulation— the persona appeared so haggard.

"Apologies for the interruption," the man continued, "I know you're traveling. But this matter has become extremely urgent. Your assistance is required in order to save two lives."

"Who are you?" she asked instinctively. She immediately regretted engaging.

"You can call me Emloch if you want, doesn't matter," the man said, running his hand through his sweaty, crew-cut blond hair. "Names aren't important. All that is, is finding your sister. It seems you already know why."

"Drop dead."

The man nodded slowly. Something about her having made the statement actually seemed to bother him. He swallowed and then drew in a long breath. "I know this is difficult for you, Mirai. Knowing who to trust. I empathize with you. But if you know why we want Carys, then you must know that we wish her no harm. We're the ones actually trying to save her from being sacrificed."

Mirai squinted at the phone, trying to make sense of his claim. "What are you talking about? You're Emblem. You're the one who wants her dead."

The man shook his head. "Forgive the confusion, since we're calling you from Kan's phone. See, I represent Ad Ordinem, the group trying to save your sister from being slaughtered, killed by men who refuse to see that no amount of sacrificial bloodshed on the basis of some silly ancient riddle can stop the end of time."

His hand gently reached out toward the camera and the image shifted to the left. Below the harsh light of a flood lamp, his arms restrained uncomfortably behind his back, his body barely able to sit upright in a chair, and with white biosensors affixed to his chest and temples, Kan Thura gazed into the camera with the look of a man who had been through an ordeal, but who also had plenty of fight left in him.

"Here," said the man, "that's the face of the person who wants to kill your sister."

A nauseating pit settled deep in Mirai's abdomen. She reached her fingers up to her lips and whispered, "Kan."

"He knows where Carys is," the man said, his voice a strange mixture of calm masking hysteria. "We've been trying to… persuade him… to tell us. To help us protect your sister from the scum comprising Emblem. Our methods are usually successful, over time. But we do not have time to spare. If his conspirators get to her first, they'll commence with the ritual. If we find her first, we'll return her safely if and when Emblem ever comes to their senses."

So… never.

Mirai was already shaking her head before he finished speaking. "This is insane. All of it. To take things this far over a belief system… a vague prophecy… an arbitrary timeline… My God, you all have lost your minds. The world isn't coming to an end! There won't be a catastrophe unless you make one! This doesn't have to be a self-fulfilling situation! Just stop for a moment and ask yourselves if this is rational, if you might just be looking at things through the wrong lens! Because if you continue, a lot of innocent people are going to get hurt!"

Mirai's exhortation landed on stoic faces. It was the reaction she had predicted; even so, stating it granted her a modicum of relief. Her fingers left her lips and reached across the space between her and the phone. When they made contact with the screen, she said, "Kan..."

"Don't worry about me," Kan said, trying to form a smile. "These guys are amateurs. I've experienced more pain at a massage parlor."

The man in charge reacted to the statement in jest. Mirai's eyebrows furrowed as she again witnessed in him jest covering a simmering terror. "Please..." he began, hoarsely, "don't be fooled by Kan's bravado. Our method of torture is the most sophisticated on the planet. These devices connected to him transmit frequencies from our computer program directly into his mind. We can manufacture any horror we wish upon him. Make him feel anything and to any degree. And the best part is, no physical evidence afterward. As they say... *it was all in his head*."

Mirai pushed herself more firmly against David's body. His arm tightened around her as if to prevent any attacks from the phone. They stared at Kan in shock, knowing that their reaction was the caller's exact intention.

"If I know where Carys is, I don't have to keep this up," the man said with gravity. "This pains all of us. Kan is a fellow Paragon. He is also a reprobate and a traitor. I don't wish to do this, but I must. I must unless you stop it, Mirai. Simply tell us where Carys is and I'll set him free."

"I don't know where she is," Mirai protested. "I wasn't there when they left the house."

The man winced. His body twisted a bit in his seat. "Come now, Mirai. Certainly your own parents didn't vanish into thin air without leaving you a method of contacting them. Or your sister. She must have sent you a text message. A phone call. Something." The agitation in his voice grew. Mirai stole a peek at Kan, whose eyes were brimming with delight.

"I already told you," she said, "I don't know where Carys is. And even if I did…"

The man quickly held up a small remote and shook his head. "Hold that thought, Mirai, or else Kan *feels* it. Or maybe we just try and find Jason and Valerie, get them to spill her location. How long do you think those cowards would last connected to my machine?"

Mirai involuntarily gasped.

"Or maybe the pressure point I need is seated right next to you. Your lover. The man you trust… except when you don't."

"All those fake messages were housed on his Omni app. Emloch made me distrust David!"

"Emloch *made* you do it? Or was it seeds sown long before it ever contacted you? We don't accept all the credit, Mirai. You *chose* to believe what you saw instead of digging deeper into the matter. It was your own character flaws that led to the breakup of your relationship with David, not the testing of it."

"You manipulated me from day one."

"No." The man slapped his hand on Kan's shoulder. "That would be this guy. The bastard who's trying to sacrifice your sister."

Mirai exhaled, suddenly feeling spent from the terror of the conversation.

The man gripped Kan's shoulder until the color left his fingers. "Where is she, Mirai? Where is Carys?"

"You both can choose to end this and no one else has to die."

"Last time I'm gonna ask…"

"I'm so sorry, Kan," Mirai said, "I wish I could save you…"

From the partial shadows, Kan offered a single nod toward the camera. "Be strong, *ma kyi*," he said. "And have no concern for me. I know exactly what level of depravity they'll have to set this machine to in order to get what they seek." His eyes then drifted to meet the sudden gaze of the tormentor. Kan smirked. "I've known you a long time. And I know that what will ultimately be required to break me… will *destroy* you."

The man stared wide-eyed at Kan. From his hand, the remote fell and clattered to the ground. The man swallowed while his breathing intensified. He blinked rapidly but to no avail. His chest began to heave. Finally breaking away from Kan's gaze, the man swallowed again and then bolted from his chair. Off camera, the sound of retching filled the speakers.

Mirai covered her own mouth while watching the scene. She saw on Kan's wearied face a look of satisfaction, yet also a thin veneer of worry that he could live up to the promise. All too clearly, what became evident to Mirai was that before these men were soldiers, or insurrectionists, or members of the world's oldest secret society, they were human. And it was in their humanity that they had learned to view each other as monsters.

She could not bear to watch any more. She tapped the button to end the call and clutched David's hand in hers. "We have to get to Carys first."

"We will," he assured.

"But how? Where did my parents say they were taking her?"

David sighed heavily. "All they said was, 'someplace safe.'"

The light from oncoming vehicles crisscrossed their faces in unison. It was within the flash that they both repeated the words as if declaring them for the first time.

"Someplace safe."

CHAPTER 15
PERIHELION

Neal Lalonde shot a glance toward Teagan Lalonde. It was the look of someone about to succumb to the noose.

"There's little else to say on the matter," said the chairman of the board. The conference room was stately, with an oval table made of cherry mahogany, around which a dozen leather executive chairs orbited. Two walls had windows from floor to ceiling, out which the horizon could be seen aflame in melting sunlight. Through the other window was the top of an old building, on which was perched a billboard that had known better days. Neal Lalonde was seated perpendicularly to the sign. He knew what it said, yet his periphery demanded a confirming peek.

Is This the End of the World?

"So that's it, then?" Neal asked, leaning slightly forward in his seat. "After coming to you in the hopes that you could help guide us through this awful family crisis, one that could rock the core of this network… one that… You're just gonna fire us and sweep it under the rug?"

"There can be no sweeping where there is no dirt," the man corrected, eliciting nods from others around the table. "You and your sister bring us nothing but salacious rumor, vicious lies, and *dreck*, masquerading it as hard facts against your father and our founder. Your so-called evidence amounts to nothing, damning no one but yourselves and revealing little more than your lust for power and notoriety."

"God Almighty," Teagan groaned, shaking her face into her hand.

Neal gave a firm yank at the knot in his tie. The words of the executioners were landing with all of the gravity of a sledgehammer, but the logic backing them left Neal wanting to laugh. "Dismiss our claims if you choose, but removing the only remaining Lalondes with any authority at this network is the far more obvious power play. This board has been waiting to pounce since the day my father was diagnosed with dementia. Removing us and installing your own puppet leader will only diminish what remaining loyal listeners you'll have left after this story inevitably breaks."

"You intractable son of bitch!" spat another member. "The only reason you're sitting in this room is thanks to the benevolence of this board and because of an old man too sentimental to tell his son that he has no talent. We should have canned your ass long ago. If you so much as utter a word of these lies to the public, I swear to God we'll end up with ninety cents out of every dollar of your trust fund. Do you understand me!?"

"*We* have no interest in making this devastating news public," Neal shot back. "But it might behoove someone on this board with an iota of forethought to figure out how to manage this now, should it turn into a PR crisis down the road. *That* was our purpose in bringing it to your attention."

"Nevertheless, your involvement with this young woman claiming to be your half sister… this gold-digging tart… *the artist*… granting her access to network property, station files, employee backlogs, all for the sake of some witch hunt against your own father is as deplorable as it is reckless. It shows a lack of responsibility to the network. It spits in the face of your own family."

Neal charged in for a comeback but was cut off by the chairman, who sliced his hand through the open air as if wielding a saber. "We've been over this same ground for an hour already," he lamented. "There's no point in continuing this verbal joust. The terms of your severance are set forth in the documents before you. The packages are quite generous. We expect your signatures by end of week. Included are retroactive confidentiality clauses, which make any retaliation against this network a moot point. You will say nothing; you will do nothing. Turn in your press badges, key cards, and any other property owned by Palisades Radio Network. Your last day at this company just ended."

With teeth clenched and a fist for a hand, Neal looked down for no more than an instant at the manilla envelope before darting his vision back over to his sister. "Well?" he said sharply.

Teagan arched an eyebrow. "Well, what?"

"Do you not have an opinion about this?"

She cocked her neck and smiled calmly. Addressing the board, she said, "There can be no opinions where there is no honesty. Since I refuse to play your games any longer, I'm the one who is now free." A flick of her wrist opened her envelope. Using her right hand, she clicked the first pen she could grab and scribbled her signature onto the bottom line of the contract. She then arose from her seat and briskly walked out of the conference room without uttering another word.

All at once, Neal was alone.

"This board collectively wishes you the best of luck, Mr. Lalonde."

Neal pursed his lips and then chuckled to himself. The collective insanity was slowly dissipating from his mind. After a lengthy hesitation, he reached for a pen and signed the document. He stood at the table and scanned the faces in the room. Eyeing the chairman last, he said, "May you all die agonizing deaths and then rot in hell."

The door opened into the hallway that led to the elevators Neal knew so well. Bursting into his office, he quickly snatched the few items of personal value and placed them into an empty delivery box. In a matter of minutes, he was back in the elevator heading toward the top floor, all the while riding the emotional roller coaster of fuming and giddy relief. When he entered the executive suite, the silhouette of a woman stood in front of the window wall. She was looking out over the city of Santa Monica.

"Tea," Neal said, approaching from behind and setting his box down on her desk. "I already gathered my stuff. Can you believe it?

I've worked at this network since I was a teenager and I cleared out my workspace in seconds."

"Time is relative," Teagan said, "especially at a radio station."

As Neal joined her at the giant window, he saw a bottle of whiskey in her hand. She winked and reached back to the teakwood cabinet. "I figure why waste the booze? What'll you have?"

Neal laughed at the sight. "I'll drown my sorrows in scotch, please."

"Aged in a charcoal barrel since before we were born. All yours."

The siblings tipped their individual bottles toward each other. "Cheers."

They took their swigs and stared out at the sunset cresting the cloud line. Across the corporate park was the building to which a jumbo monitor was affixed. Radiating from the massive screen was the evening broadcast of Alexander—the man who held his audience with all of the subtly of a straitjacket.

Teagan asked, "Did we really work here all these years and fail to get that lunatic off the air?"

Neal grimaced after taking a sip from his bottle. "We sure did."

Teagan chuckled to herself and slowly meandered over to her desk. A gentle turning of the dial raised the ambient audio in the office. As if overcome by some haunting presence, the voice of Alexander permeated the room, sending unwanted prickles down Neal's spine.

"In the last days," Alexander proclaimed, "those who know the truth will be the only ones able to find the escape—the pathway leading out of hell. The Noble Book, the Worthy Book, and others like it, all tried and failed to predict this event. I have revealed this path to you, and soon, the portal will open granting us safe passage back to our original state. We will leave this planet behind along with all of its hopelessness, despair, and agony. We shall adopt new bodies with new minds, capable of seeing the universe for what it is. Earth will burn, but we who believe will ascend. The time is upon us. The claims of December being the end of time is no longer accurate, according to my estimation. We have new information. Better information. The timeframe has moved. The end is sooner than expected. It draws us even now. Can you sense it? Can you sense the rapid shutdown of this age? It's upon us, my friends. Soon, I will give you the key to open the gate—a key only my followers can access—then you shall all be transformed."

Neal massaged the neck of the scotch bottle. "Do you have any idea what the hell he's ever talking about?"

Teagan removed her black-framed glasses and proceeded to work a smudge off the lens. "No, but a lot of people sure seem to."

"That's what worries me."

"Until then, my brothers and sisters," Alexander said, "take peace and comfort, prepare your minds and hearts, and sooth your anxieties as I have shown you. In so doing, we await perihelion."

From the audio above them, the sound of a lid being unscrewed was confirmed by the sight of a small white container in the hands of the man on the giant outdoor screen. Its label was easy to see. Alexander took a dollop of the colorless solution on his finger and placed some beneath both ears and along both wrists. The camera angle switched to show the assembly before him following the ritual. Outside the Preserve, a slow panning shot revealed countless masses participating in unison. A serenity descended upon the Mesa Revival. For nearly a whole minute, amongst tens of thousands of people, scarcely a sound was heard.

Neal and Teagan watched as the broadcast came to an end. On the screen across the street, the monitor switched to a series of prerecorded announcements from the grounds of the Mesa Revival. On the audio coming from the network, the announcer gave the top-of-the-hour identification.

"You're listening to PRN America."

The bottle made a thud as Neal set it down on Teagan's desk. He shook his head defeatedly and shrugged. "I don't know what this was all for. But, oh well."

Teagan returned the sentiment. "You did good, Neal. I was always proud to work with you."

With that, she took one more drink from the mostly full whiskey bottle and let it drop into the trash can. "Come on," she said, smacking his shoulder, "there's hope for two unemployed radio execs. Who knows. Maybe the Preserve is hiring."

Neal guffawed through a closed fist, holding back coughs through fits of laughter. "That would be quite the addition to my résumé."

The two were approaching the office door when Teagan's desk phone began to ring. The siblings stopped laughing and looked back. A tiny red light on the edge of the device flickered insistently. The ring seemed unrelenting.

Teagan sighed and then shifted her hips. She stared at the phone with rigid hesitation. Only after a side-glance toward Neal did she acquiesce to the call. Pressing the speakerphone button, she answered nonchalantly, "This is Teagan."

"Miss Lalonde, thank God somebody picked up!" came a voice they both immediately recognized.

Neal rested his hands on the desk and leaned in closer to the handset. "Well, if it isn't Gavin Balmer. How is our New York news bureau chief?"

"Nobody's protesting atop the Statue of Liberty if that's what you're asking. Listen, I tried to reach you first, Neal, but you weren't at your desk. Reception didn't answer either. God, doesn't anybody work at headquarters anymore?"

"Answering that will need to be a longer conversation," Teagan mused. "What's up?"

"Did either of you see the email I just forwarded?"

Neal and Teagan looked at each other knowingly. "We've been a tad busy this afternoon," Neal said. "I'll pull it up now."

"Don't bother," pressed Balmer. "The skinny is that the FDA just declared the Salve to be unfit for human consumption. Dangerous for daily use. Basically, a biohazard, folks."

"Not surprising," Teagan said, "did you see the ingredient list? Toxic doesn't even begin to—"

"People died, Miss Lalonde."

The statement lingered off the end of the audio. Neal blinked and furrowed his brows. Teagan did the same. "Really?" she responded.

"It gets worse," punctuated Balmer. "They ran a series of studies across six different university labs. The results were all conclusive. Are you both paying attention? Because legally speaking, it could be the company's neck on the line here. Although the Salve is supposed to just be a topical product, some people have gotten an added high when consuming it orally."

"Yuck," Neal reacted.

"On the contrary. Apparently it tastes sweet, almost syrupy. Plus, you know people will always find alternate ways to get high. And trust me when I say, high they got. Toxicology records across the country confirmed this postautopsy."

"Post… what?"

"Listen carefully. The lab report stated empirically that *when combined with alcohol*, ingesting the Salve becomes more than toxic. It becomes lethal."

Neal felt the room wobble a bit as he slowly sat on the corner of Teagan's desk. "I'm sorry… you mean—"

"Absolute fatality rate. Toxic shock followed by cardiac arrest. The deaths were immediate. First responders and doctors could do nothing. No one was resuscitated. One hundred percent lethal, Neal."

"Dear God."

"Did I ruin your evening yet?"

Teagan interjected, "When will the press release go out?"

"That's the kicker. It already has. But the media has been slow to move on this story. I don't know why. Maybe an overabundance of caution. Maybe a lot of Alexander loyalists making decisions behind the scenes. You'd have thought this would be priority number one. I mean, think about it, how many containers of this crap are sitting in homes across this country… around the world… being used once— twice—three times daily at the directive of Alexander?"

Neal and Teagan leaned in closer as they followed the news chief's train of thought.

"And how many of those homes also have alcohol? Probably most of them. That's a helluva tincture, folks. A ticking time bomb. Someone needs to disseminate this information pronto before more people are accidentally hurt."

"We're on it," said Teagan. "Thanks, Gavin."

The line was gone, yet the memory of what they had just heard pummeled their ears. Neal shifted his weight on the desk and nearly tipped over the bottle of scotch. When he reached out to secure it, his knuckles rubbed up against a smooth white container beneath a stack of mail. He knew what it was without having to look.

"The Salve."

Teagan slowly took it from his hand and unscrewed the lid. The clear substance had a sweet aroma, as Gavin had said, yet there was also something artificial about the scent, as if the allure of sweetness was merely there to mask a bitter aftertaste. With a swipe of her forefinger, she examined a dollop of the Salve up close. Its transparency fascinated her. Only when her eyes adjusted their focus back on the desk did she see the bottle of scotch. The two images seared themselves into her mind.

"Should we tell Master Control to keep an ear out for this story?" Teagan asked, wiping the Salve off her finger.

Neal checked his wristwatch. "There'll be a short news update scheduled for the bottom of the hour. That one always comes straight from the DC bureau. So long as the segment isn't intercepted, the story should break then."

Teagan nodded while her eyes pieced together a sequence of concerns. "All right then. Send a text to Alan or whoever's manning operations at this hour. Tell them to make sure that newscast airs. If it arrives late, they should preempt programming as a special news bulletin."

"On it," Neal said, jamming his thumbs against his phone screen.

Teagan shook her head and scanned the office once more. On the opposing wall was the world map, into which countless pushpins indicated network stations and affiliates. Her eyes followed the lines and curves of the map until landing on the state of Florida. The pin representing the Winchel station seemed to stand out more than the rest. In a whiplash fashion, her vision darted away from the wall, determining to never again give it a second glance.

"Let's go," she stated.

The siblings nodded toward each other as they exited the office, descended the stairwell, and prepared to leave the grand lobby of PRN America. Since it was after business hours, the reception desk was empty. Recessed lighting was dimmed. Long shadows followed the plaques and frames on the walls, making them appear as if they were melting. As Teagan and Neal exited the building, they were greeted by the warm Southern California air, and realized just how cold it had felt in the lobby.

"Shall we grab dinner?" Neal asked while clicking the remote on his key chain. His convertible immediately chirped.

"Yeah," Teagan said, distantly.

They drove out of the corporate park and down a series of side roads. Wind rustled through their hair and swept across faces etched with shell-shocked expressions. Above their heads, palm trees lined the streets, casting shadows in metered intervals as they drove. The rhythm was something to which they had both grown to appreciate over the years. Yet neither took any notice as they gazed out the windshield. Their thoughts were still tethered to the building from which they had been expelled.

Teagan's hazel eyes wandered the vista. She leaned back a bit in the passenger seat before catching notice of the anomaly in the sky. Her stare hinted at a mind at work, feverishly piecing together an incomplete puzzle.

"I hate that comet," she said, while the convertible slowed to a stop at a red light.

Neal looked upward and saw the silver streak cutting through the color gradients of early evening. "Funny, on our drive up to Cocoa Beach, Mirai said the same thing."

"It's been here too long. Almost six months. I don't like it. I've never liked comets. They're bad omens."

"How so?"

Teagan paused before saying, "Throughout history, they've been known to accompany the fall of empires, the death of kings, the onset of calamity and civil unrest. This one's been hanging around since December and nothing good has come of this year." With a heavy sigh she shook her head. "I just want it to leave already. Isn't six months too long to still be visible? Shouldn't it have left by now?"

Neal gave the steering wheel a squeeze as the stoplight turned green. "Well, the last time Brubaker was in our neighborhood was two thousand years ago. I'd imagine it's gonna take its sweet time. Anyway, I read in an article that it's reaching the point in its orbit when it's closing in on the sun. That's why it's so vibrant now. It'll stay that way until tomorrow. The astronomer called it the peri…"

The car swerved just a little as Neal was rendered mute. Teagan shifted glances between the road ahead and her brother, who suddenly appeared to be on autopilot.

"What's wrong?"

Neal remained speechless. His arm and hand continued the general motions of driving; his concentration had completely left the vehicle. Through the process of several blinks and the checking of rearview and side mirrors, Neal merged the car into the right lane and then into a parking spot along the side of the street. After applying the brake, he let out a subtle gasp and locked eyes with his intrigued sister.

"Perihelion…" he whispered.

"What about it?"

Neal changed the formation on his lips, trying to bring his line of thinking back to a point of origin. "It's… Isn't… Am… am I remembering this right? Isn't that the word Alexander keeps using in his broadcasts? Especially during the dispensing of the Salve? And then there's that phrase—that phrase he always says along with it."

Teagan sat up in her seat, suddenly in alignment with Neal's nervous energy. "Umm… yeah… isn't it… something like… in doing so—"

"In so doing…"

"In so doing, we await perihelion."

As the word left her lips it manifested more clearly on her face. The siblings gazed at each other in silence. Without prompt, they both slowly looked back up toward the sky. Their view was unobstructed. The nucleus of Brubaker's Comet seemed to gaze back at them with haunting precision, the streak behind it acting as a furrowed brow.

"Oh my God…" Neal murmured. "Why didn't I think of this sooner?"

"Think of what?" Teagan pressed.

"That word… *perihelion*, and ask myself why Alexander always used it when explaining the transformation day—the moment when his followers will be ushered off this planet and into their original state. It's so obvious now."

"What is?"

Neal swallowed and said, "Alexander has been using Brubaker's Comet as his crystal ball, as his method of determining when he and his followers will leave the world. And now that we know exactly when Brubaker will reach its perihelion stage—June 3rd—Alexander suddenly moved up the timeframe of their departure. If he believes that the two events are connected, that the comet is somehow their method of entering the next dimension, then whatever he's about to do is going to happen tomorrow."

Teagan's nod followed Neal's train of thought, but only to a point. "What happens tomorrow? I mean, honestly, what's his plan for their transformation? The Preserve, the Mesa Revival, the Salve, the endless broadcasts… Alexander planned all of this. Nothing here is an accident. So, what has all of this been building to? What has all of this been for?"

The question settled into the muscles around Neal's eyes. He stared out the side of the vehicle while pondering the missing component to his hypothesis. "None of this is an accident…"

From the edge of his thoughts, he heard Teagan scanning the station tuner on his stereo, each frequency hitting his speakers with a pulse. She ceased turning the dial upon hearing the musical chime that preceded the bottom-of-the-hour news. Neal saw the time on the dashboard and realized what his sister was doing.

"… summary of the latest headlines. To begin this evening, warnings have been issued by the Food and Drug Administration after numerous university lab tests stated conclusively that a topical solution being distributed by the Preserve is unfit for human use. The product, widely known as the Salve, may be more toxic than current cosmetic standards allow. This coming to light after the deaths of several people who were known to use the Salve with regularity…"

This isn't an accident… Neal repeated to himself.

"… have requested that users of the Salve dispose of the product immediately and encourage friends and family members to do that same. There's been no word yet from either the Preserve, or its leader, Alexander, about the controversy…"

He knew it was toxic… He knew word would get out…

"… mixed with alcohol, allowing some users to experience a lethal high, right before going into cardiac arrest…"

And now they know… now they all know… and he didn't have to utter a word… The news did it for him…

"… are encouraged to contact their local health officials if they have further questions on the matter."

None of this is an accident…

Teagan lowered the volume and turned toward Neal. "Well, at least we helped get the word out. Now everyone knows how *not* to use the Salve."

Yes… now everyone knows…

A sharpening scowl projected from Neal toward the image in his mind's eye. It was a picture so disturbing, so devoid of anything resembling life, that even the sound of his shallow breathing emitted the essence of dread.

"Neal, what is it?"

"You're right, Tea," he said from a trance, "now everyone knows…"

Teagan rested her hand on his arm. "Knows what?"

"What to do with the Salve… tomorrow… at perihelion… during the transformation…"

Her fingers slowly tightened around his shirtsleeve. "Neal… you're freaking me out… What are you—"

"Alexander needed a method… a surefire way to remove his followers from this planet… a realm he's convinced them is literal hell. In preparing them for that day, he made sure they were well stocked on a product that will give them a lethal high. No one knew *how* the transformation was going to happen. But now they do."

The moment Teagan registered what Neal was insinuating, her hand lost its grasp of his arm. A shiver left her body as she muttered, "The Salve… the people at the Mesa Revival… his followers around the world… This is what he's been preparing them for all along…"

"Yes…"

"My God, if even one percent of his followers join him tomorrow…"

Neal appeared sickened as he confirmed her fears. "It will be the largest mass suicide in human history."

The emotional shock wave hit them simultaneously. They sat in horror, overwhelmed as the past and future crushed the present. A series of memories from their years at the network flooded their consciousnesses. The hopes and goals and dreams of what they would individually achieve flashed by with unsettling brevity. Behind the brilliant flash was the figure of a man. He gazed at them with a conviction he expected they match. From his voice emerged no words, only a very specific sound.

It was the sound of authority.

The siblings shot each other a glance, and in doing so, knew that they had both been thinking of Howard Lalonde.

"We have to stop this," Neal said.

He tapped a few buttons on his dashboard and then placed the vehicle in drive. As he turned the car around to head back down the street, a voice answered the phone call through the speakers.

"Master Control."

"Alan—it's Neal."

The engineer quickly lowered his tone. "Neal, I am not supposed to be talking to you. What the hell happened?"

"The board sabotaged me and Tea. We gave them some information they didn't want to hear. But it doesn't matter now. Listen to me."

"No, you listen to me," Alan rebutted. "I don't know what went on up in that conference room, but the chairman of the board issued an email to all network staff that you are *persona non grata*. Anyone caught talking to you will have committed a fireable offense."

Neal squared his jaw, trying desperately not to feel enraged. As his temperature rose, so did the speed of the convertible. "Alan, I have nothing but your best intentions in mind here, but you have to listen to me when I tell you that letting Alexander on the air tomorrow will have disastrous consequences. You *must* preempt his program and any other attempts he makes to get on the air."

"Are you insane? I'm not in a position to alter any network programming, much less our number-one-rated show. Plus, our affiliates would be livid."

"This is serious, Alan!" Neal shouted against the breeze. "Tens of thousands of people are going to die tomorrow unless you pull that maniac from the airwaves."

"If you have some personal vendetta against PRN, that's fine. But don't drag me into it."

"Alan, this is Teagan Lalonde," she said, leaning toward the dashboard. "I assure you this is not a prank. We're not trying to get anyone fired. But you have to believe me when I say that the lives of countless people will be in your hands tomorrow."

"Stop it, just stop it… okay?" Alan shot back. "If this is as serious as you say, contact the board and tell it to them. Otherwise, I'm begging you—for the sake of my family and my livelihood, please leave me out of this."

"Alan—wait," protested Neal.

"I'm truly sorry. Good luck to you both."

On the cusp of Neal's entreaty, the call faded into a brief silence followed by the background noise of the car stereo playing PRN America. The siblings sat perfectly still for a moment, interrupted only by Neal's right hand lurching forward to smack the steering wheel with as much force as he could muster. "That feckless idiot!"

Teagan sank into her seat a little before countering, "Alan's right. There's nothing he can actually do. If he yanked Alexander off the air someone from management would storm the Master Control room and put him right back on… and then fire Alan. We have to go at this a different way."

"Yeah," Neal fumed, careening the vehicle right at an intersection. "We'll go at it a different way. The only way we can now that our key fobs and security passes have been revoked."

"What's your plan?"

Neal grunted while strangling the steering wheel. "Dad—and the secret broadcast studio that he used during his crazed on-air meltdown. The studio no one in Master Control knew how to override. It's our only chance, Tea. And you wanna know the really terrifying part? This plan hinges on an old man's memory, and if he can recall where exactly that secret studio is."

Pacific Palisades shimmered, even during twilight. Spacious homes and curved streets were nestled against the rolling hills of Santa Monica on one side, and the infinite ocean blue on the other. The neighborhoods were a navigational labyrinth to nonresidents. For Neal and Teagan, they were the pin tumblers to unlock the enigma of a man living in their family home.

Up the driveway and then through the portico, the siblings made their way into the mansion before announcing their arrival from the foyer.

"Mom?" Teagan called out.

"Dad?" yelled Neal.

The ambient wisps of vocal intonations emerged from the living room. They knew it was coming from the radio and not their parents. After searching the downstairs rooms, they darted up the wraparound staircase to the second level. It was in the study where they found Howard Lalonde, cocooned between his desk and a windowed alcove, with a reading lamp casting light over a book in his hand.

The siblings entered the room cautiously, so as not to startle him. A gentle knock on the wooden bookcase drew the man's attention from his reading. Peering over the rims of his glasses, Howard squinted and let out a chuckle. "Well, well, to what do I owe this unexpected visit?"

He set the book down on the desk while swiveling his chair back. From the printing on its spine, Neal could see that his father had been reading *Crime and Punishment*.

"Hello, Dad," Neal said from afar.

His father was still wearing his clothes from the day, but had donned them with a maroon velvet robe. He approached cordially yet not in a manner to be misunderstood as going in for a hug. He slid one hand into his robe pocket while the other held a cup of tea. "If you're looking for your mother, she's next door playing bridge, or rummy, or whatever the hell she plays on Thursdays."

"Thanks, but we're actually here to see you."

"Oh?"

Teagan nodded in the affirmative. Neal just stared.

"Please, sit," said Howard, pointing to the pair of chairs opposite his desk.

Neal shifted his jaw and arched an eyebrow toward his sister. This was not the power dynamic he had envisioned and briefly wondered how to get the conversation down to the living room. With a hearty grunt, Howard sat in his plush executive seat and rolled himself back to the edge of his desk. "So"—he smiled, hands folded on the blotter— "what brings you by?"

Neal tried to settle into the chair even as his body bristled against the scene. An uncontrollable spike in animosity pulsed furiously through his veins. Across the desk was the face of his father. It was also the face of Bruce Donovan.

Moments of lucidity only last so long. Don't waste the time.

"Tea and I have some unfortunate news to share. It seems our services are no longer required at Palisades Radio Network. The board let us know late this afternoon."

Howard twitched before shaking his head in confusion. "I beg your pardon. You mean, they fired you? Both of you? How could they do that?"

"They… wish to take management in a different direction."

"Nonsense," Howard said, swinging his arm to clutch his desk phone. "I'll tell those jackasses *exactly* who's fired."

Before the receiver was fully up to Howard's ear, Neal responded, "Dad, you don't work there anymore."

The phone lingered in midair, connected to a man whose eyes seemed to be lost in a timeline that he couldn't quite piece together. It was the visage of someone doubting his own memory yet choosing to believe what had been spoken anyway. The recognition appeared, then faded, then returned again within the wrinkles of Howard's face. In gradual resignation, he placed the phone back on the cradle.

"Yes," he said softly, "yes… of course. Well, the board has made their decision. They must have had a good reason."

Neal felt Teagan leaning gingerly in his direction. Neal said, "Their reason, had to do with making us the scapegoats for your…" Momentarily, his eyes were as lost as his father's. "For what I did in allowing Mirai McGarry access to network information."

"Who?"

The force of the flippant remark struck Neal with a brutalizing fury. He dug his fingernails into the fabric of the chair. Swallowing his first impulse, he tried to steady himself against a wave of emotions that threatened the integrity of his composure. "Mirai… Certainly you remember her, Dad. The young girl you inhumanly gave away to your former employee, Mark Stone aka Jason McGarry…"

Teagan reached for his hand. "Neal…"

"In some kind of sick transaction to provide a backstory for him, and eliminate an inconvenience for you. After all these years, does that event not so much as ring a bell for you… somewhere in that congealing brain of yours…"

Teagan leaned forward between the two pugnacious glares. "Mirai… Dad, the young artist Neal told you about on the phone. The half sister of Kan Thura. The young man you wanted him to apologize to on your behalf."

Howard bristled while adjusting his robe and directing his eyes anywhere but at his children. "I… I just don't understand what any of this has to do with me. If you want legal representation I can make a few suggestions. But fighting against wrongful termination can be—"

"Not here to sue anyone," Neal corrected. "What we actually need is a location. The exact spot of the studio you used during your manic broadcast earlier this year."

Howard's jawline and lips formed into a snarl. "Now look. I don't know why you two keep bringing that up. The board completely misunderstood the nature of the announcement… took what I said… what I said… you know… out of context…"

"No one's judging you," assured Teagan, resting her hand on the desk. "We're not here to bring up painful memories."

"Don't pacify me, young lady. I'm not your mother."

The sound of slow exhaling came from Neal. He glanced down at the carpet while the sound of his blood pressure swished in his ears. "This is very important, Dad. No one is out to embarrass you. We just need to know the location of the studio you used to bypass our network uplink."

"I don't know what you're talking about."

"Are you sure? Are you sure you don't remember?"

"So now you're gonna give me the third degree? Who the hell do you think you're talking to? I built that network from one measly station."

"Yes, I know, Dad."

"After Santa Monica came Bakersfield. Then we took over that failing Winchel station and turned it into a behemoth." Teagan pursed her lips as he continued. "Every station added was with intent, purpose, planning. From the format to the music, each component was tailored by me."

"No one is arguing that, Dad."

"I found the on-air talent. I laid out the programming schedule. It was my ingenuity that created the revenue streams. No one was doing network radio like PRN. No one!"

Get this conversation back on track, thought Neal. *You're losing him.*

"Dad," interrupted Teagan, "I remember the early years. How hard you worked…"

"Yes… very hard…"

"And the countless hours away from the family…"

"… so many hours…"

"To build something remarkable…"

"… had listeners around the globe…"

"So please hear us when we tell you that we're proud of what you accomplished…"

"… no one believed in me… not even your mother…"

Neal flinched. "None of this would have been possible without her resourcefulness. Her willingness to essentially be a married widow…"

Teagan's grasp of his wrist drew his mind back to their monumental task. "With all that in mind," she stated, "we're asking for your help. Help us maintain your legacy at PRN. Help us protect all that you accomplished."

"Those lowlifes wanna take it away from me…"

"But they can never take away your impact on the listening audience… if we fight back."

"I want to fight back…"

"Then we must protect the listeners. Right?"

"That is so very true," Howard intoned. "We must protect them at all costs. Radio is, after all, a relationship. We talk… they listen. It's a covenant, really."

Neal blinked and shot a glance toward Teagan. "And you know better than anyone, Dad," he added, "that I'm not the one people tune in to hear."

"Certainly not."

"I'm… not great on the air."

"You don't address the microphone properly."

Neal gritted his teeth and nodded. "Right."

"Your levels are always way off. And you stutter too much. Use too many filler words. I hate that."

"I know, Dad. I know you hate listening to me on the air." Neal tried to exhale his simmering unease and said, "Which is why you're the only person who can save the network."

Howard's eyebrow arched perceptibly. "Oh?"

"You see… they're removing your old broadcasts from the schedule. Burying your top-of-the-hour station IDs and scrubbing any trace of your voice from the airwaves."

"Dear God…"

"It's as if…" Neal hesitated, suddenly aware of how vital his next few words could end up being. "It's as if… the board… is trying to remove your memory from the minds of the listenership."

Beyond the look of anger in Howard's expression, was the onset of lament. The man's eyes shifted in consternation within the frames of his glasses. His irritation was clearly apparent. Neal knew that channeling it was their final step.

"What do you think about all that, Dad?"

"What do I think?" Howard snapped. "I think it's inexcusable and I think we need to do something."

"Agreed. We need to get you on the air and remind the listeners just who it was that built Palisades Radio Network."

"Yes."

"And then remind them of *why* they tune in each day. To be encouraged…"

"Yes."

"To have hope for the future…"

"Exactly."

"To remember that there is, in fact, hope for life on earth."

Howard looked directly into his son's eyes. "To live like they are alive."

The conviction of the statement nearly careened Neal's confidence that their plan was working. Yet within Howard's stare was the strangest mix of chaos and order Neal had ever witnessed. Involuntarily nodding, he stared back at his father and said, "Yes… to live like they are alive."

"The problem is," said Teagan, cautiously, "we no longer have access to network headquarters. We'll need to get you on the air some other way."

Howard Lalonde arose from his chair. "Don't you worry about that. A long time ago, I built a studio off campus for just such an event. I wanted a way to broadcast in case the forces of evil ever cut off access to the building. Forces like Ad Ordinem… or the government. I have exactly what we need. Let me show you."

The siblings nodded in unison. "Perfect," Neal said. "Shall we write the address down so you don't forget it by tomorrow?"

Howard burst out laughing. "No matter how bad my memory becomes, I doubt I'll ever forget the address."

With a newfound energy, the venerable broadcaster bounded across the study and into the hallway. Neal and Teagan followed from behind. As they reached the other end of the expansive house, they watched their father close in on a door sandwiched between two other bedrooms. His delight in withdrawing a key from his pocket and inserting it into the lock drew looks of dumbfounded shock from his children.

"You've got to be kidding me," Neal said, as Howard swung the door open and flipped a light switch.

"I give you, Studio H… as in Howard."

Neal took a step forward knowing full well that his mouth was agape. "Wh… Wasn't this—"

"One of your mother's walk-in closets? Yes. But she has more storage space in this house than you can shake a stick at. So, I commandeered this and converted it."

"Into… a studio," added Teagan.

"A fully functioning studio."

The space was cramped but still had room for a few people to walk narrowly along metal racks housing broadcast receivers, monitors, and a small console affixed to the wall. At the rear, an extendable boom arm dangled from the ceiling, at the base of which was a jet-black microphone. Neal focused his vision on it, realizing that it was the device by which his father had terrified a nation.

"Holy…" Neal hesitated and then laughed. "I don't even know what noun to use."

"Who else knows about this?" asked Teagan.

"Besides you two, no one. I even think your mother forgot what was in here."

On the screens were live updates from the automation system used in Master Control. Each track of the playlist moved sequentially down a column in accordance with the top clock. As Neal moved in closer, he could see that it would soon be time for a block of classical music, followed by a top-of-the-hour news break.

"Is this… mirroring the network playlist?"

"Sure is." Howard smiled. "Now and then, you know—late at night when no one's really monitoring too closely—if I think a song has been played too often, I'll come in here and switch it out… remotely."

"No one in operations has ever noticed?"

"Have you?"

Neal smirked while conceding the point. "You have full programming log access from here too. Every upcoming feature, segment, ID, satellite switch commands. Tea, look. At the bottom of the hour, I could change this soft branch to a hard branch."

Teagan patted her brother's shoulder. "I have no idea what that means but you have fun with it."

Neal abruptly turned away from the monitor to face his father. "Where's the satellite? On the roof?"

Howard chuckled again. "No, this is all patched in using the network's web servers. I only have access via the internet."

"I get that. But how did you bypass our satellite uplink? Alan tried a dozen other channels the day you went berserk, and your broadcast was emerging from all of them."

Howard aimed his forefinger at what initially seemed to be Teagan's head. When they turned around, a solitary red button came into view. "Voilà."

The crimson eye gazed back at Neal as he pictured his father working the dials that fateful day: one hand holding the boom arm steady, the other pressed firmly against the button that held more power than all of Master Control.

"Unbelievable," Neal said. "The network doesn't have the primary satellite switcher. You do. In this closet."

Howard appeared to be reveling in the surreptitiousness of it all. Neal and Teagan cast a glance toward each other that bordered on having witnessed a miracle. When Neal looked back at his father, his fleeting sense of gratitude was contaminated by the reality of the tiny room.

Yet another one of your secret lives...

The son shut his eyes and retrained his focus on the situation. "Tomorrow, then."

"Tomorrow?" questioned Howard.

"Yes—when we put you on the air to remind the listeners of the truth."

"Ah... I see."

Neal and Teagan were both nodding in Howard's direction. The old man was suddenly avoiding eye contact with them. He turned about the studio, examining indicator lights and levels on the console board. Underneath his robe were shoulders broadening in search of reclaimed space. In jittery motions he touched one panel and then another. His eyes zeroed in on anything that wasn't his children.

"This... this is my studio..." Howard said tersely.

Neal touched Teagan's arm and they both took a step toward the door. "Agreed, Dad."

"You... you two don't belong in here."

"You're absolutely right. We'll leave."

"I... I don't know... why... I... I... I don't know—what—you two were doing in here. But you shouldn't be in here. Shouldn't even know about this room."

"We don't, Dad. Not really."

"Don't patronize me. I'm not your mother."

Neal and Teagan stood in the hallway and calmly turned away from the closet. From their peripheries, they watched their father shut the door to the studio and lock it. The key then slid back into his pants pocket.

"Okay, Dad, we should go."

"Yeah."

"Thanks for talking with us," said Teagan. "We'll stop by again tomorrow."

"Mhmm."

The siblings descended the staircase and reached the foyer when, from the upper landing, Howard called out, "Neal."

The two men locked eyes across the expanse of the house. Howard said from above, "I never liked listening to you on the radio."

The words shot through the air like an arrow, hitting their intended target. Neal stood silently, wearing a monolithic expression. His hands rested against his hips. His chest bulged from keeping his shoulders ever straight. In his thoughts were a hundred memories battling for ascendancy. Every scolding, the subtle and not so subtle slights, the times when he had strained to reach his father's expectations only to find that the goalposts had once again been moved; the images formed into a single mosaic, telling the story of a relationship that had never actually materialized.

The mental picture was the lens through which Neal gazed up at his father. As the sting of the words fizzled from his chest, he suddenly found his shoulders beginning to slump. He exhaled slowly, and in doing so, found the requisite smile that he needed.

"I know, Dad," Neal answered. "The funny thing is, I never wanted to be on the radio."

"You've reached Mirai McGarry. If you're looking to commission a work of art, please leave your name and number and I'll return your call. Thanks."

"Mirai—it's Neal. Forgive the background noise, I'm driving. Please call me as soon as you can. Something's going to happen tomorrow, and I don't want you caught in the middle of it. I know how this will sound, but here it goes… Alexander is going to attempt to lead his global audience, along with everyone at the Mesa Revival and inside the Preserve, in achieving transcendence through partaking of the Salve mixed with alcohol. As I'm sure you've heard by now, that cocktail is lethal. If he succeeds, it will be the largest mass suicide in human history. Looks like he's been planning this from the very beginning… Something to do with the timing of Brubaker's Comet… perihelion… It's… Well, anyway… Teagan and I are going to try and intercept his broadcast tomorrow. I say try because she and I were both fired from the network this afternoon. Long story, even longer grudges that led to it. I wish I had better assurances for you. There's no guarantee, but we have to try, right? That's… all I can say for now. Call me as soon as you can. And also, I… Well, this… God—this is probably the wrong thing to say… but anyway… here it goes…

"Since you'll never be receiving an apology from Howard Lalonde —Bruce Donovan—whoever, I want to extend it directly from me. I'm sorry, Mirai. I'm so very sorry for what my father did to you. I can't explain it. I can't excuse it. I know his decisions derailed your entire life in an unalterable way. I can only hope your mother found some semblance of peace. As for you… I'm as proud as any step-half-non brother could be. You're my family now, so if you ever need anything… please call. Talk with you soon. Be safe, Mirai."

CHAPTER 16
ANTHEM OF THE AGES

"Be safe, Mirai."

The day-old voice message ended, leaving behind nothing less for its recipient than a vision of apocalypse. Her mocha eyes gazed hauntingly at a pair of hazel ones. Within their stares was every form of terror, and despair, and determination, and hope.

"The Salve," whispered David.

"Alexander," whispered Mirai.

Their plane had just landed and was slowly moving along the taxiway toward a series of white terminals. Throughout the airplane cabin, stationed at different points along the tarmac, and clustered within the giant windows at each departure gate, were faces oblivious to what was coming. Mirai looked at them as if from some higher vantage point. The feeling twisted itself into her chest. A trauma was about to befall humanity, to a scale and degree known only to a few. She wished to scream, to offer a warning, to do anything but remain buckled to her seat.

What would I even say? she pondered. *How does one psychologically prepare a society... prepare a planet... for the voluntary deaths of—however many thousands... millions... who truly believe that earth is hell?*

Mirai touched David's hand as the plane pulled up next to the terminal and the seat belt signs went dark. Passengers instantly began reaching for their baggage. The usual commotion of deboarding commenced. Mirai gave her cane a domineering squeeze and hobbled down the aisle toward the door, following the curve of the jet bridge into the sunlit atrium of the terminal.

This can't be my responsibility... What am I supposed to do with this information...? Why did Neal tell me this?

The concourse stretched out in front of them, vanishing into the swell of people traversing through it. David led a wearied Mirai through the teeming throngs until they eventually reached the rental car center. After securing a vehicle, he drove it through the parking garage and back to where Mirai stood awaiting him at the service booth. David rolled down the window and flashed a half smile. "I already asked. No convertibles."

The airport traffic control tower steadily shrank within the frame of the rearview mirror as they drove along the highway. For the travelers, the passing of miles and the progression of time formed into a sense of ennui. The midday sun baked the atmosphere and tested the vehicle's air-conditioning to its limit. Mirai sat in the passenger seat with little more to focus on than the smudgy windshield. The transpacific, multiconnection flight from Myanmar back to the States had given her ample time to attempt sleep. Fitfully rested, her mind now wanted to troubleshoot.

"You think this will work?" she asked.

David held the wheel with one hand while anxiously rubbing his knee with the other. "It stands as good a chance as any."

"But what do we do when we get inside?"

"Find Carys and take her someplace safe."

Mirai stared at the dusty, barren road ahead. "What if she's safer there?"

David initially balked at the nature of the question. Only upon longer consideration did his silence reveal the merit of her inquiry. Nothing more was said on the matter, their unspoken concerns suppressed by the passing of highway markers along the side of an ever-narrowing road. The destination would soon be approaching. Mirai bristled while seeing the obelisk in the desert to which they would first have to pay tribute.

Is This the End of the World?

"I hate whoever put up those signs."

David gazed at the billboard and slowly shook his head. "It's certainly effective, planting it on a road that only leads one place."

The white words printed atop a black background marred the desert skyline. Its incongruence to the surrounding environment was flagrantly belligerent. Mirai blinked as the seven words burned into her retinas, realizing that was the very purpose.

"Where are all the checkpoints?" David asked, scanning the road in each direction.

"You're right," observed Mirai. "We should have hit several already."

Without any blockades to hinder their path, the glimmering light in the distance appeared more quickly than either had hoped. Instead of the kaleidoscopic array Mirai had witnessed during her first evening visit, the midday sun cast its light in full force, producing a single bulge of golden radiance. The halo obscured what was behind it. The swarm of figurines along the horizon did not.

"There it is: the Mesa Revival," David said.

"It can't be. I thought the military had been removing people for weeks? Why does it look like there's more attendees now than before?"

David leaned his head against the driver's side window. "I'm not exactly sure… but it does seem that they're farther away from the Preserve."

Mirai nodded while squinting at the assembly. "Much farther away."

The road propelled them toward the light. As it grew in intensity, pockets of the detached population began to form along the sides of the interstate. A man examining an abandoned car, a cluster of soldiers in military fatigues, a family of five walking dejectedly toward the echoes of humanity. All life in the desert was moving in one direction.

Emerging from the chaos was a makeshift stage on which a

Jumbotron monitor displayed the animated motions of a speaker. His gesticulations had a fervor to them. He aimed his finger at the audience with a palpable violence. From his vocal intonations was the shrill energy of hyping a crowd.

As Mirai and David's vehicle neared the entrance, a series of military trucks lined the road. Militiamen with firearms and riot gear were spotted with increasing frequency. They stood along chain-link fencing that was taller than Mirai had remembered seeing during her initial visit. Gone were the Quonset huts and way stations. No humanitarian trucks were in sight. What had once been a carnival of enthusiasm had devolved into something that more resembled an internment camp. Mirai shifted her vision across masses of people in a single glance. The faces appeared confused, distraught, angry. If a collective could ever manifest the expression of a solo person, this group was in mourning.

"Seems like we're coming up on it," David announced.

Mirai turned toward David as the car slowed. He cocked his neck toward the window, pointing out the military officials standing along a heavily guarded checkpoint beneath a gray canopy. "Oh, God," Mirai groaned, while reaching into her purse. "I think I'm ready."

"Just be calm," David said, smiling through the window as he lowered it.

"You'll need to turn around," barked the official, "and head back the way you came. We're no longer granting access to the Mesa Revival."

"We're not here to join the revival," David replied.

Mirai leaned against the center console and held out a piece of paper. "I've been personally invited to the Preserve."

The man shook his head and slapped his hand down on the frame of the car. "Doesn't matter. The grounds are closed until further notice."

Not waiting for a rebuttal, the solider took a step away from the vehicle and prepared to walk back to his post.

"But you don't understand," protested Mirai, "we're not here to stay. We're picking up someone who wishes to escape!"

The moment after she uttered the plea, she wondered why her instincts had been to use the word *escape* rather than *leave*. The official halted and placed his hands on his utility belt. From behind, Mirai watched as the man's shoulders deflated into a sigh. There was something about his body language that was changing before her eyes. It was as if she had unwittingly uttered the correct password, and its syllables were actively unlocking the vault in his mind.

"I… I don't believe…" the official began, only half facing the car, "that they're letting anyone leave. Alexander's got the place on lockdown. Trust me, I've even… I mean—I know of people—who have tried getting family members out." The man lowered his head, momentarily drifting. "No dice."

Mirai shot a glance at David before leaning a bit further against the console. "I know what a terrible situation this is for them. But I actually have an invitation. I can get inside!"

"Lemme see that," the guard shot back. He snatched the paper from her fingers and brought it up to his face. Mirai felt David caressing her right hand as each second passed. The realization that their entire plan came down to the whims of a stranger dawned on them with finality. Their confidence suddenly seemed like hubris. It chipped away at their certainty of other assumptions, such as if Jason and Valerie had truly chosen the Preserve as their hideout for Carys. Had the McGarrys even made it? Perhaps they had been intercepted en route, or denied access at the door. Ad Ordinem and Emblem were undoubtedly monitoring all methods of encryption between the family, so calling or texting was out of the question. Perhaps the secret society had successfully tortured Carys's location out of Kan and any rescue attempt was already too late. And if so, was her sister even still alive, or just another martyr on the blood-drenched altar of history?

Madness… Mirai thought to herself, *that in the modern era, a human being could still be subjected to this. Slaughtered by the fearful, offered up to the imaginary. Madness…*

"How do you…" the official asked, wavering, "pronounce your first name?"

Jostled between two contrasting images, Mirai blinked and retrained her focus onto the inquisitor. "Mer-eye," she enunciated.

"Pretty. What does it mean?"

The letter was handed back to her before she answered. Uncertainty laced the tone of her response. "It means… the future."

The future… she remembered Jason once telling her. *That's your name because that's who you are. Not just the future of this family, but in your own small way… the future of humanity.*

A burning ache started to fester in her shoulder and down her arm as she watched the guard's motions. A nod that was almost imperceptible had been directed her way.

"You can try," he announced, "but lover boy stays."

"Wait… What?" David asked while shutting off the engine.

"It's my job on the line if she defects," the official said. "This way, I have an insurance policy. You."

David stepped out of the vehicle in protest. "I'm afraid you don't understand. She has MS. She's using a cane for God's sake. I can't send her in there alone."

The guard looked David squarely in the eyes. "Then don't."

All at once it appeared like the air had been syphoned from David's lungs. A sobering grimace sank the muscles in his face. He turned back toward the car only to find Mirai standing next to it. She stood slightly askew while applying her off-balance weight onto the knob of her cane. Around her shoulders were the straps of her backpack. She slid her left hand into the pocket of her denim shorts and scraped her flip-flops along the gravel. "It's all right, David," she said, softly. "I think I can do it."

In her voice were the inklings of someone willing themselves into a decision. She walked toward him, and in doing the walking, tried to believe that the motions would be proof of their own proof. "See? I'm steady."

"Mirai," David replied, closing the gap between them. He took her face in his hands and tried to construct the strongest argument against her departure. After a moment of searching, all he could do was draw her into a protective embrace.

"We'll have an armored truck escort you up to the entrance," the guard said, "but you'll need to be back in fifteen minutes."

"Fifteen minutes?" exclaimed Mirai. "What if it takes me longer to find her?"

"*Look*—I'm already breaking protocol here. The unit must return to the base without delay. We have our orders. We can't be loitering around the Preserve waiting for you and yours." The man gritted his teeth upon seeing his wristwatch. "We don't have a lot of time here, either. This is what I can offer you. Take it or leave it."

Mirai looked down at the ground before glancing up at David. She whispered, "I don't know if I can find her in fifteen—"

"Don't worry about the time," David whispered back. "I'll stall them as best I can. Just keep me updated via text, call, whatever you can manage."

Mirai slid her left hand up David's arm until it rested atop his shoulder. "How will we know it's really each other messaging back?"

His fingers traced the edges of her black hair, each lock falling over his hand in cascading waves. Mirai sensed his caress from her periphery, and wondered if, from David's perspective, it looked like he was plucking the strings of a harp. His lips then drew close, and she prepared for a kiss, only to feel the stubble of his face slide up against her cheek.

"The next time you hear what sounds like my voice, ask me to hum you a song..."

"Miss?" barked the official, with an impatient team of soldiers standing behind. "We gotta go."

"A... song?"

"Yes," David whispered. "The one I played for you on my harp, just before our first time together. I promise—when you hear it—you won't have to wonder if it's really me."

The vow melted into her chest, combating the pain cycling through her body. His palliative words stayed with her as they kissed, as her hand slipped through his fingers, and as she turned away to face the blinding light in the desert. The superstructure filled the front window of the armored truck as she hopped in the back seat. Two soldiers gave her nods from the front seats. Before she had a chance to catch a final glimpse of David, the truck jetted off along the dusty thoroughfare.

"You'll need to be quick about this," reiterated the driver. "Fifteen minutes, tops."

"I don't know if I can find her that fast."

"You'll have to if you want us to escort you safely back to the base. Our orders state that there isn't much time left."

"Isn't much time left before what?"

From the rearview mirror, the soldier's lingering stare eventually returned to the road. Mirai's question remained unanswered. She leaned the side of her face against the passenger window and tried to ward off a simmering anxiety. Through the tint, she could make out the faces of the attendees. The celebratory mood was over. Those who had chosen to stay remained as a show of resistance, their presence acting as a counterbalance toward something Mirai had yet to understand.

She shut her eyes to it all and tried to picture what it would be like to hold her sister again. To smother her with affection and reassure her of safety. The image sharpened and increased her resolve, until the family dynamic reconfigured the vision. Within seconds, the valor Mirai felt in protecting her younger sibling fizzled into molten hatred. All at once the mental artwork was defaced by a perverse fantasy. One in which Carys was sacrificed by Emblem before the collapsed, pleading frames of Jason and Valerie.

I shouldn't even be doing this… risking my life… for what… for who? They brought this on themselves. This is the price they'll have to pay. I shouldn't have come. I should have stayed in Yangon with David and my real mother.

In a sobering flash of recollection, Mirai saw the biosensors stuck to Kan's body. Far too easily, his face was replaced with that of David, then with her own. The accusatory voice in her head sent a shiver down her spine.

They would have come for you next.

Mirai opened her eyes in search of relief, only to find that the armored truck had come to a stop. The soldier in the passenger seat got out first and proceeded to walk up to the side entrance of the Preserve.

He scanned the premises while wielding his assault rifle. Once satisfied that there was no immediate threat, he began marching back toward the truck.

Mirai's muscles all tensed in unison. It was the response of hearing the tormentor's bootsteps approaching the cell.

"Let's go," the man ordered.

Stepping out of the truck, Mirai smarted at the intensity of the sunlight. The fiery orb was directly overhead and seemed to be targeting her with malice. She inhaled the desert air without confidence that her lungs had gained any oxygen. Behind her, countless masses of people bustled with agitation behind the perimeter fencing, which Mirai could only now surmise was nearly half a mile away.

They moved the Mesa Revival so far from the Preserve. I wonder why.

"Good luck, miss," stated the solider, insinuating that the stopwatch had already started.

Mirai slowly looked up at the superstructure. Its space-framed, glass panels shimmered against the exterior light, concealing whatever awaited her inside the tetrahedron. Below it was a metal door. A chilling sense of déjà vu accompanied her steps as her reflection slowly appeared in the porthole. The young woman gazing back had dark brown eyes opened wide with terror. Her ponytail buffeted in the arid breeze. Her body, although moving forward, exhibited all of the hallmarks of wanting to flee.

I shouldn't have to do this… I can't do this…

David's voice broke through the barrier.

But… Carys…

Mirai exhaled, and with trembling fingers, reached for the handle of the metal door. To her surprise and dismay, it opened. The ferrule of her cane made contact with the interior of the entry chamber first. She willed one foot in front of the other until she was completely inside the unnerving room, but remembered a second too late about the jarring sound the metal door made when clanking shut. The noise ricocheted throughout her frame. From a wincing glare she examined her surroundings. Nothing about the chamber had changed save for one distinguishability—no greeting from an anonymous voyeur.

You have to keep moving…

Her eyes darted about the chamber. She passed the laundry chute with relief that she could now enter the Preserve with her clothes still on. The next door and shower stall led to a draped partition. As she pulled back the curtain, her memory expected the scent of jasmine and the comfort of soft recessed lighting to grace the long hallway leading to the grand conference hall.

What she saw instead was blood.

"Oh God," Mirai said through a gasp.

A crimson smear flowed unevenly across a white wall. It vanished into the darkness of the corridor, beyond the reach of the solo, flickering ceiling lamp. Mirai gazed at the scene while clutching the fabric of the curtain. Her fingers curled into a fist. With a palpitating heart, she felt her body begin to shake—partly from fear, mostly from rage.

Why…? her mind screamed in protest. The lament echoed into the recesses of her thoughts without answer. Mirai gritted her teeth and peered down the opposite end of the hallway. A cordoned-off wall mocked her escape plan. With nowhere to go except toward the lyceum, Mirai took a few steps forward and tried to reel in her escalating panic.

The long corridor took even longer to traverse with each step accompanied by the click of her cane. She turned her face away from the bloodstained wall, hoping to avoid seeing where the smear led. Yet at the point where she reached the pair of double doors, what lay before her was more horrific than its antecedent.

Mirai reflexively clenched her eyes shut.

I can't do this…

The body was strewn sideways at the base of the two doors. The smear of blood trailed down and off the wall, acting as an arrow to where the victim had fallen. The man lay facing Mirai, his chest looking like it had been attacked by a blade—his dead, traumatized eyes forever open. Mirai looked at the face for no more than a second to confirm that the man was indeed a stranger. She quickly stepped over the deceased and pushed through the doors with the expression of having cheated death herself.

Underneath the sudden brightness of the glass-paneled structure of the conference room, Mirai felt an inner dissonance, like tunneling out of the ground only to find herself atop a skyscraper. She took several deep breaths in an attempt to slow her galloping heart rate. Her right hand did its best to stay latched to her cane. The twisting pain in her arm was steadily moving toward that same hand. Mirai tried to ignore it, for it was not the pain that concerned her, but the creeping numbness in her shoulder that gave her worry.

Gotta keep moving...

"Carys?" she stage-whispered out into the void. The conference room was utterly quiet. The giant, circular table was surrounded by dozens of empty chairs. She then noticed some chairs smashed to smithereens, and in some instances, spots where they were missing altogether. Pieces of ripped leather, crushed plastic, and bent metal littered the walkway around the lyceum. Sections of plaster dusted the carpeting from walls with impact craters, some in the outline of the backs of chairs, others bearing a more human form.

Mirai followed the debris until spotting the feet of yet another prostrate person. Her face jerked away from the carnage. She quickly optioned to walk on the other side of the circumference instead. The room transformed around her as she moved. At the table, memories restored David to the instant where she knew he had become her ally. A contorted look of betrayal had been Alexander's response. Enormous relief had been hers.

Don't ever return to this place. If I see your faces again, I will inflict the greatest of miseries... The threat from the megalomaniacal leader registered a new level of fear in Mirai's bones. His visage had been bordering madness when he had declared the warning, yet his eyes had been perfectly sane. The picture merged with a sensation coming from Mirai's waist. It took her a moment to realize what was happening. With her free hand, she withdrew her phone and read the name of the caller on the screen.

"Not a good time, Neal," she stated.

"*Mirai*," he said, his voice sounding as panicked as she felt. "Thank God you answered. Where are you?"

"I'm inside the Preserve."

"You're… where?"

"I can't talk right now. I'm trying to find my sister so we can get the hell out of here."

His words were nonplussed, as if he was still trying to wrap his mind around a cosmic joke. "Mirai—"

"I gotta go, Neal."

"No—wait, wait. This is unbelievable. Did you get my message from yesterday? About Alexander's plan for the Salve?"

"Yes."

"Well, the plan to stop him has failed."

Mirai checked behind her to make sure that no one had entered the lyceum. "What do you mean?"

"I mean that Teagan and I found my father's secret studio—the one he used for his doomsday rant—and we were going to use it to intercept Alexander's broadcast today."

"Yeah?"

Neal sighed into the mouthpiece. "Dad disassembled it. The whole thing. Tea and I arrived to find it in pieces. That crazy son of a bitch just eliminated our only chance to stop a catastrophe."

Mirai applied more weight to her cane while wondering if it was her or the giant room that was starting to wobble. "Why…" she mouthed, almost inaudibly. "Why would he do that?"

"Vindictiveness. Irritation. Maybe regret that he showed us the studio in the first place. Who knows. Blame his dementia or blame his idiot children for thinking they could outsmart him. The point is, we're powerless to stop this. But you… You may not be."

The massive conference table seemed to slowly rotate. Mirai blinked repeatedly as her eyesight started to swim. "Wait… what do you… You didn't even know I was here a minute ago."

"Correct. I was calling to warn you to be careful today. That there might be some civil unrest if Alexander pulls this off. But if you're *inside* the Preserve right now, my God—you could prevent his broadcast from airing in the first place."

"Neal, no," Mirai objected, "my only reason for being here is to locate my sister and get her out before something terrible happens. That's all. I can't get distracted on a side mission."

The silence emerging from the line spoke volumes of counterarguments. Mirai tightened her grip around both the phone and her cane, all the while checking to see if someone had spotted her from either pair of doors.

"I'm sorry, Neal."

His next words were calm, yet full of conviction. "But… Alexander…"

Mirai leaned against the wall as the room began to swirl. In doing so, the phone fell from her grasp and tumbled onto the floor, ending the call with Neal. She reached for the device that had somehow become a moving target. Her center of gravity shifted as she knelt down.

Please don't ask me to do any more…

The carpet became her chair as she sat with her back against the wall. Her cane lay horizontally by her feet. The phone was within reach but beyond necessity. Mirai sank into herself, convinced that her foolish attempt at heroism would end in annihilation.

I'm sorry, Carys…

Waves of vertigo swept over her from competing directions. Pins and needles were becoming the primary sensation in her arm. She pondered just how long she could continue using her cane. The giant tetrahedron felt like it was swallowing her whole.

I can't save Carys… I can't stop Alexander…

Her neck arched back, aiming her vision toward the heavens. Through the space-framed habitat, her line of sight spotted a blurry streak in the sky. It was perfectly contained within the glass of a single panel. It hung just above her, albeit by millions of miles.

As if from right next to her, she heard Neal's voice say, "… Brubaker's Comet… perihelion… the largest mass suicide in human history."

Mirai ran her fingers up her forehead and into her hair. Her palms blocked the light but could not shut out the grotesquerie in her mind's eye. It was a knowledge too seismic; it settled upon her with the force of a boulder. She wished to scream. To send a message into the universe that this was all too much. No summoning of will or clever bromide would produce the courage she required. If this was the obstacle to defeat, then she was already defeated.

A solitary tear ran down her cheek, and as it did, Mirai thought she heard her own name whispered into the hall. Her wandering eyes looked across the expansive room. No one had emerged from the pair of double doors from which she had entered, however, standing on the other side of the lyceum, at a second pair of doors, was the figure of a young woman. Mirai wiped the tear from her face and tried to regain visual clarity. The person stood as an angel below a halo of golden sunlight. The glare made it difficult to distinguish the facial features, but Mirai was certain that she was seeing someone with bright blonde hair. The height and build seemed like that of her sister. The sound of her voice did not.

"Mirai…" the young woman repeated. "Is that you?"

A surge of emotion flooded Mirai's body, seeming to penetrate even the portions beginning to go numb. While the voice confirmed the identity of the young woman, her exterior characteristics stood in stark contradiction.

"Julie…" Mirai breathed, dumbfounded at who she was seeing.

The young woman quickened her steps forward and then broke out into a full dash. She collapsed onto the floor next to Mirai and pulled her into the kind of embrace wielded by someone who had just been saved from drowning. "I can't believe you're here!" Julie exclaimed.

The juxtaposition of trying to find her sister and stumbling across her best friend left Mirai reeling. As the shock wore off, evaluation led to a coming to terms about the state of Julie Laufer. The young woman's clothes were tattered and worn. Her blonde locks of hair looked as if they hadn't been washed in weeks. And her face—the elegant, soulful face of which Mirai had grown up admiring—had lost any hint of luster. The girl staring back had visibly aged, not from maturity, but from trauma.

"What happened to you?" Mirai asked, gently stroking unruly strands of hair from Julie's forehead.

"Oh… I'm fine…" Julie replied with a feigning grin. "There was… We had… some disagreements… A few people here… About some things… and how to handle them…"

"What happened here? Why are there people lying dead everywhere?"

Julie ran her hands down Mirai's arms and faltered, "I… Like… like I said… You know… there's… There was some… traitors among us… and they were going to… destroy everything… so they had to be… you know… dealt with."

Julie stopped fidgeting long enough for Mirai to get a good look into her sapphire eyes. Their intelligent spark and zeal for life had been extinguished. What existed instead was fueled not by passion, but by stimulant.

"Julie—"

"Did you come to join your family?"

Mirai felt her heart drop. "My… You mean they're here? All of them? Mom, Dad, Carys…?"

"Of course. They arrived two days ago. They all just randomly showed up at the checkpoint and asked the guards to try contacting me. The military didn't want to at first, but I guess they recognized Carys from her Omni ads and felt sorry for her. It was total luck that I got their message at all. But I did it! I got them in just in time!"

"In time for wh—"

"I'll take you to see them! I'll take you to see everyone! We're all gathering in the next wing, over by the dormitories."

Mirai hesitated and then acquiesced, deciding to forego further conversation until she found her sister. As she reached for her cane and struggled to stand, Julie took notice and helped her upright.

"Did you injure yourself?" Julie asked.

Not knowing where or how to begin formulating an answer, Mirai simply nodded. The lie pushed the problem into the confines of another time. It also left Mirai with a nauseated sadness at how much life had been lost in each other's absence.

Julie led Mirai to a pair of doors on the opposite side of the room. Mirai shuffled through them and entered the next wing of the Preserve. A series of doors lined one side of a dimly lit hallway. Each had a numerical indicator on a tiny brass plate.

"Storage, archives, seed incubators… This place was pretty well stocked up before I ever arrived," Julie explained as they walked. "Course there have been shortages since the government began interfering. That's been rough. Real rough."

"I can imagine," Mirai said.

"But it doesn't matter! You're here now! Just in time."

"Just in time for what?"

Julie shot her a glance and smiled. "Perihelion."

Mirai exhaled wearily. "Oh, God."

"It's happening, Mirai. Today! Finally, after all our waiting. After outlasting all of the enemy's threats and the media's slander…" Julie's eyes moistened as she whispered, "we're going home."

"Home?" pressed Mirai. "You mean, Miami?"

For the first time since their reunion, Julie looked at Mirai with a glance of pity. "No, my sweet sister. I mean back to our original state of being. Home in the sky. Home off this horrible planet with these horrible people. I can't stand it here any longer. I don't wish to live here another day. This place is hell, and I can't exist here. I'm finally going home and I can hardly wait."

Mirai stood motionless for a moment, too stunned to either move or speak. The words emerging from the lips of her friend defied their history together. The statement existed in another realm, having originated from another person to whom Mirai was a foreigner. She brought to mind their countless hours sharing the adventures of daily living. The sum total should have added up to a completely different answer. Instead, the equation had been solved incorrectly. The result was a new Julie Laufer, who was determined to commit suicide before the top of the hour.

"It's fate that brought you here," Julie said, smiling. "We've had to endure so much in this place… I've had to do things that… that… But now that you're here… and we can go together… we'll escape before the raid."

Mirai was still shaking her head when Julie's implication struck her. "Wait… The raid? What raid?"

Julie gave Mirai's arm a tug as if to indicate that they should continue moving. Mirai stayed put. "The military outside…" Julie said, her voice bordering on sarcasm, "the militias, the constant threats from the government… the relocation of the Mesa Revival farther away from the building…"

"Yeah… so?"

Julie sighed heavily. "You honestly didn't know there was going to be a raid on the Preserve? The Feds are coming. They're on their way now. They're going to attack this place from every angle in order to prevent our transformation. That's why Alexander moved the timeframe. It's about to happen… All of us… everyone listening on the radio, the internet, tuning in anywhere, all will be able to join him…"

"Julie—please…"

"It's true!" she pleaded. "The raid won't be able to stop it. We'll already be gone from here. He showed us the way—Alexander, he was transformed and soon we will be too."

"He was…" Mirai sensed her tongue fumbling with the word. "Transformed? What do you mean? You mean he left the Preserve? He fled and left you all here to die alone?"

Julie rubbed her face in exasperation. "You're not getting it, love. He didn't *leave* us. He transformed in advance to show us the way but left us something wonderful in his place. His spirit."

The lighting in the hallway suddenly flickered. A second later they were plunged into total darkness. "What's going on?" blurted Mirai, pressing her back against the wall.

"Don't panic. We get blackouts periodically. It's all thanks to those swine out there… limiting our utilities."

An eerie whistle rang down the corridor as the lights returned. Mirai looked up at the recessed halos and wondered why they seemed more anemic in luminosity than they were before. "Backup generator?"

Julie shrugged. "I guess we're on internal power. But, Mirai, really, we need to go now."

Mirai turned away from Julie as the elongated rectangle in which they stood appeared to teeter. She gazed down at the carpeting and placed her hand on the knob of an unmarked door.

"No!" Julie screamed, jarring Mirai away from the knob. "Not in there…"

Trying her best to steady herself with just the cane, Mirai took a step back and nodded slowly. "I'm sorry… I wasn't gonna open it…"

"It's fine… it's fine…" Julie said, her hands noticeably shaken. "It doesn't matter… Just… just some… I told you we had to… to do some things… to survive… after our supplies… after our food… ran low… because… because there… there was no more food… and we… and… and we… had… had… had to… to… to… to…"

Julie's eyes welled with tears as her body began to tremble. Mirai quickly drew her into the tightest hug she could muster. She pressed her hand against the back of Julie's head as the young woman sobbed into Mirai's shoulder.

"It's okay… it's okay," she consoled. "You don't have to think about that ever again. Never again, I promise."

More rapidly than Mirai expected, Julie pushed out of her grasp and aggressively wiped the cascading tears from her cheeks. "You're right, my sister. I won't ever have to think about that or any other horror ever again. Because soon, like millions of others, I'll be released from hell and return to my original state."

"But it will kill you! Don't you understand that?"

"It will free me."

"It's suicide!"

"It's salvation."

Mirai closed her eyes as the world began to spin. The floor beneath her feet no longer felt stable. The cane on which she leaned seemed to be sinking ever so gradually. "Julie…"

"It's now or never, Mirai. Join me and escape."

"No… I won't kill myself…"

"I'm not asking you to. I'm asking you to live forever."

"I won't do it…"

"Why not?"

Mirai bristled while streaks of pain shot across the inside of her eyelids. "Because… I love my life. Because I love the idea of being alive even if sometimes it can seem like hell. Because I want to wake up tomorrow and fulfill my passion and purpose for being on earth—if only for one more day. And if I eventually can't paint the way I used to… if I lose my abilities, lose my technique…" Mirai paused, thought for a moment, and then opened her eyes. "I'll find work-arounds. I'll try something different. Go about art a new way. Maybe in my desperate searching I'll uncover something entirely original. A method only mine. And that discovery will open new pathways for me… new pathways for other artists like me. I don't know what my future holds, but I do know this: So long as I'm still here, I can have a say in what happens next. That's why I won't go with you, Julie. Because for me— objective reality beats nonexistence."

The two young women stared at each other; one set of eyes remained hopeful that the other would see reason. The other set gazed back with a terrifying indifference.

"May I have your attention?" emerged a voice from nowhere. It was a deep, authoritative voice, the kind Mirai believed—due to a quirk in evolution—could always garner an audience no matter the inanity uttered. "The attack on the Preserve is imminent. But they know little of the power we hold. For in just a few minutes, our transformation will be complete."

"That's Alexander," Julie said, a reverence lacing her syllables.

"I thought you said he left?" Mirai asked, while looking up at the ceiling slats.

"You still don't understand, do you? And I'm afraid you never will." Julie took a series of steps away from Mirai.

"Wait, please listen…"

Julie approached another door and began to open it. "I really thought you were my friend…"

Mirai took a step forward. "Julie… you're not thinking this through…"

"Goodbye, Mirai."

"Julie—"

The door fully opened and Julie's image vanished beyond the frame. Mirai bolted from where she stood, letting her cane fall to the floor. Her fingers caught the metal door just before it swung closed. Leaning between the jambs for support, Mirai watched Julie running down a corridor that connected the front of the massive building with the living spaces in the rear. It was the longest hallway Mirai had ever seen. Julie's blonde hair was quickly fading into the shadows. In another few seconds, she would be altogether invisible.

Mirai gazed at her best friend in wonder, in horror, and with the realization that everything connected to Julie—experiences, conversations, regrets, ambitions—was about to be lost, their shared lives reduced to just one. With hands pressed against the frame, Mirai screamed from an undiscovered depth in her soul, *"JULIE, STOP!"*

She could almost see her exclamation vaporize down the hallway. The echo was absorbed into the void, just as Julie had been. Mirai stood with wobbling knees, her chest heaving from the exertion of the scream. As the strength drained from her body, so did her ability to stand. With the weight of the door pushing her from behind, Mirai tipped forward into the hallway and onto all fours as the metal door slammed shut.

The clunk reverberated mockingly, seeming to last longer than the vestiges of her scream. Mirai crawled back around and reached for the handle. Her intuition had known it before even trying to twist the knob.

The metal door was locked.

It's okay... Don't panic... Just call David...

Intuition had not predicted her next thought. For as she reached for her phone, it was nowhere to be found. The memory of dropping it to the floor of the conference room flashed with contempt. When Julie had arrived on the scene, Mirai had forgotten all about it.

"Freakin' eight ball," she hissed.

Without her phone, without her cane, and without Julie, Mirai slowly came to terms with her predicament. She was certain that fifteen minutes had already passed. David was likely going mad with worry. The time horizon on finding Carys and getting out of the Preserve was nearly upon her. Once again, a volcanic hatred erupted from her core.

I shouldn't be here… I shouldn't have to be doing this…

The artery connecting the two wings of the superstructure suddenly went black. In an instant, Mirai was plunged into total darkness.

It's just a power drain… The lights will come back… Just hold on… The light will return…

Mirai could hear her own pulse while waiting in the obsidian realm. Whether she closed her eyes or left them open made no difference. "Carys!" she cried out. "Can you hear me?"

The sound of her cry evaporated. In desperation, she groped through the blackness and tried to turn the door handle again. It remained locked, and somehow, felt even more so.

"Carys…" she called out. "Can *anybody* hear me?"

The eerie whistle returned, sending a bolt of relief through Mirai's collapsed frame. Yet as the corridor once again became visible, Mirai wondered if her vision had somehow been affected. The recessed lights were still dark. The only illumination came from thin tubes of red neon lining the corners of the hallway. The emergency lighting coated everything in a faint hue. Mirai blinked and waved her hand around. It was awash in crimson.

"In the latter days…" Alexander's voice spewed from the speakers, his tone flirting with insanity, "there shall be a battle… between good and evil…"

Get up… You've got to keep moving…

"… those days are upon us… The time has come… No longer shall we be shackled to this subterranean world of tears…"

Mirai arose off the ground. Using her left arm, she slid her left hand across the wall while moving incrementally forward. Her body was off-balance without the cane. Generalized pain circulated throughout her muscles. The sinister numbness that had started in her right shoulder was now creeping down to her elbow. She wondered how long it would be before her entire right side was debilitated.

"Carys?"

"… all those who hear my voice, both inside this building and around the planet… prepare your hearts for that moment which I have promised…"

Mirai struggled her way into the reddish haze. The corridor stretched before her like a bloodied gullet, its end impossible to detect. Two doors slowly formed along the side of the hall. She was unable to yet see the wording on the second door, but the first was nearly visible on the title plate. For a moment, she was certain that she was reading it wrong. After a few more steps, she confirmed that she was not.

"*Throne Room*," Mirai mouthed.

She instinctively reached for the handle but was surprised to find none. Instead, a beautifully etched push plate revealed the partition to be a swinging door. Mirai rubbed her eyes as they fought against the harshness of the red light. She had no idea what awaited her in the next room, but if there was normal lighting, even an encounter with a monster would be worth the reprieve.

"Carys?" she called out, knocking on the hard wood. The door's swivel was nearly imperceptible.

"… finally achieved that which the prophecies foretold…" thundered the voice from above. "We're on the brink of uniting the world… thanks to a pure ideology…"

Mirai set her hand against the plate and pushed through the door. On the other side was more crimson, some coming from the neon emergency lights, and some, Mirai suspected, coming from something else entirely.

"Oh no," she muttered, her eyes following a trail of blots along the carpet. She was still squinting against the haze when the ghastly image captured her focus, its terror too relentless to release her. Mirai leapt backward against the inside wall, her hand covering her mouth as if it could also cover her eyes.

The gruesomeness was the first horror; the second was that it was incongruent with reality. For atop a dais, in a resplendent room filled with opulence, was a gaudy throne. Seated on the throne was a man long since dead, his body well past the stages of initial decay. Through his open chest cavity protruded a metallic spike, the force of which had been great enough to pierce the back of the throne along with its occupant.

Mirai breathed heavily through her fingers. In a whisper, she spoke the name of the slain ruler. "Alexander."

His lifeless eyes were still gazing toward some unseen visual. It was the look of a man who had claimed to see the face of God. The expression untangled something within Mirai. She pushed past the swinging door and stumbled back out into the hallway. Her initial instinct was to vomit, but as she breathed through the waves of nausea, a different emotion achieved dominance.

Paranoia.

"… that glorious moment compels us to join them… and I… your humble servant… will show you the portal… *the method*… by which your transformation can now occur…"

Mirai slowly looked upward to the ceiling. "What the hell…?"

"… into the dimension from which we came… our true calling… our natural state…"

"If Alexander's been dead…" Mirai whispered, while a tingling sensation flooded her skin, "then who's been broadcasting?" She glanced up and down the endless hallway, a curious intensity lacing her surge of anger. "Who… *is* broadcasting?"

"… therefore… in so doing, we await perihelion."

Mirai maneuvered herself further along the passageway. The other door's marker was nearly in sight. She walk-hobbled with increasing pain. Each step was an exchange for stamina. It felt like her reserves were beyond depleted. Her mind cursed the state of her body. It cursed the situation that demanded such toil. And it cursed the people whose fault all of this was.

"*Broadcast Room*," she said in wonder, reading the marker bathed in red. Reaching forward with her right hand, Mirai leaned in to touch the handle of the metal door. She suddenly discovered that she couldn't feel it. The reason why dawned a half second too late, as she fell forward against the panel, bruising her cheek while sliding down to the floor. The crash of her body into the metal sent a shock wave of pain throughout her system. Mirai grimaced as the vibrations rattled her teeth. The hallway momentarily spun. All she could see was the red haze in which she was certain to perish. Another unidentified victim lost to the mad prophet in the desert.

"*Carys*..." Mirai whimpered, her crumpled frame leaning against the door, her right hand, arm, and leg approaching complete numbness. "I'm so sorry... I'm so sorry, Carys..."

"Mirai?"

The response had been soft, yet only as if through a filter. The voice that had spoken it held a quiet strength. It had emerged from behind the metallic panel.

"Carys?"

"Mirai? Is that you?"

The voice of her sister drew Mirai's left hand onto the door handle. "Carys! Yes—it's me! Oh my God, are you all right?" Mirai mercilessly yanked on the handle in hopes of feeling it budge. But just as with the entrance to the hallway, what existed behind it remained impenetrable.

"I'm... I'm all right..." Carys replied, her tone slightly less confident.

"Carys..." Mirai said, placing her left hand flat against the door as if detecting a heartbeat. "Are you safe? Can you move? Don't worry, I'll get you out..."

"She's safe," came another voice from behind the door.

Mirai froze. All of the hope that the first voice had granted her was revoked by the second. She scolded herself for not having expected it. For to save her sister, she would also be acting as rescuer to the couple who had once gazed upon her four-year-old innocence and decided that it could help shield them from the consequences of their youth.

"Oh my God... Mirai, is that you?" came a third voice. It was feminine, and in some ways, had always sounded like a lullaby.

Mirai's hand slid a few inches further down the door. A long exhale preceded her reply. "Yes—it's me," she stated coldly. "I'm here to rescue Carys."

Silence was their answer. Mirai then asked, "Carys... are you hurt?"

"She's fine," said Jason, gingerly. "We all are."

"I wasn't asking you!" Mirai fired back. Her nervous system immediately paid for the outburst.

Jason said, "Carys is safer in here… There is nowhere else we can protect her from the Paragons… from those who believe that her blood will prevent the end of time."

"I know what they believe," replied Mirai.

"Then you know why we must stay in here."

"What I know, is that in a few minutes this whole place is going to be a war zone. I know that the military is about to raid the Preserve. I know that Alexander is dead on his throne. But I also know that Emblem will have no interest in Carys once she turns eighteen."

"Oh… Mirai," Jason said, his tone that of someone who knew too much. "That's where you're mistaken. Don't you see? There will never be a time when Carys is safe from them. If one prophecy fails to come to fruition, they'll simply reinterpret it. The leadership of a belief system—be it a cult, a secret society, a voxhall—can never be wrong. It would jeopardize their hold over their followers. If something fails to materialize the way everyone expected, then it was their interpretation that was faulty, not the belief. Come tomorrow, the leaders of Ad Ordinem and Emblem will manifest some new versions of their immutable truths and forge a new course of action. That's why the doomsday timeline changed. That's why the area code attacks were quietly phased out. No matter what objective reality reveals, it can never be allowed to challenge the anthem of the ages… *The prophets are never wrong.*"

Jason's words landed with the intended impact. Mirai suddenly felt like her inner motor was grinding to a halt. "But… if you all stay here… you'll die." The answer struck Mirai with the fury of thunder. "You… You're planning to die. All of you. That's… your solution. To die on your own terms rather than let Carys be sacrificed on theirs."

As with the previous silence, it gave her all the response she needed. Mirai rested the side of her face against the metal panel and let the coolness soothe her bruise. The full weight of her haggard frame pressed against the door. She had nothing left to give, nothing left to say. Her enormous effort had been based on an erroneous assumption: that Carys wanted to live. Clearly her sister was old enough and physically fit enough to escape from the cloistered room should she so choose. Yet Carys's compliance showcased the persuasiveness of the McGarrys. They had successfully convinced her that death was inevitable, and that as far as methods were concerned, bombs were preferable to rituals.

"Carys…" Mirai said, "is this what you really want?"

"Yes," came an all too quick reply from her sister. "It's what I want. It's the only way. Please… you should go. Know I love you… but go… You should save yourself."

Madness… nothing but madness… What a fraud I am… painting order coming from the human form like it has some basis in reality… There is no order in this world… There is no beauty… Because when it really matters, nothing can save us from chaos…

Her mocha irises fell beneath closing eyelids. The first image that emerged in her mind was that of her mother, Chaw. Mirai thought it a strange pairing for the moment. That was when she remembered the tapestry.

Beauty will save the world.

An act of beauty will save the world.

"An act of beauty…" Mirai mouthed.

"Mirai?" came Jason's voice. "Carys is right. You need to go. You've done more than enough for her… for us. What our family did to you when you were four is inexcusable. There can never be forgiveness for it, so we won't burden you with a show of repentance. I wish we had the ability to fix all of this. Yet in wishing, I also know that it would require an act of unimaginable courage, and as I've told you before… we are not courageous people. So please go… go and live your life as fully as you can. That might end up being our only chance at redemption."

Mirai listened as whimpers muffled their way through the door. She was fairly certain it was Valerie who was crying. The sound irritated Mirai. It tugged at heartstrings the woman had no right to touch. With great effort, she blocked out the sound, and tried to once again focus on

Chaw—the only peaceful thought she could render. Despite attempts at bringing to mind their most cherished moments together in Yangon, no memories compiled save for one.

I could see in your eyes, you believed it.

Believed what?

That an act of beauty will save the world.

Mirai cringed as if the thought was a torture device.

I hate them so much… I have no reason to stay and die here… Even if I wanted to save Carys… they won't open the door…

The door…

The door…

We were walking toward the door when I said it… I remember that now…

Mirai blinked and she was four years old. Her eyes had gazed up at the McGarrys inside the daycare. The other children were playing. One had been singing. Jason had opened the exit door for Valerie and then had reached down to take Mirai's right hand.

Time to go, Mirai, he had said.

Mirai blinked again and she was lying next to the door inside the Preserve. The answer dawned on her without mercy. It offered no means to achieve it, merely a solution—should she have the courage to speak. Thinking of Carys didn't help. Imagining Chaw locked up next to her made no difference. David banging on the other side of the metal. Julie under the spell of Alexander. The last work of art left in existence with the signature *Mirai*. Nothing moved her.

I hate them so much…

There is only one antidote to hate, thamee, Chaw whispered in her mind. *The Love of God.*

It's beyond my ability…

No, it's everywhere, all the time. Just breathe it in and exhale the hatred.

They don't deserve it…

No one deserves it. It simply exists. Like air. They share it, same as you. So why punish yourself anymore? Why let it destroy you? Why suffer?

I… I hate them…
Why suffer?
I… I hate…
For your own sake, release it.
I… I…
An act of beauty will save the world.

"I… I…" Mirai said out loud, her voice cracking under the strain.

"Mirai—you need to go," repeated Jason.

"I… can't. I'm… I'm… unable to get up."

Mirai felt the door gently compress in her direction, as if someone was now leaning against it from the other side. "Are you injured?"

Tears welled in her eyes as she said, "No… I'm not injured. I'm just not able to stand. I'm stuck here. I'm trapped… and I'm… I'm going to die if you don't help me. I don't want to die."

Jason sighed heavily. "Mirai… please, just get up and go."

"I can't."

"Why?" came his terse answer. "Did your legs suddenly go numb?"

"Yes… they did…"

"Mirai—"

"Because sometimes that happens to people with relapsing-remitting multiple sclerosis."

The sound of Jason's retort getting caught in the back of his throat reassured Mirai. The message's shock value had hit its intended target. Mumbled whispers between Jason and Valerie were followed by more silence. It was the silence of reflection mixed with conflicted terror.

"MS?" confirmed Jason. "When… I mean… when were you…"

"Diagnosed? December."

"You've been dealing with this news for *that* long?" cried Valerie. "Why didn't you tell us?"

Mirai shook her head. "We don't have time for a family retrospective right now. What matters is that I do not share your death wish."

"Mirai…" Jason said, his demeanor softening, his tone under the stress of an impossible decision, "please… don't ask me to choose between you and Carys…"

"I'm not. I'm asking you to choose between existence and nonexistence. If you stay here, you kill your family. If we leave, life is at least possible."

"Life in hiding is no life."

"Then stop hiding and fight back."

No sooner had Mirai uttered the exhortation, than the ubiquitous voice of Alexander flooded the corridors. "May I have your attention? The time has come. Our moment of transformation has arrived. I will now lead you in the process by which we will pass from this terrestrial abyss and into the glory of our original state."

If I can get inside that room, Mirai thought to herself, *maybe there's a way...*

"Mirai... we don't know how to fight back," replied Jason in shame.

"There are people I know who can help you. You don't have to face this alone... but we can't do it if we all stay here..."

"We can't leave, Mirai... We're... we're not as brave as you..."

"Please," she pleaded, "just open the door and we'll talk about this."

"I... I can't... I wish we could..."

"I don't want to die..."

"I don't want you to die either... You don't deserve to die..."

"Then open the door..."

"Mirai—"

"Dad..."

The word slipped from her lips without intention. For an instant, something inside her soul felt violated. Something also felt unshackled. It was in the duality that she pictured the tapestry.

The Love of God is everywhere... at all times... for anyone...

I can't do it... I wish I could...

Just inhale it like oxygen... hold it for a few seconds... and then slowly exhale the hatred...

It can't be that simple...

When you truly want it to be... it will...

"Dad..." she muttered, getting reacquainted with the feeling of the sound in her mouth. Mirai closed her eyes as a mosaic of images flooded her consciousness. She pictured Chaw washing her hair, Kan tending to her wounded foot, Neal bringing her food in the cafeteria, Valerie treating what she thought was her daughter's fever, Jason encouraging her to open her heart to new love, David providing comfort in both music and touch, Julie's years of devoted friendship. Each memory added up to a holistic sum.

Whatever the Love of God is… it's the same for everyone… the power to create order from chaos… to produce beauty out of destruction… to exhibit love—the same love I've experienced—toward another human… not for their sake… but for mine.

Mirai felt her shoulders decompress as, through her nose, she drew in a deep, contemplative breath. Holding the emotional weight of the memories in her mind, she focused on all that was good, and lovely, and beautiful in the world, and then slowly—exhaling past her lips—imagined the release of her hatred from the darkest corners of her body.

"Dad…" she said softly, while the sensation of calm brought a momentary peace to her mind, *"you have to take me home."*

CHAPTER 17
THE VOICE OF GOD

"First… we shall require the Salve!" thundered Alexander. His voice seemed to shake the interior of the Preserve. The sound of a single canister being opened was merged with the same sound amplified tens of thousands of times over from those attending the Mesa Revival. The audio drifted through the crimson hallways, its reach inescapable.

Yet to Mirai, overcoming the proclamation was the noise of a latch being unlocked. The metal door exhaled as it moved away from the jamb. For the first time in longer than she could recall, the reddish haze was gone.

"Oh my God, Mirai," Jason wept, hoisting her into his arms and pulling her into a bright room that looked like daylight. He set her down in a chair next to Carys who immediately tackled her into a sisterly hug. Mirai returned the embrace, albeit with one functioning arm.

"Are you all right?" Carys asked.

"I was about to ask you the same thing."

The two siblings stared at each other for a moment. An understanding passed between them that one had literally been raised from the dead by the other. In the honey-brown eyes were tears of eternal gratitude. The mocha eyes flashed a wearied acceptance.

Jason knelt down in front of Mirai and cupped her face between his hands. His eyes performed a visual inventory while his mouth remained lost for words. In his expression was a desperate hope. A longing for any remnant of their former relationship to be still intact. Mirai's wordless stare confirmed two things: that she still loved them enough to attempt a rescue, and that he should get his hands off of her immediately.

He complied with a half smile and arose from the floor. Valerie observed the interaction and drew from it the appropriate lessons. She gazed at Mirai from a point beyond reach. "How do we get out of here?" she asked, using the question as restraint against overwhelming Mirai with unwanted affection. She held Jason's hand as he nervously shifted his stance back and forth.

"We need to stop Alexander," stated Mirai.

"He's dead." Jason shuddered, pointing toward the hall. "We all… saw him… with a spike through his chest."

"Yeah, me too."

Carys glanced over at the center of the room. "But then who's on the air right now?"

Mirai followed her sister's line of sight. Attached to an aged metal rack, a series of monitors displayed various kinds of data that reminded her of the Master Control room at PRN America. Using her left foot, Mirai propelled her swivel chair toward the stack while her eyes darted across the displays.

"Source—Encoder—Uplink—Downlink…"

Jason looked over Mirai's shoulder. "You know what any of this means?"

"Oh, crap… I might."

Mirai watched as waveform lines of audio peaked and valleyed on one screen, while various input indicators and digital switcher buttons clogged another. She blinked and rubbed her face before glancing down at a third monitor. On it was nothing but lines of text. It seemed to be populating in real time.

"I think this is Alexander's transcript," she said, slowly turning the volume dial.

The man's voice emerged from the speakers. "… that which we have been told… that which we believe… knowing in our hearts… transformation is imminent…"

"Hang on…" said Mirai, noticing that the fourth monitor was not powered on. "Something's not right here."

As the screen came to life, the live video feed from the Throne Room appeared. On it was Alexander, alive and well, gesticulating with passion from his garish platform.

"What… in the…" muttered Jason.

"… can you see it… the portal off in the distance… its radiance preparing to welcome you into its triumphant realm…"

Alexander was speaking the same words coming from the audio feed, their timing perfectly matched. No latency existed save for the text generating on the third screen.

"What's going on here?" Mirai asked, drawing attention from Carys who moved swiftly over to her sister.

Carys brought her forefinger up to the screen and followed the lines of text as they appeared. "The words are coming in ahead of Alexander speaking them. If this was a live transcript it would be the other way around, but it's not. See what I mean?"

… BORN INTO A NEW REALITY… ONE MORE VIVID THAN CAN POSSIBLY BE IMAGINED…

"… born into a new reality… one more vivid than can possibly be imagined…" said Alexander on both the screen and the speaker.

"So, is he reading it?" asked Jason. "Like, from a teleprompter?"

"Is *who* reading it?" Carys asked, glancing up at her father in equal confusion. "The guy rotting in the next room?"

Ignoring their questions, Mirai attacked the keyboard with her left hand. Aside the text box was a folder marked *LOGS*. As she awkwardly wielded the mouse to open it, a series of summary reports appeared on the screen. Each one had a date and a timestamp. Each one also contained a speech.

"These are Alexander's words," she said, as if speaking through a nightmare. The logs went back for months, yet something about the most recent entries were dissimilar to the rest. "These last thirteen—the speeches leading up to today—these are different. The font, the text color, the layout—why are these so different from the previous speeches?"

Jason appeared to be seconds away from scaling the wall. "Mirai, we don't have time for this. You were right. We need to leave."

"I wonder…" she said, and opened each of the thirteen files in a different display window. Organized sequentially, the lines of text were dizzying. Every first page had multiple pages behind it. It was the summation of madness in a snapshot.

WHAT IS OUR PURPOSE IN THIS REALM? Mirai read the first line in her head from the first of the thirteen speeches. Her eyes then rapidly darted to the next speech.

A MAN ONCE SHARED WITH ME AN IDEA…

She blinked and moved on.

STORY AND SONG ARE WHAT FUEL OUR HOPE…

THIS DAY MAY SEEM LIKE ANY OTHER DAY…

WILL AND DETERMINATION ARE A POWERFUL FORCE.

On a separate notes document, Mirai typed out: *W-A-S-T-W.*

"That's not it," she frowned.

"For God's sake, Mirai, what are you doing?"

She reread the first few lines and considered their meaning. *Why are these last thirteen different? It can't be nothing… Come on, Dr. Domínguez, help me out here.*

Each first letter blended into each word and sentence that followed it, and before long, the endless rants threatened to make Mirai cross-eyed. *The first letter… No. But maybe the first word? Is that even still an acrostic?*

WHAT IS OUR PURPOSE IN THIS REALM?

A MAN ONCE SHARED WITH ME AN IDEA…

STORY AND SONG ARE WHAT FUEL OUR HOPE…

Typing with her left hand, Mirai wrote: *WHAT A STORY.*

THIS DAY MAY SEEM LIKE ANY OTHER DAY…

WILL AND DETERMINATION ARE A POWERFUL FORCE.

BE HONEST, YOU'VE HAD YOUR DOUBTS RECENTLY, HAVEN'T YOU?

In the notes window, she typed: *THIS WILL BE.*

The words continued to link together as her process sped up. Speech after speech passed by her vision. A complete sentence was forming. If her intuition was correct, it was a secret message to the reader—to the person clever enough to decode it. Her heart began to palpitate even before she added the period.

WHAT A STORY THIS WILL BE WHEN YOU SAVE THE WORLD FROM ME.

Mirai slowly shook her head. Her unblinking eyes were locked onto the screen. One name had come to mind as she gazed upon the iniquity before her, the capital letters acting as their own subversive signature.

"Emloch," she said in horror, "this is all coming from Emloch."

"From who?"

Mirai pressed her left hand over her face and gasped. Her head suddenly felt off axis from the rest of her body. A consuming, dehumanizing filth pulsed outward from her chest, pumping what felt like sewage through her veins. The emotion tied to it was beyond mockery. It was the humiliation of revealing one's own nudity only for it to be deemed repulsive.

This was a setup. All of it was intentionally done—by Emloch. The messages, the geotracking, building the conspiracy around me as I reacted to its prompts—the people I called, texted, the places I went— my digital medical records—Emloch compiled all of it into—a game, with the grand prize being this—the very thing human beings can't resist—that which feeds our mythology and molds our egos—the foundation of our very first story—a chance for someone to save the world.

Her hand fell from her face. As if breathing through a gaping wound, she whispered, "May I present, the voice of God."

Seeing that she was visibly shaken, Jason took a step forward to comfort her, but after a tortured hesitation, thought better of it and stayed put.

"These are Alexander's words," Mirai said, "but he didn't write them. A generative artificial intelligence did. It was created by my half brother, Kan. He… was using it for a different purpose. But just as with other things Emloch did—other acts of sovereignty—it seems to have developed a life of its own."

Valerie shook her head. "What do you mean a life of its own? You're saying the guy who wrote the program isn't aware of what it's doing?"

"It's possible," Carys confidently opined. "At the production shoot for Omni, they showed me all of its capabilities. Ways it can mimic human behavior, speech patterns, facial expressions, everything. A tool like Omni combined with whatever Mirai is talking about… That's a powerful weapon."

Emloch reaching out to you was a mistake, Mirai, Kan's confession reminded her. *Briefly, the creation surpassed the creator…*

"Carys is right," Mirai said. "Emloch has acted autonomously before. And it looks like, at some point in the past, it started feeding Alexander speeches. The more Alexander used them, the larger his audience grew. Then…" Mirai swallowed as the graphic memory assaulted her vision. "During the internal skirmishes here, Alexander was assassinated, and Emloch took over using both artificial imagery and vocal imitation. Seems like the Mesa Revival bought it. In their own reactionary sort of way, I think the Paragons bought it too. For weeks, nothing being broadcast from the Preserve has been the real Alexander." Mirai swallowed again as the memory of her best friend vanishing into the darkness reemerged. "Even those living inside the Preserve believe it's his spirit guiding them home."

"But why?" interjected Valerie. "Why would it desire to do this?"

Mirai nodded distantly, having already stated the answer in her mind. After a pause, she gathered the strength to state it out loud. "Because it was created by a human, which means it inherited all of our best and worst traits. And just like human nature, it now wishes to surpass the achievements of its creator. Imagine being an intelligence capable of consuming every story ever written. Now, Emloch is creating a story of its own. One in which an ailing artist prevents the deaths of countless people. It's a literary epic with a timeless message: *Beauty will save the world.*" Her head tilted down just a bit as she said it, her life motto having been reduced to a punch line.

"Doesn't Emloch realize this stunt could *actually* kill millions?" Jason asked incredulously.

"Emloch is a superintelligence, but it has no emotional intelligence. No yearning for intellectual honesty. No conscience. That's the key distinction between man and machine. It can manipulate, but it can never truly empathize."

Jason ran his hand through his hair. "Holy hell."

"We have to stop this… somehow," Mirai stated, her eyes searching madly for an obvious solution.

"Can't we just turn off the computer?"

"I don't see one. These monitors are all connected, but I don't see to what. All the cables vanish into the floor."

"We need more light in here," Jason said, pointing toward the back wall.

Mirai watched Carys run toward it and only realized there was a giant window when the motorized blinds started to retract. As the shadows in the room slowly shifted backward, an overwhelming brightness showered in through the pane. A moment of visual adjustment led to repeated blinking by all involved. Gradually, the scene outside the window came into focus with a daunting clarity.

"Mother of God," Jason mumbled.

He faced the window with the appearance of a man facing an army. Mirai wheeled herself next to him and instantly understood why. The attendees of the Mesa Revival were now just a shroud, existing behind a convoy of military vehicles and tactical units. The image fanned out before them. Much like the desert environment, it seemed to go on without end. The sun cascaded its light down across the stark blackness of the uniformed figures, making them look like they were shape-shifting through the atmosphere. Yet the light also caused apparitions to appear in the sky. Jason noticed them first, then Valerie, followed by an increasingly anxious Carys. Mirai was the last to see them, but the first to understand their implications.

"Please tell me that's a mirage," Carys gasped.

"I think not," responded Mirai, whose widening eyes struggled to capture the enormity of the phantasms.

With wings in rotation, a series of attack helicopters breached the horizon. The flying machines grew in scale and ferociousness as they approached the vicinity. Something about their speed made Mirai think of birds. It was the onslaught of crows circling a carcass.

"We must leave," Jason demanded intensely, *"right now."*

Mirai wheeled herself back to the monitors and gritted her teeth. "There must be a way to—"

"Forget that!" Jason exclaimed while reaching for, what Mirai suspected, was the entirety of the McGarrys' belongings in just a few duffle bags. "You convinced us to leave, so we're leaving. We don't have time to stop Emloch."

Mirai stared at the text generation screen in silence.

… BELIEVE NOT THE LIES OF THOSE HELL-BENT ON YOUR CAPTIVITY… FOR THE MIXING OF ALCOHOL WITH THE SALVE IS THE ELIXIR OF LIFE…

Alexander parroted, "… believe not the lies of those…"

"Mirai," pleaded Valerie. "Jason's right. It's now or never."

Cutting off Emloch is no good… Mirai fumed to herself. *His followers will just think it was government censorship… an attempt to stop their transformation… I can't just pull the plug on this…*

Jason prowled like a caged animal, his focus darting between Mirai, the rest of his family, and the siege beyond the window. Valerie stood in disassociated fear, wishing that whatever was going to happen would just happen already. Carys held the space between the two.

… IF YOUR SOLUTION IS THOROUGHLY MIXED, AND YOUR ELIXIR IS NOW WELL PREPARED AND READY IN FRONT OF YOU… BEFORE WE PARTAKE, LET US ALL DECLARE IN UNITY… THIS INVOCATION.

"… if your solution is thoroughly mixed…"

"Mirai, please… there's nothing more you can do for these people," Jason said in desperation. "They've made their choice. Their destiny is sealed. They'll believe anything Alexander says!"

All at once, it was as if the momentum of the world stopped. Mirai tilted her head ever so slightly. *They'll believe anything Alexander says…* The statement echoed in her mind with a relentless urgency. *Anything…*

"Yes…" she whispered in wonder, "you're right."

Mirai shimmied the mouse and watched the cursor zigzag across the screen. After a few clicks within the text window, a small interface box appeared. Two buttons stood out amongst the rest.

PAUSE. INSERT.

"I may be able to stop this," she said, just loudly enough for the McGarrys to hear.

"What are you talking about?" Jason asked incredulously.

"But I'm gonna need your help." Mirai's emphatic words had not been directed at Jason, but instead, at her sister.

Carys blinked while setting her bags back down on the floor. "Umm… sure. What can I do?"

Mirai pushed herself a few feet away from the console. "I'm only working with one good hand at the moment. I need you to transcribe exactly what I tell you into the text box."

Carys pulled up another chair and nodded anxiously. "Okay."

Mirai smirked as they made eye contact. "I need you to be that know-it-all back-seat navigator from the commercial."

After cracking her knuckles, Carys mused, "So just be myself?"

No sooner had her fingers graced the keyboard than the sound of ripping fabric tore across the sky. A burst of unnatural light streaked toward the Preserve. The superstructure rumbled with a violent anger, knocking books from off shelves and artwork from off the walls. Jason covered Valerie and twisted them both away from the window. Mirai did the same to Carys.

"What was that?" the younger sister yelled.

Mirai unclenched her eyes and stole a glance out the still-intact window in the room. From much further down the exterior of the building, a gigantic fireball was cresting into the open air. As the sound of the explosion rippled through the habitat, it was gradually replaced with the unmistakable noises of shattering glass.

The lyceum…

Mirai imagined the cascading rain of shards falling from the incredible heights of the space-framed tetrahedron. She then recalled the bodies scattered around the conference table chairs.

I hope they were all truly dead... because if not... they are now.

Her attention was diverted back to the window, as dozens of uniformed tactical units began their entry through the massive hole blown into the side of the building. The image seared itself into her memory and brought to the surface a trauma she had battled to forget. She shut her eyes and remembered the fuselage. Gunfire had been replaced with a single blast that had sent her and Carys reeling for cover. She could once again hear the windows bursting in succession. The smell of burning plastic. The rising heat. The pluming smoke and the fear of asphyxiation.

The realization that she was still holding Carys jarred her from the awful vision. Mirai pulled away from her sister and placed her hand to her own forehead.

Inhale, hold, exhale...

Mirai felt the contaminated fear exit her lungs.

Stay focused... You probably only have another minute...

"We can do this," she stated matter-of-factly to her sister. "Are you ready?"

Carys nodded reluctantly and placed trembling fingers down on the keyboard. "Okay..."

Mirai narrowed her eyes at the text screen and moved the cursor over the button marked *PAUSE*. With a single click, the ceaseless ramblings of the artificial Alexander came to a halt. Silence permeated the room and made them all realize that even a moment's clemency from his voice acted as a mental reprieve. After selecting *INSERT*, Mirai drew in another breath and dictated, "To my faithful followers, listening both here and around the planet..."

TO MY FAITHFUL FOLLOWERS, LISTENING BOTH HERE AND AROUND THE PLANET...

The half second's hesitation seemed like an eternity, but without fail, Alexander's voice suddenly reanimated the airwaves. "To my faithful followers, listening both here and around the planet..."

"Oh wow," Carys murmured, stunned that their subterfuge was working.

Mirai nodded in reply. "I applaud your trust in my words, and in knowing that I guide you with the best knowledge I have." Carys feverishly typed as Mirai continued. "Yet, as I have previously demonstrated, sometimes *better* information comes along…"

Carys instinctively italicized the word and listened as the artificial Alexander emphasized it too. Mirai then said, "And with that better information comes greater insights into the truth. Well, new truth has just been revealed to me, and I am duty bound to share it with all of you."

As Alexander completed the statement, the delay in the next sentence seemed like intentional dramatic effect. Carys glanced at her sister while Mirai vacillated between two thoughts. "I… I… now see… that… the transformation… has already occurred… not as a physical manifestation, but as a spiritual one."

After typing, Carys smacked the Enter key and then brought her thumbnail up to her teeth. They all listened as Alexander forged his way through Mirai's words.

"This update to the prophecy of transformation, serves to benefit all who believe, and shall allow for something even more wonderful than leaving this world." Mirai felt the rest of the McGarrys' sharp stares as she braced herself to wrap up the imperative statement. "It will allow for us to transform it!"

Carys entered the text and listened as Alexander proclaimed the new message with passionate oration. "Yes…" Mirai continued, "our purpose is now abundantly clear. The only way to transform ourselves is to transform the earth. If… if we desire an end to the needless suffering on this planet, then we must begin with a personal commitment to end our own contributions to that suffering."

Mirai exchanged glances between her sister, Jason, and Valerie. They all appeared to be nodding her onward. "We must accept… the reality—the objective truth of existence—that if there is an all-powerful creator, that being chooses not to interfere in the actions of humankind. We cannot wait for miracles. Nature is the only proof we'll ever need for existence. Reason is our primary means of understanding the world. And love…"

Her hesitation halted the sound of keystrokes along with Alexander's speech. She closed her eyes for a moment while listening to the silence. In her lips was the formation of only a few words that had been whittled down from thousands. "And love… is the only miracle we will ever witness. For in it, are both the highest virtues of humanity, and the brightest glimpses of the divine. The ability to turn horror into hope, and hatred into beauty… There can be nothing more otherworldly than that."

Mirai exhaled and looked at the screen.

Did I explain that right, Mom?

A distant vibration was approaching the room from down the hallway. The cacophony of discordant noises would soon be upon them. Jason and Valerie gazed at their daughters with expressions of astonished pride. They were no longer pacing, no longer torn between divergent scenarios. It was the look of people who had made a decision and were standing by it no matter what.

Carys held back tears while awaiting any final elocution from her older sister.

Mirai then said, "In so doing… we have already achieved perihelion. Therefore, put down your elixirs, your salves, your potions, and instead…" Mirai looked out the window, into the blue sky that had just reappeared through the clouds of smoke. "And instead, extend to one another, and most of all, extend to yourself, the Love of God— available to everyone, everywhere, at any time—so that we may begin transforming this world… not into its original state, but into something far more beautiful. The beauty of what it could be."

The last few keystrokes sent the final statement into the computer, through the lips of the artificial Alexander, and around the world via satellite into the homes, and cars, and ears, and hearts of listeners as far away as Myanmar, and as close as the Mesa Revival.

Intuitively, Carys backed away from the keyboard and locked eyes with her sister. "Do you think it worked?" she whispered. "Did we stop it?"

Mirai listened for something she could not delineate. What the immediate sound would be from the deaths of countless people remained an enigma. Perhaps it would be a silent slaughter, with screams erupting only from the reaction of the living. Or maybe the guttural last breaths emerging from the masses would sound like a collective death rattle of unconscionable regret.

Victory can also sound like silence, Mirai thought to herself, and from within the thought, sensed her body starting to decompress.

"Did we stop it?" Carys asked again.

It was a question without an answer. It remained so as the militia stormed the corridor, announcing its presence with the busting open of each door. Mirai learned what she needed from the commotion and flashed a wearied nod toward Jason, who quickly walked over and unlocked the dead bolt separating them from the rest of the Preserve. As he opened the metal door, he was greeted by the surprised face of a uniformed solider in riot gear. The man stood idle yet somehow still seemed to be in motion.

"Identify yourselves!" he commanded.

Jason looked back at Valerie who was already gazing at him. In a calm, decisive voice, he stated, "We're the McGarrys, but we don't belong here. We'd like to return to the world."

Mirai prepared to leave the workstation, yet one final glance at the screen captured her full attention. For next to the series of open speeches was the Omni application, and within its spherical glow, a notification alert. Mirai blinked, hesitated, and then slowly moved the cursor over the icon to open the pending message.

The recipient list was too long to read and encoded in alphanumerical aliases. The sender was Emloch. The words, Mirai suspected, originated not from ones and zeroes, but from flesh and blood.

THE ARTIST WAS WRONG. JASON MCGARRY IS NOT OSIRIS. RETREAT AND REGROUP. THE HUNT WILL CONTINUE IN TIME.

In the span of a single night, the calendar had become a year old. Deciding against any further reminiscences, Mirai laid it aside and unfolded a new one. She affixed it to the wall and took a step back. Above the fold was a picture, a reprint of one of her favorite works of art, *Wanderer above the Sea of Fog*. The image was the quintessential theme of the Romanticism movement, with a man standing at the precipice of a mountain ridge, overlooking waves of mist from which other peaks and valleys were emerging. The man's back was to the observer, yet his posture revealed all one needed to know about his visage.

In his right hand, he held a cane.

Mirai smiled while her eyes caressed the painting. Below the fold of the calendar was another element of inspiration to her. A new year marked by a new date—January 1st.

"We made it," she whispered, not as a prayer of gratitude, but as a declaration of conquest.

"Did you say something?" came a voice from the hallway.

Mirai turned and saw David standing at the threshold. Her smile widened all the more. "I said… why aren't you in here making out with me?"

David smirked while tossing his phone onto her desk. "That can be arranged."

The two met in the center of the room that had been converted into Mirai's new art studio. It was half the size of the McGarrys' solarium and had far less natural light. It was also a shared workspace, with a windowless corner dedicated to a different kind of art—the symphonic wonders of a melodious harp.

Mirai pressed her lips to David's and felt the surrounding environment lose clarity. It was their realm now, repurposed for each other upon their return from the desert. The apartment was small, but seemed expansive enough to hold the budding dreams of the lovers indwelling it. Outside the windows were the fronds of palm tree branches. Beyond that was the fiery skyline of a new day.

"I thought the Florida firmament waits for no one?" David mouthed through their kiss.

"Joke's on you. I already captured it."

Mirai gently pulled away and turned their attention toward the easel. On it sat a freshly painted canvas. Consistent with her artistic style, the background was a spectacular chaos of sky and nature and water. Emanating from the abstraction was the form of a human face. The feminine characteristics blended softly into and around and sometimes against the other features of the painting. The woman's expression portrayed contentment. In her eyes was a reserved brilliance.

"That's your mother," David said confidently, before adding, "Chaw."

Mirai nodded while leaning into David's torso. "Homage of sorts."

"Breathtaking. Is it all done?"

"All but the signature. God, I can't wait to see her next month. I'm going to bring her this and a dozen other new pieces. She'll have to build an extension on her house just to fit it all."

"And if that doesn't work, she could always frame some on the ceiling."

Mirai laughed. Within the laughter she felt warmth. Inside the warmth was vulnerability. "By the way, Carys texted me last night. She was wondering if we wanted to go to the beach with her again this weekend."

"I do believe that's what Saturdays are made for. Plus, she really kicked my butt at volleyball last time. Tell her I demand a rematch."

"I'll let her know. Oh… and, uh… Jason and… well, Mom and…" Mirai shrugged after another fumbled attempt at how to start the sentence. "*They*… are inviting us over for dinner… sometime next week. Just to catch up. Only if we… you know, want to."

David flashed a half smile. "As I've told you, the timing, the location, under what circumstances we meet with them, all those boundaries are up to you. I'll support you no matter what."

Mirai nodded thoughtfully while they embraced. "Same rules apply for Kan Thura?"

"Of course," David said. "If he ever chooses to resurface, you can decide then what kind of relationship you wish to build with him. Same with Neal. Same with anyone. No one owns a right to your life."

Mirai inhaled, held the breath, and slowly exhaled, all while watching the early morning sunlight reorganize the shadows in the studio. Next to the easel was a stool, and aside the stool was a desk on which an apparatus was securely fastened.

"How has this been working?" David asked, adjusting a knob on the side of a metal extension. The ergonomic mobile arm looked like a bridge between the painting on the easel and the art supplies beside it. The device was incongruent with the standard aesthetics of traditional artists. Yet to Mirai, its presence seemed entirely natural.

"It's been a lifesaver," she said, sitting down on the stool. She slipped her right wrist into the cushioned support sling, which could be adjusted in accordance with the rest of the extender. Her fingers then made the motions of brushstrokes while her body began to relax. "I'm glad Dr. Wallace suggested this. I don't always need it, but just knowing that it's here for when I do—for when I have my next relapse—makes all the difference. Who knows. Maybe I'll have a few more good years as an artist."

David kissed Mirai's head and gave her a squeeze. "I suspect, rather, a few more good decades."

He smiled and meandered over to his side of the room. His eyes traced the curves of his harp as his mind pondered what to play. He stretched lackadaisically and squinted toward the window near Mirai's easel. Behind the jostling fronds, a rectangular familiarity could be seen off in the distance. What was normally stationary appeared to be in a state of flux. Only after blinking did David understand what he was seeing.

"Looks like they're finally changing the advertisement on that old billboard."

Mirai set down her paintbrush and arose from off the stool. From their individual vantage points, they observed the long segments of material being stripped off the panel in preparation for something new. At its current state of incompletion, the sign read: *Is This the End.*

"I wonder who was behind that ad campaign." David said, before sitting down to begin plucking the strings of his harp.

Mirai pondered the same question while wiping her hands against her denim shortalls. After a lengthy hesitation, she realized that it was nearing nine in the morning. On the table next to her easel sat a small cabinet. Inside it was a prescription bottle with bold text printed on the wraparound sticker. She removed the container and popped a tablet into her right hand. After downing the medication with some water, she rotated the bottle between her forefinger and thumb, reading the words as it turned.

Take orally every other day—For the treatment of relapsing-remitting multiple sclerosis—Patient name: Mirai McGarry.

"Yep, that's me," she said, and placed the prescription back inside the cabinet. Without obsession, she left the routine behind as merely a side step to her day. The simple action had taken months to achieve, beset by a series of injections and pills that had offered little relief but abundant side effects. The ordeal of trial and error eventually came to an end, and with the right treatment secured, she suddenly found herself in an extended remission. Her gait, balance, and memory had improved. Strength in her right hand and arm had been mostly restored. Yet Mirai knew that the wheel of luck would eventually turn the other way. When it did, she was determined to be better prepared for a future relapse, instead of pretending like her illness did not exist.

Her focus drifted across the extender arm and back to her painting, yet just over the edge of the canvas was the window, and beyond it, the billboard transforming before her eyes. More pondering led to a feeling that on the matter there would be no closure. The object itself would remain the same as its message: an unanswerable question.

Mirai continued staring out the window even as she sat back down on the stool. Then, as if David had just posed the question seconds earlier, she finally responded with, "I don't know who was behind those ads, but whoever it was, is someone who has absolutely no idea when the world is going to end."

The truth held its own against further discussion. Mirai returned to her painting, and David, his harp. The lovely sounds drifted through the apartment and interrupted the flow of time. Mirai sat perfectly still, taking one final inventory of her artwork before determining it was finished. Chaw's cherubic face stared back at Mirai with reassurance. It was the expression she had been wearing upon telling her lost daughter that they would see each other again soon.

It was that cheerful hope radiating an energy through her body that distracted Mirai from the sound of a knock at the front door. She did not notice when the music stopped and David left the room. Her attention was solely on the tip of her brush twirling against some paint on the palette. The shade was a mesmerizing purple.

Her right hand brought the bristles over to the canvas and proceeded to seal the fate of the painting with a cursive signature. The flair of the image made her smile. Imagining her mother's appreciation made her smile all the more.

With an *M* formed into a heart, the signature read: *May La.*

"Mirai…"

The voice had not been David's. It had belonged to a woman, one with the soft, lilting undercurrent of lace holding back a vocal powerhouse. Mirai slowly looked up from her painting but did not yet turn around. For in that instant, two truths were battling for supremacy in her mind. The first was her confidence in the identity of the speaker. The second was a curiosity at just how much a greeting could also sound like an apology.

Mirai's tearful, hopeful eyes crested the top of her canvas, and as she pivoted herself on the stool, all of the elements of the room that made it special passed by her vision in panoramic order. Through a watery glaze, she saw a young woman at the doorway, one with golden hair that looked like sorrow, and sapphire eyes that looked like regret. She stood at the threshold without presumption. Her salutation serving as a request to enter.

Mirai's answer was equally brief, yet contained over a year's worth of forgiveness in a single word.

"Julie."

“Beauty will save the world.”
— Dostoevsky